## WOMAN HUNTER

Marty Doyle was sup
now Angie is looking
betting loss out in a serious beating. Marty's
manager, Chuffy, figures the only way he can keep
Marty alive and healthy is to pay back Angie, so he
agrees to help Barth make his last big strike,
bringing Marty in as driver. Barth is an old-timer
with one more job to pull. But he's losing his grip,
and needs the comfort of Sophia. While Sophia finds
herself drawn to Marty, Chuffy falls for Jasmine, the
daughter of the lawyer who set up the strike in the
first place—and who is having her followed, thinking
she's carrying on with Marty. The crazy set-up is
complete when Barth holes them all up in a cabin,
and prepares for his heist. It's a set-up for disaster.

## KISS OF FIRE

Mady is mad as hell when she is accused by her
neighbor of seducing the woman's husband. All she
did was talk to the man. But that's the way it goes
on the Gulf Coast. Tempers fly. Things get out of
hand. So when handsome Tuck Rossiter jumps in
and beats the hell out of the guy who actually
accused her, she finds herself falling for him. But
Mady doesn't know the real Tuck. This guy is also
playing around with Ida, his boss's sister, while
trying to con Mady into helping him locate the man
who has stolen a small fortune from her father. Tuck
is playing a complicated game, and nobody—not
Mady, not Ida, not his boss Leo, and certainly not the
neighbor's son, Bass McNulty—is going to stop him
from grabbing that loot for himself.

# WOMAN HUNTER
# KISS OF FIRE
## LORENZ HELLER

### INTRODUCTION
### BY BILL KELLY

STARK
HOUSE

**Stark House Press • Eureka California**

WOMAN HUNTER / KISS OF FIRE

Published by Stark House Press
1315 H Street
Eureka, CA 95501, USA
griffinskye3@sbcglobal.net
www.starkhousepress.com

WOMAN HUNTER
Originally published and copyright © 1952 by Falcon Books,
Inc., New York, as by Laura Hale. Re-written and published
as *Lessons in Lust*, Beacon Books, 1961.

KISS OF FIRE
Originally published by Rainbow Books, New York, and
copyright © 1952 by Magazine Productions, Inc., as by Laura
Hale. Reprinted in Australia as *Kiss Of Death*, Phantom, 1953.

"Beyond Sex: the Role of Women in the Laura Hale Novels of
Lorenz Heller" copyright © 2021 by Bill Kelly

ISBN: 978-1-951473-48-8

Cover design by Jeff Vorzimmer, ¡caliente!design, Austin, Texas
Book design by Mark Shepard, shepgraphics.com
Proofreading by Bill Kelly
Cover art by Edmond Gray

First Stark House Press Edition: September 2021

# Beyond Sex: the Role of Women in the Laura Hale Novels of Lorenz Heller

## BY BILL KELLY

KISS OF FIRE, one of three titles Lorenz Heller produced as "Laura Hale," was published in 1952 by Rainbow as one of sixteen criminous titles produced between 1951 and 1953 by this short-lived publisher. The prolific Norman A. Daniels' long history in the pulp market included editorship of several magazines as well as producing an incredible number of novels and short stories using both his own name and a galaxy of pseudonyms. Of the sixteen books published by Rainbow, ten were by Daniels using either his own name or one of two pseudonyms, Mark Reed and David Wade. Lionel White's SEVEN HUNGRY MEN was the only hardback title produced by Rainbow, while Laura Hale was the only title bearing a female name.

In a practice that would soon become more common, publishing provocative titles by female authors (or female pseudonyms used by male authors) was calculated to increase the titillation factor for newsstand and paperback rack browsers. If the implication was that a woman author could offer even more torrid and intimate accounts of romance and unbridled passion than could a male, both KISS OF FIRE and WOMAN HUNTER probably delivered on the expectations of most readers experienced in purchasing magazine rack fare. Typical of the period, the content of these novels would almost always be less provocative than the cover art blaring its clarion call to the customer at the newsstand or magazine rack. Also, the scenes pictured on the covers might not resemble anything to be found in the text, another common phenomenon of the time. The original cover art for WOMAN HUNTER would have been more appropriate for an Orrie Hitt or Harry Whittington novel set in the rural South. I imagine that it didn't take long for fans of these so-called "sleaze" novels to take these covers with a grain of salt. Both Hale novels do feature the sexual content (subdued, of course) promised by the covers, but as one comes to expect from Lorenz Heller, there are deeper themes to be explored after the fun is over.

KISS OF FIRE's steamy Key West, Florida setting provides a suitable background for the overheated romantic and criminal ambitions of its principal characters. Mady Lamont is hoping that rugged Tuck Rossiter will be able to locate her missing father. Mady fears her father is in trouble, but exactly what that trouble is, she can only guess. After being rescued by Tuck from the violence of a woman accusing Mady of seducing her husband, she falls in love with him and Tuck promises to rescue her father from his enemies and Mady from her life of being merely a spectator and not a participant:

> But now she was not a spectator, but was on the stage herself, a living performer in a play that wasn't a play at all but was life itself, at a breathlessly accelerated pace. There were voices around her like a mounting roar, sounds that glittered and whirled by like comets. And from some unseen orchestra there was music like a tempest, a whirlwind, a maelstrom. She could almost distinguish the wild skirling of the violins, the clarion silver of the trumpets, the flutes in headlong fury, the timpani thundering.

Mady and Tuck thrill to kisses of fire, but complications ensue, of course. Tuck's business, hidden from Mady, is that of being a go-fer for gangster Leo Brunn. Tuck has a driving ambition to climb the criminal food chain and to help achieve this he has developed a relationship of convenience with Leo's not-so-bright and very spoiled sister, Ida, whose near infantile behavior revolts him. Tuck starts to fall for Mady, but is frightened by the depth of his feeling for her:

> He was still unsure of himself, a feeling he had never experienced before. He had always been able to take this kind of stuff in his stride and laugh it off afterward. It had never meant anything to him, had never really touched him. He had always known no dame would ever be able to get her hooks into him. For that reason, he had always played the field. If one went sour on him, hell, there was always another just around the corner, there were always three or four just around the corner. But what the hell had happened to him now?

Mady's preoccupation with resolving her father's disappearance and Ida's cloying affections distract Tuck from his criminal ambitions and he reduces them both to pawns serving a higher purpose in his master plan to rise to the top. Leo and Tuck are seeking the whereabouts of pilot Joe Menagh, who after crashing his plane, robbed Leo's dead courier and is on the run. Local fisherman, Bass McNulty (Bass for Bascom, not for the fish) is suspected of harboring Joe, and Tuck turns Mady into a cat's paw to work her charms on Bass. Although Bass falls for Mady and inserts himself into her quest to find her father and duels Leo and Tuck over Joe, his behavior and decision making in the end owe more to his good character than to his attraction to Mady or her influence over him.

KISS OF FIRE is a novel of tangled romance, shifting alliances and emotional manipulation that typically, for a Lorenz Heller story, moves along briskly and offers crisp dialogue, fully realized characters, skillfully inserted humor and a slam-bang finish.

WOMAN HUNTER was a paperback original published by Falcon in 1952. Falcon would publish thirteen criminous titles between 1952 and 1953. Once again, Norman A. Daniels would head the list with five titles, one under his own name, three as by Mark Reed and one as by David Wade. In this brief period, Falcon would also publish "JUNKIE!" by Jonathan Craig (a pseudonym of Frank E. Smith), THE EVIL SLEEP by Evan Hunter and DAGGER OF FLESH by Richard S. Prather. And again "Laura Hale" would be the sole female author name.

A plot summary of WOMAN HUNTER may appear at first to be that of a typical heist/caper novel from this era. From the back cover of the Falcon paperback original:

It was a wholly desperate plan—and it called for wholly desperate men to execute it. Barth picked his men carefully. ... four rugged, hard-hitting men filled with the will to succeed and let nothing stand in their way. But what they hadn't counted on were two eleventh-hour confederates who made a considerable difference in their plans. They were both young, both beautiful ... One was Jasmine, blonde and lovely with the face of a teenager—and the style of a streetwalker. The other was Sophie, a streetwalker in fact—with the touch of an angel. ... four men of action and two lonely passionate women. ... caught up in a web of violence when their own basic flesh-and-blood desires and emotions conflict with and threaten their only chance for survival.

Lionel White's 1955 caper novel CLEAN BREAK (filmed as *The Killing* and reissued by Stark House) could be cited as an archetype for the story in which a group of professional criminals, each of whom has a specific and well defined role to play, are led by a ruthless and supremely capable leader in the successful commission of a crime. Throughout a typical heist novel we see methodical planning, preparation and execution of a daring crime conducted by talented and experienced professionals. In WOMAN HUNTER, we immediately get the impression that both the crime and its actors are on shaky ground; in fact, each of the participants, for various reasons, are on the verge of collapse from the very beginning of the story.

Marty Doyle is a boxer in trouble with a gangster for not throwing a fight and is badly in need of money to make good on the gangster's betting losses. Marty's manager and father figure Chuffy has an underworld connection that offers Marty the opportunity to earn money by driving for a crew hoping to hijack a heist gang after they have completed a robbery. For Marty, this is an act of desperation, rather than a career opportunity. Throughout the novel, Marty is disturbed by the implications of his upcoming criminal activity and attempts to rationalize his role in the hijacking. When Sophie attempts to dissuade Marty from participating in the crime, he responds:

"All I'm doing," he said woodenly, "is driving a car for Barth. I don't know anything about anything else. I'm just driving a car."

Gerald Barth, the brains of the hijack crew, is a career criminal on his last legs, both financially and emotionally. Devastated by the death of his sister and the loss of a fortune accumulated over the course of his career, Barth engages lawyer Walter Thomas (The Eye) as fixer/bankroller for his crew. Thomas is in deep trouble himself, both professionally and emotionally, as he is about to be indicted for previous crimes. Additionally his daughter, Jasmine, has chosen to forsake her cushy middle class lifestyle for a life of "fun and thrills" as a prostitute. Barth hopes his share of the hijack loot sets him up for retirement and a life of peace; Thomas is looking for getaway money and a last opportunity to bond with his daughter. Barth has replaced his lost sister with ex-prostitute Sophie. Barth and Sophie have taken turns rescuing each other from dire situations, but for Sophie they seem bound together more by loyalty and obligation than by love. To Barth, however, Sophie is a woman whom he regards as both his savior and his good luck charm:

It was only in Sophie's arms these days that he could renew himself, for she gave so generously of herself, in tenderness and gratitude, that after he had been with her, it was like being reborn.

Barth, leader of the hijack team, is a career criminal burnout:

In the past, there had always been a lifting excitement before a strike, an anticipation, an eagerness—but this time he was dead inside. ... In the past, he'd had to do nothing but walk into a room for everyone to know who was boss. This time it had been an effort. He felt as if he had been drained dry.

Overly dependent upon alcohol and Sophie's support, Barth's tenuous grip on controlling his crew provides much of the tension and suspense in the novel. In a conventional heist novel, key components for success include each member maintaining a rigid focus on the job and performing the duties required to ensure the job's success. The preparation stages of the hijacking in WOMAN HUNTER are portrayed in a series of scenes each containing its own hint that a careless action here or a wrong word there will bring down the whole scheme. This creates the problem that although each of the male characters is deeply committed and desperate for the successful outcome of the hijacking, each has emotional conflicts that threaten to subvert whatever efforts are being made toward achieving the prize. So rather than being a linear story of the conception, planning and execution of a daring crime, the crime in WOMAN HUNTER is a backdrop for the playing out of the emotional highs and lows of its principal characters. Heller, however, never loses the thread of the story and there is plenty of action and suspense. Although the success of the heist is doubtful, Heller is skillful enough to tell a story where the reader is always thinking, "Hey, they may just pull this off, anyway."

The title WOMAN HUNTER was typical for the time: more appropriate for bookrack appeal than serving as representative of the novel's content. Women do, however, lie at the work's thematic core: can I rescue my man, can I rescue myself, and must I do both to ensure my survival? Jasmine's fling as a prostitute serves the dual purpose of spiting a father that has never taken time for her and of relieving the boredom of a comfortable middle class life. Jasmine views her love for Chuffy and his commitment to her as the stated first real love of her life as a way of escaping the life she was born to and the life she has chosen.

Together they can be something more and something better from what they each are now.

Sophie finds the relationship between her and Barth to one of mutual self-destructive dependency, rather than one of a powerful love that will enable each of them to be happy. Sophie finds love with Marty, but because of the criminal path that Marty has chosen, she suffers from visions of Marty becoming another Barth. Neither woman ever assumes a passive role in their relationships. Marty and Chuffy are always quite clear about their partner's wants and needs. Heller's skill as an author of crime fiction was to create a work atypical of the genre, where the danger and fears inherent in a crime's commission are eclipsed by the more visceral dangers and fears in acting out the impulses of the human heart.

In KISS OF FIRE, Mady (the sole female protagonist) requires rescue as well as love—falling distinctly into the "damsel in distress" category. She looks to two different men for love and rescue and although not completely passive in her relationships, Mady lacks the emotional depth of a Jasmine or a Sophie. In KISS OF FIRE, the men were probably "gonna to do what men are gonna do" whether Mady was around or not. Jasmine and Sophie, however, play decisive roles in WOMAN HUNTER and have importance to their male partners far beyond their sexuality.

—May 2021
Mesa, AZ

# WOMAN HUNTER

## LORENZ HELLER

writing as Laura Hale

## HOLED UP
## CHAPTER ONE

Marty Doyle lay on the bed, disinterestedly leafing through the copy of *The Ring* that Chuffy had brought him. This was the fifth day he had been holed up in his lousy Market Street fleabag, ever since that Friday night when he had gotten out of the Arena by the skin of his teeth, dressed in nothing but his robe and trunks. Chuffy had brought him clothes—if he hadn't, Marty would still be sitting around in his trunks, for he didn't dare to leave the room.

He was a light-heavy, weighing in at about a hundred and seventy, most of it in his chest and shoulders, like old Fitzsimmons. He was practically hipless and his legs were long, lean and tough. He had a tough but somehow boyish Irish face. His ring name was Irish Jack Doyle and he had been good. He was fast, could hit with both hands—and his boxing was steadily improving, though he was far from being a Sugar Ray Robinson. He had definitely been on the way up—until Friday night.

There was a light, tricky knock at the door—shave-and-a-haircut-bay-rum. He dropped his magazine and snatched a stubby .38 from under his pillow. He said nothing but sat tensely, gun pointed at the door.

A voice outside said cautiously, "It's me, Marty-boy."

That was Chuffy's reedy voice. Marty slipped off the bed and lithely crossed the floor. He was more quick than graceful but there was grace in his controlled balance. He turned the key and stepped back, screening himself with the open door. He stiffened when he discovered Chuffy was not alone. He had a girl with him, a blonde with adolescent breasts, a small face and slender legs. Her hair was very fine and silky, like baby hair. Chuffy liked them immature but there was nothing immature in the look she gave Marty. It was an eager, greedy look.

Marty said angrily, "What the hell's the idea?"

Chuffy winked. "Jasmine's okay, Marty-boy. I thought you might be getting lonesome or something. She's a good kid." He winked again and pinched her.

She jumped and cried, "I told you not to do that, damn you!" Her voice was shrill and childish. She gave Marty a languishing smile and sat down, curling her legs under her with a deliberate show of underdeveloped thighs. "What's the matter, handsome? Don't you like me?"

"Get her out of here," said Marty.

Chuffy protested, "Aw now, Marty-boy ..."

"Get her out of here!"

The girl flushed and sprang to her feet. "The big baby doesn't want a girl," she jeered. "He wants his mama. Hand it over, Rover." She held out her hand and Chuffy, looking pained, put a twenty in it.

She bent and pulled up her skirt, showing peach-colored panties appliquéd with blue flowers. She slipped the bill into her stocking top ostentatiously, gave Marty a cocky, contemptuous grin, tossed her head high and walked out. Chuffy closed the door after her.

"That was a dumb trick," said Marty bitingly.

Chuffy made placating gestures with his bony hands. He had a long simian face and bright black eyes. He was a thin little man and always moved and spoke with jerky rapidity, as if there were never enough time for all he wanted to do and say. He was addicted to gray pinstripe suits, bowties, and homburgs. His sponge rubber boutonniere resembled a chrysanthemum.

"Yeah," he admitted. "Maybe it was a bum idea."

Marty gave him a hard glance, then walked over to the bed and put his gun back under the pillow. "How'd you make out?"

Chuffy spread his hands and shook his head. "You're up against it, Marty-boy, and no mistake. But honest to God, I don't see why when they said dive you had to make an operation out of it."

"I don't dive for anybody!"

"Okay—but you should've picked somebody else not to dive for. They're rough and they're sore—'specially that Angie. They dropped something like fifteen grand when you flattened that Hunky in the third."

"I told them I wouldn't dive, didn't I?"

"Sure—but they're guys they don't believe it, you don't do what they say—tough. You could square it for fifteen grand. I think."

"I haven't got fifteen grand. What did Lieutenant Flannery say?"

"Cops!" Chuffy made a wry face. "He said, why didn't you squawk to the Commish before, instead of afterwards? He said he's tired of crooked pugs and the hell with you. That's what he said, not me," Chuffy added quickly. "I don't know what to say, Marty, honest. If you can't dig up fifteen grand, you're up against it and that's a fact."

Marty crumpled *The Ring* and threw it across the room. "I wouldn't pay it if I had it!"

"But that's the only kind of deal you can make, Marty-boy. It ain't like slapping a guy in the snoot, then saying you're sorry and everything's okay. It's fifteen grand."

"The hell with them!"

Chuffy took off his pearl gray homburg and looked unhappily inside at the satin lining. "I wish I could feel that way about it," he said. "But lookit what they done to Young Griffin from Detroit that crossed them—busted his hands! With you it's worse. It's fifteen grand worse. You can't stay holed up here forever, that's a cinch. They'll catch up with you sooner or later—and it's too late to get out of town now. They know you're around, and that Angie, he's wild. Where could you go, anyways? There ain't no place you can fight again. They got connections all over the country. Maybe you could get back in stock car racing like you usta ..."

"That's not racing—that's a hassle." Marty returned incredulously to Lieutenant Flannery. "You mean he said he wouldn't do anything? You told him what I was up against, didn't you? You told him I wouldn't take the dive?"

Chuffy nodded and avoided Marty's eyes. He couldn't tell Marty everything Flannery had said for most of it had been scathing, obscene and highly uncomplimentary to all fighters.

Chuffy himself felt lucky, for Angie had slapped him around a little, nothing busted. He was Marty's manager and, had it not been absolutely clear that Marty had disobeyed his ringside instructions that night, he'd have gotten the same that was in store for Marty. The old bumpus. It was a mess and no way out.

"But what are the police for?" Marty protested.

Chuffy shook his head again and took a cigar from his pocket. He bit off the end and, after looking around unsuccessfully for an ashtray, fastidiously spat it behind the chest of drawers.

He could tell Marty what the police were for—but he didn't. He knew all about the police. He had carried a gun in the old Prohi days and after, hanging around on the fringe of the rackets, but mostly acting as a free agent for hire when he needed the money. He had been pretty good with guns, all kinds. They came natural to him. But there had always been some mitt to grease, always some cop with his hand out.

Marty paced the room, slapping his fist into the palm of his hand. "All your life you go around honest and sometimes it's tough. You try to be straight and turn in a good bout and here's what it adds up to. The first time you need a cop, he spits in your face. What the hell?" His voice was bitter.

Chuffy watched him. He had never been able to figure Marty out. The kid had been fighting since he was eighteen, he had been around. But he talked like a mark. He should know better. He wasn't any Winchell. Chuffy couldn't figure him out at all. He was a tough boy, a sweetheart in the ring. But sometimes his ideas were strictly apple, like expecting something from a fixed mitt like Flannery. It didn't add up. There was an essential honesty and integrity in Marty that Chuffy regarded with amazement. Chuffy could see no percentage in it. He himself preferred to bet on rigged ponies, to use heavy dice, to take every advantage that was offered. Sometimes he regarded Marty with awe—when he wasn't actually feeling sorry for such unworldly naiveté.

"I'm trying to raise the dough, kid," he said. "A little something came up today. In fact, that's where I'm on my way. I just wanted to stop in and tell you."

Marty said sharply, "Not for me!"

"Okay, for me then. You ain't doing me no good stashed away in this crumbtrap. You don't get no fights that way. I been talking to Angie," he lied, "and they think you're a good bet. Know what I mean? You're on your way up—and they'll go along—only I gotta pay off that fifteen grand."

"Nuts. I'll get out of this by myself."

"Yeah, out of this and into a wooden overcoat. Jesus Christ, you dumb ox, this ain't Boy Scouts. You're on the punklist and nobody gives a damn but me! Get that through your thick Irish skull, will you? The cops don't care, nobody cares!" Chuffy punched his hat angrily. "They can pick you up dead tomorrow and nobody'd care even then. Nobody'd give a damn how holy you were when you were alive and kicking. You beginning to get the idea? So do me a favor and shut your big trap for a minute!"

Marty threw himself on the bed and stared up at the ceiling, clenching his big fists behind his head. Chuffy stood at the foot of the bed and jabbed the air with his cigar.

"You ain't got a chance unless I pay off. That's the reason I'm taking this job, to pay off. Maybe you don't think you crossed nobody—but they think so and that's what counts! And all this baloney about taking a dive. Listen to me for a minute. Your last ten bouts down the Arena was rigged. Not by me. By Nick that runs the Arena. And because why? He likes you and the crowd likes you. He's building you up. But even him, he can't understand why you didn't take the dive. It wouldna hurt you none ... you listening to me?"

"Keep talking," Marty said in a stony voice.

Chuffy watched him apprehensively, realizing there was a change under way in the boy. The face was growing smaller and harder.

"It wouldna hurt you to take a dive just onct," said Chuffy warily. "The crowd likes a guy that don't win all the time. Even Dempsey lost a few times before he was champ. You just gotta play ball, kid. That's the answer. If you want to get any place in this town or any other town, you just plain gotta play ball. That's all. Nothing against you. It's just business."

Marty's face had grown quite pale. "And what about Flannery?" he asked.

"Forget Flannery. He's just a stooge. A fixed mitt."

"And Nick down at the Arena?"

"There are times even a promoter's gotta do what he's told. Believe me, kid."

Marty's mouth was rimmed with white and his eyes were wild. His eyes had looked funny from the moment Chuffy told him his last ten fights had been tank jobs. He rubbed his big hands down his thighs and looked at Chuffy. His eyes were getting meaner.

"Get out of here," he said in a low voice. "Get out while the getting's good. I'm warning you."

Chuffy said, "Sure, kid, sure," and edged toward the door. "But like I said, I'm working on it." He ducked out as Marty sat up and swung his legs over the edge of the bed.

Chuffy found Jasmine waiting for him in the lobby, slouched down in a lounge chair, her childish mouth sullen. She looked more like a schoolgirl than ever. He took her arm and led her to a dark niche in the shadow behind the telephone booth.

"Go up there again, honey," he said. "I think he's in the mood now."

"And get slapped around?" she jeered. "Uh-uh."

"No, he's okay. He's calmed down. I want you to go up there and stay with him for a while."

She gave him a narrow glance. "What's going on?"

"Well, he's kind of mixed up. He just found out there ain't no Sandy Claws, know what I mean? I want you to stay with him so he don't take it into his head to do somethin' dumb."

"What's that gun he's got?"

"Nothing." Chuffy showed her another twenty. "That's one of the things I want you to get away from him before he hurts himself. It's under his pillow. Throw it out the window or something."

A speculative glitter came into her eyes. There was something odd about her eyes but Chuffy couldn't decide what it was. There was something odd about all of her, as far as that went. She wasn't any regular whore. He had known the minute he picked her up, out in the swanky Forest Hill section. She looked more like a kid just out for the kicks. There was something disorganized about her eyes, something reckless and sick.

"If you want me to get the gun," she said, "it's worth more than twenty."

Chuffy opened his wallet. He had one ten dollar bill and that was all. "That's all I got," he said.

She took it. "Can I keep the gun?" she asked eagerly.

"I don't give a damn what you do with it. Just get it away from the kid, that's all. What's your name again?"

"Helen Thom ... it's Jasmine, dahling," she laughed. "It's Jasmine Vine." She laughed again. "I bloom at night. Is that what you wanted to know?"

"Just out for the kicks, eh?"

"And this." She tucked the thirty dollars into her expensive alligator handbag, a bag no ordinary pro would ever carry. She smiled and looked at his tough simian face. Her eyes became hot and she leaned toward him. "Why do I have to bother with that square upstairs? Why don't you and I go someplace and have a little party? You can raise some more money, can't you? You look as if you knew how to enjoy yourself. I don't like kids. Just you and I. What do you say?"

Chuffy licked his lips. He was tempted. Her perfume, an expensive one, was heady. And the feel of her young body against him set his pulses churning. And she was his kind of girl, too—the adolescent schoolgirl type. Christ! He wrenched his skittering thoughts back onto the track and stepped away from her, shaking his head.

"Later, baby," he said. "Right now I got something I gotta look into. Where can I pick you up?"

"The corner of Broad and Market. What time?"

"Let's see. It's nine-thirty now. Make it midnight."

"Midnight." Her eyes danced recklessly. "I'll pick up a bottle of something and you can pay me back."

"Make it Scotch. Now look, when you get up to the kid's room, you knock like this," he raised his hand and gave that shave-and-a-haircut-bay-rum knock on the wall of the phone booth. "Got it?"

"I've got it. Don't forget now—the corner of Broad and Market."

She turned and walked off with an insolent swing to her narrow hips. Chuffy watched her hungrily.


### BEAUTIFUL TEASE
CHAPTER TWO

Marty felt his rage explode when the girl walked past him and provocatively sat herself down on the bed, crossing her legs. He had been smoldering and now needed only a target for his fury. He gave an inarticulate growl and made a grab for her but she laughed and rolled to the opposite side of the bed out of his reach, with a flash of slender white thigh above her stocking top. He started around the foot of the bed and she poised, still laughing at him, ready to leap across the bed again when he approached.

He made a rush and once more her legs flashed whitely as she dove across and came up on the other side on her feet.

"Well really, dear," she said, "if I'd known you wanted to play, I'd have worn my rompers. Shall we sit the next one out, dear?"

It was her voice more than anything that stopped him cold. It was a custom voice, cool and snooty, a private school voice that tinkled like ice cubes in a tall glass—not the voice of a little tart.

"Why don't you beat it?" he said heavily.

"Because I don't wish to, dear."

"Light a rag, will you? Nobody wants you here. Scram, dangle, take a powder."

"My, we have quite a vocabulary, haven't we, dear? And so picturesque. Where did we ever learn it?"

Marty threw himself down on the bed and she darted away—but this time he was not pursuing her. He bunched the pillow under his head and lay staring moodily up at the ceiling. She hovered at the foot of the bed.

"Why don't you like me?" she asked. "Everybody likes me."

He ignored her. She leaned on the footboard and looked down at him, smiling faintly.

"Don't you ever have any fun, dear? Or are you the serious type? Don't you ever get any kicks?"

Her eyes narrowed angrily when he continued to ignore her. His eyes were withdrawn. She stood up straight, tilting her chin.

"You're making it very difficult for me, dear," she said too sweetly.

He was scarcely aware of her. His mind was coursing down frustrating alleys, into the deadends. Every word Chuffy had spoken at the end had been like a solid right hook to the jaw and Chuffy had not pulled any of his punches. All Marty could think of was—his last ten fights had been set-ups. He remembered his elation at winning, his keyed-up nervousness before entering the ring, his hard, conscientious training for each bout. And what for? He could have trained on lemon meringue. But what was worse, there was nothing ahead. How could he ever tell again, when he stepped into a ring, if it was going to be a straight bout or a set-up? How could he ever fight again? How could he ever believe in anything again? In Chuffy, in Nick, the cops, anybody. Everybody was out for a fast buck. That's what it amounted to. The fast buck. It didn't matter how honest you were or how straight you tried to be, the fast buck always caught up with you in the end. It was always faster than you were.

He was snapped out of his bitter reverie by the sudden violent shaking of the bed. He looked down and saw Jasmine shaking the footboard with both hands. He didn't say anything. He just glowered.

"I thought you were dead," she said calmly.

He dropped his head back on the pillow and stared up at the ceiling again. He heard her cross the room and a few moments later the small radio on the chest of drawers burst into music.

"Shall we dance, dear?" she asked. "No? I'll dance for you, then. Maybe you think you won't watch—but you will. You really will ..."

It was a few minutes before Marty realized she had taken off all her clothes except for her garterbelt, stockings and shoes. Her body was as slim as a candle-flame, a creamy white, her feminine contours somehow childlike, only half-formed. Her long legs were slender and there was a hint of coming fullness in the straight, smooth thighs.

"I told you you'd watch!" she cried triumphantly when she saw his glance flicker over her.

But when she began to dance, he looked up at the ceiling again. Her mouth thinned angrily. She walked over to him and sat down, running her fingers through his thick black hair.

"Poor baby," she crooned. "He's all upset and bothered. Tell Jasmine all about it."

He turned his head on the pillow and looked up at her. "Why don't you go home and do your arithmetic lesson?" he asked stonily.

She flushed, then laughed. "But dear," she said, "I simply can't tear myself away from you. My poor little heart is going pit-a-pat. Feel it."

She seized his hand and placed it over her heart before he could pull away.

"Why, heavens to Betsy!" she murmured. "Just look at him. He blushes."

He lay there stiffly, his rage building up inside him again. It was not her precocious chatter—but the feeling that she had come from that cynical Outside to torment him.

She saw none of the danger signs or, if she did, she paid scant attention—the bunching of his thick black eyebrows, the gathering of his lips into a tight knot, the swift, slashing sidelong glance, the slow beginning movement of his hands over his thighs as if he were rubbing the sweat from them.

She chattered away, poking fun at him, running her fingertips lightly over his face, tracing the outline of his mouth with a feathered forefinger, feeling the hard ropiness of the muscles in his arm. She was very sure of herself, of the ultimate effect she would have on him. She had accepted the challenge and she was beginning to enjoy herself, teasing him little by little, gloating as he became more and more aware of her.

In the end, she had decided, she would refuse him. She would leap away from his urgent, reaching hands and laugh at him. Then she would walk out. He had it coming.

She bent over him. "Let me see how you look when you smile, dear," she said. She lifted the corner of his mouth with her finger.

She gave a cry as he turned on her and tried to spring from his grasp but he was faster than she had imagined—and stronger. She struggled but he held her arms tight and pulled her roughly to him. His grin glittered for a moment before her eyes, then he ground a savage kiss into her lips which were parted to cry out again. She tried frantically to squirm away but he grasped the hinges of her jaws between his thumb and middle finger and held her rigid while he raked her mouth with kisses. When he finally moved his face from hers, she watched him with wide, frightened eyes.

"But really, dear," she said shakily, in an attempt to recapture her light, superior tone. "Really ..."

Her eyes followed his hand as he reached to turn out the lamp.


## WIN, LOSE OR DRAW
### CHAPTER THREE

Chuffy slipped from the hotel entrance into the stream of pedestrian traffic down Market Street toward Penn Station. His destination was the Pastime Pool & Billiards on West Market Street where he was to ask for Petey McKim. Chuffy had known McKim since the old Prohi days. McKim had called him at noon to ask if he'd be interested in a job—and he didn't mean racking up balls.

Chuffy had asked cynically, "Who's that hard up? I ain't handled heat for ten years."

"Are you interested or ain't you? That's all I want to know."

If it hadn't been for Marty and the fifteen grand, Chuffy would have turned it down. But he was anxious to get Marty fighting again. His win over the Hunky had made him bigger than ever with the crowd and Nick was talking about working him into the finals. But first he had to square the beef with Angie. Chuffy wanted no part of McKim's job—but this was different.

"How much is in it?" That's what it came down to.

"I wouldn't know. Not peanuts. Well?"

"Oke."

"Be here at ten tonight."

It was twenty of ten now as Chuffy lengthened his stride. He walked into the Pastime at five of. McKim, fat and disgusted looking, was seated on a high stool behind the cigar counter, sucking at a cup of coffee. Chuffy threw a quarter on the counter and pointed to a box of cigars. McKim held out the box and Chuffy took a cigar, sticking it into his breast pocket.

"What gives?" he asked.

McKim moved his ponderous shoulders irritably. "How would I know? Anyway, I don't wanna know. Back room. You're early."

"So I'm early. Gettin' much?"

"My share. You?"

"I do all right." Chuffy's lips quirked as he thought of his midnight date with Jasmine. He was doing all right, all right. He nodded at McKim and moved slowly down the room, stopping at one of the tables to watch a hard masse shot bungled. He laughed softly and moved on.

The room was quiet. It was always quiet—just the murmurous hum of low-voiced conversation and the brittle click of the balls.

He drifted into the men's room and stayed there a few minutes. Then he came out and slipped into the back room. In the center of the small room was a round table and several wooden chairs. A slim, dark-faced man sat at the table, playing solitaire. There was a bottle of rye at his elbow but it was still sealed. He glanced up as Chuffy entered, then his eyebrows arched.

"Hiya, Chuffy," he said. There was just a trace of accent in his liquid voice.

Chuffy said, "Cuesta," and sat down at the table. "What gives?"

Cuesta shrugged delicately. "You know McKim. Any ideas?" Cuesta was Spanish—or said he was—a hothead but steady when the cards were down. A good man. For this kind of stuff, Chuffy amended. Johnny Dillinger was a good man too—and Cuesta didn't come anywheres near Johnny. He'd end up like Johnny, though. That's how good he was. That's how good they all were. Suckers.

He voiced his thought, "It's gotta be big or they can include me out. I need a stake."

"Who don't?"

The door opened and McKim stuck his head into the room. He beckoned silently to Chuffy, who stood up and went over to him.

McKim whispered, "One of Angie's extra special tough boys walked in right after you. I thought you squared that beef."

"I did." Chuffy's tongue darted nervously over his lips. "It's the kid they want. They got no beef with me."

"And you got him stashed away."

"Not me. I don't know where he went after he ran out of the Arena."

"You're a goddamn liar. So you got him stashed away. So what? I wouldn't hand over my worst enemy to a maniac like Angie. All the same, I don't want any trouble. You better talk to The Eye when he comes. Maybe he can put the pressure on."

"I thought that was the guy you were calling for," said Chuffy with satisfaction. "I went up and looked at his house, big place up Forest Hill. Don't look at me like that. If it was anybody but The Eye, you'd have said so. Anyways, you done business for him before."

McKim growled, "Wise guy, aintcha? But you put it up to The Eye. He'll square it."

"Fifteen grand worth?"

"Are you kiddin' yourself, chump?"

"How?"

"Angie don't want the dough, he wants the neck. You better talk to The Eye or you'll have a dead boy on your hands. Jesus," he said disgustedly, "that pug of yours must have rocks in his head."

"He's a clean kid."

"He's a dead one, on'y he don't know it yet. Look, chump, I'll cover for you as much as I can. If that jerk out there starts nosing around, throw him out on his can. I can get away with that much with Angie— but no more. Better keep this door locked."

McKim's head disappeared. Chuffy closed the door and shot the bolt. Cuesta looked up from his cards.

"What was that all about?" he asked.

"McKim says The Eye'll be here any minute."

"I thought it was him. It's big if he's mixed up in it. I hope to Christ it's big—or I'll have to start rolling drunks."

He went back to his cards and Chuffy sat smoking his cigar, trying to conceal his growing agitation. He hadn't thought Angie would put a tail on him—but the fact that the tail had followed him here was reassuring in a way. At least they hadn't found Marty in that fleabag up the street.

About ten minutes later there was a sharp knock at the door leading out to the alley. Chuffy opened it. A bulky man in a chauffeur's uniform sent a sharp, searching glance over the room, then turned and walked out into the alley. Chuffy closed the door and waited. In a few minutes there was another knock and this time a tall, imposing man with a senatorial manner came in. He had iron gray hair and a stern face. He had an air of unshakable confidence and was quite obviously prosperous.

This was Walter Thomas, known in criminal circles as The Eye. He operated only in Newark. He was a fairly successful attorney but his real money came from his criminal connections. If a criminal arrived in Newark with an adequate amount of money and wanted to pull a job, he went first to Thomas, who always had a variety of jobs lined up. For a percentage of the take, he could furnish a blueprint of the job, line up the necessary hired help and make the fix. This was a lucrative pursuit that depended largely on City Hall good will but of late there had been talk of a gubernatorial investigation coming out of Trenton—and Thomas did not feel as secure as he once had. There was no hint now, however, of nervousness as he walked into the room, gave both men a small, impersonal smile, and looked carefully around to make sure things were as they seemed. Then he went back to the doorway and said, "All right."

Chuffy's heart gave a lurching bound when a stocky, compact man walked in and closed the door. There wasn't a criminal in the country who wouldn't have recognized that round hard face set with gray eyes as cold as January ice. Gerald Barth was Big Time, credited with a list of bank robberies that sounded like a roll call of the Federal Reserve membership. He had not actually committed all of them, of course, but he had pulled off enough of them to deserve his fantastic, if somewhat exaggerated reputation.

He looked from Cuesta to Chuffy, then turned and said sharply to Thomas, "I wanted three men."

Thomas' answer was a little stiff. "It was the best I could do on short notice. I told you it wasn't going to be easy."

Barth made an impatient noise in his throat and turned back to Cuesta.

"I know you," he said. "You're Angel Cuesta. I worked with you in Fargo. Do you still get the shakes before a strike?"

Cuesta's teeth gleamed in a brief smile. "Always—but I'm all right after. I didn't let you down, did I?"

"No. You were okay." Barth swung around to Chuffy. "You the driver?"

Chuffy shook his head and Thomas said smoothly, "Chuffy's a wizard with guns. McKim gave him an especially strong recommendation."

Barth said drily, "That's fine. But what are we supposed to do—make the strike on bicycles? We have to have a driver—and I don't mean just some punk who knows how to shift gears."

"I'll get you a driver! But please do me the favor of remembering that these are peculiar circumstances. Neither of us can operate in the usual way. Now, you two"—he turned to Chuffy and Cuesta—"this is your boss. What he says goes." He nodded shortly at Barth and went out through the alley door.

Barth swung a chair around and straddled it, resting his arms on its

back. Chuffy could feel the force of the man even before he spoke. It was
partly, of course, Barth's reputation for daring and successful coups—
but the force was there, the impact. Chuffy immediately knew this man
was hard all the way through—up and down, inside and out.

"I'm not going to tell you two a goddamn thing," said Barth without
preliminaries. "That's the way I operate. I don't want anybody
masterminding the strike before we make it. If you don't like it, say so
now and get your can out of here."

He waited a moment but neither Cuesta nor Chuffy said anything.
Barth nodded.

"Okay so far," he said. "Now for the dough. There's no split. I never split.
That works both ways. You get paid, win-lose-or-draw. On a split, you'd
stand a chance of getting nothing but lumps. You're both supposed to
be good men and you'll be paid accordingly. Ten grand apiece, half down
and the rest after the strike, win-lose-or-draw. Yes or no?"

Cuesta said, "Okay by me," and looked at Chuffy.

Chuffy said, "Oke." He was disappointed. He had thought working
with Barth would mean a really big score. He wanted to argue but the
will went out of him under Barth's cold, steady gaze. There was no
arguing with Barth; he knew. It was take it or leave it.

"Everything understood now?" asked Barth. "I don't want any squawks
from here on in. This is a good strike and it's all laid out. It can be
rough—or it can be a walkaway. I think it'll be a walkaway. I'll tell you
this much and that's all—you won't have to worry about the law. That
part of it'll be all over by the time we move in. But nothing," he added,
"is ever a walkaway until it's over. Now if anybody's got anything on his
mind, let's have it. We've got to start clean. You, Cuesta?"

Cuesta shook his head.

"Not me," said Chuffy.

"Then everybody's happy and satisfied," said Barth with irony, as if he
knew from experience how happy and satisfied they would remain. He
took two slips of paper from his pocket and handed one to each of them.
"That's the address I want you to be at tomorrow morning. And I mean
tomorrow morning. That's where you'll get your dough and that's where
you'll stay until we make the strike. You're going to live like hermits for
a while, so you might just as well make up your mind to it. I don't want
anybody going on the town and getting his brains picked."

Chuffy glanced at the slip in his hand. It read: "*Birch Cottage, Sunset
Drive, Lake Powhatan, Hazelview, New Jersey. Take Erie train or Public
Service bus No. 314 or Route No. 6 by car.*"

"Tomorrow morning," repeated Barth with emphasis. He stood up.

Cuesta gathered up his cards and put them in his pocket. He glanced at the whisky bottle, changed his mind, and pushed back his chair.

"Can I drop anybody any place?" he asked. "I got a car." Neither Barth nor Chuffy wanted a lift so Cuesta walked out with a brief, "See you."

Chuffy waited till he had gone, then said to Barth, "I think maybe I can get you a driver."

"Why didn't you say so before?"

"I just thought of it."

"Is he any good?"

"He used to race stock cars. That good enough?"

"How would I know till I talk to him?" said Barth roughly. "He can be the best driver in the world but he can be chicken, too. Jesus Christ, you should know that much!"

Chuffy was surprised at the outburst. Barth might look as cold as ice—but here he was blowing hot.

"I don't know if he'll be interested," Chuffy said warily. "I'll go get him and you can talk it over."

"The hell you will. There's been too much coming and going here tonight as it is."

"If you want, he's just down the street ..."

"I'm not going down any streets," Barth exploded. "Use your head!" Then he seemed suddenly to regain his composure. "You know where Thomas' place is, out in the Forest Hill section? Okay. Get him there about one o'clock. Thomas should be home by then. Anything else?"

"The dough. How much?"

"The same as you and Cuesta."

"I'll tell him but I ain't making no promises."

Barth shrugged as if he didn't care one way or the other. Chuffy started for the door leading out into the poolroom, then he remembered Angie's man might still be out there so he turned and went out through the alley.

Barth went over and locked the door after him. Then he leaned against it and closed his eyes, fighting down that sick quivering inside him. He pushed himself away from the door and said angrily aloud, "Washed up, hell!"

He went over to the table, tore the seal from the whisky bottle and drank straight from the neck. He stood still for a moment, letting the hotness burn through him. He didn't want to make this strike. Two years ago he had made up his mind never to make another strike. Hell, only two weeks ago he'd thought it was all over ...

## THE FASTIDIOUS STREETWALKER
CHAPTER FOUR

Two weeks ago he had walked out of prison. He'd served eighteen months. Deliberately, as part of his plan to get out of the racket and stay out. He had held up a gas station and bungled it purposely, let himself get taken. In prison he had been apathetic, as if he had finally broken. Then, after eighteen months, they let him out. He knew he'd be under police surveillance from the moment he walked through those prison gates, and he acted accordingly.

The first thing he did was to get himself a pint bottle of gin. The second thing was to empty the gin down a toilet in the railroad station and refill the bottle with water. Then he had gone on what looked like a ten day binge, drunk every minute—Barth, the guy who was known never to touch a drop. He could always spot the tail the police had on him and at the end of ten days the tail was no longer there and the word went around that Barth was all washed up and hitting the bottle.

Well, he was all washed up—but not the way they thought. He was tired. There were heavy lines in his face, trenched from the sides of his nose to the end of his mouth. His eyes were crow-footed. But worse, he was bone tired, bone and marrow tired, tired to the core, tired of the everlasting running-away of the criminal life. In his last two jobs, there had been none of the hard bright joy of pulling a big strike—and even the plans had been a little sour. Not sour enough to spoil but sour enough for him to know they were sour. That was what had decided him to get out and stay out. He was washed up. And once he admitted it to himself, he felt nothing but relief.

He had fifty grand stashed away in three safe deposit boxes and his sister in Philly was holding the keys for him. Fifty grand would buy him a motel in Florida and, with Sissie, that was where he intended to spend the ten or fifteen remaining years of his life, drowsing in the sun, fishing, unharried by the police. But anything as wonderful to anticipate as that, couldn't come true. Maybe he had known that all along, too. Fluffy dreams just didn't pan out for men like Gerald Barth.

It took him two days to reach his sister's home in Philly for he went by a circuitous route to shake any police tails that might still be dodging around. And when he got there, they were waiting for him. They took him down to Headquarters, where they told him his sister had been killed in a motor accident. They dangled a ring of keys in front of his face.

"Take a look at these, Barth. Take a good look. Safe deposit keys. What banks are they from? Come on, sit up! What banks? We know you got stuff stashed away and we're going to find out where—if we have to keep you here from now on!"

They kept it up, hour after hour, even after he could no longer pretend to be drunk. And then he simulated the shakes and begged for a drink, just one little drink. He didn't have to fake much, either, for his hands had really begun to shake.

They finally gave him up in disgust—after they had pounded his kidneys with padded nightsticks and slapped him around. "Come on, Barth. What banks? What banks?"

He didn't know anything about any safe deposit keys. He didn't know anything about anything. All he wanted was a drink. His eyes watered from the beating they gave him—and they thought it was because he needed alcohol. His head and hands shook. And he pleaded constantly for a drink.

In the end, they believed him and turned him loose.

He was, in fact, not far from madness—Sissie dead, fifty grand gone, eighteen months served for nothing. And gone, too, that opium dream of peace and security.

They let him go, and he made a beeline for the nearest gin mill, the one just across the street from Headquarters. It was full of off-duty cops, politicos, lawyers, bait-bondsmen, wardheels, and just plain political crumbs.

He downed one drink after another until he was really drunk. When he reeled out, a detective followed him. As drunk as he was, he noted that—so he reeled into the next gin mill he came to and drank some more. He had about a hundred dollars in his wallet and two more fifties sewn into the cuffs of his trousers. He went on a real binge, staggering from one bar to another, winding up in a really tough joint near the railroad terminal. There he sprawled over a table, weeping for his fifty grand and for Sissie. But mostly for Sissie. And no one dared to approach him, for the detective stood watching from the bar, sipping at his beer.

The girl who came in a little later was either too tired to take in the situation or too inexperienced to realize it even existed. She was a tall girl with broad Slavic cheekbones. She had a wide mouth—a wide, tender, gentle mouth. She shied away from the men at the bar and walked over to Barth's table with a self-conscious swagger. She slipped into the chair beside him and reached for his bottle.

"Buy a girl a drink, sailor?" she asked in a husky, tired voice.

The barkeep made a move to interfere but the detective put out his arm and stopped him, then hooked his elbows over the edge of the bar and watched interestedly, weighing the value of an idea that had just come to him.

The girl poured herself a drink, but she barely touched the glass with her lips. Asking for it had just been her opening gimmick. She set down her glass and gave Barth a mechanical smile. He had said nothing, for he was almost incapable of articulate speech by then. And she did not seem to know how to go on.

"What's your name, sailor?" she asked finally.

He kept ogling her foggily. He could see that she was female but that was just about all he could see. He felt a faint, futile stirring of desire. He reached out but she took his hand quickly before it could touch her. It seemed a most curious fastidiousness in a streetwalker.

"Now now, sailor, be nice," she said hurriedly.

The barkeep gave the detective a worried glance and mumbled, "Look, friend, I don't like this—I don't run that kind of place."

The detective grinned, "Oh, sure."

Now the girl, with uneasy side glances toward the men at the bar, was trying to get Barth out of the gin mill. "How about a little walk, sailor? Let's go down to my place and have a party, just me and you, eh?"

He mumbled something that made no sense except possibly to himself but the girl took it as acquiescence. She stood up and helped him to his feet.

"Let's go, sailor," she said. "Up we go. That's right. Now straight ahead ..."

No prostitute had ever before picked up a mark so clumsily—nor with such an interested audience.

He was almost bonelessly limp but he managed to keep his feet as she steered him toward the door. He grinned fatuously and pawed at her. She pushed his hands away.

The detective slid off his stool and, without offering to pay for his three beers, followed them out of the gin mill. He caught up with them halfway down the block.

"I'll give you a hand, sister," he grinned.

The girl's eyes spread with fright. She was not so inexperienced that she couldn't recognize a cop, especially an obvious cop like him with that air of arrogance and that hard flat voice that was like a slap across the face.

"It's not a pinch," he told her. He leered, "Paid your dues, didn't you? Where's your crib?"

Wordlessly, she pointed down the street. He took Barth's left arm around his shoulders and jerked him upright.

"Let's go," he said.

He paid no attention to the hate in her eyes. He was used to that. He saw it every day—he was that kind of cop. He'd probably have missed it if it hadn't been there.

Together, they half-dragged Barth down the street and up into the house. Her room was on the third floor. The stairway sagged soggily under their weight and the detective cursed as Barth's feet kept getting tangled in the spindles of the handrail.

Her room contained a bed, a chair, a chest of drawers, a toilet and a handbasin. The toilet and basin were not in a separate room but were screened by a cheap cretonne drape.

The detective dumped Barth on the bed. Amazingly, Barth was not yet unconscious, despite the tremendous amount of liquor he had downed. There are times when a man just can't drink himself out of misery, no matter how much he drinks. Barth just lay there miserably, tears running down his face, mumbling over and over again, "Sissie, Sissie, oh Sissie...."

The detective said with disgust, "This is what I get stuck with all the time, some goddamn rummy. All right, sister, all right, come on—get his clothes off."

They undressed him, throwing his clothes on the floor.

Then the detective said to the girl, "Go ahead, sister, peel."

She undressed slowly, with more than reluctance. She did not mind nudity. Men had seen her naked before—but this was different. With the detective standing there, his eyes never leaving her. There was no desire in his eyes, no heat, just that cold hard flat appraisal.

"Come on, come on," he said. "What's the matter with you?"

She hung her skirt and blouse carefully over the back of the chair. She was not wearing a slip. She hesitated—and he became really angry.

"What do you want," he demanded, "ninety days? Now, take it off!"

She shrugged out of her brassiere and took off her panties. Her stockings were held up by a garter belt. She started to unfasten it but he slapped her hand away.

"You look better that way," he grinned. He eyed her voluptuous, full curves from her lovely long neck to the gracefully rounded thighs, on down to the slender ankles. He winked. "If I wasn't on duty, I'd give you a little attention myself. And that's something I wouldn't do with every mud-kicker that comes down the street. You're well stacked. All right, get to work on him now. Put your arms around him. Ask him where he's going, what he's going to do—all that. I'll be right here listening, so make it good."

She obeyed stiffly. Barth mumbled and moved against her. The detective crossed the tiny room and sat down on the toilet, pulling the curtain closed in front of him, leaving a crack through which he could watch.

"Go ahead," he ordered. "What do you want me to do, teach you your business?"

The girl said mechanically, "Where you bound for, sailor?"

Barth mumbled, heaved a deep sigh and fell asleep.

"He's sleeping," she said shortly to the detective.

"Well, for crissake wake him up. You know how."

"He's dead to the world."

The detective swore and came striding across the room. He lifted Barth's head from the pillow by the hair. He slapped his cheeks back and forth, palm and backhand, palm and backhand. He let the head fall back, then twisted Barth's ears until the girl cried out. But Barth did not even moan. The detective snapped his fingers and said, "Wait a minute."

He went over to the toilet and came back with a bottle of ammonia. He sniffed at it and jerked his head back. He said, "Whew!" Then he held it under Barth's nose. Barth turned his head away but the detective followed his movement with the bottle. Finally Barth's eyes opened a little.

"Wassa matta?" he said thickly.

"Got any liquor?" the detective demanded.

The girl pointed hostilely to the chest of drawers. There was a pint bottle of whisky standing on it. The detective brought it back to the bedside.

"Sometimes," he said, "a snort brings them around again for a while." He opened Barth's mouth and poured a little whiskey into it. Barth coughed and swallowed. The detective poured a little more and this time Barth swallowed without coughing. The detective gave him a little more, then put the bottle down on the floor. He looked down at Barth with satisfaction.

Barth had revived a little. His hand was moving sluggishly over the girl's smooth white flesh and his eyelids were open in narrow slits. He was mumbling. The detective gave the girl a nod.

"Now go to work on him," he said. "Get him talking. If he starts to go under again, give him another whiff of that ammonia."

He went back and sat on the toilet. He kept the drape open and told her what to do and exactly how to do it. She did whatever he told her but she kept her eyes closed tightly and she kept counting to herself— one-two-three-four-five-six—so she wouldn't have to think about what he was making her do.

All night long, through hours that stretched endlessly, he kept her at it, kept her working with the ammonia bottle, kept her talking.

"Where you bound for, sailor? Going any place special?"

It was all right and she kept it up as long as Barth was too drunk to know what was going on. But at dawn, when his eyes opened and she saw that he was aware of her alongside him, she bent over him, screening him from the detective, whispered quickly in his ear, "There's a cop taking it in. Watch it!"

Then aloud she said, "Coming around, sailor? How's about a little drink, a little eye-opener?"

She reached over to get the almost empty pint of rye. Barth held it with trembling hands and took a long swallow. "Cop?" he whispered into her ear.

She nodded and said loudly, "You had quite a night, sailor. How you feeling?"

"Don't ask," he groaned—loudly enough for the detective to hear.

"Staying long in Philly?"

"Not if I can get out of it. But what comes after? I'm busted, broke, flat. My sister had some dough but she's dead. Dead," he repeated slowly as he remembered. "She's dead ..." Tears crept into his eyes.

The girl put her hands to his cheeks, moved by his tears.

"Just a lousy rummy," said Barth thickly. "That's all I am, just a lousy rummy. But who gives a damn anyway? This all the liquor you got?" He held up the empty bottle in his shaking hand.

"We can get some more, sailor."

She looked back over her shoulder. The detective was standing outside the curtain. He motioned her to keep Barth covered and tiptoed to the door. The latch clicked as he went out, satisfied now that Barth was really washed up. That would be his report at Headquarters. Barth was broke and a rummy.

Barth said clearly, "He's gone?"

The girl sat back wearily. "Yes."

"This must have been a nice night for you."

"What could I do?"

"Cops!" he said.

He patted her gently and sat up. He put his hands to his eyes and the sudden movement made them throb painfully. She looked at him softly.

"Want me to run down to the gin mill and pick up a bottle?" she asked.

"Nix. Last night was enough. Got any coffee?"

"I can get some from the lunch wagon."

"Good. Here's some dough."

He looked around, saw his pants on the floor, reached down into the pocket and gave her a five dollar bill. He watched her, his eyes kindling, as she jumped out of bed and pulled on her dress. When she left, he went over to the basin behind the curtain and splashed his face with cold water. He lifted his head and stared at the haggard face looking out at him from the mirror. It was a shock. It was as if he were seeing it for the first time, seeing the gray, sagging cheeks, the tired lines, the lackluster eyes, the down-curving, defeated mouth.

Washed up!

He made an effort and stood straighter, throwing back his broad shoulders. He tightened his mouth and looked steadily into the mirror. That was better. A shave would help, too. He wasn't quite washed up yet. He had the makings of another strike in him, one more last strike. He had to have money. He couldn't live without it. He could make one more last strike, then lose himself in Florida. He still had it in him.

As he turned from the mirror, a wave of loneliness passed over him like a sudden sickness. Perhaps it was the sober sight of that mean room, perhaps it reminded him of some of the dreary hideouts he had vegetated in from time to time—but more probably, it went deeper than that. More probably, this drab slattern of a room showed him in a flash what the end of hope looked like. The Florida dream had been very real to him for eighteen long months. The contrast was shocking.

He had always been a loner, self-sufficient. But now, for the first time, he found himself listening desperately for the returning footsteps of another human being. The decision was not conscious—he was totally unaware of having made it—but he resolved at that moment never to be so alone again as long as he lived.

Newark was a haven for him. He had local connections and had never made a strike there, so the police had no personal reason to remember him. He had brought Sophie along with him from Philly. That was the biggest change in him. He had always had women—sex was his torment—but they had always been call girls, women of the urgent moment, nothing more. Johnny Dillinger, among others, had had the finger put on him by a woman. Barth was never going to let that happen to him. But he had persuaded himself Sophie was different— and anyway, this was his last strike, so there was no danger. And he needed her. Not just for sex—but for the tenderness and gentleness that was in her. When she was with him, he could forget his sick melancholy.

His Newark connections were the best and within a matter of hours he had learned that a big strike was pending and the spark-plug was Jack Niles. Niles was a wild man with a bad reputation for savagery. No one knew where the strike would be made but there were three guesses—the National City and County Trust, the Eastern Electric payroll, or the Citizens State Bank. None of the three had ever been scored on. And everybody agreed, too, that Niles must surely have secured his blueprint from The Eye, Walter Thomas.

Barth's first thought had been to go to Niles and tell him he wanted in. There wouldn't be any fuss about that. Niles, even if he were a mad dog, would be more than glad to have him. But he could not bring himself to go to Niles. His stomach churned with revolt at the thought. It was plain, ordinary fear—though he told himself if he did cut in on this strike, Niles would be eager for him to plan it—and then it would fall into the typical Barth pattern, which the police knew pretty well by this time, so that was out. But the truth was, he didn't have it anymore—didn't have the necessary drive to walk in calmly with guns, make the strike and maintain control until the getaway. He couldn't face it anymore, the thought that there might be shooting, that something might go sour, that the police might crash in before the strike was finished.

He could not go to Niles and he told himself it was because Niles was a mad dog and could not be trusted. Niles' style was to crash in, make the strike and blast out, carrying it off by sheer savagery.

What Barth really wanted was a safe, simple way to make a strike, with no repercussions afterward. That was how far he had slipped. But he was to slip still farther, for the idea that came to him was one that would never have occurred to him in the past. He would let Niles do the work, then hijack the take after it was all over. It was simple and reasonably safe, for Niles would never know what hit him. There was one difficulty and that was to get Niles' blueprint from somebody in the know. That was when he braced Thomas, after nerving himself with Scotch.

It was a curious meeting, for Thomas was just about washed up, too. The Trenton investigation was imminent and he had the jitters.

When Barth said, "Jack Niles is going to make a strike and you laid it out for him," Thomas had turned so white that he looked like a drained corpse.

But Barth hardly noticed, he was so busy holding on to his own nerve with both hands. This was the hump he had to get over. If Thomas kicked him out and repeated it to Niles, it would be curtains. Niles would be sure to rub him out—or chase him out.

Barth went on in a desperately calm voice. "The best cut you'll get from Niles will be a quarter of the score. I'm offering you a better proposition. Fifty-fifty."

Thomas squirmed. His broad plump face was bathed in perspiration. But his mind was clicking. Fifty-fifty. That would give him enough to get out from under before the investigation reached out and tapped him on the shoulder. He wasn't going to get a quarter from Niles. He was going to get only a seventh. There was a big difference.

He said hoarsely, "Niles would blast us off the map."

Barth managed a grin. "He'd have to be alive, wouldn't he?"

In the end, it was Barth's own reputation that persuaded Thomas—that, and the fact that he would have enough money to get out of the country and stay out until the investigation had petered out.

"But for the love of God," he said, "don't bobble it—or we'll both be dead meat."

Now that he was over the hump, now that the danger was past, Barth could relax and give a fair imitation of the way he used to be—cold, hard, and decisive. Niles' escape route was what he wanted. Thomas sketched it rapidly on a sheet of blank paper with a hand that shook only a little.

"Here's the strike," he said, touching the map with the tip of his pencil. "The Stratton Armored Car Service. It's never been scored on and it's ripe. The take should be close to a million. After the strike, they'll cut down to Mulberry Street, turn north to the Clay Street bridge, over the bridge and north again on River Road in Kearny. Here," his pencil touched another point on the map, "is where they'll change cars, on River Road. The original car will be taken to Weehawken and abandoned in the Forty-Second Street Ferry parking lot, to give the impression that the getaway was into New York. They'll leave some of the money bags in the car so that it can be identified."

Barth said, "So far, so good. But where does the second car go? The farther you run, the more chance of being picked up before you get to the hideout."

"Right. The second car cuts back over the Belleville Turnpike bridge and heads north into Nutley. The hideout is right here on the river, a three-story Victorian house with a cupola. Niles and the boys have been staying there for the past three weeks to give the people in the neighborhood a chance to get used to seeing somebody around."

Barth looked down at the map, nodding. "Here's where to take them," he lied, putting his finger on the spot where Niles planned to switch cars in Kearny. "We'll take the car that's waiting and get them when they try to switch. We'll have them out in the open."

He lied because he didn't trust Thomas. His actual plan was to hit when Niles rolled into the hideout in Nutley. The less Thomas knew about that, the better. Thomas was pulling one double-cross and there was nothing to prevent his crossing back again.

"Now that's settled," he said crisply, "we can get on with the rest of it. I'll need two cars, a driver, and two good—and I mean good—boys to handle the heat if Niles spooks on us. That'll be your end of it, to get me the cars and the boys ..."

Now, alone in McKim's back room, Barth took another pull at the bottle. The reaction from the strain had left him a little shaky—the reaction from his pretending to be Barth. It had been a shock, seeing Cuesta, for Cuesta had worked with him before and would be quick to see the change, should Barth show in any slight degree how far he had slipped. Cuesta could have blown the whole thing up right there—but Barth had carried it off and now he wanted to get back to Sophie at the hotel as fast as he could.

It was only in Sophie's arms these days that he could renew himself, for she gave so generously of herself, in tenderness and gratitude, that after he had been with her, it was like being reborn. He turned to the door, hurrying now, almost frantically eager to be back in her strong, comforting arms. He thought of her breasts, those wonderful deep maternal breasts ...

## THE THIRD MAN
### CHAPTER FIVE

The radio was still playing when Chuffy walked into Marty's room for the second time that night. Chuffy looked around swiftly but the girl Jasmine—or whatever her name was—had gone. He felt a little stab of disappointment but it sharpened his anticipation of seeing her at midnight.

Marty slammed the door shut and said heavily, "That little bitch ran off with the gun."

"I'll get you another one."

"Suit yourself."

Chuffy gave him a sharp glance. There was a definite change in Marty. He looked tough. He had always looked tough but there had been a kind of boyishness about him, too. Now he looked just plain tough.

Marty snarled, "Well, what's the matter with you? Whattaya lookin' at?"

"Nothin', nothin'," Chuffy said hastily. He was beginning to wish he had never said anything about Marty to Barth. It had been a cockeyed notion. He hedged, "Get along all right with that little tomato?"

"I gave her what she was asking for," said Marty grimly. "She won't be so goddamn smart for a while."

"You smacked her?"

"Forget it, will you? No, I didn't smack her."

Chuffy walked over to the radio and diddled with it until Marty snapped at him to leave it alone. Chuffy nervously lit another cigar.

"Say listen," he blurted, "how'd you like to make a fast ten grand?"

Marty said thinly, "Why not?"

Chuffy was too surprised for a moment to answer. Curiously, he felt betrayed. He had expected furious resistance. It was then he saw that the boyishness was really gone from Marty's face.

"Yeah, why not?" he said. "It's a kind of heist and they need a driver. There's ten grand in it."

"Good."

"Wait a minute. Maybe you ain't got this straight. You know what a heist is? If it backfires, the law'll throw your can in jail."

"The hell with the law. What'd the law ever do for me? But that sounds like a lot of dough for just driving."

"It ain't just driving," said Chuffy in a flat voice. "It's a kind of driving you ain't never done before in your life. It ain't like a race. They won't be wanting to pass you—they'll be wanting to stop you."

"So?"

"That's all. Think you can handle it?"

"I can handle it."

Chuffy mumbled, "I ain't got the last word on it. I gotta take you to see a guy at one." He edged toward the door, suddenly wanting a drink. "I'll pick you up about quarter to one."

Marty nodded. Chuffy opened the door and slipped out. "Christ," he said unhappily.

He was at the corner of Broad and Market at midnight but the high, tingling anticipation had left him. He felt a kind of emptiness inside. He didn't care if Jasmine turned up or not.

She didn't.

Chuffy took a cab, picked Marty up at the hotel and drove out to Thomas' Forest Hill home. Thomas himself let them in and Chuffy could see right away that Thomas was sore.

Thomas said curtly, "In here," and led them into a kind of library. Barth was seated in a lounge chair, a glass of whisky in his hand.

He looked coldly at Marty and said to Chuffy, "This the boy?"

Chuffy nodded. "Marty Doyle," he said. "He used to drive in stock car races. He's good."

"This won't be a stock car race," said Barth drily. "Know what it's all about, Doyle?"

Marty matched his tone. "I got an idea."

Barth sized him up and after a pause said, "Tough boy, eh?"

Marty shrugged as if Barth's opinion was a matter of indifference to him.

Thomas, whose face was covered with perspiration, started heavily, "I don't like using amateurs ..."

Barth interrupted flatly, "It's what I like, not you. He'll do. You, Chuffy, bring him up to the cottage with you tomorrow morning."

Chuffy started to say, "Yessir ..." when the library door opened and a girl looked into the room. It was only for an instant, then the door closed again. Neither Barth nor Thomas had noticed, for their backs were to the door—but Chuffy froze. The girl was Jasmine. A thousand thoughts ran through his head. Had she followed him here? Had Marty really slapped her around? Was she going to make a mess?

Barth looked at him and said sharply, "What's the matter with you?"

Chuffy stammered, with great presence of mind, "Where's the john? I don't feel so good."

Thomas said sourly, "That's all we need—a gunman with the G.I.'s! It's out in the hall, third door to the right."

Chuffy walked out quickly, his heart pounding. He found Jasmine lurking outside in the hall. He grabbed her by the wrist and pulled her into the shadows under the stairway. Her thin, immature face was frightened.

"What is this?" he hissed.

"Let me go. You're hurting me!" She tried to pull away.

"What's the idea?"

"No idea. I live here."

"You work here?" he asked incredulously.

"I live here."

Chuffy glanced over his shoulder and pointed wordlessly toward the library door. "You mean ..."

"I live here," she repeated defiantly.

"And that's your old man?"

"Yes, that's my father. Now let me go, will you? You hurt!"

"I don't get it."

"There's nothing to get. Lots of us girls do it."

"You mean, go around picking up guys?"

"Lots of us do it."

"Jesus!" Chuffy was genuinely shocked. A girl of good family, with everything she could want, a good home and everything, acting like a whore. He could see she was scared, deeply and badly scared.

"I won't tell your old man," he said. "But all the same, I don't get it."

She turned her childish face from him. "It's fun."

"How old are you?"

"Twenty."

"How old?"

"Nineteen—and I can prove it."

"Nineteen? How long have you been running around like this?"

"None of your business."

"Okay, okay." Then, "What happened with you and the kid tonight?"

Her young face clouded. "He's a jerk!" she said viciously.

"What happened?"

She was recovering her poise. "I think I remarked, dear," she said insolently, "that it was none of your business."

"Listen to the duchess," jeered Chuffy.

"Really, though, I should be annoyed with you."

"Oh reely, should you reely?"

"Yes, I should. He's psychopathic."

"You don't say—whatever the hell that is. Listen," he pulled her closer and grinned down at her. "You stood me up tonight and I don't like that, so we're gonna do something about it. You come to my place tonight after I get out of here. Hotel Sherman, Room 303."

"How much?" she asked impudently.

"Never mind that. You be there."

She looked frightened again. He tightened his fingers around her wrist. "You be there!" he repeated.

"All right," she said sullenly. "But you don't have to hurt me, do you?" She pulled her wrist away and rubbed it.

He looked up and down the hall, then pressed her close in his arms. He was suddenly on fire. Christ, what did this kid have for him that nobody else had? She gave him a charge like he'd never felt before.

"You be there," he said huskily for the third time. Then he turned and walked quickly back into the library.

As he walked in, Barth was pouring himself another drink from the decanter on the Chippendale desk. He had been drinking steadily for two hours and he was in a mood of high arrogance.

"There's nothing the matter with you, is there?" he snapped at Chuffy.

"With me?" Chuffy had forgotten his impromptu excuse.

"Yeah, you. I don't want anybody with the G.I.'s."

"No," said Chuffy, remembering. "It's just something I et."

"I hope," said Thomas gloomily.

Barth swung around on him. "And what's the matter with you?"

"Nothing's the matter with me."

"The hell there isn't. You're sweating like a pig."

Thomas made a formless gesture with his hands. "Family trouble," he mumbled. "I'm a little worried about my daughter."

Chuffy's pulse jumped.

Thomas went on mumbling, "It's nothing serious, of course. She's a little wild. Her mother pays no attention to her, always off playing bridge. A girl that age needs a mother. It worries ..."

Marty watched him with hard, intolerant eyes. Hell, he thought, was this the big shot, The Eye, Chuffy had been telling him about? He noticed, if no one else did, the slight tremor in Thomas' hands. And he saw, too, that Barth was slightly drunk—not sloppy, but high. For Thomas he felt contempt but Barth was something different. Barth was the boss. Even though Barth was high, Marty had an idea he'd be a bad man to cross.

Marty himself was in a highly intolerant mood. Suddenly he wanted to get out, to go some place and do something. Something in him needed the release of action, needed to be doing something, not just sitting listening to Thomas' mutterings about his daughter.

He pushed back his chair and stood up. "Is that all?" he asked Barth shortly.

Barth raised his eyebrows at Marty's tone. The kid had stuff, he thought. "That's all. See you tomorrow morning up at the Lake."

Marty turned and walked across the room. Chuffy trotted hurriedly after him, stopping him at the door.

"Wait a minute, kid," he said. "Wanna talk to Thomas for a minute. I wanna see if he can square that beef with Angie."

Marty glanced back at the hunched figure of Thomas and said contemptuously, "He can't even square a beef with his own daughter."

"Don't be dumb. The guy's got influence."

"All right. He's got influence."

"Wait for me now," said Chuffy anxiously.

"Yeah. I'll wait outside."

Marty had no intention of waiting. He didn't want Chuffy hovering over him like a nursing mother. The moment he was outside he ran down the, steps and walked briskly down the long, curving driveway through the maple trees. On Mt. Prospect Avenue he hailed a downtown bus and got off at the corner of Broad and Market. It was pretty deserted at that late hour. The all-night cafeteria across the street bloodily stabbed the night with neon and down Market Street, aside from the street lamps, the only lights he saw were from other cafeterias and, of course, the gin mills. That's what he wanted, a gin mill. He felt in his pocket. He still had the ten bucks Chuffy had given him. That was good for all night and that was the way he felt—like making a night of it. He walked down Market Street with a cocky, free-swinging stride. Christ, he thought, and this afternoon I was scared to stick my nose out of that crummy room! He was in a state of stern elation. Nothing could happen to him—he could handle anything. He turned into the Novelty Bar & Grill across the street from the narrow Newark News Building.

The bar was crowded and he elbowed himself in to the rail. A tall, thick-shouldered Negro turned his head and grinned at him.

"Yeah man," he said good-naturedly. "You just 'bout gettin' in undah the wiah for that drink. They closin' in a quartah an houah."

"There are other gin mills."

"Suah, one right down the street, othah side Penn Station. You got yo'self a thirst, man?"

"Is it against the law?"

The Negro's good nature fled at this rebuff. "Guess not," he said shortly, turning back to his beer.

Marty had one drink and left. It was too quiet for him. He wanted a place with a juke box, with dancing, with something going on.

The gin mill at the other side of Penn Station had a juke box but no dancing. There were *No Dancing* signs on all the walls. But there was a shuffleboard and a noisy, half-drunken crowd around it. He ordered himself a beer and leaned his back against the bar, watching the progress of the game.

At the far end of the bar sat a man with the crumpled ears and flattened nose of an ex-prizefighter. When Marty walked in, he was morosely making circles on the bar in front of him with his beer glass. He had spent his last dime and he was grumbling to himself. He knew there was no chance of wheedling a free drink but he kept turning it over and over in his mind, childishly hoping to hit on a magic formula that would get him a free beer. It was twenty minutes before he noticed Marty. His eyes shone under the craggy broken cartilage of his eyebrows. There was his free beer! Better than a free beer. A whole flock of beers, even hard liquor. He knew certain people who would shell out a fin, maybe even a sawbuck, to find out where Marty was.

He put a cigarette in his mouth and shambled down the bar. He stopped in front of Marty and said in a hoarse voice, "Got a match, cap?" He looked hard into Marty's face to make sure he wasn't making any mistake. He was too stupid to be subtle and he continued to stare into Marty's face, even after Marty had handed a package of matches to him. Marty started to scowl, then he noticed that the man was a little punchy. There had been several punchies around the gym where he had trained and they all had the same kind of battered face and a way of looking at you with puzzled uncertainty as if your face was familiar but they couldn't recall the name. Marty suddenly felt sorry for him, excessively so. He'd had five beers and he was not accustomed to drinking. He was in a mood to fight, or dance, or feel excessively sorry for all the punchies in the world.

"Think you'll know me the next time, Battler?" he asked.

"I know ya now, cap. Yer Irish Jack Doyle that flattened the Hunky in the third down the Arena Friday night." Then, anxiously, "Right?"

"Right, Battler," Marty patted his shoulder. "Right the first time. Buy you a drink?"

"Well," the pug licked his lips and glanced toward the door. "Yeah sure, thanks. Rye."

Marty turned and called to the barkeep, "Hey, handsome, two ryes down here." He was beginning to feel very happy.

"Wit' beer chasers," the pug told the bartender quickly.

"With beer chasers," agreed Marty. He wanted the punchy to have everything he desired. "How about a hamburger, Battler? Feel like a hamburger?"

"Yeah sure, thanks."

"A hamburger for my friend, handsome. With onions, Battler?"

"Yeah, wit' onions. Here's how, cap."

"Here's how." With a swagger, Marty imitated the pug and drank it down. "Another one, Battler? How's about another one, champ?"

"Yeah sure, thanks, cap."

The pug drank three more ryes and ate his hamburger. There was no conversation between them. Marty was happy merely buying drinks and whatever else he could think of for the punchy. Piled up on the bar in front of the pug was a pack of Luckies, two cigars, a bag of potato chips, a box of pretzels, a tiny can of kippered herring and a package of razor blades. When he saw how things were going, the bartender had managed by then to shortchange and overcharge to such a degree that there were only three quarters left on the bar from Marty's ten dollar bill. One more pair of drinks cleared the board of that. The pug began to gather up his newly acquired possessions. Marty, quite drunk, regarded him with affection.

"Tell you what, Battler," he said. "Listen to me. Tell you what. You wanna bout, right? Right. Sure you wanna bout. Tell you what. I'll get you a bout. M'fren Chully'll get you a bout. Globe Hotel, up Market Street. Chuffy. Great li'l manager. Get you a bout. How zat?"

"You oughta lay off the liquor, cap," said the pug earnestly. "Y'll never get noplace fightin' the bottle. You can't handle it. Leave it alone. Y'gotta live right. The ring ain't no place for rummies. Y'look like a clean kid, so take my advice and lay off the liquor. Okay?"

"Okay."

"That's the kid. Don't lead wit' y'chin."

The pug stood there for a moment with a slightly puzzled expression on his face, as if there were something more he wanted to say but couldn't quite think what it was. Then he turned and walked out. Once outside, he started to shuffle rapidly toward the Market Street gym where Angie had his headquarters.

Marty slouched against the bar and called for another drink. The bartender picked up the glass.

"Can you pay for it, fella?" he demanded.

Marty looked down at the bar, then fumbled in his pockets. He was swaying. "Money s'mplace," he mumbled.

"No dough, no drink, fella."

Marty continued his aimless fumbling, finding nothing but his hotel key and handkerchief, which he placed carefully on the bar. The bartender walked away from him. Marty stood swaying and humming happily to himself. In a little while he remembered about the drink again and called to the bartender. The bartender didn't ever bother to come back down.

"Gwan home," he called, bored. "You ain't got no dough. You had enough anyways."

Marty grinned hazily. He was very amiable. He nodded several times. "Right. Hadda nuff. Had plenny. Go home."

He stumbled out of the gin mill and staggered down the street toward the Ironbound, the slum. He was still feeling wonderful and he lurched along out in the street, humming happily. Fortunately the street was deserted, for it was almost three A.M. A couple of cabs crawled past him and called out but he waved them on. He wanted to walk. Walking was wonderful. And he wanted to sing. He sang. He sang *"The Rose Of Tralee,"* and it was such a success that he sang it again, giving himself an encore with *"Roses Of Picardy."* It was during the encore that a cab tore out of a side street and swerved around him with screeching tires. The driver took the time to slow down, lean out through his window and swear. Marty waved happily, nodded and staggered toward the sidewalk. He sat down on the curb, leaned back against the lamppost and continued his rendition of *"Roses Of Picardy."*

The cab went about a block, then made a squealing U-turn and came tearing back. It stopped in front of Marty and a stocky man jumped out.

"Oh, Jesus!" he said in disgust. It was Barth.

He grabbed Marty by the arm, jerked him to his feet and shoved him into the cab. "I ought to break your goddamn neck," he growled. Marty collapsed gently into the cushions and went to sleep.

It took Barth and the cabbie together to carry him up to Barth's room in the Ironbound Hotel. Sophie was sitting up in bed, reading a Hollywood fan magazine. She always waited up for Barth. She looked very different from the tired, frightened, hostile girl who had picked Barth up in that Philadelphia gin mill. There was a kind of peace in her steady gray eyes and her wide mouth had more than a defeated gentleness now. It seemed fuller, more voluptuous, more capable of giving deep pleasure.

The cabbie stared when she leaped out of bed in the transparent nylon nightgown Barth, the sensualist, had bought for her.

"Oh, the poor baby!" she cried, immediately sensing Marty's condition. "Here, put him on the bed."

"Put him on the bed, hell!" growled Barth. "And for crissake put on some clothes or get back in bed yourself." He handed the cabbie two dollars. "Beat it."

He dragged Marty across the room and dumped him in the lounge chair. Sophie had obediently returned to bed. She watched as Barth angrily pulled off Marty's shoes—not because Barth wanted to make Marty comfortable, but because taking off a drunk's shoes was one of the things you did automatically.

"You shouldn't be mad at him," said Sophie. "You get drunk yourself sometimes."

"Shut up." Barth stalked into the bathroom and slammed the door.

Sophie slipped out of bed and ran to the closet. She took out a worn cotton blanket. She snatched up her pillow from the bed and went over to Marty. She pulled off his jacket and opened his shirt at the neck. Then she arranged him comfortably in the chair with the pillow under his head and covered him with the blanket. She smiled down at him tenderly.

"Poor baby," she murmured again.

At the same moment, two men walked heavily into the gin mill near Penn Station. They looked around, then one of them went back to the men's room. He returned, looking annoyed.

"You see a tall, black-haired kid in here?" he asked the barkeep.

"Yeah. He left about a half hour ago."

"Where'd he go?"

The barkeep looked at the men carefully. He did not know them personally but he knew what they were and he didn't want trouble. He glanced toward the cash register, next to which he had placed Marty's hotel key and handkerchief. Reluctantly, he went over and got them. He put them on the bar. He didn't want to—but he was afraid someone else would give him away if he didn't.

"He left these," he said shortly.

The man picked up the key, looked at it, nodded, then left, walking out quickly and purposefully. The bartender picked up the handkerchief, looked at it for a moment, then threw it into a small garbage can under the bar.

There was nothing on his conscience. He hadn't told them anything. But he had to protect himself, didn't he? He didn't owe the punk anything. Was it his fault if the key bore the name of the Globe Hotel?

## IMPACT
### CHAPTER SIX

Barth was up early the next morning in a dour mood. He'd had very little rest. Marty had made several trips to the bathroom during the night, making anguished vocal noises, stumbling into the furniture coming and going. He now lay asleep on the floor, curled up in a position of exhausted misery.

In the old days, Barth would have bawled the hell out of Marty and held his head under cold water until he sobered up. Maybe he would have laughed at him, too. But this time he had just lain in bed, swearing soddenly, a little drunk himself and too bone-tired to get up and give Marty what he deserved. And, to make it worse, Sophie had giggled every time Marty staggered urgently into a chair or let out one of those moans of alcoholic anguish.

Now, Marty was asleep and Sophie was asleep, her deep, beautiful breasts rising and falling gently beneath the sheer nightgown, her tawny hair a nimbus of spread gold on the pillow. Barth looked at her with resentment, then glanced at Marty with dull hatred and plodded across the room, stepping over the sleeping boy, into the bathroom where he slammed the door loudly behind him.

The cold shower did nothing to lift his sodden mood. He stared into the mirror as he smeared shaving cream over his face. His hand moved slowly, then more slowly until it finally stopped. Those deep tired wrinkles around his eyes, those brownish-pebbled sacs beneath them. His eyeballs were yellowish with threads of red. He stared at his image, not thinking of what he saw—not thinking at all, in fact. It was just a kind of revulsion that coiled within him like a sick animal, a revulsion against having to think at all, about anything. Mechanically his fingers started to work again, massaging the cream into the bristles.

The mornings were always bad. It wasn't until a few drinks had stirred his reluctant vitality that he could whip up any semblance of his old force.

When he went back into the bedroom, now fully dressed except for his tie, Sophie was awake and bright-eyed. She smiled at him, then put her finger to her lips and pointed to Marty asleep on the floor.

Barth growled, "The hell with that," and snapped his tie from the doorknob where he hung it at night. He stood before the mirror over the chest of drawers and knotted it into the V of his collar. "I'm going downtown for the other car," he said as he donned his jacket. "I might be back and I might not. If I'm not back in an hour, take the Buick and go up to the Lake. You know how to reach the cottage?"

She nodded. "Sunset Drive, Lake Powhatan. Up Route 6."

"Right." Barth turned and looked sourly at the sleeping boy. "If it don't come to life, throw it in the bathtub and turn the water on." He nodded shortly and walked out.

Sophie's reaction to his brusqueness was one of surprise. It was the first morning he had failed to kiss her before leaving the hotel room. For some reason, he had always been especially amorous in the morning, demanding greater tenderness from her. She understood more about him now and he touched her deeply, particularly when he clung almost with desperation, as if she were a last haven and a refuge.

He was not a lover, although he made love to her—nor did he arouse that fundamental maternity in her. It is the quality of a mother not merely to love but to prepare the child for what lies ahead in life, to protect it from premature shock. Barth was not a child. And he was not a lover, for he had nothing, emotionally or spiritually, to give her. His exercise of the sexual function sprang more from his desperate need than from any warming growth of passion. The most Sophie could give him, for it was all he was capable of receiving, was comfort, tenderness, and gentleness. There was gratitude, too—but Barth was not interested in gratitude.

Sophie did not know all this consecutively and coherently. But she knew it. She was not a woman who needed words to give form to what she knew.

She did not know about the strike but she did know Barth was doing something he didn't want to do. She was sorry for him but there was nothing she could do about it. He would not tolerate interference or advice from her. She had only one function as far as he was concerned— and, oddly enough, it was not entirely sexual. In fact, the sexual part of it was only incidental.

First making sure Marty was really asleep, Sophie slipped out of bed and put on her negligee. She gathered up her shoes, stockings, underthings, skirt and sweater, and tiptoed toward the bathroom. She stopped beside him for a moment and looked down. As she did, he turned over on his back, mumbling in his sleep.

Defenseless in sleep, there was nothing tough in his young Irish face. His mouth was slack and his eyes were folded. His fists were clenched. "Watch that left," he mumbled, "watch that left ..." and he made a vague warding motion with his own right fist.

Sophie laughed, said, "Poor baby," and walked on into the bathroom. She stayed there longer and made more noise than was necessary to give him time to come around and crawl up from the floor. When she returned, filling out her sweater in a manner hopefully visualized by the manufacturers, Marty was sitting at the edge of the lounge chair, holding his head in his hands as if it would fly apart were he to let go. He did not even look up when Sophie crossed to the chest of drawers and picked up a bottle of nail polish. Smiling, she sat down on the bed and slowly began to do her nails. She had more tact than to say anything. When he felt like talking, he would. He was still sitting with his head between his hands when she finished her nails. She stood up and blew on them, waving them gently in the air. Then she took her handbag from the night table beside the bed and, giving him a commiserating glance, walked out. Let him recover in peace, she thought.

She came back about twenty minutes later with a brown paper bag that contained a carton of hot coffee from the diner, a quart of tomato juice, an egg, a bottle of Worcestershire, a bottle of Tabasco, and half a dozen ice cubes.

Judging from the sounds that came from the bathroom, Marty had come sufficiently alive to crawl under the shower and turn it on. It was another fifteen minutes before he reappeared, very scrubbed-looking and fresh, though puffy-eyed, with his harsh black hair already beginning to curl out of its flattening wetness. But he still carried his head as if it were a time bomb.

Sophie held out to him a tall glass that she had filled with a mixture of tomato juice, egg, Worcestershire and Tabasco. "This is on the house," she said, keeping her face straight.

He shot her a quick glance, to see if she was laughing, then took the glass. His hand, she noted, was as steady as her own. He raised the glass to his lips and drank. Watching the smooth muscular rise and fall of his throat as he swallowed, she felt an unaccustomed emotion and to cover it—or smother it—she thought, again, "Poor baby ..." When he lowered the glass it was empty and he grinned at her.

"That's the house I should of had them on last night," he said. Then with embarrassed confusion, "This ... uh ... your room?"

"Half of it," she said gravely.

"Oh? And the other half?"

"Mr. Barth."

Mr. Barth. She could have said Gerald Barth or even Gerry Barth but she thought of him as Mr. Barth. She called him "Barth" but never felt really easy when she did it. When she thought of him, it was as "Mr. Barth." He was so much older.

The name didn't mean anything to Marty for the moment, for he had only a hazy recollection of the night before.

"Your husband?" he asked.

She shook her head and reached for the tomato juice can. "Another one?"

"Uh-uh. Thanks. That'll hold me. How'd I get here, anyway?"

"He brought you."

"I really tied one on, didn't I?"

"Everybody does, sooner or later."

"I tied mine on sooner."

"You don't drink very much, do you?"

"Whattaya mean?" he asked defensively.

"Oh ... the way you snapped out of it. Lushes don't snap out of it so easy. They need a hair of the dog or something." Then, guiltily, she remembered how Barth always sneaked down to the gin mill for a couple of fast ones after a hard night. "I don't mean lushes exactly," she added hastily. "I mean people who, well—drink. You know—drink."

"I could've drunk a lot but I'm usually in training. I'm a fighter."

The instant the words were out of his mouth, he remembered Angie and what was in store for him if Angie caught up with him.

Something constricted in his stomach. And then he remembered who Barth was.

"Barth!" he exclaimed, aghast.

"What's the matter?"

"He's the—well, he's the boss, ain't he?"

"The boss of what!"

Marty knew he had made some kind of slip, and he tried to cover it by asking, "And he brought me in?"

"Him and the cab driver."

"I didn't ... make any trouble, did I?"

"No. You just went to sleep. He took off your shoes."

The fact that Barth had taken off his shoes seemed to relieve Marty immensely. He said, "Whew! I'm certainly glad I didn't make any trouble. He's one guy I wouldn't want to cross. Was he sore at me?"

"If there was anything to worry about, you wouldn't be here to worry about it," said Sophie practically.

"I guess you're right about that!"

An odd, slightly strained silence fell between them. Marty stared at her as if he were seeing her clearly for the first time—and it was not merely her wonderful body with her deep bosom and full long thighs and slender legs that riveted his attention. He had been successful in the ring and there had been women. Some of them had been what Chuffy called tomatoes—but not all of them. There had been that dark, intensely passionate little stenographer who worked at Prudential—(what was her name?)—the one who threatened to commit suicide but ended up by just getting drunk and marrying an assistant buyer from Kresge's Department Store.

Then there was that quiet girl with light brown hair and rather shy hazel eyes—Phyllis—or was it Lucy? He had gone out with her a couple times and necked with her—but that was all. You didn't try anything with nice girls and he had seen right away that she was a nice girl. He still felt funny about her, because it had ended in such a bewildering way. It was the night of his fight with that guy from Perth Amboy, Swede Widlund. What a scrap that had been! And she had been at the ringside. The Swede wasn't much for boxing but he was as tough as they came and Marty had been willing to mix it with him. They were both down in the first round and it was ding-dong right up to the sixth round when Marty dropped the Swede with a hard right cross to the jaw and the Swede didn't get up. But what a terrific mill it had been! The crowd kept yelling as if it wanted Marty to come back for an encore. He had a date with Phyllis (or was it Lucy?) after the fight but she didn't show up. That is, she didn't show up for the date—but when he got back to his hotel, there she was in his room without a stitch on and there was something in her face when she looked at him that had never been there before. Not a wantonness, exactly, not lust—but a passion so urgent that nothing else mattered.

Marty had been profoundly shocked. But it was funny—after a fight, especially after a tough fight like the one with the Swede where you took almost as much as you dished out—instead of wanting to crawl into a hole and lick your wounds or sleep it off or something, you were wild inside, especially when you'd won. You wanted to stand on a high place and yell at the top of your lungs, you wanted to go on the town; you wanted to bust things wide open.

But most of all you wanted a woman.

God, what a night! He had barely touched her when she was all over him as if she had hungered for him so long that further waiting was an agony not to be borne. The passion in her was like a storm in a high tree on a windy hill. Maybe the fight had done it to her. She had been right there at ringside, she had seen it all, had heard—even smelled—the violence of it. Perhaps that was it. Some women are like that.

The aftermath was even more bewildering. Instead of drifting into that peaceful after-languor the way you always did, he felt her go tense in his arms. Then, with a cry, she had sprung from his grasp and dressed as quickly as she could, hiding her face from him as he stared at her in a kind of numbed amazement. She didn't sob or cry or anything like that but her face was frozen in a desperation of shame and horror at what she had done. She ran from the room and he never saw her again.

There had been others, though none so bewildering. Some of them had been tomatoes and some had been nice girls.

But compared to Sophie, they had been nothing more than the shadows that go before substance. For the first time in his life he felt as if he were looking not at a women—but into her. It was as if there were a window in the sky, through which he gazed at the whole universe beyond.

Sophie felt the impact of his gaze and, more profoundly, felt the answering surge inside herself.

Shakily, she turned and reached for the carton of coffee.

"Coffee?" she asked, proffering the carton.

He started. "What? Oh. No. No, thanks."

She took a sip from the carton and put it back on the night table. More to keep herself from looking at him than anything else, she glanced at her watch.

"Oh! We've got to go. We're twenty minutes late as it is. Mr. Barth said, leave in an hour if I'm not back. And now it's an hour and twenty minutes. We've got to go!"

"Yes," he said, "I guess we do."

They avoided looking at each other as they went down the stairs.

## GOOD THINGS IN SMALL PACKAGES
### CHAPTER SEVEN

Chuffy turned on his pillow and let the beginnings of wakefulness wash luxuriously over him. He did not open his eyes but he stretched out his arm and curled it around the sleeping girl beside him. He was tired. Goddamn, he was tired! His muscles felt like boiled spaghetti— but he did not mind this awakening.

He had been tired before, in many ways and for many reasons—and there had always been a kind of defeat in the terminal fatigue, as if he had expended all his energy to the profit of someone other than himself. This was different. And not merely because there was a girl beside him. In spite of his small thin jockey-like body—or possibly because of it— he had always been very successful with women, especially big women. Big women with blonde hair, big breasts and voluptuous hips, thighs like fleshy columns—big women who smothered him with a devouring love that never satisfied, even meagerly, their special inner hungers. He had always attracted big women and they always seemed to feel he needed to be petted and pampered—like a little boy.

Strangely enough, that kind of success had never touched him. In his hard tough core, Chuffy was an obdurate realist. He took big women in his stride, accepted their caresses and their pettings—but he despised them eternally. He took what they offered because he could not get the kind of woman he wanted. He wanted a small woman, as hard and tough as himself, so that when they lay, lip to lip, all passion spent, they could talk the same language. He had never met such a woman. Oh, he had met them, all right but they had always belonged to other men— big, meaty men. Sometimes when he saw a small, desirable woman in the company of one of those big beefs, he amused himself by thinking how little it meant—that largeness of bone, that strength of muscle, that illusion of size. One small leaden slug, not an ounce in itself, propelled by a light charge of powder, could—in less than a second—reduce all those pounds to dead meat not worth a thin dime on the open market.

He was a realist. If he couldn't get the kind of woman he wanted, he took the kind of woman he could get. And some of them had been very beautiful. In a large way. They satisfied his immediate longing for love and he had come to believe, a long time ago, that the satisfaction of that need was so evanescent, so easily accomplished, that to rot one's self with jealousy or to make a violent issue of it, was as stupid as paying twenty dollars for a two dollar watch.

The yearning was there. The yearning had always been there. But because he was a realist and because he always negated the things of the spirit in this attitude, he never hated or wanted to revenge himself on those big men who had what he could not have himself. Possibly, he did hate them. But it did not emerge actively as hatred. It came out in a twisted form as a kind of savage amusement. Sometimes he laughed aloud, just thinking how the smug, possessive face of the small girl, clinging to the arm of some six-footer or other, would change if somebody stepped out from behind a corner and pumped two .38's into that two hundred pounds of masculinity. Goddamn, how their faces would change—and they would never be the same, once they realized that mere size no longer mattered! A little man was as good as a big man— perhaps better, because he offered a smaller target. That's what you had to be in this world, a smaller target. Bigness was a handicap. If you faced things realistically, you were bound to realize it was desirable to be small.

His mind was a patchwork of rationalizations.

Jasmine's thin, immature body stirred beside him. She was the kind of woman he had always desired—a small woman with adolescent breasts, hipless, legs as slim as candles.

As they lay side by side, they were curiously alike. They were smaller than life-size, both with thin, hard bodies, yet each with a quickness that was beyond human quickness, as a mink is quick beyond the quickness of a human. And, in its way, a mink is a beautiful animal, an animal with a sinuous grace no human could ever hope to attain.

Their faces were alike too—both narrow and sharp. And even in passion there was the identical quality of feral questing in them. The consummation of their love was a cry, sharp as pain—but because they were so alike, the satisfaction was deep and dark-running, like a subterranean river.

That was the one thing Chuffy had never felt before—warm satisfaction, then a sense, upon awakening, not of defeat nor exhaustion, but one of accomplishment. That was probably the closest he would ever come to a sensation of the spirit. But he knew now, as he stirred somnolently on his pillow, his arm lightly around the girl, that he would go great lengths to keep her, now he had found her.

She opened her eyes. His arm lay curled around her neck and her first words were, peevishly, "What the hell are you trying to do, strangle me?"

He chuckled. "If I wanted to strangle you, baby, I'd do it with a hunk of wire. It's quicker."

She turned her head without lifting it from the pillow and looked at him. "Have you ever—well—done that to anybody, Chuffy? I mean, with wire?"

"Me? Hell, no! Too damn much fuss. Christ, I'd have to climb halfway up his back to get the wire around his neck. I knew guys that did do it but they're dead now themselves. Jerks. Strictly from hunger. Nuts."

"You saw them do it?"

"Saw them? Me? Uh-uh. I'm too smart to hang around for that kind of stuff, baby. You hang around for that kind of stuff and you end up with the warden asking you what you'd like for your last dinner. The hell with that. The way to do is, do it fast and get out, and none of this stuff with wire or putting the boots to a guy or getting fancy other ways. Do it fast and get out is the only way."

"And that's the way you did it?"

"Me?" he said warily. "I never wanted no part of that stuff! Say, what the hell is this? You the D.A. or something?"

"I was just wondering, that's all."

"Well, wonder about something else then. You sound like you're leading up to somebody you want knocked off or something."

He laughed and reached for the crumpled package of cigarettes on a nearby table. It was empty. He squeezed it into a ball and threw it across the room, asking lazily, "Got any cigarettes, baby?"

"In my handbag."

He slid sinuously out of bed and crossed the room to the chair she had indicated. She watched the small, lean muscularity of his body, remembering what it had done and anticipating what it would do again. She felt a rising excitement. There was something in him that answered the thing that was in her. Greedily, she watched him.

He opened her handbag. He lifted out the gun she had taken from Marty the night before.

"What the hell are you carrying this around for?" he asked sharply, glancing at her over his shoulder.

"You told me to take it, didn't you?"

"Sure—but for crissake! I thought you had sense enough not to carry it around with you. What're you trying to do, stick your neck out? That's all they need is to find something like this on you. What're you carrying it around for?"

"I forgot it," she lied sullenly.

"Forgot it, hell!" He threw it down on to a chair.

"I want it!"

"You what?"

"I want it!'

"What for?"

"I just want it, that's all."

That was something Chuffy could understand. A gun was a good thing to have. But you didn't carry it around unless you had to. You put it away until the time came.

"All right," he said. "But, Jesus, don't carry it around in your purse. Leave it home."

"I'll leave it home but let me have it, please!"

"Okay, okay, it's all yours. But don't get any ideas, that's all. Now where are the cigarettes?"

"In the silver case."

He opened the case. His eyes narrowed as he raised it quickly to his nose and sniffed. He gave her a hard glance.

"What the hell do you smoke reefers for?" he demanded. "Are you crazy? What do you want to do, kill yourself?"

He walked into the bathroom and a moment later she heard him flush the reefers down the toilet. He came back, his face dark with anger.

"If ever I catch you with them things again," he snapped, "I'll beat your brains out. Use some sense!"

"I didn't smoke them very much." she said weakly.

"Any you smoke is too much. Hell, baby, them things rot your insides. Smart guys don't have nothin' to do with them. I wouldn't walk around the block with a guy I thought was on the gauge. It ain't smart."

"I said I only smoked them sometimes, didn't I?"

"No more!"

"All right!"

"You don't need them. You're groovy enough without the weed. Forget it. Use your brains or you won't have any to use."

"All right!"

He grinned at her, then winked. Her face was furious.

"Sure," he said in a conciliatory voice. "I know. You were just doing it for the kicks. Right?"

"Go to hell!" Her tone was sulky but she was actually delighted that he had talked to her in that fashion. He was tough. He knew what he was talking about. And, anyway, marihuana always made her faintly ill afterwards. She was glad enough to have a real excuse for giving it up.

He had been deeply shocked at first to find the reefers but now he felt easier. He had it solved in his mind. She was young and she had smoked them merely for the kicks. That was okay. When you did a thing for the kicks, you could forget about it. He had a definite code of conduct. He drank very little and did not use drugs. He did not do anything that would jeopardize his survival in a predatory world—and anyone who did was a jerk. It was as simple as that. The moral aspects interested him not at all. It came down to a matter of survival, pure and simple.

He was going through his jacket for cigarettes when a sudden thought struck him.

"Cripes, what time is it?"

Jasmine lifted her thin arm and looked at her wristwatch. "Twelve-thirty. Why? You going someplace?"

"Twelve-thirty! I gotta get outta here!" He scrambled into his underwear and, sitting at the edge of the chair, leaned over and picked up his socks from the floor.

She watched him in dismay. She had been looking forward to a whole day with him, talking, making love, filling herself with all he had to offer her.

"Go where?" she demanded, adding viciously. "To look for that jerk Marty again? You didn't get in until three o'clock this morning looking for him. I shouldn't have waited. Now you're going to run out on me again, looking for him. What's Marty, anyway? Are you one of these in-betweens?"

Chuffy said savagely, "Shut your lousy mouth! He's a clean kid. I'm tryin' to keep him out of trouble."

Oddly enough, Chuffy felt a deep affection for Marty. Perhaps it flattered his ego to have to take care of someone so big and physically dangerous—a hundred and seventy-five pounds of fistic dynamite was the way Marty had always been introduced in the ring. But that period had passed and Chuffy's deep affection for Marty remained—almost the affection of a father for his son.

Jasmine sat up in bed, her thin chest heaving in complement to the fury in her eyes.

"You're leaving me to find that Marty!"

Chuffy thrust his feet into his shoes. He paid no attention to her anger.

He said, "Shut up," and stood up, pulling on his pants. He stuffed in his shirt and reached for his tie, crossing the room to the mirror. Her voice lashed out at him. He ignored it until suddenly he realized what she was saying. Then it felt as if someone had put his heart in a vise and turned the screw.

"You and your Marty!" she spat at him. "You and Marty and my father and that big shot, Mr. Gerald Barth! You don't think I know about it—but I do! I know all about it! You're going to make what Mr. Gerald Barth calls a strike. I know! And I can spoil it all this very minute by calling Jack Niles and telling him exactly what you're planning to do. I can have you all killed if I want to. I know all about it. I heard everything."

Feeling very small and cold and murderous, Chuffy turned around slowly and said evenly, "What did you hear?"

"I heard it all!" she flung at him. "I even know Jack Niles' phone number—that's how much I know!"

That was the first Chuffy knew about Niles' connection with the strike. But he knew Niles' name and reputation as a mad dog, an indiscriminate killer.

"How'd you hear it?" Chuffy asked tonelessly. "Eavesdropping last night?"

"Last night! Don't you think I know what my father is? I've known it for years. There's a fireplace in his library and if you go up on the roof and listen at the chimney, you can hear every word. I've been listening. I know what he is. He's no good. He's never been any good—and this time he's even double-crossing his crooked friends. He's double-crossing Jack Niles, because Mr. Gerald Barth promised him a bigger cut of the take. That's what my father is—he double-crosses even the people he works with."

Chuffy said carefully, "So if I walk out now, you'll call Jack Niles. Is that the idea?"

Jasmine suddenly knew if she took one more step she would die. Chuffy would kill her. He would have to kill her. She burst into tears, covering her thin face with her hands, rocking to and fro, shaken by sobs.

"No, Chuffy, no! I'd never do that! I'd never call Jack Niles—or the police, either. I'm not a stool pigeon. It was just that you were leaving me to look for that Marty. I hate him! I hate him!"

Chuffy snatched up the gun from the chair and crossed softly to the bed. He sat down, not touching her.

"You hate him?" he said. "You hate him enough that if I walk out you'll put the boots to him?"

"No, no! I was just trying to keep you here, that's all. I don't want you to leave. I was just saying that. I was just saying it!"

Chuffy had the spot picked out, a spot just to the right of her small left breast. All he had to do was press the muzzle of the gun to that spot and pull the trigger. His instinct told him it was what he should do now, without delay. Now. But he held the gun in his lap.

"Why do you hate Marty?" he asked.

"The way he was last night."

"What way was he?"

"You made me go up there. It was your fault!"

She was speaking the truth. He had made her go up there. And something had happened. Uneasily, he felt that it had been his fault. Marty had been different afterwards. And now Jasmine was blowing her stack. But what had happened?

"What happened?" he asked sharply.

"He made me feel like ... dirt!"

Chuffy relaxed. Was that all? "He didn't smack you around or anything?"

"It was worse than being smacked around!"

"Nothing's worse than being smacked around. If you'd ever been smacked around, you'd know that. Come on, baby, come on," he said, touched by her misery. "Cut it out. He didn't do nothing to you. Cut it out."

"I don't care anymore what he did, Chuffy. It's just that you were going out looking for him, that's all."

"I gotta look for him, baby. He can't take care of himself. Any objections?"

"No objections, Chuffy."

He smiled a twisted smile, as if half of him knew that the smart thing to do would be to kill her there and then, as if this same half were telling him there was nothing but grief in store if he let her live. But Chuffy was not a man all of one piece. He was divided into many pieces. Here was his kind of girl, the kind he'd always been looking for, who'd hitherto been unattainable. Now he had her. He could not bear to lose her. If he put a slug into her, that would be the end of it. There would be no more worries. And he knew that otherwise, knowing what she knew, there would be worries or worse. But he could not make his hand bring up the gun—he could not end it, though it was the smartest thing to do. She knew too much and she was hysterical. He would never be able to trust her.

But half of a man is made of hope and the gun remained in Chuffy's lap.

He said heavily, "I'm crazy about you, baby."

She threw her arms around him. "And I'm crazy about you, Chuffy. That's the only reason I said what I did. I'm so crazy about you that I'm jealous even of this Marty. I'll do whatever you say, Chuffy, honestly I will. If you want to go out and find Marty, you go right ahead. I won't be jealous. I promise you. We must do what we have to do, isn't that right, Chuffy? We do what we have to do!"

This was a little abstruse for Chuffy but he said, "I guess you're right. And now I gotta go out and see if Marty's okay." He watched her narrowly.

Her eyes were liquid with tears but she smiled. "You look for him— and I hope you find him, Chuffy. Honestly I do. Not that I care about Marty—but because you do. All I care about is you, Chuffy!"

He was genuinely touched but the smile touched only half of his mouth. "Thanks, baby," he said. "That's what I wanted to hear." He looked down at the gun in his lap then, impulsively, put it in her hand. "Now for crissake, don't carry it around with you. Take it home and put it away. The cops like nothing better than to find a gun on you. Here," he gave her the key to his room. "I won't be able to see you tonight but I'll see you tomorrow night. Be here around ten—and you can forget the liquor. We don't need liquor. Okay, baby?"

"Okay, Chuffy."

"Now I gotta be on my way."

He finished dressing, not hurriedly for he was fussy about his appearance. He stood before the mirror, making sure his tie was knotted just right, that his handkerchief came up in just the right three white points from his breast pocket, then he set his homburg on his head at just the right angle, debonair but not zoot. He went over to the bed and kissed her, running his hands lightly over her adolescent body, not with desire but possessively.

"See you tomorrow night, baby," he whispered. Then he turned and went out quickly, before her reaching arms could disturb the angle of his homburg or his haircomb. He was empty of desire—except for the abstract desire of anticipation.

He took a cab to Market Street and got off at Pennsylvania Station. From there he walked up Market toward Marty's hotel, keeping well within the moving crowd on the north side of the street. As he approached the hotel he walked slower and slower, his eyes sharply raking the opposite side of the street. He stiffened. He had been around Newark a long time and he knew most of Angie's goon squad. He spied one of them across the street now, loitering in the doorway of the pawn shop next to the hotel. He stopped. There was a second one standing at the newsstand just ahead of him at the corner. He turned and walked back toward Penn Station. He didn't have to worry for the moment. If Angie was having Marty's hotel watched so closely, it meant only one thing—Angie had not caught up with Marty last night and Marty was still on the loose. Marty might even be up at the Lake by now. Chuffy crossed his fingers in his pocket. That would be the ideal solution, if Marty was up at the Lake with Barth and Cuesta. Barth and Cuesta would take care of Marty—Barth especially. Now that the strike was set, Barth would let nothing happen to the boy—particularly when the threat came from a local like Angie. Barth was big-time and the locals meant nothing to him. Chuffy walked back to Penn Station and into the bus terminal. There he boarded a bus to the Lake.

Jasmine did not linger in the hotel after Chuffy had gone. His absence left an unbearable ache in her. The moment he was gone, she saw the sordid meanness of the room and wanted to leave at once. Only his presence had made it habitable. She went into the bathroom but there was unwashed slime on the walls, so she did not shower. She washed her hands and face, applied make-up, then dressed and left as quickly as she could.

She had no real stomach for the degradation into which she had thrust herself. She had no stomach for rooms like that—unless Chuffy were there, too.

Thomas was not a good father but the home he provided was one of graciousness and dignity. It had been appointed by the best decorator money could buy. At the time he'd furnished his home, he'd had the money. Jasmine's room alone, with its canopied Louis XV bed, had cost five thousand dollars—not counting such odds and ends as lamps, pictures and accessories. They had amounted to another fifteen hundred. He'd been in the money at the time, the real money.

He was waiting haggardly at the window of the living room when she clattered up the pillared verandah in her absurdly high-heeled shoes. He met her at the front door.

Out of his anxiety, he spoke harshly. "Where have you been? What do you mean by staying out all night without calling me? I've been worried."

She looked at his pouchy, sagging face with distaste.

"I stayed with Imogene," she said shortly.

She had taken the precaution of calling Imogene before going home. Imogene had an apartment on Mt. Prospect Avenue.

"Why didn't you call me?" he demanded. "What do you mean by staying out all night without calling me?"

"You said that once."

"And I'll go right on saying it! What do you mean by staying out all night without calling me? I'm your father and I demand to know—what do you mean?"

She slid through the doorway and, facing him, said thinly, "It's a little late, isn't it, to remember that you're my father?"

"And just what do you mean by that?"

"Oh, I suppose you're my father, all right. Mother was never interested in anything but her bridge. She wouldn't have had the time to cheat on you. You're my father. It's down on the records in City Hall. But that's as far as it goes. You're not my father in anything but name. You've never bothered with me, any more than mother's ever bothered with me. I'll go my own way and I don't want any interference."

His face clotted and he reached for her. "I'll give you interference!"

She easily evaded his grasp. He had been drinking all night and was more than a little drunk. She stood back against the newel post at the stairway and faced him like a spitting cat.

"You'll give me nothing! You've never given me anything and you're not going to start giving me anything now. I'll do what I want! I spent the night with Imogene and it's none of your business."

"I'll make it my business."

"How can you make it your business?" she jeered. "You've never bothered to make it your business before. What is this, all of a sudden? All of a sudden you've decided to play the father? Why? Is it going to make some money for you? Is that it?"

Thomas' eyes were blinded with tears. All night long he had waited anxiously for her, not daring to call the police, afraid to call the hospitals. And now, this was her response.

Suddenly he found himself lonely and friendless. Afraid and alone. The investigation was looming from Trenton. He could not ride out an investigation. Not this time. His wife was in Chicago at a bridge tournament. She was always at bridge tournaments. She had never loved him. She had married him for position and money. Now he was alone in this crisis and friendless. The only person to whom he could turn was his daughter. After Barth's strike, he wanted to take his cut and the money he had stashed away, and take his daughter and go to South America. He wanted her with him. She was his daughter.

His law practice, once the investigation began, would be worth nothing. Nothing would be worth anything. His freedom was seriously threatened. He had to get out of Jersey, out of the country—but he was afraid to go alone. Afraid of the terrible loneliness he knew would follow.

He did not threaten any longer. He turned to her but pressed back against the door so she would not even think he was threatening. He held out his hand to her.

"Is it so strange," he asked, brokenly, "that a father should be interested in the welfare of his daughter? Is that so strange? I admit I haven't been a good father but I want to make it up to you. We'll take a trip together. We'll go to South America. You've always wanted to see South America. We'll go to Buenos Aires. They call it the Paris of South America. We'll go together. We'll call it a get-together tour. Just you and I ..."

"You're about ten years too late. I don't even want to get acquainted with you anymore!"

"But you don't know me. And I don't know you. It's my fault, I know— but it's not too late. We can have fun. We can travel. We can see things. We can make up for all that lost time. I can be a father to you!"

The appeal, piteous though it was, did not seem to touch the girl at all. She stood at the foot of the stairway, hard and composed, in an attitude of defense, as if this appeal were in reality an attack on her.

"You can't be anything to anybody," she said brutally.

"Just give me a chance."

"You've had your chance. You had your chance with mother and you drove her out of the house, away from me."

"I didn't drive her out. All she was interested in was bridge ..." The injustice of it brought tears to his eyes. He had worked so hard all his life to give them a good home—and he had given them a good home. But first his wife had left, for following bridge tournaments around the country was exactly that—and now his daughter was slipping away from him. It wasn't fair ...

The sight of his tears disgusted her. "Oh, leave me alone!" she cried and ran off up the stairs.

He went up after her but she had locked herself in her room. He tapped on the door. She didn't answer.

"Baby-doll," he pleaded—that had been her childhood name—"Baby-doll, listen to me ..."

Her voice came like a slap. "I said leave me alone, you ... crook!"

He started and stared at the closed door, aghast. "What?" he mumbled. "What was that?" Then in a burst of anger, "I demand to know where you were last night. You come home smelling of liquor and cigar smoke—and I demand to know where you were. I ... of course! Now I know where you were. You were out with that young ruffian, Marty Doyle. He suddenly disappeared and nobody knew where he'd gone. And that's where you were—you were out with him."

"Oh, Lord!"

"I won't have you running around with people like that, do you understand? I won't have it!"

"What are you going to do, put me in reform school? Please go away, won't you? If only you knew how ridiculous and pompous and silly you sound. Go away. You're making me sick to my stomach!"

Thomas clenched his hands; then abruptly turned and stamped down the stairs to his library. He went straight to the cognac bottle on the desk and poured himself a stiff drink. He downed it at a gulp. It burned, hot and acrid, in his throat. He'd had too much to drink and his face felt swollen. There was a vast trembling inside him, as if every nerve in his body were slowly being stretched to the breaking point. His lower jaw shook so, he could hear the chattering of his teeth.

He made a conscious effort to compose himself, then walked around the desk and picked up the telephone. He stood for a minute trying to remember the phone number that was almost as familiar to him as his own but his mind repeated senselessly, "Now let me see, let me see ..." over and over again. Finally, he had to take up the phone book and even then it was a little while before he could remember the name of the private detective agency he wanted to call. He dialed the number with some difficulty because his hand was shaking so.

When he was connected, he said very rapidly, "Hello, Maury, this is Thomas. There's a little job I want you to do for me but I want you to handle it personally."

Maury said, "Whoa, whoa! Come again. I didn't get it."

Thomas repeated it slowly and Maury said, "What's the matter, you got a cold or a mouthful of oatmeal? I can't understand a word. Say, are you soused? That's just the way you sound—soused. Now try it again and see if you can give it to me in English."

Thomas spoke very slowly, slushing only a little. "I want you to follow my daughter. You, personally. I think she's running around with a young hoodlum named Marty Doyle—a tall, black-haired Irishman. You, personally. Did you understand that?"

"Sure, sure. Okay. This is Thomas, isn't it?"

"Yes," said Thomas wearily, "This is Thomas."

He hung up and sat down, laying his head on the desk. He was very sleepy and was beginning to feel the first churnings of nausea. But there was something else he had to remember, something about this Marty Doyle, something somebody had said last night. Yes, yes, somebody was out to get Doyle. What was the name? Angie? That was it. Angie, that fellow down at the gym on Market Street. His hand moved slightly toward the phone. No, he was too sleepy. He'd call Angie after he'd had a nap ...

## A CHANGED MAN
### CHAPTER EIGHT

Sophie and Marty were more than an hour late when they finally arrived at the cottage at Lake Powhatan. The float in the carburetor had been stuck and it had taken Marty a while to repair it.

The cottage was at the north end of the lake on a small hill overlooking the water. It was a white clapboard structure with a broad veranda that faced the shore. Below was a small wooden dock to which was tied a green and white rowboat.

The northern end of the lake had not been developed as had the southern end where the shopping center was. Also at the southern end, two miles off, were the diving boards, the bathing beach, the floats and the boat livery. The nearest neighbor was a half-mile south on the eastern shore.

The cottage itself, though attractive enough with white clapboard walling and gay red roof, was actually quite primitive. There was no electricity nor telephone. Kerosene lamps were used for lighting and bottle-gas for cooking. For heat on chilly nights, there was a fieldstone fireplace in the living room and there were woolen blankets on the beds.

There was a black Ford sedan parked alongside the house when Sophie and Marty drove up and Cuesta was sitting out on the veranda at a card table, playing solitaire. He glanced at them briefly, then with no other form of greeting, dipped his dark slim face back over the spread of cards. Barth came around the far corner of the cottage carrying a bucket of water he had drawn from the well.

"You're late," he said shortly. "Where's that friend of yours—Chuffy— or whatever his name is? He's late, too." He set the bucket down and stood glowering.

Marty got out of the Buick and glowered back at Barth. He didn't like a dressing-down in Sophie's presence, even from Barth.

"We'd have been here on time but this crate you bought," he slapped the fender of the Buick, "needs an overhaul. The float in the carburetor got stuck on the way up—and that's not all."

"What do you mean, that's not all?"

"It needs a valve and carbon job, maybe a new condenser and points—and I'll have to look at the plugs, too. And the carburetor needs a new carburetor."

"It was all right when I bought it."

"Want to take it around the lake? I'll show you."

"I'll take your word for it. What do you want, a new car?"

"I can fix this one up. How much time do I have?"

"A few days. Four at the outside."

"I want a new car. There's too much work on this one."

Barth swore. "Take a look at the Ford."

Marty went over and started the Ford, looking through the rear window to see how much exhaust smoke it was throwing. There was none. He backed it out in a short arc, then shot down the driveway to the road. He drove it about half a mile down the road at varying speeds, then turned and came back, giving it the gun all the way. It responded instantly to the accelerator and, when he jammed on the brakes, it stopped in a spray of flying gravel. He got out and nodded at Barth.

"She needs a tuning-up but that's about all. She's in good shape. If I had the time, I'd put a supercharger and twin carburetors on her. Then nothing on the road would be able to touch us. The best I can do with the time I've got is to tune it and soup it up a little. Going through traffic, it'll be more a matter of driving, anyway."

"And you're the best, eh?"

Sophie said quickly, "He is good, Barth. He can handle a car."

She had spoken so quickly and had so obviously jumped to Marty's defense that Barth shot her a hard, suspicious glance, his eyes swiveling to Marty, then back to her. He felt a stab of jealousy. What had gone on back in that hotel room after he left? Sophie met his eyes steadily and if she felt any guilt, she did not show it.

Marty was saying belligerently, "No, I'm not the best driver on the road—but I'll be as good as anything we'll meet, including cops."

Cuesta laughed softly from the veranda and Barth turned and looked at him sourly.

Cuesta tilted his chin at Marty and said, "The wonder boy."

Barth said, "Shut up." Then to Marty, "We'll see, when the time comes.

If you're half as good as you think you are, I'll be satisfied."

"He's good," said Sophie again. She knew it was a mistake but she couldn't help saying it.

"All right, all right, so he's good," snapped Barth. "Everybody says so, so he must be. Now let's forget it. Come inside."

He turned and walked heavily into the cottage, followed by Sophie, Marty and Cuesta. The latter gave Sophie a slow, appraising glance as she passed him, watching the movement of her long thighs against the fabric of her skirt as she walked, the movement of her hips, the swell of her breasts.

He pursed his lips in a soundless wolf-whistle and, grinning secretly, lounged from his chair and followed them into the cottage, erasing his grin as he crossed the threshold.

Barth said curtly, "Shut the door."

Cuesta negligently closed the door with a flip of his foot. Then he leaned against the wall and put a cigarette between his lips. He sensed a weakness in Barth but it was something he felt more than consciously realized.

Barth stood in front of the fieldstone fireplace, facing them.

"Sit down," he ordered, and waited until they found chairs. He wanted to get this over with but he had to show his authority first. He had not had a drink that morning—the Ford had not been ready for him when he went to the agency—and his hangover was a nagging ache.

Each day he had been saying to himself—I am not going to take a drink today. I'm going to ride this hangover out, then let the stuff alone till after the strike. But each day he had taken a drink, then another—and another—to get rid of that nagging ache so he could think more clearly. In the past, there had always been a lifting excitement before a strike, an anticipation, an eagerness—but this time he was dead inside. He didn't want to make the strike but he had to. He had to have the money. And it had to be right, too. Going up against a mad dog like Jack Niles, it had to be damn good and right—or they'd all be dead meat within the space of time it took Niles to pull a trigger. If it went wrong, they'd be dead meat, all of them. It had to be right.

"This has to be right," he said aloud. "And the time to start making it right is now. Right here and now. I didn't bring you up here for a vacation. You're not here to enjoy yourself. Until we make the strike, nobody leaves the cottage, nobody goes downtown for anything, even a pack of cigarettes. Sophie will do all the shopping. Understand?"

He looked directly at Cuesta, who shifted uneasily in his chair and would not meet Barth's eyes.

"Okay with me," he mumbled.

"That goes for everybody, not just you. There's only one boss—that's me. Another thing—no liquor. No liquor in the cottage at any time. After the strike, you can drink all you want. But before—nothing. Understood?"

He kept his eyes from Sophie, as if to avoid an accusation he knew would be in her gaze—for she knew there were four bottles of Scotch in his bag. She had packed the bag and she had seen him put the bottles in first. But that was all right. He could handle it. A hothead like Cuesta, now, couldn't handle his liquor. And the kid, Marty, had damn well proved he couldn't. Anyway, he couldn't have them drinking. It was rough enough waiting to make a strike without roughing it up even more with liquor. Their tempers would be raw, especially Cuesta's. Cuesta always got jittery before a strike. He was good while he was in there during the strike but beforehand he was a sonuvabitch to live with. Barth had a feeling the one dependable member of the whole outfit would be Chuffy. The kid, Marty, didn't know what it was all about and Cuesta was all nerves—but Chuffy was okay.

Barth thought, I'll build the strike around Chuffy and me, with Cuesta in support, and the kid, Marty, to bring up the car.

"No liquor," he said flatly. "Understood?"

Marty flushed, as if the words had been directed at him. Cuesta merely shrugged. He was not a drinking man anyway, except wine, and wine he could do without for a while. He looked at Sophie. He didn't like the idea that Barth had allowed her to come along. A woman could lead to more trouble than liquor. Maybe there was nothing between her and the punk, Marty—but he'd lay eight to five there would be. He had an instinct about women. He had seen the way she looked at the punk. She had a yen. But that was Barth's business. She was Barth's woman. Thank God for that much. If the punk made a pass at the dame, Barth wouldn't make any trouble before the strike. The strike'd go off like ball bearings—but afterwards there'd be one dead punk who'd have nobody but himself to blame. All the same, Cuesta didn't like it that Barth had allowed the woman to come along.

Barth was saying in a hard voice, "Any questions?"

Cuesta shook his head and looked at Marty.

Marty said, "I can't work on a car without tools. Are you going to get me tools?"

"Make a list," said Barth. "I've got to go back to town for another crate and I'll pick up your tools at the same time. Put down everything you want—everything, because I don't want to go back twice. Anything else?"

Cuesta looked significantly at Sophie but Barth did not appear to notice. Cuesta shrugged and hunched down in his chair behind his cigarette.

"You have guns?" he asked. "I like to go over my own gun. I don't trust nobody to go over my gun. I go over my own. It gives me greater confidence."

"You can go over all the guns," said Barth. "I'll check up after you on mine and this Chuffy can check his if he wants. You want to go over all the guns?"

Cuesta spread his hands. "It will be something to do."

"They're in the black suitcase," said Barth to Sophie. "The oil and grease and cartridges are in the gray box. The shotgun shells are in a box wrapped in brown paper."

"Who takes the shotgun?" asked Cuesta.

"You can have it. You want it?"

"I prefer it. I find a shotgun very effective."

"It's all yours. You," Barth looked at Marty, "probably won't have to handle a gun. You just worry about the cars. But I'll give you a .38 just in case. Cuesta here'll show you one end from the other."

"I can handle a gun," said Marty truculently. "I've handled them before. I was with the Marines in Korea."

"Give him a howitzer," murmured Cuesta, cynically amused. "Give him a burp-gun. A .38 will be too tame for him."

"That's the second time—now cut it out!" Barth lashed savagely at him. "I don't want any bickering. We're all in this together. Leave the kid alone."

"I can take care of myself," said Marty, glaring at Cuesta.

Barth said heavily, "Whenever I hear a guy saying he can take care of himself, I know he's thinking about taking care of somebody else, so let me say this right now—the minute I find any of you trying to take care of anybody else—and you know what I mean—I'll take care of that guy myself, personally. You've got your own job to do. And you, Cuesta, you've got yours. Stay out of each other's hair. If you don't like the set-up, say so now!"

He looked from Cuesta to Marty. In that moment, he was the old Gerald Barth—a force not to be opposed, a blazing fire.

Cuesta hid behind his cigarette and mumbled, "I ain't looking for trouble. I didn't mean nothing."

And Marty said, "I didn't ask for it."

Sophie smiled at him, a quick smile to soothe his vanity that had been ruffled by both Cuesta and Barth. Barth saw the smile but ignored it. All he wanted now was to get out of the cottage and have a drink. He had said all he wanted to say and it had been an effort. In the past, he'd had to do nothing but walk into a room for everyone to know who was boss. This time it had been an effort. He felt as if he had been drained dry. All he wanted was that drink. He had them now, they knew he was boss. He wanted to leave quickly before he betrayed his own hollowness.

He said brusquely to Marty, "Tell your friend Chuffy I want to talk to him. I told the sonuvabitch to be here and he's late. I'll be back tonight if I can."

He nodded once and walked out. As he slid into the front seat under the wheel of the Buick, he felt as if he couldn't get away fast enough. There was something in him that cried out for peace and rest—but there would be no peace and rest until after the strike. In the meantime, all he needed was a drink ...

## A GOOD CATCH
### CHAPTER NINE

Chuffy showed up at the cottage about an hour after Barth had driven off in the Buick. Cuesta was sitting out on the veranda playing solitaire again. He had a pencil and pad beside him on which he recorded his wins and losses. He was playing against an imaginary gambling house. He paid an imaginary fifty-two dollars for the deck and realized an imaginary return of five dollars per card for each card he was able to play out of the set and onto the aces above the spread. He was an imaginary five hundred and twenty dollars ahead when Chuffy walked up the driveway.

"*Amigo!*" he called to Chuffy in high good humor. When Cuesta was in good humor, he larded his speech with Spanish phrases. Otherwise he spoke a sullen or sardonic English. "*Com' esta?*"

"Mamzel from Armenteers," said Chuffy, to whom all Spanish was Greek. "Wee, wee." He was in a very gray mood. It had been a two-mile walk to the cottage from the bus stop at the other end of the Lake. And, besides that, he was worried about Marty. His eyes darted to the Ford sedan parked near the cottage and he saw a pair of legs protruding from under the open hood. He strode over and, half angrily, brought down the flat of his hand across the buttocks.

"I thought I told you to wait for me last night!" he snapped.

Marty grinned back over his shoulder. "I went out bouncing."

"Well," said Chaffy grudgingly, "maybe you're lucky at that. I went to your hotel just before I come up here and found Angie's boys sticking around like tar to a fender. You didn't have no trouble, did you?"

"Hell no," said Marty. "Just a hangover this morning. From now on, remind me to remember that stuff has more backlash than a worn bearing. How're you?"

"Terrible. I could sleep for a week. Where's the bedroom? I want to hit the sack."

"Barth's sore."

"At me?"

"For being late."

"It's not my fault," said Chuffy virtuously. "I was looking for you. If you hadn't 'a run out on me last night, I'd 'a been here. Hey ..." he stared as Sophie came out of the cottage in shorts and a halter. She was carrying a fishing rod. "What's that?" he asked incredulously.

Marty lifted his head from the motor. He felt something quicken inside him at sight of her. Her feet were bare and her long legs were ivory in the sunlight. The halter molded the proud thrust of her breasts. But she was more than just another girl in playclothes. There was an excitement in her body. Not in the way she walked or exhibited herself, for she was not exhibiting herself—she was entirely unconscious of the effect she was producing in the three men—the excitement lay in what she was. The excitement was in the full, flowing lines of her body, in the rhythm of her long-thighed legs, the lift of her head.

Cuesta stopped playing solitaire and Chuffy let out a long, low wolf-whistle. Marty flushed.

"That's Sophie," he said shortly.

Chuffy grinned. He did not like big women but Sophie was not actually big. Ordinarily, she was a dame he wouldn't mind taking on—but now he had Jasmine. He had not really thought of Jasmine since leaving Newark. But now, at sight of Sophie, the thought of her came to him again and it was as if something had shot through him, like electricity.

I've fallen for the dame! he thought with a kind of dismay. Jesus, I've gone and fallen for her!

The dismay passed, leaving in its wake the most pleasurable sensation he had ever felt in retrospect. He had fallen for her. So what? She had fallen for him, too. And tomorrow night he would see her again. He had never understood what it meant before to fall for a dame—but now he knew. Jesus! It was a tingling all over, a sense of power, of power and glory. Christ. The little sonuvabitch!

He gazed after Sophie and was about to make the remark that she must be Barth's girl friend when he saw the look in Marty's eyes and he shut his mouth fast.

"Nice looking tomata," he said carefully. "What's she gonna do with that thing she's carryin', catch fish or something? Nothin' I like better'n a good fishfood dinner. Now where's the sack, kid? I wanna hit it."

"Yeah, you better hang around," said Marty, glad to be back on firm ground. "Barth said he wanted to talk to you. You'd better ask Cuesta about the sack. I wasn't here when the room keys were passed out."

"Right. Enjoy yourself, kid. Get that thing ticking like a watch. We're gonna need it when the cards are down, if you know what I mean."

He slapped Marty on the shoulder and walked up to the veranda.

"What's the idea of the tomata?" he said *sotto voce* to Cuesta. "What's goin' on here, for crissake?"

Cuesta lifted one shoulder. "Ask Barth. Maybe he knows."

"That his girl friend?"

"He thinks so!"

Chuffy glanced at Marty, then back toward the girl, who was awkwardly handling the fishing rod on the dock below. "It's always something," he said unhappily. "Say, where do I flop around here?"

Cuesta turned and pointed through the open door. "The door across from the kitchen. Mine's next to yours, and Barth and the dame have the big room at the end. We ought to ask that dame, maybe she's got three sisters."

Chuffy said, "That would be a mess," and walked into the house yawning.

Marty straightened up from the car and wiped his hands on a piece of rag. He started up the motor, made another adjustment on the carburetor, then closed the hood. That was as far as he could go without tools. He cut the motor, glancing down toward the dock where Sophie was still trying to manipulate the fishing rod. He had been sending sidelong glances down there right along but had not been able to think of a good excuse to join her. He was finished with the car now and just stood there, undecided about his next move. Cuesta watched him, cynically laying a mental bet that it wouldn't be five minutes before Marty was down at the dock with the girl. It was a bet he promptly collected, for even as he was making himself odds, Sophie managed to get the hook caught in her shorts and Marty went loping down the path. Cuesta picked up his pencil and marked down "50¢" on his pad under "Winnings." The odds had been a thousand to one. He had stood to lose an imaginary five hundred bucks.

He sat watching them with what might have been polite interest had it not been for the hard thinning of his eyelids. Then slowly his eyebrows arched and a small smile lifted one corner of his mouth. Maybe this was going to work out okay. Sophie was Barth's girl but if she let the punk make a pass at her, that made her anybody's meat. She was a good-looking dame, she was really built and, best of all, she was blonde and Cuesta had the Latin's predilection for blonde women. He relaxed in his chair and watched them with anticipatory amusement, with almost amoral detachment, like an actor awaiting a forthcoming cue in a play.

Marty knelt beside Sophie and said, "Don't pull on the rod. You'll get that hook in your leg."

"I didn't know fishing was so dangerous," she said.

"It's very dangerous. That's why fishermen have to have licenses, like dogs. Now hold still."

The hook had penetrated not only her shorts but her skimpy white nylon panties underneath, and Marty felt himself flushing as he tried to work the barb back through the fabric without touching her. It was impossible, of course. Each time his fingers touched the softness of her flesh, he felt the flush bite deeper into his cheeks, and the long curve of her thigh was so close to his face that he could have brushed it with his lips. He worked doggedly, trying to concentrate on the hook. And Sophie was not unaware of the touch of his hand. She wanted to lean into it each time it brushed her but instead, she held herself stiffly and looked out across the polished surface of the lake.

She wanted to say something—anything—just to break the tension that was growing between them. There was peril in that tension, a threat to them both, if they allowed it to develop. It had to be kept under the surface, unacknowledged, for once it was brought out into the open, she had a premonition they would be helpless before it. But she could think of nothing to say that would not heighten the tension and she stood there dumb with the dread growing inside her—a dread not born of fear but of yearning.

It was finally Marty himself who, momentarily, broke the tension. He straightened up with the hook dangling free from its leader. His face was still flushed a deep red.

"I'm sorry," he said awkwardly, "but I kind of tore your shorts a little. The hook was right through."

"It doesn't matter. Really it doesn't. What I can't understand is why I couldn't get it to throw out—I mean, I've seen them throw out, people fishing, I mean—and I tried but I just couldn't get it to do it."

"Well ... uh, you should have a weight on your line just above the leader. That's what carries it out, the weight. There ain't no weight and there should be one."

"Oh, should there? I don't know anything about it. I mean, I thought if you had a fishing pole you just kind of, well, fished. No wonder I couldn't get it to throw out! I should've had a weight. I see just what you mean," she prattled. "There should've been a weight to take it out!"

"And bait," Marty added. He was prattling, too. The flush, born of his nearness to her, was still deep in his cheeks. He did not quite know what to do or say—but he did not want to leave her.

"Bait?" she queried brightly. "You have to have bait, too? I have a lot to learn, don't I? I never fished before. I'll have to remember that. You have to have a weight and you have to have bait. I'll remember that. What is bait?"

"Well, uh, some people use worms."

"Worms!"

"Yes. You put there on your hook like, well, like spaghetti kind of. Worms."

"Live worms?"

"Yes. They have to be live. Live worms."

"Ugh! I couldn't touch them. They're like little snakes, only worse."

"Well, other people use flies. I don't mean flies, exactly. They just call them flies. They're kind of like colored feathers tied to your hook to look like kind of bugs. Fishes like kinds of bugs and when you find out the kinds of bugs fishes like, then you catch a lot of fish. But you gotta train, I mean, practice," he floundered. "There's a trick to it. Like trouts. Most people fish for trouts—but you have to know how. They say trouts are different from other fishes. I don't mean they look different but they kind of act different. I mean, they like different kinds of bugs."

"You know, I never knew any of that. I thought when you went fishing, you—well—just went fishing. There's a lot to it, isn't there?"

"Oh, yes. You have to know how to throw it, too. Not everybody knows how. You have to throw it a certain way. Like the bugs. I mean, you have to kind of make the fishes think it's a real bug, not just a bunch of feathers tied to a hook. Some fishes are real smart, like trouts. The trick is to be smarter than them," he told her earnestly. "The reason most people don't catch trouts is, they ain't as smart as the trouts. That's the way it works."

She said admiringly, "You really know a lot about fishing, don't you, Marty?"

"No, I don't. Honest, I don't. This is just some stuff I picked up reading magazines like *Field & Stream*, and *Argosy*, and like that. There's a lot about fishing in magazines."

She was eager to praise everything he did and to believe everything he did was praiseworthy. "You read a lot. You must read a lot to know all that about fishing and never did any fishing yourself, I mean, just picking it up out of magazines."

"Someday," said Marty wistfully, "I want to do a lot of fishing. Reading in the magazines, it sounded like what I'd like to do a lot of. Not in the Passaic River. I was raised in Newark near the Passaic River but there ain't no fishing in the Passaic. And if there was, you couldn't even eat them on account of the chemicals in the water. I read in the paper you couldn't even go swimming in the Passaic on account of the chemicals. But some day I want to do a lot of fishing. Like in Florida or Canada."

"I'd like to go to Florida some day, too. I ain't never been out of Pennsylvania. I mean, Pennsylvania and Jersey. Some day I'm going to Florida."

"Me, too."

They had run out of prattle—though behind and through the prattle they had been trying to tell each other what they were—and a yearning silence fell between them.

At length Marty said hesitantly, like a man about to walk on eggs, "Do you want me to get you some bait? So you can go fishing, I mean."

She laughed artificially. "Worms?"

"Well, yes—like worms."

"Oh, no thank you! If it comes to worms, I don't think I'll do any fishing. I couldn't even touch them."

"Would you like to go for a row in the boat?" he asked eagerly. "I used to do a lot of rowing when I was a sparring partner up at Pompton Lakes."

"Well, yes, thank you, I think I would like to go for a row in the boat. I've never been. Isn't that funny? I lived right in Pittsburgh and lots of people went rowing in boats on the river but I never did. I'd really like to go for a row in the boat, if you don't mind."

"Mind! I asked you, didn't I? If I minded, I wouldn't've asked you. Here, give me your hand. You don't have to be afraid to step down into it. It won't tip over. Flat-bottom boats don't tip very easy. That's right. Sit in the back. It's easier to row for me and we can talk because I gotta face the back when I row. That's a funny thing about boats, you have to row backwards, if you know what I mean."

Sophie sat precariously in the stern of the green and white rowboat, as if expecting it to up-end and plunge her into the water. She dabbled her fingers in the cool water. She had shed years, talking to Marty—all the long and disillusioning years since her fifteenth birthday. It was at her fifteenth birthday party that an older cousin, drunk on applejack, had attempted to rape her and she had fought him frantically, thinking he wanted to kill her. Her father had come upon them and had beaten the cousin into a bloody, repulsive ruin. Then he had beaten her, demanding to know how many times she had done that before, calling her awful names. Until that moment she had not known what "that" meant—but in his berserk rage, her father had soon enlightened her. In short, hard, brutal words, her father had furiously demanded to know how many times her cousin had this-and-that and if she had unspeakable and how many times. Even up to the present, nine long years later, Sophie had not been able to bring herself even to think the words her father had flung at her while he was beating her with his belt ...

Marty cast off the lines, pushed off from the dock with one oar and settled down in the seat facing her, seating the oars in the locks.

Up at the cottage, Cuesta had darted inside and returned to the veranda after a minute with a pair of cheap field glasses he had noticed earlier in the living room. They were low-powered and brought the boat scarcely any closer to him but holding them to his eyes and watching from the shadows gave him a feeling of omnipotence. He watched.

"Well," said Marty cheerfully, poising his oars, "where'd you like to go? Europe?"

"I'd like to go to that island over there," she pointed. "Let's make believe we're shipwrecked or something, on the island, like Robinson Caruso. You know, the book."

Marty said, "Ship ahoy." He had read that, too, in a magazine and it sounded like the sort of thing you should say in a boat. He dug the oars into the water and with an easy, powerful stroke, sent the tubby rowboat shimming toward the island.

It was not much of an island. It was only two hundred feet long and about fifty feet wide, thinly wooded, thrusting up through the skin of the lake like a fist, rising to what, at water level, seemed a considerable height, though it was actually no more than sixty feet at the rocky peak. It was sparsely grown with scrub birch and pine and had an anemic undergrowth of weed. Marty had to row completely around it before he found a ten-foot scrap of beach on which he could ground the rowboat. The rest of the island rose shearly from the water, twelve feet of solid rock. With a strong pull on the oars, he sent the boat into the beach. There was still six feet of shallow water between the bow and solid land, so he took off his shoes and socks and stepped over the side. He held out his arms.

"I'll carry you in," he said. "You take my shoes."

With small, laughing cries of apprehension, she stepped from the stern to the bow—though the water was a bare fourteen inches deep—picked up his shoes and, grasping his shoulder, let herself sink into his cradled arms.

A feeling of such unutterable warmth flowed through her at the tightening of his arms that she clung to him, her fingers digging into the hard, molded muscles of his wide shoulders. Red-faced and more breathless than the short distance warranted, Marty set her down on the beach. Again, they avoided each other's eyes.

He said awkwardly, pointing to the rocky crest of the island, "Like to go to the top?"

"Oh, yes! We've got to go to the top, now we're here."

He crouched to put on his shoes but more to hide his flaming face. He too, young as he was, had shed the years. He was older than she was but inside he was back at that period of bashful adolescence during which even the drawing of a breath in the presence of a woman is an agony. He had never felt that way with a girl before.

Up on the veranda, sitting cross-legged in the shadows with the field glasses to his eyes, Cuesta watched, disappointed for the moment that Marty had not kissed her. Hell, the guy had her in his arms, didn't he? Her face hadn't been any farther than that away from his, had it? What was the matter with the punk? Didn't he know which way was up? Cuesta knew what he would have done, had he carried Sophie ashore like that. Christ, her bare legs were hanging out of her shorts and her breasts half out of that rag around her chest—and the punk didn't even try to kiss her! Once a punk, thought Cuesta derisively, always a punk!

He adjusted the glasses slightly and settled himself more comfortably against the wall of the cottage to watch.

Straightening from tying his shoes, Marty picked up a thin piece of shale and, with a lithe sweep of his arm, sent it skipping over the calm surface of the water. Gleefully, he counted each skip, then watched it end in a feather of spray as it finally dived.

"Twelve skips!" he crowed. "That's a record. We gotta get it in the books. Now let's go to the top. Ready?"

Hand in hand, they went up the first shallow rise in a rush, the shale noisily sliding out from under their feet. They stopped at the first hard outcrop of rock and eyed the face of the steep, rocky climb ahead.

Marty said, "Phew!" and grinned. "Maybe we should have an elevator. You still want to go to the top?"

"All the way!" Sophie panted, clinging to his hand.

The rest of the way up was not as hazardous as it had first appeared. The alternate rains and freezes of many past winters had split wide fissures in the rock and there were many foot- and handholds. Marty was in splendid physical condition and was breathing almost normally when he reached the top. But Sophie had to lean against a tree, panting and a little dizzy, but laughing.

"Remind me," she said, "the next time we go mountain climbing, to start two hours ahead of you. It'd make me feel better if you'd pant a little, too."

Marty grinned. "A couple hours a day of road work, rope skipping and punching the bag would put you in condition."

"Condition for what?"

"Oh ... for whatever comes along."

"Thanks—but I've never had any trouble handling whatever came along. 'Specially if it whistled at me. And the kind of road work you have in mind wouldn't be any good for that. Oh Marty, isn't it pretty up here!"

She walked to the lip of the rocky promontory and stood looking over the placid water. There were a few rowboats scattered here and there, motionless, containing motionless fishermen contemplating their motionless lives. Three small sailboats with white triangular sails skimmed over the surface as happily as bits of paper caught in a spring breeze. They could hear the far-off cries of splashing children from the beach at the far end of the lake. Around the shores and stretching far back into the hills stood the quiet trees, chartreuse in the sunlight and blue-black in the shadows. Sophie felt a deep glow of peace.

"It's so pretty," she breathed.

She turned to Marty as if to ask him to share in this flowing tranquility. Her lips were parted to speak, but, suddenly, there were no words. They stood not a foot apart, looking into each other's faces. Then, drawn by what they saw there, they moved together and poised for a breathless instant before they surged into a deep and searching kiss.

Back at the cottage, Cuesta's thin mouth quirked and he pressed the cheap glasses more tightly to his eyes as if by doing so he could draw Sophie and Marty closer. Cuesta was a man who liked watching almost as much as doing. His eyebrows lifted as Sophie broke from the kiss and turned sharply away....

Her back to Marty, Sophie said agitatedly, "We must never do that again, never!"

Marty stammered, "I'm crazy about you."

"That doesn't make any difference. We mustn't do it again. It'll just lead to trouble, that's all. It'll just make trouble for you."

"I don't care. You're not married to him."

"That doesn't make any difference either."

"It makes all the difference."

"You don't know what you're talking about. You don't know Barth. He's not like anybody you ever knew. He'll ... do something bad to you."

"I can take care of myself. And I can take care of you too, if it comes right down to it. I'm not afraid of Barth."

"I know you're not, Marty, but sometimes it's smarter to be afraid—and this is one of those times."

She turned and faced him, pleading, but as he took a step toward her, she backed off, shaking her head. "No, Marty, no—not again, please!"

"But you don't love him...."

"He was good to me once when I needed somebody to be good to me—and he needs me now. I won't cheat on him."

Marty said, "Oh," in a deflated voice and looked down at his muscular hands. "That makes things kind of different, I guess."

"It makes all the difference, Marty." She hesitated, "Marty...."

"What?"

"I ... don't know what Barth is planning but I know the kind of business he used to be in. He was what they used to call a public enemy or something. All this talk about guns and things, I guess he's going to hold up somebody or something...."

"So?"

"It's not for you, Marty! You've never done anything like that before. Get out before it's too late. Get out before they put your picture in the post offices! Barth used to be one of the biggest in the country and look at him now. You don't have to do this, Marty. Get out of it!"

Marty's mouth compressed as if she had attacked his pride.

"All I'm doing," he said woodenly, "is driving a car for Barth. I don't know anything about anything else. I'm just driving a car."

"But you'll still be mixed up in it, Marty. I have to stay with him but you don't. Get out now, today. Just walk away and never come back."

"Why?"

"Because I don't want you mixed up in it."

"Don't worry about me."

"But I am worrying."

"So you're worrying," he said with sudden ferocity. "What about me? Don't you think I can worry, too? I know what kind of guy Barth is. I used to read the newspapers. Do you think I can just walk away and leave you here with him? Do you think that's the kind of guy I am? Maybe I used to be that kind of guy with dames, but I was never crazy about one before. I'm crazy about you and I'm going to stay right here where you are."

"But it won't do any good!" she cried in despair.

"And besides," he said stubbornly, "I'm going to talk to Barth. He looks like the kind of guy you can talk to. And I'm going to tell him that we...."

"You're crazy!"

"Maybe I am—but I'm going to talk to him, all the same. And he'll listen, too. He might be the toughest guy in the world and all that but he's not a sonuvabitch."

Sophie stared at him in horror. It was as if he were about to put his head in a lion's mouth, claiming it was nothing more than an overgrown alley cat.

She clenched her fists at her sides.

"I told you Barth was good to me," she said harshly, "but I didn't tell you how good he really was. He picked me up in Philly in a gin mill. He took me out of the gutter."

"Then there's some good in him."

"Use your brains for a minute, will you! I didn't mean he picked me up—I picked him up! I was a whore, a lousy Philadelphia whore. I picked him up because I was out for business. He was cockeyed and looked like a mark. Is that plain enough for you to understand or should I make it plainer?"

He disregarded the jeer in her voice and said calmly, "You never were a whore."

"No? Ask the cops down in Philly. Only they wouldn't call me a whore. They'd call me a mud-kicker."

"I don't care. You never were a whore."

"Oh, Jesus!"

"I know I'm not very smart," said Marty, "but there's a difference between you and whores. I met a lot of whores and they did it because they were too damn lazy to do anything else. Or too damn something. I met them. I know. A pug meets a lot of them. Once a whore, always a whore. Look at you now. You're sticking to this guy because he was good to you. Do you think a whore would stick to a guy because he was good to her once? Not on your life. She'd stick to him because he had dough."

"Barth's got dough—and he's going to have a lot more. He's the kind of guy who thinks he's broke when he's only got five or ten grand to his name. How much have you got? How much'll you ever have? I was a whore, all right. And not even a good one. I almost starved."

"And I was a pug. Do you know how good I was? They had to fix almost every fight so I could win, that's how good I was! I'm going to talk to Barth first chance I get."

"You do that, Junior," said Sophie as coldly as she could, "and I'll tell him you've been drinking canned heat. Take me back to the cottage. I'm getting tired of this."

Cuesta lowered his glasses after watching them clamber back into the boat. He felt a deep disappointment, as if he had paid to see a hot movie and had been shown a Tarzan film instead.

## MOONLIGHT MADNESS
CHAPTER TEN

Barth wanted a drink desperately but he drove all the way into Paterson without stopping. He had connections in Paterson and wanted to get rid of the Buick before he did anything else. His suspicion of a connection between Sophie and Marty was gnawing at him and he nursed it the way another might have nursed an abscessed tooth by prodding at it with his tongue.

His connection in Paterson was a thin, tuberculous man who ran a lunch wagon on the outskirts of the city on the road to Passaic. In the sometimes senseless nomenclature of the underworld he was known as the Wop, though he was actually Irish. Barth took a stool at the far end of the counter and, after the Wop had leisurely served hamburgers and coffee to a couple at the opposite end, ordered himself a Western on soft roll and a bottle of beer. The Wop took his time filling the order, sending many sidelong glances down the counter.

When he finally did serve Barth, he said from the side of his mouth, "Heard you were out, Soldier. Things okay?"

"Fine, fine," said Barth. He filled his glass with beer and drank it down thirstily. He tapped the empty bottle with his forefinger, ordering another. "With you?"

"So-so. Kind of out of touch, if you know what I mean."

"Yeah?"

"New crowd in City Hall."

Barth nodded. The Wop was telling him that no matter what was on his mind, it was no dice—the connection was broken, washed up.

"I'm looking for a new heap. I got a Buick but it's a dog," he said casually. "I want something that'll take me from here to Florida without the motor falling out. Know any dealers around?"

The Wop looked relieved. "Sure. Franklin Motors down the highway a half-mile. See a guy named Britton. Tell him Charlie McCabe sent you. Another beer?"

Barth nodded again. The Wop reached into the cooler and brought out a dripping bottle, then went down the counter to serve a pair of truck drivers who had just come in. He did not come back.

Barth grinned a little sourly. It was the old brush-off. The word had gone around that Barth was washed up and now even a two-bit jerk like the Wop didn't want anything to do with him. Well, that was all to the good. Now the word would go around that Barth was on his way to

Florida. The Wop would spread it. Barth couldn't ask for anything better. He finished his second bottle of beer, threw a dollar bill on the counter and walked out, leaving his Western untouched.

He got a dark green Packard sedan at Franklin Motors.

"I had my eye on this one for myself," the salesman, Britton, told him, "but for a friend of Charlie McCabe ... hell, I can pick up another."

"You'll be picking teeth out of your beer if it's a lemon," Barth told him sourly.

But the car seemed all right as he drove back toward Nutley along the bank of the Passaic River. It was lively and had a lot of power. He stopped in Passaic and picked up a bottle of Scotch. He nipped at it as he drove. It usually took about four drinks to smooth him out but this time he did not smooth out at all. There was a smoldering resentment in him that burned hotter and hotter. He knew he had made a mistake in bringing Sophie to the cottage but he wanted her there with him. He wanted the reassurance that she gave him.

He knew, without having to think about it, that Marty had something he, Barth, would never have again. He pounded the wheel of the car with his fist.

"I'll break his goddamn neck," he growled. "I'll break his goddamn neck."

He was on the outskirts of Nutley when he remembered the supplies he had forgotten to get—a good pair of binoculars, a pencil and a pad of paper. He turned and drove all the way back to Passaic, where he picked up another bottle of Scotch.

He tried not to think of Sophie and Marty. This was the most important part of the strike. You didn't make mistakes when you were handling a madman like Jack Niles. Niles was as deadly as cyanide. This thing had to be planned right the first time.

Thomas had given him the location of Niles' hideout on River Road and he had it pretty firmly fixed in his mind. The thing he had to do now was get it down on paper.

The first time, he drove slowly past and went all the way to the Belleville Turnpike before he turned back, returning by way of Washington Avenue, a block to the west. The street on which he had to turn left was Hillcrest Road. He parked halfway down the hill. From there he could just see the southern arm of the forked driveway that led into Niles' lair. He took out his pad and pencil and quickly made a sketch of Hillcrest Road and River Road, marking the spot on which he was then parked with a heavy "X". On that spot, the first getaway car would be stashed, out of sight of the hideout below.

He got out of the car and walked across the street into the empty lot.

From there he could see the whole of the driveway and the garage on the bank of the river, and he could even glimpse the house through the trees, heavy bushes and undergrowth that screened it from the road. The driveway itself was about three hundred feet long from the apex of the fork to the garage. It was heavily overgrown on either side by towering, neglected rhododendron bushes. He nodded with satisfaction. That would make excellent cover for Chuffy and himself, Chuffy on one side of the driveway, he on the other. Cuesta, he would place closer to the garage on the north side. That way when Niles got out of his car, he would be subject to a murderous three-way crossfire.

This was familiar work and Barth sketched rapidly and with absorption, putting in every tree, every bush, every bit of cover, including the old wheelbarrow beside the garage.

He had a pretty fair idea of what would happen. Niles would drive straight into the garage, for the car had to be hidden. Then he and his henchmen would come out and close the doors, leaving themselves no cover. They would be standing in the open driveway and that would be the time to blast them. Barth would take care of that part of it with the submachine gun. If things went right, he could handle the whole thing himself. Chuffy and Cuesta were only reserves to take care of anybody who did manage to make a break. But if things went right, it would all be over in two minutes from the time Niles came out of the garage. And things were going to go right, he told himself.

He finished the map and went back to the car. Before driving off, he took another deep swallow from the bottle. He was feeling good. He told himself that he always felt good after things began to get set. It was only before they started to jell that he was edgy. He had always been one of the best at this sort of thing—the planning, making the layout. He had always been a careful planner. Not like Niles. Niles was good up to a point but after that, he was sloppy. After that point, Niles substituted bullets for careful thinking, blasting everything in sight to make a hole to squirm through. Well, Barth thought grimly, Niles had only one more hole coming to him—six feet straight down.

He took one more drink from the Scotch bottle, then drove back to Washington Street, turning east across the Lyndhurst Bridge. He had to take a look next at Niles' hideout from the east bank of the river. He clambered aboard an old barge that had burned out and beached there. Squatting comfortably in what was left of the cabin, he had a clear view of the river side of Niles' hideout. The house, a two-story white clapboard building with a peaked roof, stood about thirty feet north of the garage. The entrance was from the rear. Good. If anybody made a break, it would be for that door—and Cuesta would have that covered with his shotgun.

He swept the shore carefully with his powerful binoculars. The tide was low and the scummy mud flats extended a good twenty feet from the weed-grown shore.

Barth shook his head and muttered, "How dumb can one get!"

Already Niles had made one mistake. If Barth had chosen that hideout, with his back to the river, he'd have had a speedboat docked right there. Just in case. He went over the opposite shoreline inch by inch, able to see even the blades of grass with his strong glasses. But there was no sign of a boat. That was lousy planning. Niles had put his back to a wall.

Barth took a drink from the bottle he had carried with him, then set carefully to work on his third sketch. The three sketches would cover Niles from every direction. The ground to the north of the house was covered with more trees and bushes but no one would get that far because that side of the driveway would be covered by Cuesta and Chuffy. Barth was not worried about their charging his side of the driveway. Nobody charged into the muzzle of a submachine gun. The break, if any, would be away from him. He took frequent small nips from the bottle as he worked. He was in a state of high elation as he finished his last sketch. He had Niles covered like a blanket. It would be all over in two minutes. Five short bursts from the gun would clean it up. And there were no neighbors close enough to get nosy—or to worry about if they did get nosy. Within five minutes after the first shot, Barth would be on his way back to the Lake. He finished the last drink and threw the empty bottle into a corner of the cabin. He glanced at his watch and was surprised to find that he had been working on the sketches almost four hours. He was not drunk but he felt a deep glowing satisfaction.

He drove back to Passaic and stopped to call Thomas but there was no answer. To kill time, he found a Western Auto store and bought the tools Marty had ordered, also the smaller tools Cuesta wanted for overhauling the guns. He called Thomas again but still there was no answer. He did not want to call from the Lake, nor anywhere near the Lake, so he went into a gin mill and had a few more Scotches. Three-quarters of an hour later, he called Thomas for the third time. This time Thomas answered in a thick but understandable voice.

"I've been calling you for over an hour," said Barth. "Where the hell you been?"

"I was upstairs."

"So what? You got a phone upstairs."

"I was talking," said Thomas stiffly, "to my daughter. She's locked herself in her room. I, mean, she's locked herself in her room."

"Say, what's the matter with you? You drunk again?"

"I am not drunk."

"You sound it."

"I have had a few drinks but I am not drunk—and I don't like your tone."

"Okay, okay. I didn't call up to argue. Is our friend still set for Friday?"

"You know where to get in touch with me in case there's any change?"

"You gave me your address, I presume."

"You presume right. See that you don't forget it. They're still changing cars on River Road in Kearny?"

"That was the way it was set up, I believe. There has been no occasion to change plans."

"Oh for crissake, who're you trying to sound like, Arthur Treacher? Well, my plans are set too. I'll take them when they change cars on River Road in Kearny. Meantime, why don't you sober up?"

Thomas shouted, "I am perfectly sober! And if you're finished trying to tell me what to do, let me tell you something. You tell Doyle to keep away from my daughter or there'll be trouble."

Barth said incredulously, "Marty Doyle? My driver?"

"You tell him to keep away from my daughter. There's a certain person around town looking for Doyle. You tell Doyle if he comes nosing around my daughter just once more, that certain person is going to find him. And you, Mr. Barth, will lose a driver. Is that quite clear?"

"Yeah, sure," said Barth, grinning. "Absolutely. But are you sure it's Doyle?"

"Do you doubt my word?"

"Hell, no."

"Furthermore, I am having my daughter followed by detectives and Doyle won't have the slightest chance to meet her on the sly. You might tell him that also."

"I sure will, pal, I sure will."

"See that you do." Thomas hung up with a crash.

Barth laughed and replaced the receiver on the hook. Still chuckling, he walked from the booth and went back to the bar. He ordered a Scotch, to celebrate. He had to laugh again, thinking of the stew he had been in over Sophie and Marty. Well, that was the way he was before a strike started to jell—edgy, imagining things. He suddenly felt an indulgent affection for Marty. What the hell, he was only a kid. It was a dumb trick, of course, making a play for Thomas' own daughter—but that's the way kids were. And Thomas had a point, too. He wanted something better for his daughter. That was okay. Well, he'd warn Marty when he got back to the Lake. He remembered now something about a local mug named Angie, who was looking for Marty. Something about a double-cross in a fixed fight. That was it. Angie was gunning for the kid. That was who Thomas meant, this Angie. Thomas was just the kind of guy who'd let somebody else do his dirty work for him. Well, he'd throw a good scare into the kid when he got back to the Lake and that ought to hold him till after the strike. If Marty wanted to get himself shot up by Angie after the strike, that was his business.

Barth had one more Scotch for the road, then left for the Lake. He didn't realize how drunk he was by then. He had to squint once in a while to see the road clearly, for the white line in the center kept forking into a double line. But he was in such high good humor that it didn't bother him until he heard the shrill angry scream of the police siren behind him.

He went cold and thought, "Oh God!" For a moment he thought wildly of making a run for it but he didn't know the car and he didn't know the road except to the Lake. Sweating, he lifted his foot slightly from the gas pedal and drifted to the right side of the road. The police car passed him with a roar and went skirling up the road into the darkness. He stared blankly after it, then his hands began to shake. He pulled off the road to the shoulder and stopped until he could steady himself. His heart was racing and there was a coiling, sluggish sickness in his stomach. It brought back everything, his old fears, his desperate need for peace. Oh God, if only his sister had not died so needlessly! Tears welled up in his eyes. By this time, he and Sissie would have been safe in Florida, sitting on the beach or fishing, without a worry in the world, just taking it easy and drifting along—not sitting here sick because a police car had passed him on the road. He felt crumpled and old and tired and sick because he had to make this strike. If only he could forget the strike and go away with Sophie! But he had to have the money. He had to have a stake so he could go to Florida and live out the rest of his years in quiet.

After a while he started the car again and drove on at a sedate forty miles an hour. But the moment he turned into the Lake road, he uncorked his second Scotch bottle and took a deep, desperate drink. He shuddered and took another. His hands were still shaking a little.

Marty was sitting in the dark out on the porch smoking a cigarette when Barth drew up before the cottage. Cuesta and Chuffy were indoors, playing gin. Sophie was in the kitchen, washing dishes. Marty flipped his cigarette away.

Barth said curtly, "Siddown. I want to talk to you."

"And I want to talk to you."

"Fine," said Barth with irony. "We'll talk to each other. But I'll talk first. You've been playing around with a certain dame and you know who I mean."

Marty lifted his chin. "I'm not playing around. I'm nuts about her."

"I don't give a damn if you're nuts about her whole family. You're going to stay away from her, understand?"

"Now wait a minute," Marty started belligerently.

"Wait, hell! There's only one thing I'm interested in and that's the strike. Until then, you'll keep your nose clean. After that, what you do is your business. You can make love to her at the corner of Broad and Market if you want. I won't give a damn. But till then I don't want any horsing around."

Marty was dumbfounded. He had expected anything but this. He had expected Barth to get tough and he had been prepared to get just as tough. But not this!

"B-but when's the strike?" he stammered.

Barth smiled grimly. "Soon."

"And ... after the strike, it's okay with you?"

"Why not? I don't give a damn. I just told you, all I'm interested in is the strike. Now are you going to keep your nose clean or aren't you?"

Marty flushed at Barth's peremptory tone but then he saw that the man was drunk and he said quietly, "All right, we'll do it that way."

"Okay. The tools you wanted are in the back seat of the car. That's the new heap I picked up. As long as it's dark, take it down the highway and give it a run. If it's sour, I'm taking it back tomorrow and shoving it down somebody's throat."

Marty said, "Right," and walked toward the car.

Barth went into the cottage. He was carrying the small package of tools he had bought for Cuesta to clean the guns. He threw it on the table in front of Cuesta, scattering the cards.

"Now you can go to work on the guns," he said, walking into the kitchen where Sophie was waiting apprehensively.

Cuesta turned and watched him, then scowled at Chuffy. "He's soused!" he said.

Chuffy shrugged and lit a cigar.

Cuesta hissed, "I don't trust a guy that gets soused before a strike. Where's that leave us?"

"He won't be soused when the time comes."

"If he is, *amigo*, I won't be there."

But Chuffy's mind was elsewhere. He had been aching to see Jasmine ever since he had awakened from his nap. But he had not dared to sneak off for fear of Barth. He glanced toward the kitchen. Barth was swaying in the doorway. Chuffy's eyes lighted. Unless he missed his guess, Barth would be dead to the world inside an hour. Already his eyes were at half mast. What a break! The minute Barth hit the sack, he could slip out, take the Ford and be in Newark in an hour. His pulse quickened at the thought of seeing Jasmine again.

Barth stepped into the kitchen and closed the door, leaning his back against it. Things were beginning to spin a little. Sophie watched him uneasily. She knew Marty had been waiting outside on the porch to speak to him. She had tried to talk Marty out of it, she had jeered at him, had become angry—but he had remained stubbornly resolved.

"Did ... did you see Marty?" she faltered.

He focused on her with difficulty. Marty? He didn't want to talk about Marty—or think about him. He didn't want to think about any of them. All he wanted was to go to bed and think about his sister and the way they had planned to go to Florida. But they had killed his sister, she was dead. An anger rose crazily in his head, and he turned and wrenched at the doorknob. Sophie darted forward and seized his arm.

"What did you do to him, Barth?" she cried.

He half-turned and gave her a stinging backhand slap across the cheek. "You whore," he said thickly. "They killed my sister and now all I got's a whore."

Tears streaked his face again. It was all confused in the alcoholic haze and all he wanted was to go away into the peace and security of bed which, somehow, he identified with his sister. He thrust Sophie away from him with a sweep of his arm and staggered out of the kitchen. Cuesta watched him with hard accusing eyes. Chuffy pretended not to notice and blew a plume of blue cigar smoke up toward the ceiling. But the moment he heard Barth's bedroom door slam shut, he laid down his cards and pushed back his chair.

"I think I'll take a run downtown for some cigars," he said casually. "I'm out."

He walked out quickly before Cuesta could offer to accompany him. Cuesta reached out slowly and gathered up the cards. He started to shuffle them. He shuffled them over and over and over. His eyes were thin, fixed and dark, staring at nothing except, possibly, the dark turmoil in his own mind. He glanced toward Barth's closed door and muttered under his breath.

Once he said aloud, "I ought to screw the joint right now!" But he did not move. Barth's drunkenness had done something to him and he sat there in an agony of indecision. After a while, he put the cards down on the table and walked quietly back into the kitchen.

He opened the door and started persuasively, "Hoy, *querida*, how's about me and you having a little drink and ..."

He stopped and looked around with angry disappointment. Sophie was gone.

Marty picked her out in the headlights of the returning Packard about a quarter of a mile down the road from the cottage. She was walking rapidly and her face was a rigid mask. He braked and leaned out of the window.

"Hey," he said. Then, seeing the look on her face, "What's the matter, honey?"

She shook her head. He reached across and opened the other door for her.

"Get in. Come on."

She hesitated, then slid into the seat beside him. The high moon was almost full and he could see her clearly in its radiance. "What's the matter, honey?" he repeated.

She shook her head and turned her face, hiding it from him with her hand. Very gently, he took her hand and pulled it away from her cheek. She was crying.

"What's the matter, honey?" he pleaded. He fondled her hand.

She turned and looked at him, her working mouth trying to smile. "Oh Marty! I was afraid he had done something to you. He looked so awful when he came in."

"He was drunk, that's all."

"I know—but I was so afraid. Did ... did you talk to him?"

For a moment Marty looked puzzled, as he went back over the bewildering conversation he'd had with Barth.

"Yes," he said. "That is, he did all the talking. I don't know how he knew, but he knew about us. And he said for me to keep my nose clean till after what he called the strike. After that, he said, it was all right. I mean, you and me. I thought he'd be different. You know! But he said all he cared about was the strike."

"Oh. Then that accounts for it."

"Accounts for what?"

"The way he was," said Sophie quickly. She reached out and touched his cheek. "He really said that, Marty, about you and me? He really said that?"

"He said just what I told you. I said to him, after the strike it's okay with you? And he said, why not? I don't give a damn. That's just what he said. I didn't know what to say. I was all set to have it out with him right there."

"Oh, Marty!"

"Honey!"

After a while he lifted from her warm, parted lips and said huskily, "Let's drive a little."

She tightened her arms around him. "I don't feel like driving," she whispered.

"But we can't stay here in the middle of the road."

"Let's walk down to the lake. I love the lake."

"All right."

He drove down a side road until he came to a small cement block-house that was under construction. There the road ended. They walked hand in hand to the shore of the lake and sat down on the grass under the low-spreading arms of a blue spruce.

Sophie leaned her head into the hollow of his shoulder and said wonderingly, "I didn't know water could be so clean and peaceful. In Pittsburgh there was the Allegheny River and it was dirty—and there were all those factories. I never knew water could be like this." She touched his cheek again. "I didn't know anything could be like this. It's like I was dreaming."

"It's always going to be like this."

"I know—but I can't believe it all at once. I have to believe it a little bit at a time. Oh, Marty!"

She lifted her face. He kissed her. Lightly. He drew back a little and smiled at her, then kissed her again. Her arm tightened around his neck, then her hand slid to the back of his head and drew him more deeply into the kiss. He cupped her shoulders in his hands and pulled her fiercely to him. The kiss trembled on the edge of their tumulting emotion. A touch would have sent it either way, back into withdrawal or on into passion. They were suspended between the two, clinging to each other. Then slowly, ineluctably, the kiss deepened, became more demanding. Her fingers dug into the hard muscles of his neck and his hands slid down her back. For a space of time, in which the very instants erupted, their hands were as incoherent as their emotions. But then their hands found each other, at first hesitantly, groping, touching a cheek, stroking a forearm, brushing the hollow of a throat, not experimentally but with the growing sureness of a blending passion.

After the kiss, there was no point at which they could have drawn back. The trickle became a rush, the rush a torrent, and they were swept together into it, lips, hands and bodies, and beyond the bodies, the emotions and their very beings. They could no more change the course than they could have changed their course had they been directly in the path of a bursting dam. And at its very quivering peak, when there was no longer any higher reach, the climax of their love did not come with a wrench, a dislocation, a falling away—but it came and miraculously lifted them even higher. And afterwards there was the sweet drifting back, the languorous settling. They lay side by side and Marty brushed her lips with his, murmuring. There were no real words in his murmuring, no real coherence—but words were just things he would have stumbled over, trying to tell her what he felt. And she must have understood, for her wordless murmur was his answer.

It was Marty who heard the cracking branch and he whirled sharply, half-upright, covering Sophie with his body. Cuesta stood before them on the path, his mouth quirking. He covered his mouth with his left hand. His right hand hung down at his side.

"Do not disturb yourself, *amigo*," he said with a curious giggling lift to his voice. He waved his hand. "Relax, eh? We are all old friends. Are we not old friends?"

For a moment, Marty was frozen. Then, with a hoarse cry, he rolled and came to his feet, crouching. Cuesta leaped back and laughed.

"Relax, *amigo*," he grinned. His right hand came up. There was a click and six inches of bright steel sprang from the knife that had been concealed in his palm. His thumb slid down to the blade, holding it firm, the gesture of a practiced knife-fighter. He tilted his chin at Sophie. "Relax, there is enough there for both of us, eh?"

Marty moved toward him, balanced on the balls of his feet.

"Don't be foolish, *amigo*," Cuesta said sharply, lowering his knife for the stomach thrust, upward. "I do not want to hurt you."

Marty said heavily, "You lousy sonuvabitch!" and sprang at him.

Cuesta cried out and slashed in and up with the knife. Marty was accustomed to having to watch both hands of his opponents in the ring. Now, having to watch only Cuesta's right hand was like child's play for him. He feinted with his body, then pivoted, letting the knife slide harmlessly past his belly. As Cuesta drove in with the follow-through, Marty chopped him across the side of the jaw with a short, hard right hook. Cuesta went down as if his legs had been cut off at the hips. The knife flew from his hand in a short glittering arc. He scrambled wildly on the grass, reaching into his shirt for the gun that was strapped under his left armpit. Marty kicked him on the elbow and Cuesta groaned as if the pain were death itself. Marty reached down, tore the shirt away and plucked the ugly, short-barreled gun from the holster. Cuesta looked up at him with hate in his glassy eyes. Slowly he rose to his feet, holding his elbow. He said nothing but a crooked grin slid up into his right cheek. He backed away from them.

"*Buenas noches, senorita y señor*," he said with jeering courtesy. "*Va con Dios, señor*."

He turned and walked swiftly away through the spindling scrub birch trees.

Marty lifted the gun in his hand and Sophie cried out, "Don't, Marty!

Don't!"

Cuesta looked back over his shoulder, saw the gun, and broke into a panicky run. Marty lowered the gun.

"I'll kill him," he said heavily. "I'll kill him."

"Let him alone. He can't hurt us."

"He was standing there all the time ..."

"He can't hurt us, Marty. Please, Marty!"

Marty took a long, shuddering breath, then thrust the gun into his hip pocket.

"He'll try something. I know he'll try something—and the first time he does, I'll kill him."

"But what can he do, Marty? There's nothing he can do. Tell Barth? Barth doesn't care. Anyway, he won't dare tell Barth, because he knows I'll tell Barth he tried to attack me with a knife in his hand. He won't tell Barth. He's afraid of Barth. So what can he do?"

"He can make a pass at you. That's what he can do. When I'm not around."

"I can handle him."

"I know, I know—but I just can't stand the thought of him making a pass at you. I'll kill him!"

"Oh, Marty! I can handle him, honest. He won't try anything, I know he won't."

Marty burst out, "But what I can't stand was him being there all the time!"

And for the second time that night, Sophie saw tears in a man's eyes.

## LONG WATCH
### CHAPTER ELEVEN

Jasmine was waiting at the hotel when Chuffy walked into the room carrying a bottle of Drambuie. He had called her from Caldwell. Only last night she might have greeted him naked from the bed, waiting for him with a lascivious smile of welcome on her lips. But something had happened to her in those intervening hours and she no longer wanted to play the prostitute in front of Chuffy. She wanted desperately now to erase that first sordid impression he had had of her.

She was sitting up on the bed, propped with pillows. She wore a white nylon nightgown and, over it, a high-collared white nylon dressing gown. It made her look more childlike than ever, with her thin face and enormous eyes and silky light hair.

"I thought you weren't coming," she pouted. "I've been waiting for hours. I thought that horrible Marty had held you up again. I hate him."

Chuffy looked at his wristwatch with surprise. "I said I'd be here at ten and it's only five minutes to. See?" He held out his arm.

"Well, it felt like hours. And what do you know?" She sat up, bright-eyed and laughing. "A man tried to follow me. It was a private detective named Maury, who works for my father sometimes. I lost him in traffic at Broad and Market Street by making a left turn. You're not allowed to make turns there but I made a turn and the policeman didn't see me. Then I heard a whistle and looked back and there was Maury with the policeman leaning against his car, writing out a ticket. I'll bet his face was red."

"What's a private eye following you around for?" Chuffy demanded.

"That's my father," Jasmine shrugged contemptuously. "He wants me to go to South America with him. I won't go." She looked straight into his eyes. "And you know why. I hope that isn't Scotch in that bag. I hate Scotch. It tastes like an unemptied ashtray."

Chuffy sat down at the edge of the bed beside her and, grinning, held up the bottle of Drambuie for her inspection.

"Well," she said, "what have we here, dear? How'd you know I liked it?"

"You mentioned it. It's the right stuff, ain't it?"

"Huh! I suppose you're the sort who brings a girl a gift just to get her in the mood for smooching." She kissed him.

He held her off. "You ain't been picking up any more guys on the street, have you?"

She flushed and turned her face away from him. "I wish I never had," she said almost inaudibly. "I wish I'd never done it." She began to cry.

He cupped her chin in his hand and turned her face back to his. "Now cut it out, baby. If you ain't doing it no more, that's all I want to know. If you didn't do it in the first place, we'd never've got together, right?"

"But, Chuffy ..."

"Okay, okay, let's forget it, huh? It's over, it's done with. And I been thinking. When I finish up this hassle with Barth, let's me and you tie up for good and go some place."

"You mean—get married?"

"Anything wrong with that?"

"Oh, no!"

"Crazy about me, huh?"

"Well, aren't you crazy about me, too?"

"It's mutual. But don't get any ideas. The minute a dame finds out a guy's nuts about her, the first thing she wants to do is put a rope around his neck or a ring in his nose—or something. That don't work with me, baby."

"I wouldn't, Chuffy, honestly. I'm not possessive."

"I'd walk out on you."

"You'll never walk out on me. You're my man. You know what the Spanish say? *Mucho hombre.* That means, much man. That's what you are—much man. I'll never do anything to make you want to walk out on me."

"And that other stuff, it's all over now, right? I'm broadminded and all that—but I don't want my wife walking around picking up guys just for the kicks. If you can't get your kicks with me, the hell with you."

She put her hand over his mouth. "Please don't ever mention that again," she pleaded. "I'll never do it again, honestly. It was stupid. I was doing it just to get even with my father, I suppose. I've been thinking about. It was the same thing as my smoking reefers. I'll never do that again, either. I swear I won't, Chuffy. You really mean it about getting married, don't you?"

"What do you think I said it for, just to get to first base, like some guys? I didn't have to say it, did I? Okay, then. Let's consider it settled."

She peered anxiously into his face. "Are you—going to keep working with Barth? I mean, after we're married?"

"Hell, no! That's strictly, for jerks. I wouldn't even've done it this time except I needed a stake. The best of them get it in the end like Johnny Dillinger. I'm going back in the fight racket. Managing. It's what I know best."

"With Marty Doyle?" she asked jealously. "I hate him!"

"So what? I'd manage Jack the Ripper if I thought I could work him up to the big dough. It's a business, that's all."

"But he'll get you in trouble, Chuffy. I know he will."

"Then I'll get somebody else. He ain't the only light-heavy in the world."

"Oh—Chuffy, I love you so much!"

He held her tightly, then untied her negligee at the throat. "We've been wasting a lot of time tonight, baby," he whispered.

"Take it off, darling. I love having you undress me. I wish I had more clothes on, so you could take them all off!"

"Baby ..."

Across the street from the hotel was an all-night counter lunchroom, The Red Castle, specializing in cheap hamburgers. The man standing in the phone booth had no trouble watching the hotel entrance and, even as he talked, he kept his head half-turned, watching the dimly lit double doors.

"Angie?" he said into the phone.

"Yeah?"

"This is Al down the Hotel Sherman."

"Yeah?"

"You been sold a bill of goods, boss. I followed the dame like you said but Marty Doyle didn't show."

Angie swore. "Okay. Chalk it off."

"No, wait a minute, boss. Doyle didn't show but a friend of his did—Chuffy, Doyle's manager. I'll pick him up when he comes out, right?"

The silence stretched out and Al finally said, "You still there, boss?"

"Shut up. I'm thinking."

"Sure, boss, on'y I know you been wanting to talk to Chuffy too and I thought ..."

"Shut the hell up, will you!"

Al shrugged and looked hurt but he kept his mouth closed. Jeez, why did Angie always have to be such a hothead. One minute he's patting you on the back, the next minute he's shoving your teeth down your throat—and Angie could really ruin a guy when he got started, like that guy he worked on once with a billiard cue.

"Listen!" Angie's voice came sharply and Al straightened up with a jerk. "Keep yourself out of sight. When Chuffy comes out, follow him. See where he goes. I got an idea he's got Doyle stashed away some place. Now for crissake, use your head and don't let him spot you,"

"Sure, boss, but if he knows where Doyle is, wouldn't it be easier to bring him in and ..."

"Are you going to argue with me, Al?"

"Hell no, Angie. I was just ... I mean, I'll do just like you say. I'll tail him when he comes out."

"Now you're being smart, Al. Find out where he goes, then call me back."

"Sure, just like you say, Angie."

Al was perspiring a little when he stepped out of the phone booth. Jeez, you sure had to watch your step every minute with Angie or before you knew it, you were being worked over with a billiard cue. He sat down at the end of the counter and leaned against the wall, watching the hotel entrance. He ordered a cup of coffee. He wished they had beer or something. He was getting sick of coffee.

It was twenty to one when Chuffy emerged from the hotel and walked straight to his Ford with a jaunty step. The traffic was still heavy enough so that Al had no difficulty tailing him unobserved and there were enough homeward bound theatregoers on the open highway so that Al could keep a safe hundred feet behind the Ford. Chuffy was not a fast driver. He hit fifty and kept it steady. Al bit his lip when Chuffy turned into the Lake road but two other cars followed them in and Al breathed easier.

He looked mistrustfully at the crowding trees on both sides of the road. Anything outside the city was the sticks to him and he didn't like the sticks. He pretended to be contemptuous of the sticks but he was really afraid when he was away from the familiar safety of the city, where you could get a cab if you had to, and where the worst you had to worry about was a cop. Out here in the sticks, you never knew. Snakes, for instance. He'd heard of guys being bitten by snakes. Died, too. Knocked them off, just like that. How the hell were you supposed to know where the snakes lived? It all looked the same. That is, the real sticks, like this. He began to hate Chuffy.

The two other cars turned off at the southern end of the Lake and Al dropped back so that Chuffy would not get the idea he was being trailed. Anyway, the moon was so bright that Al could see far ahead on the straight road. He was three hundred feet behind when Chuffy turned off into the driveway of the cottage. Al cut his lights and stopped at the side of the road in the deep shadows of a pine grove. He watched Chuffy drive up to the cottage and get out of the car. He saw Chuffy tiptoe up to the porch, listen at the front door for a moment, then tiptoe inside. Al waited, watching narrowly. No lights went on in the cottage and after fifteen minutes, he decided that Chuffy had gone to bed, so he made a U-turn and headed back to town. The gin mills were still open and he had a double rye before he called Angie again at the gym down on Market Street.

He was feeling cocky when Angie came on the wire but he was smart enough not to let Angie hear it. Anything Angie hated, it was a guy that thought he was something.

"Well," said Angie nastily, "did you boot it or what?"

"It's okay, boss. He's shacked up in Lake Powhatan just outside a whistle stop named Hazelview out in the sticks up here. What do you want me to do now?"

"He know you were on his tail?"

"Uh-uh."

"He didn't speed up and try to lose you or do any fancy driving around or nothing?"

"He came straight up and went into the shack. I hung around a half hour to see maybe he might come out again but he didn't. He went right in and hit the sack."

"Okay. Hang around till morning and see if Doyle shows. What is it, a training camp or something?"

"Just a shack."

"Okay. Call me back in the morning."

Al went back to the bar. He liked his liquor straight but he had a rye and soda. He knew better than to get a load on at a time like this. The bar was full of vacationists from the southern end of the Lake. His eyes lighted when he noted that several of the dancing couples were girls. He gave his hand-painted tie a little squeeze to settle it into the V of his collar, then turned on his stool and hooked one elbow over the edge of the bar, watching the dance floor. Fifteen minutes later he had isolated a little plump blonde, who was just drunk enough—but not so drunk that she'd pass out on another drink or two. Just right.

He steered her out to the back seat of the car before the gin mill closed. He had just about decided he was getting somewhere when a tall brunette looked in on them and said cheerfully, "Hello, you two. Curfew, Margie."

The little blonde sat up, disengaging herself unselfconsciously from Al. She poked at her hair and said, "Oh my goodness! Time to go already?"

"What is this?" Al asked angrily.

The brunette smiled at him. "Oh, sometimes I have to tell Margie it's curfew and sometimes she has to tell me. Otherwise, how would we get any sleep?"

The little blonde kissed Al lightly on the cheek and jumped out of the car. "You be here tomorrow night, Georgie?" she asked brightly.

Georgie was the name he had given her.

"Maybe Georgie's got a friend," said the tall brunette.

"Bring your friend, Georgie," said the blonde.

Al was sore because he knew he was being given the business. All he'd ever get from these tomatoes would be the old runaround. Teasers, that's what they were.

"Yeah," he said. "I got a friend. Let's make it a foursome tomorrow night. This guy's got plenty of dough. Put on your best rags and we'll hit some of the wet spots. We'll pick you up here about nine. Okay?"

"Evening gowns?" said the blonde. The girls looked at each other.

"That's what I meant. This guy likes dressy dames. Of course, if you ain't got the clothes ..."

"Oh, we'll have them. Tomorrow night at nine?"

"Between nine and half-past. This guy owns a club in Newark and he likes to put in an appearance, know what I mean? Is there a flower shop around?"

"Right up the street," said the blonde eagerly.

"Okay. Order yourself a couple corsages and me and Jeff'll pick them up. Don't worry about the price. Just get something to match your dress. And I'll give you a tip—Jeff likes that perfume, what do you call it,

Chanel Number Five or something. If you got it, douse yourself a little. You'll make a hit. And if you make a hit, he'll really spend. He's got the dough. Now, you'll be here?"

"Oh yes, we'll be here!"

The girls walked toward their own car, talking excitedly. Al watched them, his lip curling. Yeah, be here, he thought. Me, I'll be down at Newark and the, hell with you. Now he felt better. He'd gotten even.

It was an hour and a half since Jasmine had come into the house and gone straight to her room without a word. Thomas sat in the library with a bottle of brandy on the desk before him. He had been drinking heavily and his face looked curiously swollen out of proportion.

He alternated between a dull rage and a feeling of triumph. If Jasmine had been out with Marty, Angie would have picked him up by now and that would be the end of Marty. But he was angry because Maury, his private detective, had not called him. For the tenth time, he reached for the phone and called Maury. This time a tired voice answered and it was Maury.

"I lost her," said Maury apologetically. "I think she spotted me. She made a funny turn at Broad and Market and I got picked up by a traffic cop. It was one of those things."

"One of what things?" asked Thomas coldly. "Don't you know your business?"

"I know my business."

"You bungled it."

"Have it your own way. But she recognized me. She's seen me around your place enough. You know how many jobs I did for you. But you wanted me to handle it personally, so I did, and she recognized me. Pull me off the job. I don't give a damn. I've been all over town trying to pick her up again. I'm pooped. If you don't like the way I do things, the hell with it."

"All right, all right, all right!" Thomas' anger exploded and he shook his head as if to clear it. "I didn't say anything about pulling you off the job, did I? Goddamnit, put a dozen men on the job if you have to. I never kicked about expense, did I?"

"Yeah, but this time you're paying for it yourself," said Maury cynically. "Just give me the word and I'll cover her like Sherman covered Richmond."

"I just did, didn't I? If you can't use your brains, at least use your ears once in a while."

"Okay, pal. Whenever she moves from now on, she'll be high man in the gooney parade. And let me give you a tip, pal. Lay off the red-eye.

You're beginning to unravel at the edge." He hung up, for emphasis.

Thomas stared dully at the dead phone, then replaced the receiver in the cradle. His hand was only inches away from the brandy bottle so he picked it up automatically and tilted it over his glass. He downed the drink in one gulp. It no longer had any flavor, any fire, any power to arouse him.

"Baby-doll," he thought miserably, feeling the loneliness closing in again. "Baby-doll. My little baby. My little girl. You're my daughter and I'm your father. I love you, Baby-doll."

He reached for the bottle again. He gave his head a hard shake. If only he could think clearly ...

## MISFIRE!
### CHAPTER TWELVE

Al, puffy-eyed from lack of sleep, was crouched in the grove of pine below the cottage the next morning when Marty came out with the tools Barth had bought for him. Marty went first to the Ford and lifted the hood. Then he spread newspapers on the ground and carefully laid out his tools. He was wearing only a pair of trunks, and the sun glistened on his bronzed chest and shoulders.

Al peered at him intently through a kind of telescope, the only glass he could buy in Hazelview. It was little more than a child's toy but it magnified enough for him to see it was Marty. He had seen Marty several times in the ring and had especially seen him that night Angie had all the money down on the Hunky and Marty had flattened him— but good. He knew Marty Doyle, all right. As he watched, Cuesta came out of the cottage and stood on the porch, looking at Marty. Cuesta was smiling but the smile was all in one place—across his thin lips. It did not go down into the seething fury of his chest, nor did it rise as high as his dark eyes. He walked over to the Ford and stood there for a moment without speaking. Then he said, "Look, kid, I'm sorry about last night. I was out of line. Let's forget it happened."

Marty looked up briefly over his shoulder. "Beat it," he said.

"Anything you say, *amigo*. I just wanted you to know, that's all. A guy can be wrong once in a while."

"I said, beat it!"

Cuesta's face darkened. He glowered down at Marty's back as if marking the spot between the shoulders to sink a knife into. But he shrugged and sauntered off with a swagger.

A little while later, Barth came out. He was in a surly mood. His hangover was like a fist in his head. He had no recollection of the night before, of slapping Sophie. There was Scotch in his suitcase but he had not touched it.

He watched Marty for a while, then said abruptly, "How's the Packard?"

Marty straightened up. "Okay," he said. "It's in good shape. I'll touch up the points, plugs and carburetor—but it's a helluva lot better than the Buick."

"Thank Christ for something. How long's all this going to take you?"

"A few hours on each car. When do we need them?"

"Finish them up today—and I mean, finish them up. What the hell's he moping about?" Barth glanced toward Cuesta, who was sitting hunched at the edge of the small lawn on one side of the cottage, staring out across the Lake.

Marty's heart lurched as Barth plodded heavily across the grass toward Cuesta. He stood stiffly with a wrench in his hand as Barth stood over the dark, thin man and snapped, "What the hell's eating you? I thought you were going to work on the guns. Get off that goddamn dime."

Cuesta looked up. His eyes flickered across the lawn to Marty, then he shrugged and said sullenly, "I just got up."

"Get to work. This is the last day."

Cuesta's eyes spread and something like a touch of panic spurted up in them. He had not thought the strike was so imminent. He felt a quiver run down through him and sprinkle out through his feet.

"Yeah, sure," he muttered. "I'll get right at it." His heart suddenly felt as if it were packed in ice. The quiver ran through him again. Now it was beginning, the way he always got before a strike. He would be okay while it was going on, he knew, but these hours beforehand were the bad ones. He clenched his hands, afraid they would start to shake and Barth would see their shaking. Why did he always have to be like this before a job?

Sophie came out on the porch and called cheerfully, "Breakfast, you guys." She shot a quick glance at Barth and Cuesta, then turned a reassuring smile on Marty. "Come and get it."

Below, from the grove of pines, Al watched until they had all trooped into the cottage for breakfast. Then he rose cautiously and stretched his aching legs. He collapsed the cheap telescope and put it into his pocket. He trudged tiredly down the road to where he had concealed his car. Back in Hazelview, he called Angie immediately.

"Doyle's there all right, Angie," he said. "But there's three other guys and a dame with him, counting Chuffy."

"Who're the other two guys?"

"I couldn't get that close."

"Is it a training camp or something?"

"Didn't look like it to me, Angie. Anyway, Doyle ain't doing no training. He's fixing one of the crates. Din' he used to be a race driver one time? But this ain't no race car. It's a Ford. What you want me to do now? I can't go up against no four guys in broad daylight. They can see you a mile away up here."

"Stop babbling, for crissake. Nobody asked you to take him yourself. Where're you now?"

"At this end of the Lake road, Angie. They gotta come out here. There's no other way."

"In a gin mill?"

"Well yeah, sure, but I ain't drinking nothing."

"Stay that way, buster, stay that way. What's the name of the joint?"

"It's the Deerhead Inn."

"Okay. I'll pick up Vince and meet you there this afternoon, say around five. You go back and keep an eye on Doyle. If it looks like he's getting ready to make a break, call me back right away. And look, buster, if I come up this afternoon and find you slopped over, you'll get your can in a sling. Now tell me what you ain't gonna do?"

"I ain't gonna touch no likker," said Al sullenly.

"Say it over again," Angie purred. "Say it louder. I didn't hear you."

"I ain't gonna touch no likker."

"Come on now, louder and slower. I want to hear every word."

Al shouted furiously, "I ain't gonna touch no likker. Is that loud enough or you want me to get a loudspeaker?"

"What're you yelling for? I can hear you," Angie chuckled. "See you at five at the Deerhead Inn, buster, and if you're real good, I'll let you join the Girl Scouts. So long, dearie."

Al hung up, feeling as if he wanted to break something with his hands. He looked at the bar. He badly needed a pick-up. He walked over quickly and ordered a triple rye. He drank it straight down.

"Now gimme a pack of that chloro-file choon gum, or whatever it's called," he ordered. "That stuff that takes your breath away." He put six pieces of gum into his mouth and chewed them doggedly as he walked out of the bar. He got a couple of sandwiches and a container of coffee at the delicatessen and picked up a dozen comic books from the newsstand before he went back to the car. He felt better now. Not merely because of the liquor but because he had defied Angie. He felt a stab of apprehension at the thought of Angie and popped another two pieces of the deodorizing gum into his mouth. He drove back to the same side road and left the car there. The spot he had chosen, from which to watch the cottage, was up the side of a hill, screened by wild fern. He cautiously poked at it with a dead branch to make sure no snakes were nesting there. Then he sat down with his back against a maple tree and took the cheap telescope from his pocket.

Marty was still working on the Ford and there was no sign of the other men. The girl was sitting on the porch, peeling potatoes. Once in a while she'd say something and Marty would straighten up and give her a grin. Otherwise, nothing happened. Al yawned and put down his telescope. He opened one of the comic books. It was one of his favorites—*Plastic Man.*

Chuffy came out of the cottage about one o'clock in the afternoon. He was wearing a pair of swimming trunks. Marty was working on the Packard by then, sitting cross-legged on the ground with pieces of the carburetor laid out carefully on newspapers around him.

"Soupin' her up, kid?" asked Chuffy curiously.

"Just tuning her up."

"Will that be enough?"

"Barth thinks so. He says there won't be anything after us."

Chuffy lifted his eyebrows and grimaced. If there were nothing after them, it meant Barth intended to leave some stiffs behind. In the beginning, Barth had told them they wouldn't have to worry about the law, that that part of it would be all over when they moved in for the strike. That spelled a hijacking job. It could be awful rough, especially if you ran into a bunch of trigger-happy goons with a hot take on their hands. There'd be more lead than air in the atmosphere. But Barth knew his business. He was known to be a guy who didn't take chances. And one of the best. Chuffy had faith in Barth.

"Aaaaaaeeee," he said meaninglessly. "Think I'll go down and dunk the body beautiful. Feel like taking, a break, kid?"

"Can't now, Chuffy," said Marty, indicating the dissembled carburetor. "I've got another two, three hours on this heap."

Chuffy was suddenly struck by something boyish, something sweet and ingenuous in Marty's grin. He squatted down on his heels beside him.

"Look, kid," he said in a low voice. "How much you know about this strike?"

"Not a thing, except I have to do the driving."

"Pull out, kid. It ain't for you. I oughtta have my head examined for dragging you into it. Pull out. I'll give you some dough and you go to Chi or L.A. or something. I'll join you later. Okay?"

Marty compressed his lips. "I told Barth I'd do it—and I'll do it."

"No, wait a minute, kid. I been in this stuff a long time and there's no percentage in it. Look at Barth. One of the best but where's he been for the last few years? Up the river. One of the best, and they put the arm on him. There was another one of the best. He was the best—Johnny Dillinger. He went down with a gutful of slugs. I can tick 'em off on my fingers—Torrio, Moran, Nelson. Where're they now? Look, lemme give you a couple grand and you go to L.A. It's a good fight town. I'll square Angie here and we can pick up out there where we left off. How's about it?"

Marty shook his head stubbornly and kept his eyes on the carburetor part he was cleaning. He wanted to pull out. He wanted no part of this anymore. His resentment against the police was gone. He'd had time to think it over and he could see why they wouldn't do anything about Angie. He should have gone to the Commission before the fight, not afterward when he was in trouble.

But he had told Barth he would do it. He could not pull out.

Chuffy said woodenly, "It's your funeral," and walked down the path toward the dock. He made a flashy, skillful dive and began to swim in rapid hundred-foot circles with a fast crawl stroke.

Marty finished working on the Packard at four-thirty. He washed up in the kitchen. Cuesta was seated at the kitchen table, cleaning and oiling the submachine gun. The shotgun, which he had already cleaned, stood against the wall next to the door. Marty ignored him. Cuesta glared at his back with hatred but said nothing. Barth was visible in the armchair in the living room, making a final map and course of action from the three plans he had sketched down in Nutley.

Sophie came into the kitchen, ostensibly for a glass of water but actually because she had heard Marty come in. She gave him a small, intimate smile.

"All finished?" she asked.

"All done." He grinned. "Say, how's about a row in the boat?"

"I'd love it!"

"What's that?" called Barth from the living room.

"Marty wants to take me for a row in the boat."

"Sure. Go ahead—but stay down at this end of the Lake."

Cuesta jealously watched them go. His hands were shaking as he began to reassemble the submachine gun. He muttered to himself under his breath. The memory of last night lay poisoned in his mind. He had thought a dozen times of telling Barth but he knew he had made a bad play with his knife and he was afraid.

Barth heard him muttering and looked up with a scowl. "Shut up," he growled, "I'm trying to work."

He had the final plan made now. He had gone over it again and again and he couldn't find a single flaw in it. Cuesta would be posted at the north side of the garage to take care of anybody who made a break for the house. He himself would be on the south side of the driveway in a position commanding the garage entrance. And Chuffy would be set up down in the driveway nearer to the street to cover Barth in case he had to be covered when he made the run for the car. He had put Chuffy there because Chuffy was absolutely dependable. He trusted Chuffy. Cuesta was too emotional for a spot like that. Cuesta would be in the worst spot. If anything went sour, Cuesta would be left high and dry because Niles would be between him and the getaway car. But nothing could go wrong. The plan was perfect.

But something nagged from some dark corner deep in Barth's mind. The plan looked perfect—but was it? Was there something he had overlooked? He no longer had this self-assurance. All he could think of was, in eighteen hours they'd be making the strike. He could almost see Jack Niles walking unscathed into a hail of bullets, his own guns snarling and his long jaws set in that alligator grin of his. For a moment, Barth felt like a man committed to a suicidal course and, nightmarishly, unable to turn from it. He didn't want to make this strike but he had to. He had to have a stake. He had to make it. Setting his teeth, he went over the plan once more.

He glanced into the kitchen again and was suddenly irritated beyond measure by the sheen of perspiration that glistened on Cuesta's face.

"What's the matter, Cuesta?" he jeered. "Got the meemees or somethin'?"

Cuesta muttered, "I'm okay."

"Sure—but who you waving good-bye to?"

Cuesta clenched his shaking hands.

Barth goaded him. "Feel like walking out, pal? Feel like crawling into a hole?"

"Leave me alone, will you?"

"I wish I'd left you alone right from the beginning. If there's anything I hate, it's chicken."

"Go to hell."

Barth laughed unpleasantly. "If I do, I won't get the sweats on the way." Only he would ever know how close he was to the sweats himself at that very moment.

Cuesta turned on him, his face twitching. "At least my dames don't play around with everybody in sight," he cried shrilly. "They don't have to two-time me to get what they want."

Barth felt an icy clutch and said evenly, "Just what the hell do you mean by that?"

Cuesta pointed toward the window through which they could see Sophie and Marty rowing on the lake. "I saw them last night. I saw them with my own eyes out in the woods."

Barth felt as if someone had covered his face with a hot, constricting hand. But he retained sufficient self-control to say, "What's the matter, Cuesta, are you spilling it because she wouldn't let you have any?"

"She's your dame, not mine."

"Not my dame—anybody's dame. She's a streetwalker I picked up in Philly. Finished that gun yet?"

Cuesta flushed and nodded. Barth gave a strained laugh.

"Have a drink," he said. "You'll feel better. Anybody that gets himself turned down by a streetwalker ..."

Cuesta sprang up from his chair and stamped out of the cottage through the kitchen door. Barth sat quietly, holding desperately to his self-control—but if Sophie and Marty had walked into the cottage at that moment, he would have killed them. He walked heavily into the kitchen and picked up the submachine gun. He shoved the clip in and went outside. He pointed the gun at the ground and fired a short burst.

Then he stood rigid, fighting an almost insane lust to rush down to the dock and pump slugs into the rowboat that hovered only twenty feet offshore. The only thing that deterred him was the pitiful hope that Cuesta was lying. Nothing in the world had any meaning for him without Sophie. He deluded himself with the thought that he was really making this strike for her sake, that he wanted a stake so he could take her to Florida in style.

He was beginning to see what had really happened. Cuesta had made a pass at Sophie and she had turned him down flat, the way she would. Cuesta wouldn't take a rebuff like that. He'd connive some way of sticking a knife in her back—and this was it. Barth was beginning to feel better. What the hell, Marty Doyle was nuts about the Thomas girl, wasn't he? Thomas himself had told him.

He turned and saw Cuesta watching him. He grinned. It gave him a vast, lifting satisfaction to know that when the strike was made, Cuesta would be in the most vulnerable position.

**THE BITER BIT**
CHAPTER THIRTEEN

Angie was half an hour late and Al sat at a side table in the Deerhead bar, drinking a bottle of coke and chewing on his last two pieces of chlorophyll gum. Angie came directly to the table and Vince, a compact, thin-faced man, went over to the pinball machine. Angie was thickset and blond with gray eyes so pale they seemed colorless in his heavy, brutal face.

"What you drinking?" he demanded.

Al touched the Coca-Cola bottle with a tobacco-stained forefinger. "Just coke, that's all, Angie."

Angie raised his arm to the barkeep. "Two double Scotches and a coke," he called.

"Wait a minute, Angie ..."

"What's the matter? You just said you were drinking coke, didn't you?"

"Sure—but what the hell ..."

"Can't you make up your mind, buster? If you're drinking Scotch, say so."

"You told me ..."

"I didn't tell you nothing. I asked you to have a drink with me and you said you wanted coke. Now you want Scotch. I don't get it."

Vince turned from the pinball machine, laughing soundlessly. Angie was a real comedian when he got going.

"Now come on, Al," said Angie. "Pull yourself together. If you want some Scotch, say—'Please, Angie, I would like a small beaker of Scotch.' Go ahead."

Flushing, Al mumbled, "PleaseAngieIwouldlikeasmallbeakerof— Scotch. Aw, Angie, why do you keep doing this?"

"Because you're a born sucker, buster. Hey, barkeep, make that three Scotches. Now, how's it with Doyle, Al?"

"He's still up there in the shack. And so are the three other guys."

"What the hell're they doing up there?"

"Nothing. Chuffy went swimming and Doyle went rowing in a boat with the dame. The other two guys just kind of sit around all the time."

"And there's only one dame?"

"That's all I seen."

"Maybe the other three are in the shack," said Angie, who could conceive of no other reason for four men to spend time in the sticks.

"Maybe that's the reason the other two guys just sit around. You should of gone up and given them a hand, Al." Angie was feeling good. Tonight he would square things with Doyle.

Al laughed dutifully and asked, "What do we do now, Angie?"

"We hang around till it gets dark, buster. Then we'll go up and pick Doyle like a daisy. Take it easy with your drink because you're not getting no more till we're finished."

The light began to fade at seven and they went out to Angie's car. Al saw the two baseball bats on the rear seat. They drove out along the Lake road and Al showed them where to leave the car out of sight on the side road. The Ford and the Packard were still parked outside the cottage and lights glowed from inside the house. The sun had set and darkness was beginning to seep into the sky. The front door of the cottage opened and, in the streaming light, they saw Sophie and Marty emerge and stroll slowly down the path that led away from the Lake.

Angie said tersely, "Let's go."

Vince took the two baseball bats from the back seat and the men walked quickly up the road. They went about three hundred yards beyond the cottage, then turned left into the sparse thicket of scrub birch. Angie slipped a gun from under his left armpit and handed it to Al.

"You hold it on them, buster," he ordered. "This is my party this time." He took one of the bats from Vince and hefted it in his thick hands. He liked baseball bats. They had a nice balance. Billiard cues tended to be a little heavy in the butt end and weren't thick enough at the other end to give you a good swinging grip.

Angie had calculated his angle nicely and came out in the crest of the hill ahead of Marty and Sophie. The rising moon shed good light and they could see Sophie and Marty coming slowly along the path about a hundred and fifty feet from them. Twice they stopped to kiss lightly, then they walked on, hand in hand.

"Now ain't that real romantic?" Angie chuckled softly. "Just like the movies—but better. This is gonna be better than the movies because it'll get better as it goes along. We'll put in the kind of stuff the movies leave out."

They were standing in the shadow of a small, leafy maple tree. Before them was a small clearing, through which the path ran. Angie allowed Marty and Sophie to come up almost abreast of him. Then he stepped out into the moonlight.

"Hiya, Doyle," he said. "Long time no see, kid."

Marty whirled, and saw Al standing in the path behind him, holding the gun. He stepped in front of Sophie. Angie stood there grinning, lightly swinging his baseball bat.

"You, remember me, don't you, Doyle?" he said. "I'm the guy you thought you could cross down Newark that night you flattened the Hunky. We're just gonna square things a little, that's all, kid."

He leaped forward, swinging his bat up at Marty's crotch. Marty jumped back, thrusting Sophie away from him. "Run, honey, run!" He made a grab at Angie's bat and caught it. He pulled it toward him, thinking to pull Angie off-balance but Angie let go and Marty staggered back, digging with his heels to save himself from falling.

Angie yelled, "Stop that dame!" and plunged at Marty, hitting him heavily in the face. Marty dropped the bat as he crashed into the heavy trunk of an oak tree. He fended off the next two blows Angie aimed at his face, then pushed himself away from the tree and chopped Angie twice across the jaw with a right-and-left. Vince walked in and hit him on the side of the head with the handle of the bat, not heavily, but enough to daze him. Swearing, Angie scrambled for the bat Marty had dropped.

Sophie screamed and flew down the path toward the cottage. Al put out his leg and she went down with a thud. He bent over her and hit her behind the ear with the flat of his gun—but as he straightened up, something exploded against the side of his own head and darkness enveloped him.

Barth stepped over him and roared, "Hold it, goddamn you!" He walked into the clearing with the shotgun cradled over his left arm.

Marty was leaning against the oak tree, blood streaming down his face. Angie dropped his bat and froze. From the tail of his eye, he saw Vince make a stealthy movement.

He yelled wildly, "For crissake, Vince, don't!"

Barth's grin glittered. "Drag that other mutt up here, Doyle," he ordered. "I want all three of them in a row. See if Sophie's okay. And she'd better be," he said grimly to Angie.

Angie was speechless and sweat poured down his brow. He was not cowardly but he saw death in Barth's tight face.

Barth had followed Sophie and Marty from the cottage and had seen them kiss. A need for violence roared through him but something had happened to him when he saw Al bend over Sophie and hit her with the gun. He did not want to lose her. She had taken Sissie's place in his heart and he wanted her, now more urgently than ever.

Without taking his eyes from Angie and Vince, he called, "How is she, Doyle?"

"She's all right. She's sitting up. This other guy's coming around, too."

"Bring him up here."

Al came stumbling up the path ahead of Marty and Sophie.

"Who is this monkey?" Barth asked Marty, indicating Angie with the muzzles of the shotgun.

"He's the guy that wanted me to throw a fight—and I wouldn't."

"One of them. Okay, pick up that bat and smack him."

Marty said, "No!"

"Go ahead. That's what he was doing to you. Smack him."

Barth knew exactly what he was doing. He was making a play for Sophie. He did not care what happened to Angie or Marty or any of them, but he knew he was gaining Sophie's sympathy by defending Marty. He no longer cared if she loved him or not. He needed her.

"You're making a mistake, kid," he said to Marty. "When you get a rat like this, you step on him. That's all they understand. That one over there," he tilted his chin at Vince, "he's got something under his coat. You'd better take it away from him."

Marty took the gun from Vince's shoulder holster. Vince tried to look detached.

Barth said to Angie, "Know who I am? Take a good look at me." This was still part of the play for Sophie.

Angie shook his head. "You're sticking your neck out," he croaked. "That's all I know."

"The name's Barth, Small-time. Gerald Barth. Still think I'm sticking my neck out? Is that all you know now?"

Angie licked his lips. "I—I just said that. It—was just something to say."

"Ah, for crissake, get out of here. You turn my stomach. Beat it! And take this monkey with you. Go on—dangle!"

Supporting Al, Angie and Vince went back down the hill as fast as they could. Vince had lost his detached look. Gerald Barth was a little too imminent and dangerous for detachment. With a thin smile on his lips, Barth listened to their crashing retreat through the bushes. He looked at Sophie.

"I saw them sneaking down the road," he lied easily, "and I thought, what the hell? You got nice friends, Doyle. You two better get back to the cottage before some more of your friends turn up."

He felt very cunning. He had played it just right, for Sophie was gazing at him fondly. Tomorrow would take care of Doyle. Sophie would never be able to blame him when Marty took a slug through the head at the strike.

## THE UNWRITTEN LAW
## CHAPTER FOURTEEN

Chuffy heard them come in and restlessly prowled around his bedroom. He had been dressed and ready to go to Newark since right after dinner. He had pressed his suit and tie that afternoon and Sophie had washed and ironed his shirt. He had twice polished his shoes and had just spent half an hour carefully brushing his gray homburg. There was a blue periwinkle in his buttonhole and a kerchief to match his tie in his breast pocket.

He was so nervous, he could no longer sit still. This meeting with Jasmine was going to be different from any of the others. More—well, kind of sacred, sort of. Yes, sacred, he thought defiantly. He wanted to get down to Newark before the jewelers closed their shops and he was in an agony of impatience as he listened to Sophie, Marty and Barth chatting with seeming good-humor in the living room. Earlier he had moved the Ford to the head of the incline so he could roll it down without starting the motor.

He put his ear to the door and heard Barth say, "Think I'll turn in. You'd better stick pretty close to the cottage, Doyle, just in case."

A moment later, he heard Barth's door close. He went swiftly to the window, raised it and stepped out. He trotted around the cottage and peered into Barth's room. He was startled at the look of frustrated ferocity on Barth's face. Barth was standing in the center of the room, his hands clenching and unclenching as he glowered at the closed door. As Chuffy watched, he jerked his suitcase out of the closet and took a bottle of Scotch from it. He uncapped it and took a long drink. He shook his head, still scowling. Then he went over to the bed and lay down, taking the bottle with him. He reached out and turned off the light. He was, Chuffy knew, going to make a night of it with the bottle.

Chuffy glanced at his wristwatch and clucked irritably. It was twenty past eight. He'd never make Newark in time. The jewelers closed their shops at nine.

He let the Ford roll down the hill and threw it into gear just before he reached the bottom. It started with a quiet murmur. He debated briefly with himself, then drove straight to Hazelview. He wanted to get something for Jasmine with a lot of flash and he had to give it to her tonight. This was the night. No other night would do. It was a compulsion. The night was—well, sacred, sort of.

He walked into the jewelry shop next to the movie house and said gruffly, "I want an engagement and wedding ring outfit. Something with flash."

The jeweler appraised him with a practiced eye. "I've got something very nice for eighty-nine fifty," he said, opening his case. "The diamond is ..."

"Nah, none of that Woolworth junk. I want something with flash. Show me some merchandise, pal."

The jeweler hesitated and gave Chuffy a sharp glance. He had a sudden feeling this was the prelude to a stick-up.

"Of course," he said smoothly. "I know just what you mean. Excuse me a moment." He went into the rear of the store and called Police Headquarters. "I have a feeling, Chief," he said into the phone, "and I can be wrong—but would you have the prowl car keep an eye on my place for the next fifteen minutes? You can give me the horse laugh later if you want. No, nothing like that. Just a feeling. Right. Thanks a lot, Chief. Five minutes."

He waited five minutes, then returned out front with a tray of more expensive rings from the safe. He laid the tray on the counter before Chuffy, watching the prowl car pull up outside his door.

"Now this ensemble," he murmured, touching a ring with the tip of his pen, "is four hundred and ..."

"What's this one here?" interrupted Chuffy impatiently.

"That's fifteen hundred. It's a blue-white diamond ..."

"It's a big sonuvabitch, ain't it?" said Chuffy admiringly. "That's the best, ain't it?"

"Yes, that's the best I ..."

"Sold American, pal. Now I want a nice box with that. I want your best box, with velvet. Know what I mean?"

Chuffy spent more time selecting the box than he had the rings, but finally decided on a blue velvet-lined box.

He took out his wallet and counted off fifteen one hundred dollar bills. The jeweler felt a little dazed. He went to the door with Chuffy and shook his hand.

"It's been a pleasure," he said earnestly, "a real pleasure. Come back again." He glanced at the police car and smiled a little weakly.

All the way down to Newark, Chuffy kept putting his hand in his pocket and feeling the box. Twice he pulled the car to the side of the road under a highway light and came to a dead stop so he could take out the box and admire the rings all over again.

"Lookit that sonuvabitch shine," he murmured aloud. "Just like a goddamn headlight."

He could hardly wait to see the look on Jasmine's face when she opened the box.

Jasmine, too, had made preparations for this meeting, as if some of his feeling about the evening had been transmitted telepathically to her. She was wearing a nightgown sprigged with rosebuds and, over that, a frilly negligee with a froth of Brussels lace at the collar and wrists. She was standing at the window when he walked in and turned to him with a tremulous, almost timid smile.

"I was hoping you'd come early," she said.

"Which hand?" grinned Chuffy, dancing in front of her, holding his hands behind his back.

"That one."

He quickly transferred the little box to the hand she had indicated and held it out to her. His grin grew wider as her eyes opened wide at sight of the rings.

"Whattaya think?" he said eagerly. "Like 'em?"

"Oh, Chuffy—they're beautiful! Here," she held out her hand, the third finger extended, "you're got to put this one on."

His own hand shaking a little, he slipped the ring on her finger. "Jesus!" he breathed. "I'll be a sonuvabitch. I'm engaged!" Downstairs, a bored, thickset man crossed the street and walked into the Red Castle lunchroom. He went into the phone booth and called Thomas.

"This is Maury," he said. "Your daughter's in Room 303 in the Hotel Sherman. A guy just walked in. The clerk just told me—and this is costing you another double sawbuck—that this is the third or fourth time."

Thomas said tersely, "Thank you," and hung up.

He had been drinking all day but he felt very cold, very calm now. He walked to the liquor cabinet and poured himself a double cognac. He drank it slowly. He held out his right hand and looked at it. There wasn't a tremor. He felt very stern and righteous. He ran his hand over his chin, then went out into the hall and put on his hat. He thought about calling for a cab but decided to take his own car. He knew the Hotel Sherman, a shabby red-brick building on Wakeman Street at the south end of Newark.

The clerk gave him a disinterested glance when he walked through the lobby and mounted the stairs.

Thomas found Room 303 without difficulty. He listened at the door for a moment and heard Jasmine and Chuffy laughing together inside. He took a deep breath and thrust open the door. Jasmine was lying on the bed and Chuffy was undressing near a lounge chair.

Thomas pulled the gun from his pocket and said loudly, "I'll teach you to play around with my daughter!" Then he fired.

The heavy slug caught Chuffy under the left shoulder blade and flung him into the arm of the chair. His hand made a feeble clawing motion, then slackly slid off the chair as he toppled slowly sideways. Thomas fired another shot but Chuffy was already dead.

Jasmine screamed. Thomas, dazed, stared at the gun in his hand. Jasmine looked numbly at the crumpled body of Chuffy. She was sure it wasn't real. She knew in a moment or two he would get up and laugh. She looked at her father, her face almost idiotically slack.

"We—were going to be married," she said in an odd voice. "He gave me a ring."

Thomas stammered, "I—I thought it was Marty Doyle ..." Then the full horror of what he had done flooded over him and he turned and ran wildly down the corridor. Behind him, Jasmine shrieked.

No one tried to stop him as he rushed out of the hotel. He drove straight home and went into his library. He took the cognac bottle from the cabinet and carried it to his desk. His liquor-sodden mind was in chaos. The unwritten law, he thought, that's it, the unwritten law. He could plead the unwritten law. He had to hold the bottle with both hands to pour a drink into his glass. He drank it off at a gulp and immediately poured himself another. No one could ever blame him for what he had done. Any father would have done the same. It was the unwritten law.

Jasmine was fully dressed when she heard the first police sirens. Her face was cold and dead but her eyes were a little mad. She walked calmly from the room, locking the door behind her, and left the hotel by way of the fire exit. She walked across the street into the Red Castle and called Jack Niles on the phone.

"I want to talk to Jack Niles," she said in a wooden voice.

The man said, "You got the wrong number, lady. There's no Jack Niles here."

"This is the right number. I want to talk to Jack Niles."

"Never heard of him, lady. Sorry."

But before he could hang up, Jasmine said, "This is Helen Thomas. Walter Thomas is my father. I have an important message for Jack Niles."

The man at the other end of the wire was silent for a moment, then said, "Okay. Shoot. This is Niles. What's the message?"

"My father has sold you out to a man named Gerald Barth. After your hold-up tomorrow, Gerald Barth and some other men are going to hijack you when you change cars on River Road in Kearny."

"Wait a minute, girlie. Where'd you get all this from?"

"I overheard you talking to my father and I overheard him talking to Gerald Barth. There's a fireplace in my father's library. I listened at the chimney on the roof. I could hear everything everybody said."

"Hold on a second, girlie. Where're you now? I'd like to talk this over with you. Where can I pick you up?"

"You can't. I'm going away."

"Wait a second, willya? Who else you tell about this?"

"Nobody. And I don't intend telling anybody. I'm going away. I just wanted to tell you that my father sold you out to Gerald Barth and Barth is going to hijack you on River Road in Kearny."

She hung up. She saw the police car in front of the Hotel Sherman as she walked out to the street. She gave it no more than a passing glance. She turned east on Wakeman Street and walked toward the river. She stopped at the corner of the riverside highway and looked across the street at the oily sluggish water. She waited patiently, almost somnolently, for the traffic to thin enough for her to cross the street.

A car drifted slowly to the curb near her and an insinuating voice said, "Can I drive you any place, sweetheart?"

The door swung open invitingly. She looked in but did not look directly at the man. It didn't make any difference what he was like. She looked at the river again. What difference did that make, either? She slid into the car.

"Sure," she said. "Any place at all."

Thomas was sodden drunk when the door opened and Niles walked in. Thomas looked up at him with bleary eyes.

"'Lo, Jack," he mumbled.

"How's it with Gerald Barth these days, crumb?" Niles asked softly.

Thomas was not too drunk to understand the implication of the words. The look on his face told Niles all he wanted to know. Casually, he pulled the gun from under his left armpit. Thomas struggled to push himself to his feet but his legs would not support him.

"No, Jack!" he croaked. "No, no ..."

Niles walked almost lazily to the desk and shot Thomas three times through the left breast. Thomas slumped sideways and folded over the arm of his chair. Niles gazed contemptuously at the body.

"Crumb," he said.

He walked out of the house, unhurrying. He was not worried about Barth. Barth was just an old jerk, all washed up. There was nothing to worry about, anyway. He'd change cars some place other than on River Road in Kearny—and Barth could spend the rest of his life waiting.

## LAST CHANCE
CHAPTER FIFTEEN

Barth woke up the next morning with a thundering hangover but it wasn't the hangover that kept him in bed. He had a sick reluctance to get up. This was the morning of the strike. He lay looking up at the cracked ceiling plaster and wondering with despair if there were any way out, if there were any other way to get himself a stake.

But even as he lay thinking, he knew he was going to get up and go through with it. He no longer had any choice. If he did not go through with it now, he would never be any good for anything again as long as he lived. He couldn't turn chicken now.

Marty was in the kitchen with Sophie when Barth walked in, going straight to the cold water tap where he drank four glasses of water. Sophie looked at Marty and shook her head warningly. She knew Barth had a hangover and was in a savage mood. Cuesta had come in fifteen minutes earlier for a cup of coffee. He had been jumpy and quarrelsome. Sophie had offered to scramble some eggs and make toast for him and he had spat at her like a bad-tempered cat, telling her, in short ugly words, exactly what she could do with her eggs and toast. She'd had to restrain Marty. This was the morning of the strike and they were all jumpy, herself included. Even as she spoke to Marty, she found herself consciously trying to fight down the apprehension that rose in her throat.

Barth turned from the sink and said sullenly, "Where's Chuffy—and Cuesta?"

"Cuesta's outside," said Marty.

"Where's Chuffy?"

Marty shook his head. He did not want to tell Barth Chuffy hadn't slept at the cottage last night.

"Isn't he around?" demanded Barth angrily.

"I didn't see him. I just got up."

Barth swore and stamped out of the cottage. He was back in three minutes.

"The Ford's gone," he snapped. "Did that sonuvabitch run out on us?"

Marty snapped back at him, "Don't look at me. I don't know anything about it."

"He's supposed to be a friend of yours, isn't he?"

"So what? I don't know everything he does. But he wouldn't run out. I can tell you that much."

"You can't tell me a goddamn thing. The Ford's gone. Where is he?"

"Maybe he went downtown for something."

"What the hell would he go downtown for? Christ, we gotta get out of here in an hour."

"He'll be back."

"Shut your goddamn mouth, will you? What do you use for brains, Christian Science? He'll be back, he'll be back. How the hell do you know he'll be back? You just said you didn't know anything about it."

Sophie stepped between them. They were shouting and their faces were red. "Now stop it," she said. "Why are you yelling at Marty, Barth? He didn't run out, did he? You don't have to take it out on him, do you? What's he supposed to ..."

"And another thing," Marty interrupted. "I'm going through with this with you but I'm not taking any of the money. I don't want it."

"Oh, Jesus!" Barth said savagely. "Now what?"

"I don't want any of the money, that's all."

Barth looked at Sophie and said sarcastically, "What'd he do, go join the Salvation Army or something?"

Marty flushed. "Also," he said evenly, "I'm giving you back the five thousand you advanced me."

"How sweet. And can you give me back the five grand I advanced Chuffy, too?"

Sophie cried, "Stop it, you two! Barth—listen to me. Give this thing up. You don't have to go through with it. And if Chuffy's gone, you can't, can you?"

Barth said loudly, "I'm going through with it if I have to do it alone!"

He stamped out of the kitchen. Chuffy's defection filled him with greater dismay than he was willing to show. Chuffy was the only one he had really relied on, the only steady one of the lot. And now Chuffy was gone. A feeling of impending doom began to creep over Barth. He went back to his room and broke out his remaining bottle of Scotch.

They waited three-quarters of an hour and when Chuffy still hadn't shown, Barth called them together in the living room. He was much quieter than he had been.

"I think you said you could handle a gun," he said to Marty. "You'll have to take Chuffy's place."

Cuesta said nastily, "That's all we need!"

Marty ignored him. "I'm not going to shoot anybody," he told Barth quietly. "I promised to drive the car—and I will. But I won't point a gun at anybody."

"Nobody's asking you to. Here, look ..." He spread the map of the Niles hideout on the wicker table. "Cuesta will be back here to the north of the garage, covering the back door of the house in case anybody makes a break for it. I'll be here on this side of the driveway. I'll cover the garage when they drive in. And you, Doyle, you'll be way down here on the north side of the driveway, halfway between the house and the car. All you'll have to do is cover me if I have to make a fast break. You'll have the shotgun—and you just fire over my head. When I yell, you start firing. When they hear that thing, they'll hunt their holes. Nobody in his right mind sticks his neck into a mess of buckshot. You won't have to fire at anybody at all. You can shoot the damn thing straight up in the air if you want to. All I'll need is one minute to make it from where I'll be to the car."

"I thought the shotgun was mine," snarled Cuesta.

"You'll have a pair of .38's. You won't need the shotgun. Doyle will— maybe. Maybe he won't at all. The way this figures out, I'll take Niles and everybody with him the minute they come out of the garage. It'll be all over in thirty seconds and we can walk away from it. I'll have the chopper." He glowered at them. "Everybody satisfied?"

"Who drives the car?" asked Marty. "Or do we have to make a run for it?"

"I'll drive," said Sophie. "I can drive."

Marty said explosively, "The hell with that! You'll stay right here. You're not getting mixed up in this."

"You're damn right she's not," said Barth grimly.

"I expected this," said Sophie, "so I took a wire out of the motor. If I don't go, nobody goes. You need somebody to bring the car to you. You can't park it right there. Marty can take the wheel afterwards—but I'll bring the car to you."

They stormed at her and threatened but she faced them stubbornly. And in the end she had her way. Her logic was incontrovertible. Somebody did have to bring the car down to the driveway from Hillcrest Road, where Barth had planned to park it out of sight of the house.

Barth said shortly, "Let's get out of here. It's time."

Cuesta pressed his lips thinly together when Barth handed him a pair of .38 revolvers. But he said nothing. Barth took six extra clips for the submachine gun, then filled Marty's pockets with shotgun shells. He took a long-barreled Colt .38 for himself in addition to the submachine gun.

It was a tense, silent ride down to Nutley. Cuesta sat brooding and Barth spoke to no one. He was sick about Chuffy's having run out. It was almost like an omen and he could not shake off the feeling of foreboding. He no longer had any faith in Cuesta nor did he believe in the plan he had drawn up. He went over it again in his mind, trying to pick holes, even though he knew hopelessly that his mind was no longer capable of finding flaws.

Still, he knew it was a good plan. It had been good when he drew it up originally—and it was still good. He had Niles covered from every angle. When Niles came out of the garage, three short bursts from the submachine gun would crumple the lot of them. What could go wrong?

Still, he was fatalistically certain all of them would die. Surreptitiously, he felt the long-barreled Colt in his pocket. No matter what happened, Marty was going to get his first. The first shot would be for Marty.

They drove down Hillcrest Road and Barth showed Sophie where he wanted the car. Then they drove into the hideout driveway. Barth posted Marty between the house and the road and sent Cuesta off into the bushes north of the garage. He waved Sophie off with the car and crawled under the leafy spread of the rhododendron bushes just below the mouth of the garage. He looked back toward Marty but all he could see was a leg and a hip.

"Hey, Doyle," he called. "Move a little this way."

He watched Marty shift his position until his head and chest were in view.

"Right there," he called.

He laid out his six extra clips carefully on the leaves beside him and placed the Colt on the ground close to his right hand. The first shot would be for Doyle. He shifted his position until he had a perfect, unimpeded view of the garage doors. He propped up the submachine gun in front of him. Now all he had to do was wait.

Marty lay prone, looking back over his shoulder, trying to see Sophie in the car up Hillcrest Road. But the grove of trees screened her from view. Lord, why did she have to come! He licked at the pebbles of sweat covering his upper lip. Oh Sophie, Sophie! he called out silently in despair. If only she had stayed back there at the cottage! When this was over—Lord, would it ever be over?—he was going to take her away. He was going back into stock car racing for a while, then he'd open a garage when he had enough money. He was ...

He stiffened. A car plunged into the driveway with shrieking tires, streaked up the driveway and into the garage. A window was flung open in the attic of the house and a man's voice sang out, "Watch it, Jack! There's three sonuvabitches in the weeds!"

The voice was followed immediately by a shot. Marty sucked in his breath as Barth's submachine gun chattered insanely, spraying the mouth of the garage with slugs. There were too many bushes and trees between Marty and the garage for him to see what was going on. He had a glimpse of Barth lying under the rhododendron bush but could see no more than a leg. Other guns began to answer now.

There was a lull and a harsh voice called out, "Barth! This is Niles. Put up your gun and I'll cut you in for a share."

Barth's voice answered savagely and the submachine gun chattered again. He could not see the men in the garage but he had seen Cuesta running up the riverbank, away from the hideout, running as hard as he could.

The first shot from the attic had caught him in the side, breaking a rib. Now he knew what had been wrong with his plan. He should never have laid exposed out here. He should have waited for Niles inside the house. He should have known Niles might post a lookout. He fired another short burst into the yawning open door of the garage.

There was a second shot from the attic and Barth jerked as the bullet struck him close to the first wound. He felt something warm and liquid spurting down inside him. He swore and splashed a spray of lead across the window. A man screamed.

Bullets from the garage were clipping the bushes above him and bits of leaves drifted down to him. Grimly, he fired another burst into the garage, keeping it low.

Someone cried quiveringly, "Oh, Christ!"

Niles yelled desperately, "Call it off, Barth for crissake, call it off or we'll have every cop in the county down on us. I'll cut you in for half—but call it off!"

Barth was beyond reason. He laughed harshly, insanely, and continued to pump bullets into the garage. All he wanted now was to destroy Niles. Something was running, running down inside him. He felt no pain but he could almost hear his life gurgling away.

Then he heard a car roaring into the driveway. It braked to a stop in a spray of gravel. He groaned. It was Sophie. He had told her to bring the car up fast when she heard the first shot.

He turned his head and shouted hoarsely, "Get out of here. Get out! Get out!"

The car was fully exposed in the mouth of the driveway. A shot spat from the garage. Sophie cried out and disappeared below the level of the car window.

Marty yelled, "She's hit, Barth. She's hit!"

Barth screamed, "Get her out of here, Doyle! Get her out of here! I'll cover you ..."

He picked up the submachine gun and rose to his knees. He gave the garage a burst, then lurched out into the driveway raining bullets into the garage.

Marty sprinted for the car and jerked open the door. Sophie was lying across the seat, holding her right arm. Blood seeped through her fingers.

"It—just grazed me," she whispered. Then she fainted dead away.

Marty leaped into the car and stabbed at the starter with his foot. The motor roared into life. Before slamming it into gear, he threw a last glance up the driveway. Barth was lying flat, pushing a third clip into his gun. The firing was very heavy from the garage but no one dared come out. Barth was hit twice before he was able to cut loose with the gun again. Then he staggered to his feet and charged the garage, firing continuously. Suddenly he stopped, as if he had just run into something solid. He rose to his toes, danced a few steps, then fell straight forward and lay still.

Marty heard the high keening of an approaching siren and slammed the Packard into gear. He shot out of the driveway and roared north on River Road, then turned west on Nutley. He turned north again on Washington Street and headed for the highway. He stopped under the overpass and bent anxiously over Sophie. Gently, he lifted her hand away from the wound on her arm. He let out a long, shuddery breath of relief. It was a very shallow wound across her upper arm. Already, the blood was coagulating. He pulled his shirt out of his pants and ripped off strips. Sophie recovered consciousness as he was binding the gash.

"Where—where's Barth?" she whispered.

Marty shook his head and touched her lips with his forefinger.

"He covered us while we got out," he said heavily. "He walked into their guns."

Sophie was silent. After a while she said slowly, "I think he wanted to die. He never wanted to make this strike. I knew that more than a week ago. He wanted peace so desperately. I think he finally made up his mind there was only one way to get it ..."

Police sirens were shrieking from every direction now, converging on the Niles hideout. Marty looked back. There were tears in his eyes. There was one thing he would never be able to erase from his memory—the sight of Barth suicidally charging the garage to give Sophie and him the chance to escape. Barth had really loved Sophie, after all.

Slowly he turned the car into the approach to the highway. He reached out and covered Sophie's twisting hands with his, quieting them.

"He gave us our chance, honey," he said. "Now it's up to us to make the most of it."

Sophie seized his hands, gripping them hard.

"And we will, won't we, Marty?" she said fiercely. "We will!"

**THE END**

# KISS OF FIRE
## LORENZ HELLER

Writing as Laura Hale

## TROLLOP!
### CHAPTER ONE

The knock at the door became a hammering, then a thunder that filled the small house. Hastily adjusting the halter that barely contained her full young breasts, Mady ran to answer it. Scarcely had she turned the knob when the door swung open in her face and a squat woman, with the face and figure of a wrestler, strode into the room, her hand clamped around the stub of a broken oar.

She leveled a furious finger at Mady and in a strangled voice cried, "I come for me husband, Miss Lamont!"

She brandished her club but Mady stood unflinching, her black eyes snapping. Her tumbled black hair had the dark fire of midnight in it. She tossed her head and her smile glittered as she spoke. "You're forgetting your manners, Mrs. McNulty. Say please."

Mrs. McNulty's face congested and she began a slow, ominous advance. "I'll 'please' you, you ... chippy! I'll teach you to entertain honest women's husbands alone in yer house in the dead of night!"

"And where would you have me entertain them, Mrs. McNulty? Under the bushes like you did?"

The woman gave an inarticulate howl of rage and Mady went on in the same taunting voice, "Anyway, he's probably jumped out the back window by this time, Mrs. McNulty. You'd better run or you'll never catch up with him. That husband of yours is greased lightning when he's scared."

The woman stopped and planted her feet. "He's not catching me napping that way," she said with a kind of brutal triumph. "I got two of the boys waiting outside—Roy and Clyde—and they'll be beating the living tar out of him!"

Mady's fury matched the rage of the heavier woman but it showed only in the dead white color of her beautiful face.

"Maybe you should use a few more of the boys, Mrs. McNulty," she said. "Maybe if you got the boys to tie him hand and foot, he'd stay home nights. It's not every man that can stand the sight of your face day in and day out. Maybe your husband finally took one look too many. Maybe he ran out to keep from getting the horrors!"

But the woman had reached the point where further taunts had no effect on her.

"Keep it up," she said heavily, "that's all, keep it up—but it's me that's gonna have the last word, 'cause I'm gonna break every bone in your wenching body the minute the boys lay hands on McNulty." She turned her head and yelled through the open doorway behind her, "Git 'im yet, Roy?"

A masculine voice floated in out of the darkness, "Not yet, Miz McNulty."

Mrs. McNulty swung back to Mady. "Then he's still in here," she said grimly, "so step outta the way, chippy, 'cause I'm gawn through the house."

Mady quickly reached out for an eight-ounce lead trolling weight on the table near the door. She folded it tightly in her small fist, spread her legs a little and balanced on the balls of her feet.

"First come, first served, Mrs. McNulty," she said. "Step right up and be the first to get a cracked jaw."

The woman's heavy hand tightened around the stub of oar and she slid her foot warily to Mady's left, beginning a circling movement.

Behind Mady, a grinning blond young giant, carrying a bottle of beer, lounged into view in the doorway to the kitchen. He leaned there lazily, watching them with amusement.

"Five'll get you ten, Miz McNulty," he drawled, "that Mady smacks you on the button before you can get that club shoulder high. She's faster'n a rattlesnake."

Without turning, Mady called, "You keep out of this, Tuck."

Tuck, grinned with vast good nature. "Aw," he said, "what kind of way is this? Miz McNulty don't mean no harm. She's all in a tizzy, that's all, worrying about poor old Shawn McNulty. Let her take a look around, honey, and put her poor tormented mind at rest."

"She's not going through my house!" cried Mady.

Most of the steam had gone out of Mrs. McNulty at the sight of Tuck but she half raised her club and growled, "And I'm not above beating a tune on your skull either, Tuck Rossiter!"

"That you're not, Miz McNulty," Tuck agreed solemnly. "Any lady that can lay out three rampaging fishermen on a Sattidy night with her bare knuckles'd make mincemeat out of me. So, much as I hate saying this, ma'am, I'd sure have to bust you first if you tried," he concluded.

Mady turned and stared at him, then her fury evaporated in a bright cascade of laughter. The polite apology in his voice was irresistibly funny, for Tuck Rossiter, all six feet four of him, was famous from Tarpon Springs to Key West as a rough and tumble scrapper. Not that he'd actually bust Mrs. McNulty, of course. He'd merely take her club away from her and perhaps spank her with it, that was all.

Still laughing, Mady dropped into the sofa and said, "Oh, show her through the house, Tuck. And make sure she looks under the bed, in the bathtub—though heaven knows nobody'd ever expect to find Shawn McNulty in a bathtub—and make especially sure she looks in all the ratholes along the baseboards, 'cause that's where he'll be, if any place."

Mrs. McNulty's broad face flushed. She knew, of course, her husband was not there but she plodded doggedly across the room as Tuck opened the door to the bedroom and stepped politely aside, allowing her to enter before him.

"This, ma'am," he said, "is the bedroom, the sanctum sanctorum you might say, of this timid young girl whose honor you have just insulted. Yes ma'am, that's the bed. You can always tell a bed on account of it usually has a pillow on it. It's too bad you didn't bring a shotgun, ma'am, so's you could fire a few shells under it and be right sure he ain't there. That's the closet, ma'am, and them things hanging up are dresses, though I can't say I care much for dresses unless they have females in them to kind of fill them out in the right places. Now then, ma'am, think we're all done in this room?"

Mrs. McNulty marched out of the bedroom glowering. She was making a fool of herself, she knew—but she couldn't seem to stop.

"This closed door here, ma'am," he said, "is the bathroom. And if you don't mind my saying so, I'd knock before I went in. There's nothing embarrasses a lady more, ma'am, than walking in on a gentleman while he's powdering his nose—but I'll take an itty bitty little peek first." He opened the door a crack and peeped in. "Nobody there, ma'am," he said, opening the door wide. "That white thing over there against the wall, ma'am, is a bathtub. I've heerd tell that folk git right in it and wash theirselves all over. A real curiosity, ain't it?"

Mrs. McNulty's hands were trembling and her expression was one of embarrassment.

Mady burst out impulsively, "Leave her alone, Tuck. And stop talking like a Florida cracker!"

Tuck turned and gave her an innocent stare. "Why now, honey chile," he said, "all I was doing was taking Miz McNulty here on a kind of tour of inspection, you might say. She's been busting for I don't know how long to see what the inside of this here house looked like and this is her chance. And now, if you will kindly follow me over here, ma'am, I'll be proud to point out the wonders of modern science as pertains to a kitchen. That there do-hickey in the corner is an electric range. You can cook things on it, ma'am, without first having to shove in a lot of paper and kindling and setting fire to same. Hard to believe, ain't it?"

Mady said abruptly, "Oh, shut up, Tuck!" Then to Mrs. McNulty, "Your husband isn't here, he hasn't been here and as far as I'm concerned, he never will be here. Now behave yourself and go home."

Mrs. McNulty's face went white. She was not a bad woman at heart and not as rough as she had sounded. But she had swallowed a lot of pride coming here and had been shamed in not finding him. Now, told by Mady to behave herself, she lost the little control she had left and screamed shrilly, "I'm not taking back a word I said, you ... you trollop! I had good cause to come here and don't think I didn't. Everybody knows what you are—making up to every man you see and hanging around the saloons like a tart. Shame!"

"Oh, go home, will you? Get out of here!"

"I'll get out in me own good time, missy, but not before I tell you a thing or two. A decent girl are you, hey? If you were a decent girl, you'd of taken a room at the hotel where there are rules and regulations to protect young girls that come down here to Florida for a decent vacation. But did you? No! You had to take yourself a cottage here on the beach and live all by yourself. You don't want rules and regulations. That's the reason you're living here all by yourself. You don't want to be protected. I know you and your kind, missy. I know why you took this cottage. You wanted a place to entertain the men you pick up in the saloons, that's what you wanted!"

"You ... you're crazy!" Mady crouched in the corner of the sofa, appalled by the flood of vituperation.

"So it's crazy I am!" shrilled Mrs. McNulty. "But not crazy enough to believe that that feller that comes sneaking around every once in a while is your father, like you claim. Your father! And him not over thirty. Sure—and that handsome big boat, the likes of the Queen Mary it is. That's a fine gift for a father to give a girl, aiding and abetting her to run around with men out in the middle of the Gulf of Mexico. Sport fishing, you say! Ha! More sport than fishing, I'd say. You might think you're fooling the folks of Sanibar, that don't care a fig what you Yankees do so long as you spend money—but you're not fooling me or the decent folks in the village. We know what you are ..."

Tuck said sharply, "Shut your mouth, woman!" and thrust Mady, who had half risen, back into the sofa with a sweep of his arm. "Pay no attention to her, honey," he said. "She's spitting poison because she's made a damn fool of herself here tonight."

Mrs. McNulty whirled on him. "Oh, I am, am I ..."

"Now you jest hush, ma'am," drawled Tuck, falling back into the irony of his cracker accent. "I ain't never throwed a woman out of a house yet but I'm sure willing to start now." Then, briskly, "One of the boys brought down a demijohn of mule from Georgia this afternoon and you'll find Shawn dead drunk under the fish house, where he's been ever since dark. Now you'd better go and fetch him before the tide comes in."

Mrs. McNulty's face was sick with the poison she had spewed at Mady and with her own humiliation. She stood mutely with her mouth slack and her eyes dead in her face.

"And who told you Shawn was here?" Tuck asked.

She made a meaningless gesture with her hand. There was the sound of heavy feet on the porch and a voice asked, "What was that last question, mister?"

A big fisherman in dungarees and a sweatshirt appeared in the doorway. It was Clyde. He glared with hostility at them.

"I said," Tuck said softly, "who was the liar who told Mrs. McNulty that her husband was here? Do you have an answer to that, my friend?"

"You bet I do, mister. I was the one that told her—me. I saw her," his thick forefinger jabbed at Mady, "talking to Shawn this afternoon and tonight I saw him walking down this here path—and even if McNulty ain't here now, he surer than hell has been, 'cause everybody knows what she is!" His finger jabbed contemptuously at Mady again.

Tuck cocked his head to one side and regarded the man with an amiable grin.

"You know, friend," he said finally, "I've just reached a conclusion. I've just decided that you not only talk too much but you must be feebleminded as well. And on top of that, you told a fib. I'm just naturally going to have to wash out your mouth with soap."

The fisherman broke into a loud guffaw. "You just do that, mister," he jeered. "You just do that little thing—if you want to go around breathing out of your mouth for the next six months while they graft a new nose on your face."

Tuck was still grinning amiably but there was a hotness in his eyes, a dancing flame that was more than just temper. It was a kind of savage joy. He stood, hands on hips, and continued to taunt the man.

"Now me," he said, "I'm willing to put your lying down to ignorance and general stupidity but I'm afraid I can't let it go at that. So you'll just have to get down on your knees and tell Miss Mady Lamont that you're naturally a big-mouth and that you apologize for shooting it off. You might also add a few remarks to the effect that you're not quite right in the head."

"Me apologize to her!"

"Don't you understand English, you thick-headed lout?"

For a moment the fisherman just stood gaping. Then with a bellow of fury, he leaped forward, swinging his huge, hairy fists. Tuck sprang to meet him. He easily pushed off the first wild swing with his left. Then stepping in, he shot a straight right to the jaw. The fisherman's head snapped and he went back, digging with his heels and flailing. He went back through the doorway, tripped over the mat, tumbled down the steps and sprawled on the sand.

Tuck sprang after him and caught him by the collar as he rose groggily to his knees. Tuck hauled him to his feet and swung a terrific smash to the side of his face. The man crashed back into the railing of the porch. Tuck drove in at him again. The man began to sag but Tuck held him up against the railing and drove blow after blow at the helplessly lolling head.

Mrs. McNulty clung to the side of the doorway and screamed. Mady shrieked, "Stop it, Tuck! Stop it!"

He glanced toward her and blinked. He shook his head as if to clear his eyes of the red haze. Then he laughed and let the unconscious man fall to the ground. With a light spring, he came back up to the porch.

"Get that side of beef out of here," he said, grinning at Mrs. McNulty. Then he turned and walked into the house, slamming the door shut behind him with a loud bang.

## GENTLE PERSUASION
### CHAPTER TWO

Mady looked at Tuck as if she had never seen him before. She really never had seen him before—this way. His eyes were splinters of steel and his mouth wore a thin, ugly expression of satisfaction. His whole face was harder. He noticed her thoughtful look.

"What's the matter?" he asked sharply.

"I ... I thought you were going to kill him."

The harsh look slowly dissolved into his old familiar grin—big, wide, amiable and just a little more than irresponsible.

"Aw," he said, "you couldn't kill that big hunky with a Mack truck."

"You ... looked so awful and you kept hitting him and hitting him!"

"Now, honey, you know as well as I do I could have kept smacking him till my arm dropped off. You can't kill clowns like that. A half hour from now he'll be down at the gin mill telling everybody his foot slipped. And what's more, two'll get you twenty that the next time we meet, he'll try to start another shenanigan. Listen ..." He held up his hand for silence.

From outside they could hear Mrs. McNulty's shrill voice mingling with the heavier male tones, then Clyde's voice, swearing thickly. Mady ran to the window. Three men were moving slowly down the path. Two of them had Clyde by the arms and were urging him forward to a parked car. He was stumbling and looked very weak but it was obvious that he wanted to go back to the cottage and continue the fight. At Mady's elbow,

Tuck laughed softly.

"See?" he said.

Mady shook her head and turned to him. She laid her cheek against his chest and shivered. Tuck put his big arms around her.

"Now cut that out," he said. "It's all over."

He picked her up and carried her over to the sofa where he laid her down gently. She was as limp as a jointless doll. Her long, exciting, subtly curved legs stretched out almost lifelessly from the scanty triangle of fabric, tied in perky bows at the hips that formed the trunks of her Bikini swim suit. She and Tuck had just returned from a swim in the Gulf when Mrs. McNulty stormed in. Now Mady looked like a child just beginning to feel the effects of a terrible beating. Her eyes stared straight ahead as she spoke.

"Tuck ... why did she say those awful things?"

"Aw, she's a frustrated old bag and who pays any attention to frustrated old bags? Here, now. You stay right where you are and I'll go build you a drink."

Within less time than seemed possible he was back from the kitchen with a tall glass, tinkling with ice. The liquid in the glass was deep amber, almost straight whisky. He pushed the glass into her hand but she made no attempt to drink. Tuck sat down beside her and patted her knee.

"Go on, drink it up, honey," he urged. "I'll lose my bartender's license if people go around not drinking my drinks. They'll kick me out of the union."

Mady made no response.

"Now, honey," he said smoothly, "snap out of it. You don't want to pay any attention to what a pack of goons like that think. What do they amount to, anyway? Just a bunch of two-bit fishermen and half the time they don't have that much in their pockets. What difference does it make what they think? Who gives a damn what they think? Come on, honey, forget it and drink up."

He leaned over and kissed her. Her lips were cold and unresponsive. He straightened up, frowning.

"I want to go home, Tuck," she began to cry. "I want to go back to Tampa."

"That's silly, honey."

"I hate it here. I hate it! All I did this afternoon was ask Mr. McNulty to get me some mullet for bait and look what they made of it. I hate it here."

"That'd be running away, Mady," he said.

"I don't care. I want to go home."

"Your father's depending on you."

"Dad wouldn't want me to stay here another minute if he knew about ... what went on here tonight. He'd order me to come home."

"Stop talking like a spoiled brat," Tuck said angrily. "Your father wouldn't do anything of the sort."

She stiffened. "Don't talk to me like that!"

"Then don't act like a baby. Aw honey, let's us not fight." He turned on his boyish grin again. "You're all upset and I don't blame you—but everything'll look different in the morning. You know that. Hell, tomorrow you'll be laughing at all this. Now, just take a little sip of your drink ..."

"I'm going home," she said quietly. "I'm going home tonight."

He sat back and shook his head. "All right, if that's the way you feel about it. I can't stop you. But I can tell you one thing—you're letting your father down. You know how he's depending on you to help him find that feller, Joe Menagh. If you don't want to, that's all there is to it. Nobody can make you. Maybe we can get somebody else—but I don't know."

He could see each of the thrusts went home. He patted her knee lovingly.

"Why don't you sleep on it tonight, honey," he suggested. "If you still feel the same way tomorrow, then the thing to do is go home and I won't try to talk you out of it."

She leaned her head back against the sofa. Her eyes were squinting to hold back the tears.

"Hasn't your father told you about Joe Menagh?" asked Tuck.

Mady shook her head.

Tuck looked surprised. "Nothing at all?"

She stammered, "Just ... just that he had to get in touch with him ... about a business matter."

"And he didn't tell you anything else?"

She grasped his arm. "Tuck. Is something wrong? Is Dad in trouble? What else was there to tell me?"

Tuck shook his head. "Dammit, he should have told you. It was unfair to keep you in the dark like this. You had a right to know. But probably he didn't want to frighten you."

"Tuck! What is it?" She sat up stiffly.

He seemed undecided. "I don't know if I should tell you, honey. After all, your father is my boss. If he didn't tell you, I might get into a jam if I spill it. Gosh, honey, I just don't know when to keep my big mouth shut."

"You won't get in trouble, Tuck. I promise you. You've got to tell me. I must know if Dad's in difficulty. You've got to tell me, Tuck!"

"Well ..." He looked away from her. "Let me make myself a drink, honey. I'm going to need a little Dutch courage."

He got up and ambled into the kitchen hardly looking as if he needed Dutch courage. There was a satisfied little smile on his lips and he winked at himself as he went into the kitchen. But the smile disappeared as he was seized by a new thought.

The build-up had been perfect but what the hell was he going to tell her now? He shrugged peevishly and let the liquor run into his glass from the bottle. Then he laughed. What was he getting into an uproar about? He didn't have to make a production out of it. All he had to do was follow the general outline. The facts were good enough as they stood, with a small deletion here and there. Hell, this wasn't the FBI he was telling it to.

He topped his glass with a little soda, stirred it, then started back to the living room with his natural lithe stride. He grinned a little uncertainly as he sat down on the sofa beside Mady.

"Gosh, honey," he mumbled, "I got a feeling I'm sticking my neck out on this. You don't know it but your old man can be pretty tough when he gets his back up. Honest, I wouldn't be doing this if I wasn't crazy about you. I wish we could get married. What's your father got against me, anyway?"

Mady was composed now. She leaned forward and kissed him on the cheek. "You're irresponsible, darling—and Dad doesn't happen to love you the way I do. Now please, Tuck, tell me—what kind of trouble is Dad in?"

"After this is over, honey, we're going to get married, even if it comes to a showdown with your old man."

"Please, Tuck!"

"Sure, sure, honey. But I just had to get that off my chest."

She put her hand on his. "I know, Tuck. Now who is Joe Menagh?"

"He's a pilot."

"What kind of pilot?"

"Oh, he was Mr. Guastella's pilot."

"And who is Mr. Guastella? Tuck, you're exasperating!"

"And you keep interrupting," he pointed out. "But I'll start at the beginning. You know your father's import-export business deals mainly in Cuban sugar and tobacco. Well, this Guastella, he was your father's Havana branch manager. He was a funny little guy with a waxed moustache and high heels and he was always dousing himself with perfume. I met him a couple times in Miami. He was very shrewd. I don't know how honest he was but your old man trusted him with a lot of money, so I guess he was okay. He must have been okay, because he was in complete charge of the Cuba office."

"I think I remember Dad mentioning ..."

"Sure you do. Anyway, your old man trusted Guastella with a lot of loose cash to buy small crops from independent growers. So this particular day he had a hundred thousand bucks in cash. He got in the plane with Menagh to go on his buying trip and the next thing we know, the plane has crashed ten miles inside the Big Cypress swamp around Fort Myers, here in Florida. Guastella was found dead in the wreckage but Joe Menagh had disappeared with the hundred thousand bucks. Now here's the rough part. Your old man's credit is just a little over-extended but if he had that hundred thousand he'd be okay. Or if he had the crops Guastella was going to buy with it. We didn't know where the hell to look for Menagh but we put out a flock of private detectives and one particular Saturday night Menagh is finally spotted in a gin mill right here in Sanibar. The detective tried to put the arm on him but Menagh clipped him with a beer bottle and disappeared again. We're damn sure he's still somewhere in the area, hiding out. He's a smalltime jerk and that hundred thousand has probably got him scared to death, so he'll sit still until he's sure the heat is off."

"But, Tuck, what can I do about any of this? I want to help Dad but I don't see ..."

"I'm coming to that, baby. This Menagh is a chaser and a lush. He'll stay hidden just so long, then he'll bust out again. He'll sneak into town for a drink and a woman, especially beautiful brunettes like you. That's where you come in. You just keep circulating from one gin mill to another all by yourself and he'll pick you up. Don't worry about that."

"Tuck, I'm scared ..."

"Aw, there's nothing to be scared of. The minute you think you have the right guy, just call me at the hotel bar and I'll handle it from there on in. You'll know him. His face twitches when he's cockeyed, he's got a funny kind of laugh and he's always talking about what a real hot-shot pilot he is. But there's nothing to worry about. We're not going to strong-arm the guy. All we want is to make a deal to get back the hundred thousand and by this time he's probably so scared he'll be glad to get rid of it as long as he can stay out of jail. That's all. There's nothing for you to worry about."

"I didn't mean I'm scared that way, Tuck. I meant I'm scared I'll botch it and let him get away."

"Honey," Tuck pulled her up onto his lap and looked into her face. "Just between you and me, you don't have to worry about letting him get away. With your face and figure, we won't be able to get him away from you!"

## BLONDE SECURITY
### CHAPTER THREE

Mady smiled up at him and reached up to touch his cheek with her fingertips. She said, "Tuck, Dad's not in any real trouble then, is he?"

"Well, no. Not for another month or two, when he has to start making delivery on some of his contracts. As long as we keep things under our hats. If word leaks out, he might just as well fold up."

"Is there any chance of that, Tuck?"

"There are only three of us who know. Your old man won't talk and I won't talk ..."

"And I won't talk either!" she said indignantly. Then, thoughtfully, "I did act like a spoiled brat, didn't I?"

"You sure did," said Tuck cheerfully.

"It won't happen again. It was just that I didn't know, that's all. And that horrible woman accused me of all those things. You were wonderful, Tuck. If it hadn't been for you, I'd have gone running back to Tampa and Dad would have been so disappointed in me. You were wonderful, really you were. You were very patient with me."

He started to say something but the glow of her upturned smile seemed to touch off something inside him and the impact rocked him. It was the unexpectedness of it, the surprise. Momentarily caught off balance, he reeled.

He suddenly realized he had been treating her as if she were a child—and she wasn't a child.

He slid his arm under her shoulders and lifted her roughly to meet his kiss. For a moment, her surprised lips were stiff, then he felt the quiver of her mouth as it softened and eagerly pressed into the kiss. Her arms, which had lain limp, slid up around his neck and held him tightly. And her own kiss grew warm and passionate.

He said huskily, "Honey honey honey ..."

Their eyes met for a flickering instant and hers were huge and dark. Then their lips came together again. She pressed closer to him and he felt a hot sweep of fire rise up in him. His hands swept over her curves, then tightened and held her fiercely. She seemed to melt under his touch. Her lips quivered and her arms around his neck pulled him deeper into the kiss. He reached out and snapped off the lamp, then reached impatiently for her.

She whispered, "Wait, darling, wait ..."

Her arms slipped from around his neck and he felt her arch, then heard the whisper of something light and silky slipping over her legs, heard the soft slither as it fell to the floor.

She cried out as his impatient arms tightened roughly around her, for he had twisted and hurt her. But the hurt was forgotten in the renewed and mounting violence of the kiss. She had never been kissed like this before; she had never been held like this before and at first she cringed and strained away from the raging turbulence but that reaction passed and she began to return his embrace with ardor.

It was almost as if she were in a theatre and the darkness were suddenly rent by a crashing chord from the orchestra and the black pit of the stage pierced by a jagged, flaming lance of light.

But now she was not a spectator, but was on the stage herself, a living performer in a play that wasn't a play at all but was life itself, at a breathlessly accelerated pace. There were voices around her like a mounting roar, sounds that glittered and whirled by like comets. And from some unseen orchestra there was music like a tempest, a whirlwind, a maelstrom. She could almost distinguish the wild skirling of the violins, the clarion silver of the trumpets, the flutes in headlong fury, the timpani thundering.

And then it wasn't the theatre but the ballet—and she was whirling across the stage on her toes. At the end, she sprang into the air, soaring. Her buoyancy was incredible and the speed of her ascent tore the breath from her lips. And she went up and up until the roof became the sky, the brilliance of outer space, the stars spinning globes of fire. Her flight became faster and faster until suddenly she burst through a field of meteors that flamed around her, throwing fountains of gushing sparks of beauty and color everywhere ...

It was Tuck who stirred first. He got up abruptly and strode into the kitchen. She heard the clink of bottle against glass as he poured himself a drink. When he came back, he did not sit down beside her but instead sat in the club chair opposite her. She turned on her side and smiled at him through the darkness. Against the luminescence of the window, she watched his silhouette as he tilted the bottle to his lips and drank again.

She said softly, "Tuck ..."

"Yeah?"

"I love you, darling. And don't worry about Dad. As soon as this Menagh thing is over, we'll be married. We could be married tomorrow but ... I don't want to worry him anymore right now, Tuck. You can understand that, can't you?"

He said, "Yeah," again and turned his head away from her voice, scowling.

He was still unsure of himself, a feeling he had never experienced before. He had always been able to take this kind of stuff in his stride and laugh it off afterward. It had never meant anything to him, had never really touched him. He had always known no dame would ever be able to get her hooks into him. For that reason, he had always played the field. If one went sour on him, hell, there was always another just around the corner, there were always three or four just around the corner. But what the hell had happened to him now? He had drunk too much, that was the trouble. That was a brute of a drink he had made, practically a glassful of straight rye with a little ice and soda. But Lord, she had really gotten to him.

Her voice came softly across to him. "What's the matter, darling?"

"Nothing," he said shortly. "Nothing's the matter." He put the bottle down on the floor and stood up. "I've got to go now. There's ... somebody I have to see. I'll be up to see you in the morning."

She said quietly, "All right, darling," as if she knew what was going on inside him, knew he had to get away alone and think things out for himself.

He was suddenly furious with her and it was with an effort that he kept himself from swearing at her, asking her who the hell she thought she was, pretending to know what he was thinking, acting so goddamn smug about it.

Instead, he said abruptly, "See you in the morning," and strode off. Outside in the cool night air, he swung around the path to the rear of the cottage, past the lacy clump of date palms to the macadam road where his car was parked. He got it started with angry violence and shot away from the curb, the tires throwing up a spray of sand.

Mady's cottage was about a mile south of the Sanibar bathing beach and half a mile north of the fishing village. Tuck trod heavily on the gas pedal and within a few seconds was roaring down the road. The taut canvas of the convertible thundered wildly in the wind. The thick trunks of the royal palms lining the beach road fled by. The sweeping breakers of the Gulf moved nearby like a sea in silent films, for at this speed he could not hear their heavy roar as they broke against the shore.

He slowed his speed as the clustered lights of Sanibar rushed toward him. He plucked a cigarette from a package in his breast pocket. He felt better now. Settled. Sure of himself again. But godamighty, that little black-haired canary had sure taken him over the jumps for a while. It had been just like taking a full roundhouse swing flush on the jaw.

He slowed to twenty-five, then to ten as he swung into the driveway of the Hotel Miramar, where he lived. He parked the car and walked straight into the bar.

This was the height of the winter season and the semi-circular bar was jammed. The two bartenders showed dark half-moon stains in the armpits of their white jackets. There was laughter, voices shrill and heavy, the continual clink and clatter of glasses, the rush and tinkle of the cash register—blending into a hum that sounded like a machine shop running under full power.

Tuck wedged himself in at the end of the bar against the wall, caught the bartender's eye and raised two fingers, indicating a double Scotch. A tall lanky girl standing at his side turned and looked at him.

"You're big," she said. She was a little drunk.

Tuck ignored her. His face, even in this subdued light, no longer seemed boyish. It was harder, heavier, older.

The girl pointed a finger at him. "I've seen you around," she informed him coyly. "You're a football player. Right?"

Tuck paid no attention to her. Broodingly, he watched the smoke curl from the tip of his cigarette. The exhilaration engendered by the fast drive along the beach road had left him and he felt restless and irritable again.

The girl persisted. "A fullback," she said brightly. "Right?"

Tuck looked down at her without taking the cigarette from his mouth. It bobbed as he spoke. "Why don't you shut the hell up?" he asked.

She gasped and fell back against the shoulder of a plump man standing beside her. He glared at Tuck and said, "Now wait a minute— that's no way to talk to my wife. You're asking for trouble, friend."

Tuck's eyes lighted for a moment but just then the bartender brought his drink and he turned back to the bar.

"There's a lot of riffraff in here tonight, Charlie," he said evenly.

The bartender arched his eyebrows for a moment, then laughed. "Yeah," he said, "everybody's having fun. Good crowd."

Tuck put a five dollar bill on the bar. "I'll be back in a minute, Charlie," he said. He tossed down his drink and pushed the empty glass across the bar with his forefinger. "Fill it up again."

As he turned, he looked down at the lanky girl. "If I were you, sister," he said, "I'd go upstairs and put on a sweater. You're going to catch a cold in the chest. Not enough meat on you."

He walked away grinning as he heard her outraged cries and the man's belligerent voice. He went into the lobby where the telephone booths were hidden behind a screen of potted hibiscus. He slid into the end booth and asked for long distance.

"I want to talk to Eric Lamont, Hotel Caribe, Havana, Cuba, person to person," he said.

He leaned back and lit another cigarette while he waited. When the phone rang, he picked it up and leaned forward.

"Mr. Lamont is not in the hotel at the moment, sir," said the operator. "Shall I keep trying and call you back?"

Tuck said, "Do that," and gave her his name.

He crossed the lobby to the desk. "I'm expecting a long distance call," he told the clerk. "I'll be in the bar."

It was an hour before Tuck's call came through. He had made another call in the meantime, a house call, but had received no answer on that one either.

He slid into the end booth again but this time looked up and down the lobby before closing the door.

"Lamont?" he said into the phone.

"Yes. That you, Tuck?" It was a melodious voice, soft and liquid.

"Yeah, this is Tuck. How are you doing?"

"Nothing on this end. Nobody knows a thing."

"They say."

"No, really, Tuck." Eric Lamont's voice hurried a little, as if he were anxious to convince. "Menagh was operating alone. He was Guastella's pilot and that's all. Apparently, it was something he thought up all by himself. Nobody knows a thing about him down here. He had no friends, nobody. He played poker with the crowd down at Santana's but he was strictly a lone wolf."

Tuck swore. "Sure you covered everything?" he demanded.

"From one end of the island to the other. That makes it rough, what?"

"Yeah, it makes it rough what!" Tuck mimicked him savagely.

"I'm sorry, Tuck. I did everything possible."

"You hope! And you'd better be right. Anyway, you're on your way here, whether you know it or not. Hop a plane and be here in Sanibar tomorrow. That brat of yours is cutting up."

"Mady?" There was sudden anxiety in Lamont's voice. "Tuck, do we have to use her?"

"Yes, we have to use her!"

"She's only a child, Tuck. I don't want her mixed up in this. I mean ..."

"I don't care what you mean," Tuck cut in. "She's in and she stays in. Use your head, stupid. There's a chance she might actually turn up with Menagh. A damn good chance. You know what a chaser he is."

"I know ..."

"Then talk as if you do. What do you want us to do, hire some floozie who'd sell us out the first time Menagh waved a C-note under her nose? At least we can be sure Mady won't do that—but she's getting hard to handle. She wanted to walk out on us tonight."

Lamont was silent.

"Did you hear me?"

"Yes, I heard you."

"Well, answer me then. I said she wanted to walk out on us tonight. You didn't do a very good job of getting her to make that old college try, pal."

Again Lamont was silent.

"Maybe you wanted her to walk out," suggested Tuck.

Lamont blurted, "I wish she had!"

Tuck laughed. "But she didn't. I ... talked her out of it." There was no sense in pushing the guy too far, not yet. He didn't like Lamont. Lamont didn't have guts. "You know, pal, you're lucky I'm in a good humor tonight. I should be giving you hell. Now, you're sure you're all cleaned up down there?"

Lamont said stiffly, "I was going to call you in the morning."

"Okay. Hop that plane and get up here tomorrow. I can use you here in Sanibar."

He hung up and slid out of the booth. He felt better. Lamont in Sanibar would keep Mady in line. Something rose in his chest at the thought of her and he stopped short with a surprised expression on his face.

"Jesus," he said aloud in a wondering voice.

She really did have her hooks in him. He took a cigar from his pocket, bit the end off and spat it out. He put the cigar between his teeth and thoughtfully felt for his lighter. Forget it, he told himself, you're just asking for trouble. But she stayed in his mind, and he found himself remembering her glowing smile when she looked up at him, the growing fire of her kisses ... He said, "Uh-uh," and walked through the lobby to the house phone.

"Has Miss Brunn come in yet?" he asked the girl at the switchboard. "This is Mr. Rossiter."

"I think so, Mr. Rossiter. Shall I ring her?"

"Thanks."

He heard the receiver snatched noisily from its cradle and a flat, nasal voice said, "Yeah?"

He grimaced but he made his voice warm. "Hello, Ida. I've been calling you all evening."

"Tucky-Wucky!" she squealed, as if it had been weeks instead of hours since she had last seen him. "Hiya, Tucky-Wucky. You miss Ida?"

"I've been calling you all evening, honey."

"I been to the movies. Phooey. I should of stood home. C'mon up, honeybunch, and Ida'll make her Tucky-Wucky a nice big drink."

He rolled his eyes. "I just wanted to know if you heard from Leo, honey."

"You'll never find out down there in the lobby, sugarplum. Come on up and see Ida for a little while. Come on come on come on ..."

"But did you hear from Leo?"

"Ast me no questions and I'll tell y' no lies," she said playfully. "Maybe I did and maybe I din but y'll never fine out till I tell you. Come on up, Boopsie. Ida's lonesome."

"I'm a little tired, honey ..."

"What's the matter, you got a broken leg or somethin'?" she said sharply. "Get up here fast an' no argument."

Tuck winced as she hung up with a crash. He swore and for the hundredth time asked himself why he had ever got mixed up with Ida Brunn.

He bought two more cigars, then took the elevator up to her floor. She greeted him at the door with a squeal and a wet, squashy kiss. She nuzzled his neck, took him by the hand and pulled him into the room, chattering effusively, moving animatedly, happily.

She was wearing a fluffy green chiffon negligee and not a thing more except for a pair of black stockings. She was a big girl with natural flaxen hair, baby blue eyes and a beautiful fair complexion. Her skin was truly silken. She was very vain about her complexion and never went out in the sun for fear of marring it. Her face was round and her small, heavily rouged mouth sat on it like an artificial butterfly. She was a woman who had reached the height of her physical beauty. Her figure was voluptuous with rounded, generous bosom and creamy, well-shaped legs. Her hips were gracefully curved and swayed becomingly as she moved. In a few years, all this would change and become plump, then fat. But now she had the seductive charm of a harem beauty.

But this impression was immediately dissipated the moment she opened her mouth, for her voice was as flat as a slap.

She had decorated her suite with long-legged French dolls, huge lacy pillows, Maxfield Parrish pictures and at least twenty mirrors, all with ornate gilt frames. Her bedroom was a pink and white meringue of organdy bedspread, organdy curtains, an organdy-skirted vanity and bench. Three more dolls sprawled on the bed and she had archly arranged two of them in a lovers' clasp.

Tuck let himself be dragged into the sitting room, thinking sourly that she wasn't the type to prance around like a five-year-old. There had been a time that she had amused him. She flounced down into a sofa upholstered in a white woolly material that reminded him of a sheep. She gave him an eye-fluttering smile and patted the cushion beside her. He sat on the edge of the cushion and put a cigar in his mouth before she could squash another kiss on his face.

"Did you hear from Leo?" he asked in a business-like voice.

She pouted. "That all you got to say, sweet-man. Come on, Boopsie, be nice. Le's have a li'l drinkie. That's juss what you need, a li'l drink. Ida get Tucky-Wucky a li'l drinkie."

She bounced up from the sofa and walked into the bathroom. At the door, she flounced her posterior at him, looked back over her shoulder and giggled. He glumly lit his cigar and listened as she dug around in the ice-filled bathtub. Wherever she went, she always had a bathtub full of beer and liquor. She came back with a bottle of gin but before she returned to the sofa, she went around the room, systematically turning on all the lights. Ida liked lots of light to show off her really perfect complexion. She postured a little as she reached each lamp, so he would see she was wearing nothing under the negligee. She liked to show off her body, which she thought was tops. Before her brother Leo had made so much money, she had been a stripper in the northeastern seaboard burlesque circuit and she'd been very popular. After giving Tuck what she thought was an eyeful, she walked back to the sofa with the exaggerated hip-wagging step of a professional strip artist.

There were several empty glasses and two empty gin bottles on the cocktail table. The cocktail table itself was a very special item, the kind of thing she was always buying for herself. Instead of conventional legs, the table top was supported by four black-stockinged, gartered female legs—a relic of the too consciously naughty Nineties.

She held one of the glasses up to the light, then picked up the hem of her negligee and polished it—to show Tuck she knew how to treat a guest and just incidentally, too, to exhibit a generous slice of creamy skin above the stocking top. She filled the glass with gin and handed it to him.

"Li'l drink for Tucky-Wucky," she cooed. "What's the matter, sugar-lamb? Ida's li'l Boopsie got a pain in the gut or sumpin?"

Tuck drank his gin at a gulp. He knew it was going to make him cockeyed but it was worth it. She threw her gin down with a practiced flip of her wrist. She put down her glass, then fell straight back across his lap and closed her eyes.

"Ida wants a li'l kissie," she said, bunching her lips.

He bent over and kissed her shortly but before he could straighten up, she locked her arms around his neck and moved her lips to and fro across his mouth, emitting little moans and grunts of pleasure. It was something she always did and it annoyed him. She did it so consciously, as if to stir his ardor.

Suddenly she stiffened and shoved him away. Then she leaned back and gave him a resounding slap across the face. Tears spurted from his eyes. She thrust her face toward him and screamed, "And there's more where that came from. Whattaya take me faw, a nutsy fagin?"

"What the hell are you talking about?" he roared furiously.

"I'm talking about that!" She punched his chest with her fist.

He looked down and saw a smear of lipstick across his shirt. "Lipstick," he said. "So what?"

She shrieked, "So what?" She swung another slap at him but he pushed it aside with his forearm. He grinned thinly.

"Do that again," he said, "and I'll slap your ears down."

She leaped to her feet, grasped the edge of the cocktail table with both hands and flung it into the air. Screeching incoherently, she stamped on the crunching glass. Her eyes rolled wildly and her hands made clenching motions in the air. Tuck lay back in the sofa and guffawed. She sprang at him with taloned fingers. Without shifting, he brought up his elbow and caught her under the chin. She fell to her knees, her eyes glazed from the force of the blow. Chuckling, he put his hands under her armpits and hoisted her up to the sofa.

"What do you want to go blowing your stack for?" he asked. "We had a date and you went to the goddamn movies. I went down to the bar and the dame next to me happened to turn around and smear me with lipstick. So what?"

"You're a lyin' slob!" she said quickly.

"Sure. I'm a lying slob. I met Mae West at the railroad station and before I knew what was going on, she kissed me on the shirt and told me to come up and see her sometime."

"Ha, ha, ha. Mae West woon even lookitya."

"Maybe it was Hedy Lamarr. It was dark."

"Yeah. And maybe it was some redhead, too." But her glance wavered. Then she whined, "I'll tell Leo you two-timed me, that's what I'll do."

His stomach gave a sickening lurch. He didn't want to have any mess with Leo.

"Okay," he said harshly, "and I'll tell Leo you threw another wingding and broke a hundred bucks worth of cut crystal."

"Aw, Boopsie, you woon tell Leo on poor li'l Ida. Ida oney making a big funny. Ida woon tell Leo on Boopsie—Boopsie woon tell Leo on li'l Ida. Nobody woon tell nobody about nothing. Okey-dokey, Boopsie-Woopsie?"

He knuckled her chin. "Someday," he said, "I'm going to let you have it right there and they'll send for the meat wagon." He meant it—but all the same he was relieved that she was not going to tell Leo. "When's Leo coming?" he asked.

"T'morra maybe. He said for you to meet him at the airport." She moved against him and cooed, "Come on, Tucky-Wucky, give Ida li'l ole kissie."

She bunched her lips.

This was what he hated, this having to pretend love where there was no longer any fire. He should never have made a pass at her in the first place but at the time he had thought it was a good way to get in solid with Leo. Now he was in pretty solid with Leo but he knew, too, that it depended almost entirely on his standing with Ida and in turn that meant he would have to go on pretending to love her.

Her tantrums always put her in a languorous mood. He kissed her briefly. She hooked her fingers into his shirt and pulled him close to her.

"Now give Ida a nice big kissie!" she demanded.

He bent toward her and she wound her arms around his neck. Her fingers dug into him. She made a throaty sound and began to move her lips to and fro across his. Soon, he knew, she would moan and pretend that it was all too ecstatically unbearable, that love was a terrible and beautiful thing—and there would be all the movement and clutching and smearing of her lips. Then she would begin to breathe heavily, and throw open her negligee.

Yes, he thought as he met her parted lips, one of these days something would snap and he'd break her neck—Leo or no Leo.

## A NOVEL APOLOGY
### CHAPTER FOUR

Mady awoke the next morning with a feeling of complete unreality. It was a gray windy day and cold, too—unlike the usual balmy weather. The wind came down from the North, driving lean gray clouds before it and the palms tossed and rustled like crackling old men. The curling waters of the Gulf muttered and grumbled on the beach outside her windows. She shivered, sprang out of bed and closed the windows, then turned on the electric heater that was set in the wall. She slipped into her long woolen housecoat and shivered again. She glanced at the clock and gasped. Nine-thirty! And Tuck was coming early! She ran to the chest of drawers, hurriedly pulled out clothes and pulled on a dark green short-sleeved sweater and a light ivory-colored skirt, banded at the hem with a bold peasant pattern. She postured before the mirror, anxious to look well—to look especially well this morning.

Tuck came at ten o'clock and there were brown pouches under his eyes but to Mady he looked wonderful. She flew into his arms and held up her face for a kiss.

He kissed her briefly and muttered, "Got something for a pick-me-up, honey? I feel as if I'd been up all night licking the barnacles off the bottom of a cattle boat."

"Poor Tuck." She touched his lips with her fingertips. "Hangover?"

"And what a hangover! After I left you last night, I stopped off at the bar in the hotel. If you've got something like a triple whisky sour in your pocket, I'd sure appreciate it."

She felt a little defeated by his casual greeting but she concealed it and gave him a sympathetic smile.

"You sit right down here on the sofa," she said sternly, "and I'll make you the best whisky sour you ever tasted."

He dropped into the sofa with a groan and closed his eyes. "No sugar," he said. He clasped his forehead with both hands. Lord, what a night it had been! Between them, Ida and he had killed what was left in one gin bottle, then had finished another fifth. And the drunker she had grown, the more demandingly affectionate she had become. If only he could get rid of her—but there was little chance of that with Leo around. His only hope was that her fickle fancy would tire of him, as it seemed to tire of everything else. Lord, how he hated her! Her and her soft, marshmallow cloying love! He knew she was attractive and when he was drunk enough she could still stir him as no one else could. She was utterly reckless, her abandon was unbelievable.

But how he hated her!

Mady came back from the kitchen with his drink and sat down beside him. "Here's your medicine, darling," she said, putting the glass into his hand.

Without opening his eyes, he gulped it down in two swallows. The warmth spread from his throat to his chest, from his stomach into his arms and legs. Very soon, the throbbing diminished in his temples and he could open his eyes without wincing. He looked at her and grinned. Something rose in his chest at the sight of her, sitting there looking so young and beautiful, and he pulled her to him and kissed her hungrily. How different she was from Ida!

She whispered, "Darling, darling ..." and gently put one hand behind his head, not forcing him into the kiss the way Ida did—but holding him to it as her lips parted and she melted in his arms. Her hands reached around to the back of his neck, then lovingly felt the broad, flat muscles of his shoulders and slid under his arms. Suddenly she stiffened and drew away from him.

"What's the matter, honey?" he asked.

Hesitantly she touched something under his left armpit. "It's ... it's a gun," she said.

He grinned. "It sure is. Want to see it?" He made a swift movement and the gun lay in the palm of his hand. There was a tiny metallic click as it snapped from the clip.

It was an ugly, ill-proportioned revolver with a two inch barrel and a scored walnut grip. It was a .38, a belly gun.

"It won't hurt you, honey," he said, amused. "Not unless I point it at you."

"But ... why do you carry it, Tuck?"

"Oh now, honey, use your head for a minute. This Joe Menagh is a crude character. He's got a hundred thousand bucks of your father's money. I can't just walk up to him and say, 'Now, Joe, why don't you reform?' He'll be carrying one of these himself."

"Oh, Tuck!" she said in horror.

"Now don't worry, sweetheart. Nobody's going to get hurt. That's why I carry this little gadget."

"But I never thought, Tuck ..."

"I know. You just thought we'd catch up with Menagh and he'd hand over the money like a little lamb. He will, all right, but I'm going to have to tickle him in the ribs with this little persuader first. There won't be any shenanigans."

She shivered. "I suppose you're right. Common sense tells me you're right." She tried to smile. "But ... it scares me!" She clung to him and hid her face against his chest.

He laughed and ruffled her blue-black hair. She was wonderful. He'd find a way to get rid of Ida, Leo or no Leo. This was the woman for him. She was young and sweet and clean and it made him feel clean again, just holding her in his arms, feeling her against him.

He began to kiss her, casually and playfully at first, brushing her eyelashes with his lips, then with mounting warmth. She responded with eagerness. When the knock came at the door, it was he who sprang away from her and hurriedly wiped the lipstick, from his mouth with the palm of his hand. His first thought was that Ida had followed him here to the cottage and his heart gave a sickening lurch. It would be just like her to come snooping around.

Mady laughed at him. "This is the first time I've known you to care what the neighbors think," she whispered.

"Answer it, answer it," he said, stepping back out of view of the doorway. "If it's for me, I'm not here." He turned and went into the kitchen.

Mady looked puzzled but went to open the door. The young man who stood there was a stranger. He was tall and lean and engagingly homely, with a long freckled face and a crooked, humorous mouth. His hair was sun-bleached. His eyes were that peculiar gray that sometimes seems green, sometimes blue. He was wearing sneakers, dungarees and a T-shirt.

"You'd be Miss Lamont, wouldn't you?" he said shyly.

"That's right," said Mady.

"Well ... uh ... I'm Bass McNulty."

He stopped as she threw up her head and a stony look came into her face.

"Look, Miss Lamont," he said quickly. "I know you're sore and I don't blame you. Mom never should've thrown that wingding last night and she knows it. That's why I'm here. I want to offer you a blanket apology on behalf of the benevolent and protective order of McNultys. And Mom says if you want to come down to our house and throw a wingding of your own, she'll bring out her best set of dishes and you can throw them around the room if you like, just so long as you don't break any mirrors."

"Thank you," said Mady woodenly. "Is that all?"

"No, ma'am. I don't want you to accept this apology without giving it serious thought. Too many people go around accepting apologies on the spur of the moment, then later they wish they hadn't, like getting married to the first girl you meet when you're on furlough. And I want you to know that there's nothing binding about accepting this apology, in case you want to take it back later and tell us a few home truths about ourselves, because us McNultys could use a few home truths, especially where throwing wingdings is concerned. And while you're thinking this over, I'd like to say that this apology comes from the bottom of our hearts and Mom is so 'shamed that she blushes all over every time she thinks about it. I could make a handsomer apology, I know, but this was kind of urgent and it's the best I can do on the spur of the moment. But if you want to accept it temporarily, I'll draw up a more formal one that'll be permanent."

"Very funny," said Mady, closing the door firmly.

Tuck came raging from the kitchen and grasped Mady's arm as soon as the door had closed.

"You damn fool," he said angrily. "Why didn't you use your head?"

"Tuck!"

"For Christ's sake, this is the kind of break we've been looking for and you boot it. Now go after that guy and schmooz him up a little."

"I will not!" she flamed, wrenching her arm from his grasp.

He grinned quickly, realizing he had played it wrong. She wasn't a girl you could push around.

"I'm sorry, honey," he said smoothly. "I lost my head, seeing our chance slip away like that."

"What are you talking about?"

"Look, honey. We're trying to find Joe Menagh. Right? We're pretty darn sure he's hiding around here somewhere. Right? Okay. He might be up the river, he might be hiding out in the swamp. Hell, he might only be a half mile from here, hiding in the mangrove on the beach. But we don't know enough about this country to begin to look. But these conches, like that McNulty guy, are all over the place in their boats—and if Menagh is hiding out around here, it's ten to one that those conches know just where he is. Now do you see what I mean?"

Mady said, "Oh," and glanced at the door with dismay. "I never thought of that."

"Go after him, honey," Tuck urged. "This is something money can't buy. Those conches hate us. They hate all Yankees. But this gives you an in with them. Let's make the most of it. Go on, honey, flutter your eyelashes at him and he'll eat out of your hand."

"I'm always doing something stupid, aren't I, Tuck? But I'll be good. I'll be a regular Mata Hari, you watch."

She kissed him lightly and ran out of the cottage. Bass McNulty was walking down the beach toward the fishing village, kicking idly at shells on the sand as he walked.

Mady called, "Mr. McNulty!"

He turned as she came up to him breathless and smiling. "I'm sorry I was so rude," she said.

"You weren't rude at all, ma'am. Leastways, no more than the situation called for. And all things considered, you can't hardly call that rude. You just had your dander up and I figured you'd had enough McNultys to last you quite a while. A little of us McNultys goes a long ways."

"Anyway, I accept your apology. And you tell your mother I'll be glad to come down to your house and throw your best dishes around the room."

"Yes, ma'am. But just when will that be? The reason I ask is—I know Mom'd want to have the dishes all nice and clean for the occasion. She wants to do this right. And anyway, throwing dirty dishes around the room sure makes a mess out of the wallpaper, like gravy, for instance. There's nothing makes a mess out of wallpaper like gravy. Pork gravy, 'specially."

Mady could not help laughing and she asked curiously, "Do you always talk like this?"

"No, ma'am," he said unhappily. "Only when I'm nervous. But it's a funny thing about the McNultys—if they're not trying to fight you, they're trying to make you laugh. And sometimes there's just about as much sense either way."

Mady laughed again. After all, he had done nothing to her—and he had apologized. She held out her hand.

"That's settled, then. You can come and tell me when the dishes have been washed."

He took her hand awkwardly. "Yes, ma'am. Uh ... do you want to throw them all—or just the plates?"

"We'll see. And will you do me a favor?"

"Yes, ma'am!"

"Please don't call me ma'am. It makes me feel a hundred years old."

"A hundred years old!" he grinned. "Why, ma'am, you ain't hardly reached the kissing age. I mean, Miss Lamont."

"I'd rather be called Mady, if you don't mind. It's Madeleine, really—but no one ever calls me that."

"Yes, ma'am ... Mady. I'm Bass. Nobody hardly calls me Bascom unless they're spoiling for a fight. Pop's the same way about Aloysius. Mostly they call him Muff. No sense to it and I guess it's just a waste of time trying to figure it out."

"Well ..." She suppressed a giggle. "Yes, I imagine it would be. Now don't forget to tell me when you have the dishes ready, Bass."

He stood watching her as she turned and walked up the beach away from him. Then he grinned a little to himself, stooped for a flat stone and sent it skipping over the calm blue water.

Tuck was waiting just inside the door when Mady returned to the cottage.

"How did it go?" he asked quickly.

"Wonderful." This time she did giggle. "He invited me over to his house to break some dishes."

"He what?"

"To break some dishes. It was just his way of making the apology more binding, I imagine."

"He sounds nuts."

"He did have an odd way of talking," Mady agreed. "But I don't think he's nuts. I think he was just nervous. He said he was nervous. He's nice."

"What do you mean, nice?" asked Tuck jealously.

"Oh, don't be like that, Tuck," she said but secretly she was pleased he felt that way. "He was just nice and shy and ... funny."

"Well, don't let him get too funny." He lightened his tone. "You're my girl, see? You're posted, no trespassing." And as he spoke, he made up his mind that that was just the way it would be and grimly, he knew that sooner or later he was going to have to do something about Ida.

He glanced at his wristwatch and said, "Damn." He had to meet Leo at the airport. The phone call had come through to Ida's suite early that morning. Tuck didn't want to leave Mady now but he did not dare to stay.

"I've got to run, honey," he said, giving her a last kiss. "I'll see you later this afternoon."

She noted how reluctant he was to leave and after he had gone, she danced happily around the room.

### PROPOSAL
## CHAPTER FIVE

Leo's plane was late. The sky had cleared, the wind had died down and the sun was shining brightly. It was hot now and Tuck was sweating profusely in his jacket but he could not take it off because of the gun he was wearing. And he had to wear the gun or Leo would be sore. There was no reason for a gun down here in Sanibar but Leo didn't believe in taking chances. Tuck stood in the shadows at the mouth of the hangar and smoked a cigar. He heard the drumming of propellers and walked outside to squint up at the northern sky. The small chartered plane circled the field, then glided down to the runway from the south. Tuck took his cigar from his mouth and walked out to meet it.

The plane passed him, ran down to the end of the strip, then taxied slowly back. Tuck waited until the pilot had unlocked the door from the inside, then sprang lightly up onto the wing and made a great show of opening the door.

"Hello, Leo," he cried. "You're looking great! Have a nice trip down?"

Leo ignored him. He twisted around in his seat and picked up a wire-mesh box on the floor behind him. Inside the box was a tiny chihuahua, shivering visibly in spite of the thick woolen sweater it wore.

"Send the rest of the stuff to the hotel," he grunted to the pilot.

Tuck jumped down from the wing as Leo squeezed through the narrow door. He held out the mesh box without a word and Tuck took it from him. Leo looked warily at the distance from wing to ground, then sat on the wing and slid off, slapping the seat of his pants after he alighted.

"Where's the car?" he demanded.

"Over there, Leo. Over there by the hangar. They wouldn't let me bring it out here."

Leo grunted and walked toward the hangar without giving Tuck another glance. He was a short squatty man with heavy eyes and a thick, rather shapeless mouth. His hair was darker than Ida's but his eyes were the same amazingly clear blue. There was absolutely no warmth in his eyes at all.

He was wearing a heavy weight navy suit with a double-breasted jacket and he would continue to wear it no matter how hot the weather, just as he would continue to wear his broad-toed black shoes, starched white collar and readymade bowtie that clipped into it.

He grunted a little as he slid into the front seat of Tuck's Cadillac convertible. It wasn't until they had begun to move that he finally spoke.

"Hiya, fella," he said, finally glancing at Tuck.

"It's nice seeing you again, Leo."

"How they treating you?"

"So far, so good."

"How's Ida?"

"You know Ida."

Leo's heavy face softened. "She's a one, ain't she?" he said fondly. "The world could come to an end and she wouldn't get out of bed to meet St. Pete himself. Brought down her mutt for her," he tipped his chin at the chihuahua in the mesh box that Tuck had placed carefully on the rear seat. He chuckled. "Lucky for me I remembered. She's a holy terror. You and Ida still hitting it off okay?"

"Well sure, Leo." Tuck could not suppress a guilty start. "But she's a holy terror, just as you say."

"She sure is. But you're a lucky guy all the same. There ain't many babes got what Ida's got. When're you two gonna get married?"

Tuck said shortly, "You know Ida."

"Yeah, yeah—but she's getting old enough to forget all this fediddling around. It's time she starts thinking about settling down. I'm gonna have a talk with her. What she needs is kids instead of that damn mutt she's always mushing it up with." He jerked his thumb contemptuously at the chihuahua. "What she wants is kids. I'm gonna have a talk with her." He turned his cold blue eyes on Tuck. "Okay?"

"Okay with me."

"That all you got to say?"

"That's all."

Leo's face purpled and he said angrily, "What the hell's the matter with you? Too good to marry my sister? If you been just fooling around with her, goddamn it, I'm telling you ..."

Tuck interrupted savagely. "All I said was—you know Ida. And that's what I mean. You talk to her about getting married. Go ahead. If she doesn't laugh at you, she'll spit in your face."

Leo's eyes clouded. "Don't needle me, fella," he said.

"I'm not needling you. It's just that I know Ida."

He met Leo's glowering stare and finally Leo grunted. He wasn't backing down. He was just acknowledging that Tuck had a point—Ida was a handful. After that, Leo said no more until they reached the hotel. Then all he said was, "Don't forget the mutt."

Ida had obviously been watching for them. When they stepped out of the elevator, she came flying down the hall, her fluffy negligee streaming behind her, her rounded nylon clad legs visible to the stocking tops. She hurled herself into Leo's arms shrieking, "Poodles!"

He thrust her away and said angrily, "Whattaya mean running around the halls naked?"

"Nakit!" She pretended to start to throw off her negligee. "I'll show you nakit!"

Leo grabbed her arm and rushed her back to her suite muttering, "Goddamnit, ain't you got no shame?"

This might have developed, Tuck knew, into a first class knockdown family row but just then Ida happened to catch sight of the chihuahua.

"Tootie!" she squealed. "You brung Tootie!"

She snatched the box from Tuck and carried it inside to the sofa. She hauled out the shivering, reluctant little dog and rubbed it against her cheek, crooning, "Ida's little Tootie! Tootie miss Ida? Tootie give Ida nice big kissie …"

She nuzzled the dog. It turned its head away and yelped complainingly.

Leo yelled, "Cut it out or I'll throw that goddamn mutt out the window."

Ida spat back fiercely, "And I'll kick your teeth out!"

"I want to ask you a question."

"So first you gotta throw Tootie out the window?"

Leo said uneasily, "I wanted you to cut it out for a minute, that's all. I want to talk to you."

"Nice way of talking."

"Okay, okay. Let's forget it. All I want to know is when you and Tuck here's getting married?"

"Married?" She looked from Leo to Tuck and gave one of those empty laughs that set Tuck's teeth on edge. "You're kidding."

"I'm not kidding. You're old enough to get married and have kids."

"Kids? Whatta I want kids faw? What's so much about kids?"

Leo yelled, "You get married to have kids, don't you? That's what's so much about kids. Or do you want to fool around with that goddamn mutt the rest of your life? Everybody has kids …" He stopped momentarily, took a deep breath, then continued slyly, "But it was the wedding I was thinking of mostly. Big. Down at the Saxony in Miami

Beach. Guy Lombardo—Perry Como singing 'Oh Promise Me'. Champagne, the works. You all dressed up in a wedding dress with lace and orchids. The real McCoy, Blondie."

Ida's mouth hung ajar. A wedding. A great big wedding with a lace gown and a train twenty feet long. Slowly, heavily she turned and fixed Tuck with a hostile glare.

"He ain't even ast me," she snarled.

"She means today," said Tuck, furious that he had allowed himself to be sucked into this.

"Go ahead and ask her then," snapped Leo.

Tuck looked at Ida. "Okay?" he said. "Pretend I'm on my knees."

Leo's face darkened. "Cut the comics, jerk."

"Let'm alone, you big slob," said Ida. "Who's he asting, me or you? Now ast me again, TuckyWucky—and if he doan like it, who cares? Go ahead, ast me again."

"Will you be my ever-loving wife?" Tuck said with a straight face.

"There!" said Ida triumphantly to Leo. "And look, I want an engagement party this Saddy, so for cri-sake get some stooges to throw me a shower."

Leo nodded. "Okay. Now beat it. Me and your boy friend's got business."

Ida obediently swung herself from the sofa with another careless display of creamy thigh. She never argued with Leo when it came to business. She pursed up her lips at Tuck in a pouting kiss, then went humming into her bedroom.

## ONE OF THE FAMILY
### CHAPTER SIX

Leo walked over to Tuck and gave him a shove that sent him sprawling into the sofa.

"I ought to smack you right straight in the puss," he said. "What was the idea of horsing around like that? A girl like Ida don't get married every day. I'm beginning to think you're a jerk."

Tuck snapped back, "Ida and I fool around like that all the time. That's the way she likes it." He was sure of himself—in this, at least.

"Well, I didn't like it."

"And if you'd been doing the proposing, she'd have turned you down."

"I don't know about that—but I'm telling you—watch your step. Okay. That's that. Now what about Menagh? How does it stack up?"

Tuck told him crisply that they had Menagh pinned down in this area and had everything covered. He mentioned Mady.

"What's the dame for?" Leo asked.

"The guy's a chaser and he goes for brunettes."

"Where'd you get her from? I don't want to be crossed by a dame."

"She's Lamont's kid."

"Okay, okay. Now how many guys you got here in town?"

"Eight."

"Get rid of them."

"Get—what?"

Leo's eyes fastened on Tuck's face. "I said, get rid of them. For cri-sake, stop being a mutt, will you? Get rid of them. Use your head."

"I was using them to cover the town ..."

"Get rid of them! Look, you got a lot to learn, fella. And now that you're practically a member of the family, I'll take the trouble to teach you. But when I say something, don't argue with me."

"You're the boss, Leo."

"Okay. Now I'll tell you why I want you to get rid of the guys, though you should've figured it out for yourself. Menagh's holed up around here, right? What does he eat? Grasshoppers? Daisies? He's gotta eat like everybody else. That means he's got friends."

"But we checked and double-checked, Leo. There wasn't a soul. He pulled it all by himself. If there had been anybody else, we'd have known by this time. He pulled it solo."

Leo's face reddened and he shouted, "Will you shut your goddamn face and listen? Stop arguing, will you? I'm trying to tell you something. Anybody, any place, that's got a hideout's gotta have friends or he's up the creek. Okay, Menagh pulled it solo—but if he's holed up, he's got somebody that's hiding him out and somebody that's feeding him. Now you understand? Furthermore, these friends are local. They gotta be. So you got eight guys around town and maybe you think they look like the rest of the tourists. Maybe to tourists they look like other tourists—but these local yokels ain't as dumb as you think they are and if you ask me, they got every one of your eight guys spotted. And if they got them spotted, Menagh knows about them and if he knows about them, he ain't never going to come out of his hole. So we got to get rid of the guys. Now do you get it?"

Tuck nodded. "I'll go you one better," he said. "Before they go, I'll have them ask a few questions about Sarasota and Ft. Myers, as if that's their next stop."

"It won't hurt but don't overdo it. The main thing is to get rid of them. Now—you have any idea where he's holed up?"

"Not in town. The tourists had every empty room filled by Christmas. He's either in the fishing village or in the bush. If he's got friends, they're local crackers and you know how far we get with crackers. They wouldn't tell us left from right."

"How's about putting out a little dough?"

"They'd take the dough, call me Mr. Rossiter to my face and a damnyankee behind my back. But I'm covering that angle. I got Lamont's kid working on that. She's got an in."

Leo grunted and reached for his glass. He took a small sip and put the glass back on the cocktail table.

"We gotta clean this up," he said. "It's been hanging too long."

Tuck was silent. To say anything now would be to invite abuse.

"Too long," Leo repeated. He turned his cold blue stare on Tuck. "You have any idea how much I got tied up in this?"

Tuck didn't know if he was supposed to guess or not. You never knew about something like this, with Leo. He always let you know where you stood but it wasn't always smart to let him know how much, or how little, you knew.

Tuck hesitated, then said, "Sixty, seventy thousand?"

There was no expression in Leo's eyes nor on his face but when he said, "I got two hundred grand tied up in it," he made Tuck feel like a small-time chump.

"Now that's not all clear. I've had expenses," Leo went on. "I'm telling you this because you're in the family and you gotta learn to think big. After everything's taken off the top, we'll have about a hundred and twenty."

Tuck said, "Whew!" and meant it.

Leo gave him a hard smile. "From now on, I'm cutting you in. Maybe ten, twenty percent. I'll talk it over with Ida. Now get out of here and tell your guys to take a powder."

Tuck walked out, a little dazed.

## REPAYING A VISIT
### CHAPTER SEVEN

Less than an hour after Tuck left, Bass McNulty knocked at Mady's door again. Bass had combed his hair and put on a clean striped T-shirt.

"Mady, ma'am," he said solemnly, "the benevolent and protective order of McNultys have got themselves set and braced in anticipation of your visit. Taking it for granted, of course, that your throwing arm's in good shape."

"The best!" Mady said with a laugh. "But you'll have to wait a moment until I get out of this apron. I've been housecleaning." She disappeared inside and when she came out again Bass' eyes opened wide. She was wearing a white sharkskin tie-on bra and white sharkskin shorts with a navy blue stripe down each side. Her beautifully rounded legs glowed.

"What's the matter?" she asked.

"Ma'am," he stammered shyly, "the barber ought to have you on his calendar instead of that ugly, hump-back, cross-eyed old female he's got. Leastways, that's the way she seems, seeing you."

"Now behave yourself, Bass."

"Yes, ma'am. That's what I keep telling myself. Shall we start walking, ma'am, or would you rather run?"

"We'll walk—and you'll behave yourself."

Mady felt curiously lighthearted as she walked along the hard white sand with Bass. When they reached the village, which rimmed the bank of Dogbody Bay in a quarter circle, he took her to the dock and pointed to a squat, sturdy boat moored to a buoy.

"That's the boat I'm saving to buy," he said. "The *Zoe* out there. She's a shrimper and I aim to do my own shrimping off Key West and maybe crawfishing down the Bahamas."

"That sounds wonderful! I've never been to the Bahamas. Have you?"

"I been once or twice but it wasn't so wonderful. I shipped as mate on yachts and I didn't get to see much of the Bahamas. At sea I had to take the wheel and in port I was a kind of watchman, cook and messboy. I didn't get to do much sightseeing."

"That was mean!"

"No it wasn't. It's what I was being paid for and I didn't care much for the company anyway. They didn't see much of the Bahamas, being goggle-headed most of the time. I never seen so many goggle-headed people in all my life. They seemed to be having a race to see who could drink the most liquor, get the drunkest and fall down the fastest. There won't be none of that on the *Zoe*. We'll work and enjoy ourselves. Five thousand down," he added.

Mady said, "What?"

"The *Zoe*. I can have her for five thousand down. That's why I'm working up Sanibar 'stead of being out in the boat with Pa. I can make money faster. She's a beauty, ain't she?"

"Well ... yes," said Mady doubtfully, as she regarded the broad, homely lines of the *Zoe*.

"You don't mean that, ma'am, and I don't mean it that way neither. I mean, she shure looks as if you could do a job of work with her. She's real steady and good-natured, like a fat lady. Between the money Mom's got saved and the money Pa'll make with the mullet and the money I'll make down Sanibar, I figure we can take her over by early summer. The feller said he'll wait. Anyways, nobody else wants her."

Mady found herself unaccountably impressed by his earnestness and the obvious affection with which he looked at the boat.

"I hope you're very successful with it, Bass," she said sincerely.

"I sure hope so too, because it'll be an awful mess after I've talked Mom out of her sockful. I think we better get up to the house. Mom's been peeking out of the window for the last ten minutes and she'll be getting herself into a state."

The house was a neat white cottage, the rear porch of which was built on pilings over the bay. Mady's heart beat a little faster as Bass opened the front door, for she remembered the harsh Mrs. McNulty of the night before. But there was no sign of the older woman when they stepped over the threshold.

"Mom's in her bedroom," said Bass, noticing Mady's cautious glance. "She's so embarrassed she gets red all over every time she thinks of last night. I'll coax her out to say hello in a little while. There are the dishes, ma'am, and I've cleared a space over by the fireplace wall where you can throw 'em."

He pointed to a full set of china dishes stacked neatly on a table. Mady gasped. "Oh no, that was only a joke!"

"You don't aim to throw them at all, then?"

"I should say not."

"Mom'll sure be relieved to hear that. She near threw a fit when I told her what I promised about the dishes but Mom's only a McNulty by marriage. A real McNulty'd of helped you throw 'em."

"You shut your mouth, Bascom McNulty!" cried a voice from behind the closed bedroom door.

"Come on out, Mom. Miss Lamont's here, only you got to call her Mady."

There was no sound of movement from the bedroom so Bass went over to open the door. The room looked empty at first glance. He peered in behind the door.

"She's hiding behind the door," he told Mady. "You wouldn't hardly think a woman as heavy-built as Mom could crowd in behind there, would you? Come on out, Mom. You might just as well get it over with."

Mrs. McNulty pushed his hand away and came around the door. She was blushing furiously and she would not look directly at Mady.

"There's no fool like an old fool," she said in a scolding voice to the stack of dishes. "And you're a fool if you accept the apology of a McNulty. They talk your ear off and before you know what's going on, you're married to one and you live to regret it the rest of your life."

"Now that was a real handsome apology, Mom," said Bass solemnly.

"I'm surprised Mady don't ask you up to her house tonight to do it all over again, just to have another apology like that."

Mady said quickly, "You shush, Bass. And, Mrs. McNulty, I wish you'd forget all about last night. I really do."

This was certainly not the shrill, hysterical Mrs. McNulty of the night before, Mady remarked to herself. This was a motherly, kind-faced, terribly embarrassed woman.

"If you ask me," Mady went on, "it was all the fault of that Clyde."

Bass clenched his fists and said, "That Clyde, he's a troublemaker. He's always talking somebody into something just so's he can stand back and watch the fun. I went down to see him this morning but from the look of all them bandages and the way he couldn't get out of bed, it looked like somebody beat me to it. I'll just have to wait a couple weeks, I guess."

"You stay away from Clyde, you hear me?" his mother cried in alarm. "He's too big for you—and he's been taught his lesson."

"If he's too big for me, I'll bring Pa. And if he's too big for Pa and me, I'll get some of the red-neck McNultys from Cypress City. Clyde ain't learned no lesson till he learns it the McNulty way." He grinned at Mady. "This is just talk, ma'am. Actually, I walk mighty soft when Clyde's around."

Instantly Mady knew he was not at all afraid of Clyde and that he'd fight Clyde even if he knew in advance he'd be beaten.

"I wish everybody would forget about last night!" she cried. "It's all over now and there's no sense going on about it."

"You're a good girl," Mrs. McNulty said warmly. "And I'm an old fool, even if it is the fault of the McNultys. Bass, if you're going uptown for those groceries for that feller, why don't you drive Miss Lamont along and I'll have a bite to eat when you get back."

"The feller got his own groceries," said Bass quickly. "His wife and three children and grandmother came down this morning on the train. He's figuring on taking his poor old crippled father down to Bonita Springs for the mineral waters."

He overdid it just a little and Mady looked up in time to catch the warning glance he threw at his mother. She caught her breath. So Tuck had been right. These people did know where Menagh was. Her heart began to beat rapidly.

"I ... I think I had better be going now," she said.

"I'll go with you," said Bass promptly.

"Please, no, I'd rather walk alone. I like walking alone. I mean, I do a lot of walking by myself and I like it sometimes."

"I was hoping you'd stay to dinner," Mrs. McNulty said.

She was so plainly disappointed that Mady said, "I will, another time, if you'll ask me again."

Mrs. McNulty smiled. "Any time at all, Miss Lamont, if you don't mind pot luck. Or McNultys in quantity," she added. "There might be just the three of us or there might be thirty. Sometimes McNultys come in schools, like mackerel."

Bass insisted on walking Mady back at least part of the way and as they strolled he asked her if she would like to see a movie with him that night.

"It's Bob Hope," he said. "Of course, it'd take a whole nunnery of Bob Hopes to be as much fun as one McNulty but he's in Technicolor."

"I'm sorry but I can't, Bass."

"Tomorrow then?"

"Honestly, I can't, Bass. I'm busy every night."

He said, "Well, sure," in a flattened voice.

She saw the chance. "I didn't mean that I'm too busy for you, Bass," she said. "It's that I'm doing something for my father."

His face lifted. "You work?"

"In a way, yes."

"What kind of work does your father do?"

"He's in the import-export business but this is something different." She watched him carefully. "I'm looking for a man, a certain man."

He made no comment. He just looked interested and waited for her to go on.

"This man," she said, "stole something from my father and I'm trying to find him. My father won't put him in jail if he gives back ... what he stole but it's very important to my father to get it back."

Bass' face still seemed interested but otherwise blank. Mady knew he was waiting for her to say more but she felt she had said enough, at least until she could talk with Tuck. Tuck was smart about things like that. Tuck would tell her exactly what to do and say. She did not want to make a mistake.

She stopped then and held out her hand to him. "I'll see you soon again, won't I?"

"Yes, ma'am," he said. "You sure will."

After ten paces, she looked back over her shoulder and saw that he was walking more slowly and thoughtfully than usual.

## ONE KISS TOO MANY
### CHAPTER EIGHT

Tuck was waiting at the cottage. Now that his status had changed with Leo, he had made up his mind to get rid of Mady, for he knew that sooner or later Leo would get wise to the situation. Leo was no dummy. Tuck knew he might fool Ida but he couldn't fool Leo.

When Mady walked in, Tuck was lying on the sofa, a glass of bourbon in his hand. He looked at her and there it was again, that impact and dizziness and leaping attraction to her—and he knew he'd have to get rid of her fast or there'd be a real mess.

"Where the hell have you been?" he growled at her. "I've been waiting over an hour. What's the idea?"

Mady was too excited to notice his tone. She flew across to him and sat down at the edge of the sofa.

"Tuck ..." she said quickly, "I found out something!"

"Oh for Christ's sake," he said.

"No, honestly, Tuck. I did! The McNultys know where Joe Menagh is hiding!"

"They what?"

"I think they do. This is what happened. Mrs. McNulty told Bass to go uptown and get groceries for 'that feller' and right away he started talking fast, about grandmothers and sick fathers and Bonita Springs and I could tell he was making it up. Then I saw him look at his mother as if to tell her to keep quiet. And she shut up right away."

He scowled and rubbed his chin. "It's not very much, of course ..."

"Well, one thing more," Mady said hesitantly. "He tried to make a date for tonight and when I told him I was busy, he tried to make it for tomorrow night. Anyway, I'm sure he likes me. You can tell."

"Yeah, yeah." He drank what was in his glass and thoughtfully reached for the bottle again. His face showed no unusual interest.

Mady said earnestly, "If you could have been there, Tuck, and heard the way he talked and saw the way he acted, you'd know he was trying to conceal something."

Tuck was thinking furiously. This changed everything. Mady had a lead, a real lead. He knew that. It rang true. It was right in line with everything Leo had said about Menagh's having local friends. So there it was, a real lead on Menagh.

But what the hell was he going to do about Mady? It was dangerous keeping her around, now that Leo was here and the wedding had been arranged. He had come to get rid of her—but hell, she was the only link between him and the McNultys.

He turned and faced her. "You say this guy wanted to take you out tonight?"

"Yes, but I told him ..."

"Never mind what you told him. You're going. I want you to play up to him. Make him feel like a big shot. Make him think you're nuts about him, too—but play hard to get. Don't let him get you in a clinch right away."

Mady blushed, then cried angrily, "That's going too far!"

Tuck got up, walked across the room and sat down beside her. He took one of her hands in his and smiled at her.

"Don't get me wrong, honey," he said persuasively. "I don't mean that I want you to let this guy take any liberties. I just want you to get him where when you say, 'Roll over,' he'll roll over. He'll be a pushover for you, honey, and you'll hardly have to lift a finger. All you'll have to do is look at him."

She looked steadily into his eyes and he saw the doubt in her face.

"How else would you go about it?" he asked.

"We could follow him when he takes the groceries to Menagh."

"That's okay if Menagh is holed up in the village. But suppose Menagh's hiding out in the bush somewhere, up the river or around one of those bayous or in the swamp ... See what I mean?"

She nodded.

"That's the girl. So all you have to do is get on the good side of this yokel and we won't have to follow him. He'll take you to Menagh. Anyway, he didn't look like the kind of guy who'd throw a hammer-lock on you the first time he got you alone."

"I wasn't thinking of that. It's—well, just that he's a nice boy and I don't want to be unfair to him."

"You falling for the guy?" asked Tuck.

"Of course not. Oh, I'll do it, Tuck. I'm just being silly."

"I don't want you to do anything you don't want to do, honey. If this is going to make you unhappy, we'll figure out another way. You know all I want is for you to be happy, honey."

"I was just being silly, darling. I'm sorry."

"Don't worry about it." He stood up to leave. "Go out with him tonight. Don't try to pump him. It's just a night out, understand? I'll see you in the morning."

"Aren't you even going to kiss me, Tuck?"

That was just what he didn't want to do but he grinned and said, "I didn't want to take advantage of a girl."

Afterward he felt shaken and his mind was in a turmoil. It had been one kiss too many and he knew it.

## THE LIE
### CHAPTER NINE

He stopped at the bar and had a few drinks, then went up to Ida's suite where he found Leo. Leo had a room of his own on another floor but he spent a lot of time in the suite because he liked being near Ida. Tuck couldn't understand how a man as smart as Leo could listen to her moronic chatter for hours at a stretch, enjoying every minute of it. Tuck himself had to get drunk to be able to stand her at all.

Ida was out and Leo was sitting reading the *Miami Herald* when Tuck came in.

"Sit down, fella," Leo said. "I want to talk to you." He threw the newspaper to the floor.

Tuck sat down opposite him and reached for the Scotch on the cocktail table.

Leo said, "Leave that stuff alone for a minute," but he didn't sound as offensive as he usually did. "I've been talking to Ida." He gave Tuck what was almost a genial look. "Seems I got you all wrong, fella, and I'm a guy when I'm wrong, I say so. She says you're aces and if you quit horsing around and making her laugh, she'd give you your walking papers. So if that's what she wants, it's okay with me. Hell, she's the one you're marrying, not me."

Like hell, thought Tuck.

"Go ahead, have a drink," said Leo. "I just didn't want you to be shooting the stuff into your snoot while I was having my say. Go ahead. Ida says you can handle it."

Tuck said, "Thanks, Leo." With sudden shattering clarity, he could see what his life was going to be with Ida. He was going to be more of a lapdog than that shivering little chihuahua. And if he didn't do everything Ida wanted, exactly the way she wanted it, she'd take it to Leo and Leo would crack the whip.

"Like I said," Leo went on, "me and Ida had a little talk. I told her I was cutting you in for ten percent. Right away she wanted thirty. Don't ever argue with her, fella. She's a holy terror. I didn't get no place. We settled for twenty. How's that?"

"My God, that's swell, Leo!" Tuck felt dizzy. Twenty percent of a hundred and twenty grand-was twenty-four thousand dollars!

Leo waved his hand, dismissing the gratitude. "You're in the family now, fella. You're not just one of the hired hands. And you got Ida to thank for it. She's a great little chiseler. So that's the way it is. You're in for twenty percent. Of course, Ida'll handle the dough. I'll turn it over to her ..."

Tuck felt as if he had been slapped with an icy towel. Leo glared at him.

"What's the matter with you now?" he demanded. "You think she's too dumb to handle the dough for you?"

"No, no, Leo. Nothing like that." Tuck managed a laugh. "Hell, she chiseled twenty percent out of you, didn't she?"

"That's a fact," said Leo with pride. "You're a lucky guy, and I hope you know it."

"You don't have to tell me how lucky I am."

Tuck could just see Ida with twenty-four thousand dollars. What a spree! She'd fill the place with monstrosities like that damn cocktail table and clothes and expensive junk jewelry and God knows what else. She'd spend herself blind. She had no more sense about money than a jackass. Or a moron—which she was.

"Of course," said Leo, "you'll go right on drawing your hundred bucks a week. She talked me into that, too—but that's chicken feed. Now how'd you make out in town? Everything all set?"

Tuck said mechanically, "All set."

"You get those eight goons out of town?"

"Yes."

"Okay, then. You're on the town tonight. I don't think there's much chance of Menagh turning up so quick but we can't take the chance. I gotta stick close here, so it's up to you. I got a feeling we're moving in. Don't boot it." Leo waved his hand in dismissal. Then he reached to the floor for his newspaper and began to read.

Tuck walked out stiffly, grinding his teeth in frustration and rage.

As he came into his room he switched on the light and started for the shower, unbuttoning his shirt as he walked. He threw his jacket on a chair and missed. He was unbuckling his shoulder harness when a voice behind him said, "Hello, Tuck."

He whirled with the gun in his hand. He relaxed. It was Eric Lamont, Mady's father.

"Someday," snarled Tuck, "you're going to find yourself smeared all over the wallpaper, pulling a trick like that."

Lamont said, "I've come for Mady. I'm pulling out." His weak, handsome face was pale and his right hand was sunk into his jacket pocket. He was obviously clutching a gun.

Tuck pursed his lips in a soundless whistle and tossed his own gun on the bed. He had no intention of trying to shoot it out with a desperate man.

"If you want to pull out," he said, "that's your business. But Leo won't like it."

"I don't care. I don't want Mady mixed up in this anymore. I'm taking her away."

Tuck was careful to hide the rage that spurted up within him. He nodded. "Maybe you got the right idea at that. Maybe I'll be pulling out one of these days myself. We're all riding for a fall, horsing around with Uncle Whiskers."

Lamont did not relax. His forehead was covered with a fine sheen of perspiration. "Where is Mady?" he demanded.

"She's got a cottage down the beach road."

"Take me there. Now."

"Sure." Tuck walked over to his bureau and opened the top drawer. In the mirror, he saw Lamont tense and pull the gun from his pocket. "I'm just getting my wallet, Eric," said Tuck mildly.

"Make sure it's just the wallet. I know how tricky you can be."

Tuck smiled slyly and took a wallet from the drawer. He held it up for Lamont to see, then looked inside as if checking the money. Inside was a driver's license made out to Juan Nuñez, Camaguey, Cuba. There were other papers belonging to Nuñez. Tuck slipped it into his pocket and said cheerfully, "Okay, let's go."

He walked out, leaving his gun lying on the bed where he had thrown it. Lamont walked behind and when they got to the car, he sat with his back to the door, facing Tuck. He held his gun in his lap. Tuck affected not to notice and hummed softly to himself as he backed the car out into the road.

"Have to get some gas. Okay?" Tuck asked, tilting his chin at the gas gauge. It registered empty.

Lamont nodded. He sat stiffly, his eyes darting everywhere, as they drove into town and stopped at the gas station. He was wound so tightly now that he would have cried out had anyone touched him unexpectedly. As they sped back through town, they passed the movie house but they were going so fast that neither of them saw Mady and Bass standing on line at the box-office. Mady's cry of, "Dad! Dad!" was lost in a rush of wind. It was a short run and within a few minutes they drifted to a stop before Mady's cottage.

Tuck's mouth went dry when he saw the light from Mady's living room. He had expected her to be out with Bass. He glanced quickly at Lamont, then clenched his teeth, for Lamont had stepped out of the car and was still holding the gun on him. Tuck slowly opened his own door and slid out from under the wheel. There was nothing else he could do but his mind was racing. He couldn't let Lamont talk to Mady! Lamont backed away.

"You first," he said harshly, jerking his gun toward the path.

"Why not?"

With pretended unconcern, Tuck walked around to the beach side of the cottage. Lamont followed six feet behind. Heavily, Tuck mounted the steps and knocked at the front door. Then slowly the murderous tension went out of him and he expelled the painful breath from his lungs. She wasn't home. She always answered immediately. He knocked again, then turned to Lamont.

"She's probably out for a swim," he said. "But she's never away very long. We can go in and wait."

He opened the door and walked in. Lamont stood tensely and swept the room with his eyes. Then he saw his own picture on the gateleg table near the window. His expression seemed to relax.

Tuck grinned. "This is her place all right, Eric. I didn't lead you up an alley. You can relax."

"You can't blame me, Tuck ..."

"Sure. Forget it. I'm practically washed up with Leo myself. How's about a drink?"

"I could sure use one," said Lamont.

Tuck went into the kitchen for the bottle and glasses.

"How long do you think she'll be, Tuck?" Lamont called.

"Oh, I don't know. Fifteen minutes maybe. I was supposed to pick her up at eight." Tuck came in from the kitchen with the bottle and glasses. He filled both glasses and handed one to Lamont. He raised his glass. "To hell with Leo, eh, Eric?"

Lamont smiled faintly. "To hell with Leo." He raised his own glass and threw back his head, drinking.

Tuck's hand struck out like a whip, chopping Lamont across the side of the taut neck. Lamont's eyes turned glassy and he lost his balance. Tuck stepped to one side and, with a full-arm swing, clubbed him behind the neck with tremendous force. Lamont went down headlong and lay still. Tuck bent over him slowly, lifting him a little. Lamont's head lolled at an impossible angle. His neck was broken.

Tuck quickly picked up the two whisky glasses and placed them on a table. He hoisted Lamont, threw him over his shoulder, and walked out of the house. He tossed the body into the back of the Cadillac and covered it with a plaid car robe. As he leaped into the front seat, he saw the headlights of a car approaching from Sanibar. He shot from under the poinciana tree and roared down the road. He did not turn on his own lights until he reached the fishing village. Then he turned left into the road that skirted the eastern side of Dogbody Bay. At the far end of the Bay was the bridge over the pass to Pelican Key. Here Tuck pulled over to the side of the road and stopped. He slipped into the back of the car and quickly went through Lamont's pockets, removing everything that could possibly establish his identity. Then he slipped the Nuñez wallet into Lamont's hip pocket.

There was no sound but the dry rustle of the cabbage palms and the shrilling of frogs. He lifted Lamont in his arms and carried him out to the middle of the bridge. He stopped at the rail for a moment, then toppled Lamont's body over into the swift, dark water of the Pass. He listened for the heavy splash, then hurried back to the car and in another moment was racing down the road to his hotel.

Mady stood in the center of her living room and cried excitedly, "At least they've been here. They had a drink. Look—they even spilled some on the rug. I knew I recognized Dad in Tuck's car!"

"If I could've got my car started right away, we wouldn'ta missed them," said Bass apologetically.

"Don't be silly. Tuck knew I was going to the movies with you tonight, so he probably took Dad back to the hotel."

"Is that your father?" asked Bass, motioning toward the photograph on the table. "He's a real good-looking feller."

"Dad's wonderful. I'm crazy about him. Everybody is. Let's go back to the hotel right away, Bass. Gosh, I'm so excited I can't stand still!"

"The thing to do then, ma'am," said Bass gravely, "is to keep moving."

Mady danced out to the car holding his arm and laughing happily. Bass' car was an ancient Buick that coughed and wheezed and puffed and finally achieved a top speed of thirty miles an hour. When Mady spied Tuck's Cadillac parked outside the hotel, she cried, "They're here! They're here!" and, taking Bass' hand, she ran toward the side entrance.

Tuck, standing at the bar, saw them come in. When he saw the eager expectancy on Mady's face, he knew she had somehow spied her father in his car. He suddenly felt as if he were standing with his back to a wall with eight men pointing rifles at him. He turned and waved to her.

"Hiya," he called. "Where've you been? Your father's looking for you. He just went down to the cottage. I thought you were there."

Her jaw dropped. "But ... isn't he with you?"

"No. He went down to the cottage. He blew into town with Johnny Nuñez on his way to Miami. He just had a couple of minutes and wanted to say hello to you. I sent him down to the cottage."

"We ... we just came from the cottage. But Tuck, I saw him with you in your car when you passed the movies ..."

"Not with me. With Johnny Nuñez."

"But I saw you, Tuck!"

Tuck lifted his eyebrows. "How long ago was that, Mady?"

"Almost an hour ..."

Tuck shook his head. "Not me, Mady—I've been right here for an hour and a half or more."

Mady looked at Tuck's bland face. She knew he was lying. She might have been mistaken about seeing her father because she had caught only a quick glimpse of him but she could never mistake Tuck or the Caddy convertible.

Tuck said solemnly, "It must have been Johnny Nuñez you saw him with, Mady." He lifted his glass. "Can I buy you guys a drink, by the way?"

Mady silently shook her head and backed away. She couldn't understand why he would lie about a thing like this. He was suddenly a stranger to her. If he had said, "Oh, that wasn't your old man—it was just a guy I wanted you to meet," she would have believed him, for the glimpse of her father had been so brief. But he had admitted her father was in town.

"Come on," Tuck urged. "Let me buy you just one."

"No, thank you. I want to see if I can find Dad around."

"Sure. But he's probably on his way to Miami with Johnny Nuñez by this time. He only had a minute."

Mady turned her back and walked out, followed by Bass. Tuck's mouth snapped shut angrily.

Out in the car, Mady said quietly, "Would you mind driving me back to the cottage, Bass?"

"Whatever you say, Mady."

She sat staring straight ahead all the way back. She did not say a word but her feelings were betrayed by the intermittent clenching of her hands. Tuck had lied to her. She couldn't believe it. Something had gone numb in her and she couldn't think.

When they reached the cottage, she sprang out of the car and ran inside. Bass deliberated for a moment, then followed her in. He found her examining every piece of furniture, even the walls and floor of the living room. Then she went into the bedroom. She was in there for about ten minutes and when she came out she went directly into the kitchen. Bass stood uncomfortably near the front door. At length she came out of the kitchen and looked whitely at him.

"He didn't leave a note," she said. "He would have left a note—but he didn't. Even if he had to rush to Miami, he would have taken a minute to write me a note. He wouldn't have gone off that way. Not unless something's wrong."

"Maybe he's coming back, then. Maybe he just went some place for a drink with that Nuñez feller. Maybe that's what he did."

"He still would have left me a note. He was very thoughtful. He would have left me a note saying he'd be back."

She caught sight of the whisky bottle on the table and her eyes flew to the spot on the rug where the drinks had spilled. She walked over and stared at it, then looked back at the bottle again.

"That was a brand new bottle," she said. "You can see only two drinks were poured from it and there's almost that much whisky spilled on the rug here. And it is whisky that was spilled. I could smell it the minute I walked in." She bent over, rubbed her hand across the damp spot on the rug, then smelled her fingers. "They didn't drink. They just spilled it."

She walked over to the sofa and sat down, a numbed, bewildered expression on her face. Bass crossed and sat down beside her.

"What's the matter, Mady?" he asked. "I mean, you figure there's been some trouble, maybe?"

She wailed, "I don't know, I don't know, I don't know!" and burst into tears. She turned her head into his shoulder and clung to him as if he were the one safe thing in a suddenly hostile world.

He sat awkwardly for a few minutes while the hard sobs shook her. Then tentatively he put his arm around her and patted her.

"Maybe you're getting yourself in a tizzy over nothing at all now," he soothed her. "I've always found things that look so terrible in the beginning have a way of petering out to nothing at all in the end. It could be just like that Tuck feller said—your father was in such a hurry to get to Miami that he didn't think of nothing—not even a note. Folks in a hurry can get themselves terrible worked up ..."

His voice went on softly, soothingly and gradually her sobs subsided. She looked up at him then, blinking the last tears from her eyes, smiling tremulously.

In a sudden surge of gratitude, she suddenly lifted her lips and kissed him.

His mouth was hard and startled for a moment, then his arm tightened fiercely around her. She had meant it to be a small, quick kiss but his ardor swept her along with it and she clung to him. His lips were not thrusting and demanding as Tuck's always were, and the emotion was not hard and jolting but rather seemed to lift her, not drive her before it.

It was he who broke the kiss. He started to stammer but she quickly covered his mouth with her hand.

"Don't say you're sorry," she smiled. "Please don't say that."

He shook his head. "No, ma'am. I ain't. Only I shouldn't have taken advantage when you were all broken-up."

"I'm not broken-up. I'm not even worried anymore. I'm sure that there's a very simple explanation and I was just being hysterical. Only ..." Her eyes clouded for a moment. Only Tuck had lied.

On the heels of her thought, Bass said, "That Tuck feller. Is he, uh, in business with your father?"

"He works for my father," she said. Then she added, "He's no one of any importance, really ..."

At just about that time Tuck, who had been savagely cursing himself for his carelessness, finally paid the bartender and went out to the phone booth where he placed a call to the Malaluka Club in Miami. His connection completed, he asked for Chuffy.

"This is Chuffy. Who're you?"

"Tuck Rossiter. Hiya, Chuff."

"Hiya, keed. What gives?"

"Get a pencil and paper. I want you to send a telegram."

"Shoot."

"It's to Miss Mady Lamont, Beach Road, Sanibar, Florida. Darling, so sorry I missed you at the cottage stop in an awful rush stop will make it up with love and kisses, Dad. Got it, Chuff?"

"Got it. But what gives? Who's the dame? You wouldn't be two-timing Ida, would you, keed? Leo wouldn't like that."

"Hell no. This dame works for Leo and we got to schmooz her a little. Send that in about four hours, will you, Chuff?"

"On the nose. And speaking of noses, I hope yours is clean. It don't sound like it to me. Take care of yourself, keed."

Tuck hung up and came out of the booth sweating.

## SWAMP INTERLUDE
### CHAPTER TEN

It was a clear night and the moon was so brilliant that Bass' shadow was sharply silhouetted against the white shell road. He sprang lightly up to the platform of the fish house and walked through to the dock where his father's boat was moored. He turned to glance around him once, then dropped quietly into the boat. Carefully he slid a brown cardboard carton under the seat at the bow where it was most likely to stay dry. There were groceries in the box and two bottles of rum.

He untied the lines and pushed off into the water. He started the motor and let it run for a few minutes to warm up. Then he eased it into gear and moved slowly down the bay, skirting the groups of small mangrove islands, rounding a flashing buoy, pushing the rudder stick forward, turning east. The water broadened here and for another mile or so was like a wide, placid sheet. A string of lights ahead marked the Trail bridge. After he passed under it, the river became wider and the fields of palmetto on the banks began to give way to cypress and mangrove and sea grape. He was entering the swamp. Now there was no marked channel but he chugged along carefully, watching the banks closely now. The fishermen knew these waters—and a few hunting guides, too—but ordinary residents of the town, some of whom had lived on the fringe of the great swamp all their lives, would have been lost a quarter mile inside the watery wilderness. There were false channels everywhere, inviting openings between clumps of trees and towering walls of mangrove, openings leading nowhere but into another maze where the boat would go gently aground in ooze that waited only a few inches beneath the surface, or suddenly there would be a rasping tear and a hole would appear in the boat bottom over the upthrust arm of a concealed stump. It was an eerie place, a lush, lost desert.

As the boat chugged into the swampy jungle, it grew increasingly dark and the trees began to meet over the narrowing channel. Bass knew exactly where he was going and had his own markers to point out the way—a peculiarly shaped stump to the right, a gaunt, dead cypress, a bit of white rag tied to a jutting peninsula of mangrove. He stood in the boat, a cigarette drooping from the corner of his mouth, his hand on the rudder stick, narrowly watching for the landmarks. Even for him, who knew the swamp so well, it was a chancy business at night.

Finally he relaxed, bent over and cut the gas until the boat barely crept along. Just ahead on the right bank was a crude dock made of cabbage palm logs. Beyond it was a clearing, silver in the moonlight. Someone had once lived there for part of a fieldstone chimney remained, but of the house itself there was nothing left, and the creeping vines and palmetto and other lush foliage had long since covered everything.

Bass switched off the motor entirely and drifted to the side of the dock. He tied his bow line to an iron ring stapled into the palm log, then extracted the box from the boat and laid it on the dock. Then he sprang out to the dock, picked up the box and started across the bright clearing with it.

A voice called out sharply, "Hold it, Mac!"

Bass stopped. In another moment a tall lean man swaggered out of the shadows, making a big show of thrusting his revolver into the waistband of his pants.

"You ought to be more careful, Mac," he warned. "I might have plugged you. The next time you better give me the high-sign when you come up the river. You take awful chances, Mac."

Bass said, "Hi, Joe. Here's your groceries."

Joe took the box and looked eagerly into it. He took out a bottle of rum, uncorked it and drank deeply. His face was scarred in a hundred places, as if someone had flung a handful of broken glass at him. His eyes were narrow and his mouth was small and thin. His jaw was exceptionally long and pointed but he looked more dog than wolf. He was tall and wide-shouldered and his hands were big and bony, but there was something small about him, something furtive and finicky.

He took another drink from the bottle and patted his stomach, winking at Bass. "That's the stuff, Mac," he said. "That's the real McCoy."

Bass leaned against the trunk of a fallen water oak. "There's a couple things I've been wanting to ask you, Joe."

Joe held up his hand. "Take my word for it, Mac. There's some things you're better off not knowing." He drew his forefinger significantly across his throat. "Know what I mean?"

"Nope—but I sure aim to find out."

"Nix, Mac, nix. Be smart. You'll last longer. But I'll tell you this much—if you had as many guys after you as me, you'd shoot your biscuits. Now let's relax and forget it."

Bass shifted slightly, then asked, "Did you steal something now, Joe, or didn't you?"

Joe jumped. "Now wait a minute, Mac," he started.

Bass looked at him, then pushed himself away from the tree and walked steadily across the clearing toward his boat. Joe watched him for a few uneasy seconds. Then he yelled loudly, "Just where do you think you're going, Mac?"

"Home," said Bass without turning. "I'm going home and I ain't coming back. If you want to get fed or get out of here, you'll have to do it by yourself, 'cause I ain't having nothing more to do with it or you."

Joe jerked the gun out of his waistband and brandished it menacingly. "Just a minute, Mac, just a minute. Nobody walks out on Joe Menagh. You ain't going no place. Get your tail right back here."

Bass stepped down into the boat, bent over and started the motor. Joe stared in open-mouthed disbelief. Nobody disregarded a gun—yet there was Bass paying no more attention than if he had been waving his handkerchief. Joe galvanized into action. He galloped across the clearing and pushed Bass' hand away from the bow line he was trying to free.

"Wait a minute, Mac, wait a minute," Joe pleaded. "You can't go and leave me here. I'd never get out. I'd drown. I'd starve to death ..."

"And that's a fact," Bass agreed.

"Aw, come, Mac, what kind of way is that to do?"

"It's this kind of way—I'm just plain fed up with helping you and not knowing what it's all about."

"I was only not telling you for your own good, Mac," said Joe feebly.

"You was only not telling me because you like to go around making believe you're Humphrey Bogart. You and your revolver and all that talk about plugging folks and acting like you was in a moving picture. Why, you're so scared, if I said 'Scat!' you'd fall right down."

"Yeah? Well let me tell you, if they were after you, you'd have hair-trigger nerves, too."

"That's just a fancy way of saying scared, if you ask me."

Joe made a blustering attempt to retrieve his lost prestige. He waved his gun again.

"See this, Mac? Know what this is? It's the old difference, so watch your talk."

Bass slapped Joe's hand away and untied the line, kicking the motor into gear. The boat moved away from the dock. Joe cried out and took a step as if to leap into the water to swim after it but instead he drew back fearfully. He had seen the 'gators that swam in there. He ran along the dock as Bass turned downstream.

"Mac, Mac!" he cried piteously. "Don't leave me, Mac. I'll tell you, Mac. I'll tell you anything you want. Don't leave me. Please don't leave me. Come back, Mac, come back, come back!"

Bass yelled, "Shut up, darn you!" embarrassed at having caused such an abject exhibition. He turned the boat back to the dock.

With trembling fingers, Joe helped him tie up again.

"You're a white man, Mac," he said tearfully. "Honest to God, you're a white man ..."

Bass gave him a reassuring grin. "Aw," he said, "you made me so mad. Now sit yourself down and tell me about it without trying to make like Humphrey Bogart."

Menagh took a drink first, drinking deeply.

"Now did you steal anything or didn't you?" asked Bass.

"Mac," said Menagh weakly, "so help me God, I didn't. It was Guastella."

"Who's Guastella?"

"He was my boss down in Cuba. He's the guy that was killed when I crashed the kite. Every week I brought Guastella from Havana to Ft. Myers in the crate. Well, that last trip he pointed a gun at me—this gun," he touched the butt of the gun he had thrust back into his waistband, "and said, 'Keep going, Joe.' I said, 'I can't. I gotta sit her down in Ft. Myers. I ain't got the gas.' And it was the truth. But he screwed the gun into the back of my neck and said, 'Keep going!' I tried to tell him again but he smacked me over the head with the gun. The next thing I knew, we crashed. He was laying there all smashed up but I was just cut up, like you see." He gestured toward his face. "Well, I didn't need to look twice to see that Guastella was done for, so I lifted his wallet just in case I needed dough. Then I started walking and honest to God I'd have been walking yet if you hadn't turned up that day in your boat. That's the story, Mac." He avoided Bass' steady gaze. "That's all there's to it."

"Why are all them fellers after you then, if that's all?"

"Well," Joe squirmed, "uh ... Guastella took something that belonged to them."

"Belonged to a feller named Lamont, you mean."

"That could be, Mac. I never did find out who was Guastella's boss."

Bass looked at him. "Joe," he said, "you just ain't very bright, are you? Here you been shiverin' and shakin' in here, scared of your own shadow, and Mr. Lamont's been looking for you, willing to call it all square just so long's you give him back that stolen stuff. You just plain fretted yourself into a tizzy and me along with you. You're the kind of feller that runs down the street, wavin' his arms and yelling, 'The world's coming to an end!' every time it lightnin's. And you got yourself so all wrapped up in your scare that you can't tell up from down."

"Mac," said Menagh, completely deflated, "you never said a truer word. I'm a schmoe. There's no other name for it. But it's too late now."

"Too late for what?"

"They're walking the streets with guns, looking for me right this minute."

Bass made a disgusted noise. "They're not doing any such thing. Matter of fact, I was told to tell you that if you gave back what you ... what was stole, you got nothing to be afraid of."

Menagh grasped his arm. "Who told you that?" he cried in a panicky voice. "Who knows you've been seeing me? Who knows where I am? You got to watch yourself, Mac. You got to watch every step. They'll follow you and if they find me, they'll shoot me down like ... like Dillinger."

"Nobody ain't followin' nobody," said Bass calmly. "And I was told by Miss Lamont herself. So I'm telling you plain, Joe, you give Mr. Lamont his stuff back or I'm finished with you."

The ultimatum threw Menagh into an agony of fear. His eyes darted around the clearing, as if seeking a way of escape. But he had been here too many days now not to know that the swamp completely surrounded him. And he knew that to be lost in this wilderness meant slow, excruciating death—or fast, agonizing death in the jaws of a 'gator or the venom of a water moccasin.

"How do I know this Lamont's on the level?" he cried. "How do I know he won't gun me down the minute I give him the stuff? You can't cross guys like that, Mac. They never forget and they never forgive—and sooner or later, they put the boots to you!"

"You're making like Humphrey Bogart again," said Bass. "Anyway, you got the cat-boat I brung you and you can pole yourself across the river and look him over when I bring him in. If I give you the high sign, you'll know everything is all right and you can come out."

"Mac, I'm telling you," Joe blubbered, "I'm scared witless!"

"There's not an earthly thing to worry about," said Bass serenely.


## ESCAPE
### CHAPTER ELEVEN

It was a small item tucked away on page eight of the Ft. Myers paper. It said briefly that the shark-mauled body of Juan Nuñez had been found by two Ft. Myers commercial fishermen. It was believed that Nuñez, a native of Cuba, had fallen overboard from a Tampa-bound boat. Authorities were investigating. Bass felt a chill go through him as he read it. Johnny Nuñez was the name of the man Tuck had said was with Mady's father—though Mady somehow seemed to feel Tuck was lying about it.

"What's the matter?" asked his mother. "Don't your grits sit good?"

"They sit fine." Bass quickly folded the paper and put it aside.

"Then why're you sittin' there with that sick look on your face? Didn't you and that new gal hit it off so good last night?"

"We hit it off fine."

"Well, there's something the matter."

"Nothin's the matter, honest."

"Don't lie to me, Bascom McNulty. It's writ all over you."

"I was ... just thinkin' about Clyde, that's all. He ain't been out of the house since he was beat up. I got an idea he's planning some devilment. He's a kind of grudgeful feller."

"I don't see what you're worryin' for," said his mother reasonably. "You warn't the one beat him up. If he's bearin' a grudge for anybody, it'll be that big Tuck Rossiter."

"And maybe Miss Lamont."

"So that's where the cheese binds. You're kind of sweet on her, hey?"

"I guess maybe I am," Bass got up from the table, pushing back his chair. "Though I don't see how it can lead anywheres."

"On account of her being a damnyankee and you a Florida cracker?" his mother mocked.

"Now, Ma ..."

"I'm 'shamed of you, Bascom McNulty, I purely am."

"Now stop it, Ma. Anyways; she ain't no damnyankee. She comes from Tampa. It's just, well I think she's sweet on that Tuck Rossiter—and her Pa is all kinds of rich—and anyways I don't want to talk about it!"

He walked out before she could answer and started for the beach toward Mady's cottage. He glanced over his shoulder and saw his mother standing near the window with her mouth open, laughing at him. He grinned back at her and waved. He had just been talkin' to hear himself talk on account of that story about the Nuñez feller had hit him so sudden. Mady's father just couldn't be mixed up in a thing like that, if for no other reason than that he was Mady's Pa. If anybody was mixed up in it, it would be that uppity Tuck Rossiter.

Today the walk to Mady's cottage seemed interminable. He wasn't going to say anything to her about Johnny Nuñez but he was anxious to find out if she had heard from her father. He wanted to have a talk with her father before saying anything about Joe Menagh. Joe had acted awful funny and there was no doubt he was scared clean through. A feller like Joe wouldn't admit a thing like that unless he was really bone-scared.

There was more to this whole thing, Bass was sure, than even Mady knew.

He walked more slowly as he approached the cottage. He was worried. Joe Menagh had spoken of men with guns and he hadn't meant the law. Mady just couldn't be mixed up in a thing like that.

But the thing that really worried him was how she was going to feel toward him today, after he had kissed her as he had last night. She had kissed him back, had even acted as if she liked it, but that was all on account of that Tuck Rossiter and her father. She might be feeling different today.

Mady was sitting on the porch in a deck chair, repairing the hem of a dress, when he turned into the path from the beach. She raised her head and smiled and instantly his heart turned over and became light.

"Well, if it isn't the Mr. McNulty," she cried gaily. "And how are you today, Mr. McNulty?"

He hesitated on the top step, restraining an urge to cross and kiss her lifted, shining face. "You heard from your Pa," he said.

"Last night." She reached under her chair and held up the telegram.

"It was just as Tuck said. Dad had to rush straight through to Miami."

Bass said reluctantly, "Then that Rossiter feller ... was telling the truth."

The smile faded from Mady's face and she made no answer.

That was the one thing that spoiled her happiness. Tuck had lied. And it was such a silly, meaningless lie, too, she felt. A wanton, cruel lie, for he must have known how excited she was at the prospect of seeing her father. Eric was away so much, gave her so little of his time, that every moment with him was precious. Tuck could have delayed him for just a little while. Tuck knew she had a date with Bass. It almost seemed to her that Tuck had not wanted her to see her father. But the thing that hurt the most was his lying. Perhaps he had a reason, an explanation, but by no possible stretch of imagination could she imagine that he could have a reason.

Bass said, "Did your Pa say when he's coming back?"

She shook her head. "He never says. Sometimes he's gone for months and I hear from him in South America, or Chicago, or Canada." She laughed a little. "He's a grasshopper."

Bass squatted down on his heels beside her chair and stared thoughtfully across the white sand at the gently restless Gulf.

"But how does he expect to do business with this Menagh feller?" he asked.

"He left Tuck Rossiter for that."

"Now that don't seem right. Just what did your Pa tell you about all this?"

He looked up and saw the puzzled expression on her face.

"Didn't he say nothin' to you?" he asked shrewdly.

She shook her head slowly.

Bass said at length, "I got a funny feeling about this Rossiter feller ..."

Just then, Tuck came into view around the corner of the cottage. He was smiling. "Just how funny is this feeling, chum?" he asked lightly. "Is it a personal joke or can anybody laugh?" He stood at the foot of the steps, smiling up at them, his eyes moving from Bass to Mady, then back again.

Bass flushed and rose to his feet. "I got a feeling you ain't told Miss Lamont all there is to tell," he said.

"Tell her about what, chum?"

Mady saw that Tuck had been drinking. His color was high and his eyes were very bright and she could see by the way he looked at Bass that he was spoiling for trouble.

She said warningly, "Tuck ..."

He turned his brilliant smile on her. "But sweetheart," he said, "I'm only trying to find out what chum McNulty here has in mind. Just what do you think I'm holding out on Mady, chum McNulty?"

Bass, too, felt the menace in the big man's glittering manner but he said shortly, "If I knew, it wouldn't be just a feeling."

"That's very interesting. Do you go around having feelings like that all the time, chum McNulty? Are you psychic, by any chance? Does your mother read tea leaves?"

Bass' face became fiery red. Mady put down her sewing and said sharply, "Stop it, Tuck. You came here to start a fight."

"Uh-uh, sweetheart. I came to see if we could take a little run out into the Gulf in your boat. But when I get here, what do I find? Chum McNulty looking into his crystal ball. Naturally I'm interested because it was my future he was fore ..." He stopped and a kind of comprehension came into his face. He swung back to Bass. "You've been in touch with Joe Menagh!" he exclaimed.

Bass said blandly, "I have?"

"Yeah. You've been in touch with Joe Menagh—and now you're trying to ease me out of the picture. Why you cute little son of a bitch. Come to papa!"

Grinning with bright fury, Tuck leaped up the steps and reached out with one huge hand. But Bass had moved at almost the same instant, expecting something like this. He slapped Tuck's reaching hand aside and stepped in, catching Tuck in mid-stride with a slashing right to the side of the head. To Mady, Tuck seemed to hang suspended forever on the end of Bass' fist. Then his eyes glazed and he toppled backward, falling heavily into the sand. He did not move. His jacket had fallen open, showing the darkly gleaming butt of the gun under his left arm. And it was the gun Mady stared at with horror ... not the unconscious figure of Tuck. Twice now she had seen Tuck react with violence and the gun suddenly became the very essence of his violence.

Bass was stammering, "That's ... that's what he was leading up to, honey. I didn't start it ..."

Mady cried out in despair, "Take me away from here, Bass!"

She was swaying and he caught her in his arms. She clung to him for a moment, shaking, then pushed herself away.

"I'm all right—but take me away, please, take me away. I'm afraid!"

"Sure, honey ..."

He took her hand and led her down the steps. She averted her head as they passed Tuck. They started toward the beach.

"Don't you have your car?" she asked.

"I'm sorry, honey, but the battery up and died. We'll go along the beach."

"No, no, he'll follow us. I don't want any more trouble ..."

"We'll take his car then."

"No!"

Bass said gently, "We just can't stand here, honey, and wait for him to come round and start more trouble. But wait a minute. He said something about your boat. You got a boat?"

"Oh yes, the boat ..."

She turned and fled around the side of the house. He had to sprint to catch up with her. She crossed the road and ran down a narrow shell path that led to the southernmost neck of Sanibel Bay. Her boat was moored to a rickety wooden dock at the foot of the path.

Bass whistled when he saw it. "Well, now," he said, "you sure got yourself a boat!"

It was a twenty-five foot cruiser that the impractical Eric Lamont had given Mady in one of his periodic fits of remorse. The sleek hull was painted white and the decks and cabin were gleaming mahogany. It was a beautiful, powerful boat and with its plywood hull it had a very shallow draft. It was named *Pal*.

Mady was already in the cabin, apprehensively watching the path, when Bass dropped into the cockpit. He ducked into the cabin, gave her a reassuring grin and stepped up to the controls. He turned on the ignition and pressed the starter button. The motor ground wearily but did not catch. He grunted and gave her a quick glance. The battery was low and by all counts the motor must be wet. He pressed the starter button again and the motor turned a little. He saw Mady catch her breath, saw her fingers tighten at the edge of the window, but she said nothing. He pressed the starter button for the third time and this time the motor caught. He worked the choke frantically to keep it going. It coughed and spat, then very unwillingly, very slowly increased the tempo until it was running with a deep-throated roar. He could hear that it was still missing a little but it would do to get away from the dock. He ran out of the cabin, leaped up to the dock and cast off the lines. He gave the boat a push away from the dock with his foot, then jumped aboard again. He cut the throttle but kept a ready hand on the choke as he eased it out into deeper water.

There was only one way to run and that was toward Sanibel, for the other end of the bay was a dead end. At Sanibel they could turn west through the jetties and out into the open Gulf. This was the most dangerous part of the run because Tuck could outrun them by car and catch them in the narrows where this arm of the bay opened into Big Sanibel Bay. At the Narrows, Tuck could stand on the bridge and drop aboard while they slowed to go through.

Bass opened the throttle and his eyes lit up at the powerful forward surge. The boat, he knew, could do even better than this but the motor was still missing a little. Though he could not possibly see the shore road because of the intervening mangrove, sea grape, and cabbage palm, he could not help glancing to port every few minutes.

Mady had slipped down to a seat, her body bent forward, her face hidden in the bend of her elbow that rested on her knees. She remained in that crouching position only a few minutes. When she sat up, her eyes were dry and her face was calm. She gave Bass a small smile.

"I'm all right," she said, but he knew she was saying it more to convince herself than him. She took a deep breath. "You don't know how glad I am that's over."

Bass nodded but did not answer. They were rapidly approaching the bridge. He could see it about a quarter of a mile ahead. He opened the starboard window and leaned out in order to see more clearly.

There were several motionless figures on the bridge and his eyes swept the western approach to see if he could spot the Cadillac but again the mangrove screened his view. He opened the throttle a little more and this time the motor responded immediately. He opened it wide and the boat lifted its sharp nose and skimmed the water, almost planing. He relaxed a little. He had been afraid of a cracked sparkplug but it had only been the wet. She was not missing anymore.

Now he could see the figures on the bridge more plainly but not plainly enough to see if Tuck were among them. Most of them were fishing. His heart began to beat rapidly for here was where he would have to cut the speed. Reluctantly he pushed in the throttle, keeping his eyes on the bridge, desperately trying to remember what Tuck had been wearing. But in his mind's eye he could call up nothing but a huge blurred figure leaping at him with an outstretched hand. A jacket! He remembered a jacket because it had fallen open, revealing a gun. Eagerly he scanned the figures on the bridge and saw three with jackets. The bridge loomed closer and he had to cut his speed even more. His heart leaped as one of the figures moved to the center of the bridge, directly over the channel. Then he saw the fishing rod in the man's hand and his heart thudded back into place. The fisherman paused only a moment, then sauntered to the edge of the bridge to cast his line where it would not be fouled by the boat.

They were within two hundred feet of the bridge when Bass angrily sat back behind the controls. He was getting himself into what his mother would have called a state. If Tuck intended to drop aboard, all the watching in the world wouldn't stop him. Bass said to Mady, "Can you hold her steady through the pilings, honey?"

She nodded and he turned the wheel over to her. She leaned forward to look up at the bridge and he said quickly, "You got to keep your eye on the channel, honey."

She stared straight ahead, holding the wheel tightly in both hands. Bass glanced quickly around the cabin, then wrenched the fire extinguisher from its clip alongside the controls. He ducked out of the cabin and stood in the stern cockpit. The rail of the bridge was concrete, revealing the fishermen above only from the chest up. Anyone, even as big a man as Tuck, could be crouching behind the rail, ready to drop into the boat from the far side. Bass tensed as they passed slowly under the bridge and he was still standing poised for action as they came out from under the shadows and continued unmolested through the mouth of the Narrows into the spreading Bay. He stared back at the bridge as if he could not believe their good fortune. He did not feel silly or sheepish with the heavy fire extinguisher still in his hands. It had been only good sense. One of the fishermen waved to him from the bridge and he waved back. He turned and went into the cabin.

Mady smiled at him as he thrust the fire extinguisher back into its clip and said, "I'll take her now, honey."

She stood beside him as he opened to full throttle and followed the markers toward the jetties. At the jetties he had to slow again but this time there was no danger as the channel between the jetties was a hundred yards wide. The Gulf was so smooth that the light boat did not even pitch as they passed from the jetties into the deep water. Bass sped straight out into the Gulf for about a mile before he cut the speed again. He glanced at the gas gauge. It showed a three-quarter tank. He looked at Mady.

"I can take you clear to Tampa, honey," he said, "if that's where you're aimin' to go."

The mention of Tampa seemed to startle her and she shook her head vigorously.

"No," she said, her mouth set stubbornly, "I ... I want to talk to Joe Menagh. I have to find out."

Bass stared through the windshield at the empty, glinting water. "I know where Joe Menagh is," he said slowly.

"I knew you knew."

"Then why didn't you ask me before?" he said in surprise.

"I knew you'd tell me if you wanted me to know. You had to make up your mind, didn't you?"

Bass nodded. "That's right. But not because of you, honey," he added quickly. "Because of that Rossiter feller. I didn't trust him no-ways. Not that I'm trying to protect Joe Menagh. I ain't. If Joe stole something from your Pa or anybody else I ain't gonna keep him hid out. But I ain't turning Joe over to nobody like Tuck Rossiter. He's a mean man and I got me the idea he'd hurt Joe bad if he got his hands on him. I wouldn't do that to nobody."

Mady touched his arm. "I know you wouldn't, Bass." Her fingers rested gently on his arm for another short moment.

"And I sure wish you let me handle this, honey!" he blurted. "All the time Joe was talking about men with guns being after him, I thought he was just being biggety, like Humphrey Bogart in the movies. Joe talks like that sometimes and you can't always believe him. But this time he was telling the truth, 'specially about Tuck Rossiter. I seen the gun Rossiter was toting—and a man like that, he don't tote a gun for pleasure or to shoot squirr'ls. There'll be an honest-to-God shootin' when he goes for his gun and I wouldn't like for you to be around when that happens. Rossiter ain't a man to let nobody stand in his way."

"But he wouldn't ..."

"Honey, when it comes down to what it can come down to, Tuck Rossiter won't let nobody stand in his way—you, me, nor nobody. An' I want you far away when that happens, 'cause it's gonna be happening. Let me take you up Tampa, honey ..."

"But I've got to talk to Joe Menagh," she interrupted. "I have to find out for myself."

"All right, honey. We do what we have to, I guess."

Suddenly Mady gasped and looked at him with spreading eyes.

"But you!" she said. "You're the one Tuck won't let stand in his way. You're the one!"

"I guess he's gonna figure that way, being he thinks I know where Joe is hid out. But that don't worry me nearly as much as you being there. But let's forget it for now. I can't take you to see Joe before dark tonight, on account of we'd be kind of conspicuous. I think it would be a good idea if we kind of circled around out of sight of land till then, maybe even do a little fishin' if you got the rigs."

Mady said, "Bass ..." and when he turned to look at her, she kissed him quickly and lightly on the lips.

## THE CONTRACT
### CHAPTER TWELVE

Every shade in Clyde's shack was pulled down and inside he sat slumped in the dark in a chair near the radio. There was a nearly empty jug of mule on the floor beside his chair but he was not drunk. He merely sat and smoldered and from time to time an impotent fury rose up in him and he clenched his hands and swore savagely. He had never been beaten before but after he had made all the excuses he could think of, he could not escape the bitter knowledge that he had been beaten.

His lips were bloated and his eyes peered out of purpled slits. One ear was a grotesque, shapeless doughnut. The stubble on his face now concealed the swellings and cuts made by Tuck's merciless fists and every time he took a drink of mule from the jug, the inside of his mouth burned like fire.

He was in this dangerous mood when his door opened without warning and Leo walked in. Clyde leaped to his feet and snarled, "Get the goddamn stinkin' hell outta here!"

Leo said sharply, "Sit down and shut up. I want to talk to you."

"Okay, mister. I warned you ..."

"Sit down or you'll get hurt. I didn't come here for any shenanigans."

There was something in Leo's voice that made Clyde stop and peer uncertainly at the interloper. He saw the hard stolidity, the implacability in Leo's pale eyes. He licked his lips.

"I don't feel like talkin'. Beat it," he growled.

"Sit down. You'll feel like it in a minute." Leo took something from his pocket and held it up. "Know what this is?"

"Twenny ... twenny bucks?"

"It's fifty bucks and I've known guys to sing like canaries for a sawbuck. Sit down and think it over for a minute."

Clyde sat down and said sullenly, "I don't know nothin' worth fifty bucks to talk about."

"Somebody sure kicked the hell outta you, didn't they?" said Leo, looking curiously at Clyde's swollen face.

"Go to hell."

"I just happened to hear about it—you know how those things get around. What was the fight about?"

"None of your business."

Leo held up the fifty dollar bill and waved it slowly back and forth. "What was the fight about?" he repeated.

Clyde looked at the bill. "It wasn't about nuthin'," he said. "I was jumped by a half dozen conches down Key West in a gin mill."

"You're a liar. Tuck Rossiter beat you up."

"Since you know so goddamn much, why come and ask me?"

"I want to know what it was about."

Clyde could not keep his eyes off the fifty dollar bill. It would be the easiest money he ever made. But there was a remnant of churlish pride that stood in the way.

"I got soused in a gin mill and he threw me out."

"You're still a liar. Rossiter don't beat up drunks. He just kicks 'em down and leaves 'em there. What was the fight about?"

Clyde looked at him mutely.

Leo said, "Ah hell," and put the fifty dollars in his pocket.

Clyde said angrily, "All right, all right. It was over a dame."

"A dame? What dame?"

"That chippy in the cottage down the beach."

"You tried to make time with her or something? Was that the idea?"

"Hell no. I wouldn't look at that dame twice," said Clyde. "She's been runnin' around with one of the guys here in the village, a married guy over fifty. Well, we got word this guy was down to the cottage this night, so I went down with the wife. The guy must've slipped out but this Rossiter was there, and he jumped me while I was telling the young dame what we think of her."

"You told the dame off and he jumped you?"

Clyde nodded shortly, his thoughts fixed on the fifty dollars. Leo pressed his lips together. There was something wrong with the story and he knew it. It just wasn't Tuck's style.

Sensing Leo's skepticism, Clyde said hurriedly, "You don't have to believe me. Just ast anybody around. This Lamont dame comes down here, hires her a cottage and gives out that her old man ..."

"What was that name?" Leo demanded.

"Lamont. Mabel Lamont. I think it was Mabel."

Leo said, "Oh for cri-sake." He folded the bill into a tight square and flipped it contemptuously at Clyde.

Now he knew. He had just wasted fifty bucks because he remembered Tuck saying something about using Eric Lamont's kid as bait for Menagh. It was just business.

Clyde said slyly, "Well, that was your fifty bucks worth."

"Come again?"

"That's all your fifty bucks buys. If you want more, you gotta buy it."

Leo pursed his lips once more. There was always the chance that he did know a little more than he had told. There was always that chance with everybody, even the greedy ones.

"If it's worth more," he said, "I'll pay it."

Clyde seemed satisfied. "It's about the dame," he said.

"So?"

"First she had kept company with old man McNulty and now she's goin' around with young McNulty. She switched."

Leo was more interested than he looked. "I don't get you," he said.

"There's nothing to get. I was just showin' you what kind of dame she is. First she goes around with old man McNulty, now she goes around with the son. Only today, right after lunch, I seen him walkin' up the beach to her cottage all slicked up. That should be worth something, shouldn't it?"

"Maybe it is," said Leo thoughtfully, "maybe it is. What do you know about these McNultys, anyway?"

"Crackers, that's all, just crackers. The young one gets a little biggety onct in a while but he's just a cracker like the rest of them. Goes off by hisself a lot. Thinks he's too good for the rest of us, I guess."

"Where's he go?"

"Out in the boat at night sometimes."

"Does he take the Lamont girl with him? Or Rossiter maybe?"

"Could be but I never seen him 'cept alone. Maybe he does go to meet the dame," Clyde suggested. "Or maybe it is Rossiter. I could sure nuff find out. In case it's worth anything to you, that is."

Leo walked over to the window and stood drumming his fingertips on the sill. Leo had a logical mind and he could see that if only a portion of Clyde's story were true, he might have something. Somehow he didn't trust Tuck. That was why he had decided to investigate the fight when he'd overheard some natives talking about it earlier. He thought Tuck might have something up his sleeve. He didn't want to be suckered by Tuck either. He turned.

"What kind of boat this young McNulty got?" he asked.

"Oh, just a little old fishin' boat like everybody else."

"What kind of boat you got?"

"Same thing," Clyde admitted.

"Oh hell, ain't there nothing around you could call a boat?"

"Up the boat livery. They got a eighteen-foot speedboat that'll do forty-five wide open. Faster'n anything else around."

"Get it. Here's a C-note. Get it and keep it out of sight down here. I want you to keep an eye on this young McNulty and the next time he goes out at night, give me a ring at the hotel. Now," he added briskly, "here's my name ..."

## CROSSED PATHS
### CHAPTER THIRTEEN

Tuck lay in a stupor for nearly an hour, partly from the effect of that smashing blow to his jaw and partly from the tremendous amount of alcohol he had consumed during the past few days. When he finally roused himself, he crawled into Mady's cottage. The westering sun slanted through the doorway and hurt his eyes. He groaned and covered them with a shaking hand.

His head was thundering. He staggered across the room to the table, uncorked the whisky bottle and tilted it to his mouth. He stood clutching the table and waited for the warming strength he knew would come. He felt it begin at last spreading quickly into his belly, his arms and his legs. But it did not stop the throbbing behind his eyes. He took another big drink and waited with his eyes closed. The throbbing did not go away but it lessened a little. He corked the bottle and stood looking vacantly around the room. His mouth was as tight and thin as a knife scar.

The only thought that hammered savagely in his mind was that young McNulty knew where Joe Menagh was hiding out. That was all that was important. He knew by the silence of the house that they had gone but it didn't matter at the moment. They would not go far. He put the bottle back on the table and went into the bedroom and opened the closet door. She had obviously not taken any of her clothes as her suitcase was still standing in a corner of the closet. She'd be back—and probably young McNulty with her.

It was going to be a pleasure, distinctly a pleasure, taking care of that wise young cracker. He'd wring him out dry, then pick Menagh like a grape. Two hundred thousand, Leo had said. One-fifth of a million. There were places in South America where you could live like a king on two hundred thousand. He and Mady. She was sore at him, sure, but there wasn't a shadow of doubt in his mind that she'd be back when he wanted her. He could think of Ida only with disgust.

First he would take care of the McNulty kid, then Joe Menagh, then Leo. Especially Leo. He had to laugh when he thought how easy it was going to be. Taking care of Eric Lamont had showed him that the toughest part was all in the mind.

Exulting, he walked back into the living room, had a last drink, then walked out to the Cadillac. He started the motor and began to drive slowly south toward the fishing village, keeping an eye on the beach to his right as he drove. He had an idea that Mady and Bass might be walking there.

He did not notice Ida's car, temporarily borrowed by Leo, parked out in front of Clyde's shack as he passed.

He drifted along slowly until he spotted the McNulty mailbox, standing on a post outside the cottage. He stopped and jumped out of the Cadillac, feeling wonderful now, with everything neatly settled in his mind. He walked jauntily up to the front door and knocked, whistling as he waited.

The door was opened by Mrs. McNulty. There were smudges of flour on her face, and she stood wiping her hands on her apron, so startled at seeing Tuck that all she could do was gape up at him. He gave her his most boyish and ingratiating grin.

"And how are you today, Mrs. McNulty?" he said. "Has Bass gotten in yet?"

She started, "He went down to see Miss Lamont and ..." She stopped. "And what business is it of yours?" she asked.

"Ah, you're mad at me—and to tell the truth, I've been wanting to come down and apologize to you for being so rough. I've got a quick temper and I just couldn't stand aside and listen to Miss Lamont being insulted. You'll forgive me now, won't you?"

"It's all right," she said with hostility. Then her curiosity got the better of her. "And just what would you be wanting with Bass now, Mr. Rossiter?"

"Oh, it wasn't Bass I wanted to see," he improvised smoothly. "It was Miss Lamont. Her father called me at the hotel and asked me if I would try to find her and give her a message from him."

Mrs. McNulty's hostile expression did not change. "And why should she be coming here?" she demanded.

"I didn't think she would. I just thought Bass might know where I could get in touch with her."

And it's jealous you are, thought Mrs. McNulty.

Maliciously she said, "I'll tell Bass to give her the message the minute he gets in."

"It's rather confidential and I'd rather give it to her myself."

"I'll tell Bass."

"Thanks," he gave her a winning smile. "I'll be at the hotel." He gave her a boyish wink and leaped lightly down the steps.

Again he missed seeing Ida's car as he passed Clyde's shack on his way back to the beach road. Nor was he aware of the cold blue eyes that stared at him from behind a curtain in the window of Clyde's shack. He was thinking that he had managed the interview with Mrs. McNulty rather well. She didn't like him but who gave a damn about that. He had showed her he was friendly and he knew she would pass the word along to Bass, who would probably pass it on to Mady, wherever she was. You're on the beam, Rossiter, he grinned, you're on the beam.

He had barely brought his car to a stop before the hotel when Ida came running clumsily from the patio. Her plump curves were not made for running.

"Oh, Tucky, Tucky, you're awright, you're awright!" she was almost weeping. "Jeez, I was so worried, honiss!" Her fingers tremblingly fondled his face.

He pushed her hands away with distaste. "Why shouldn't I be all right?" he asked peevishly. "What the hell's the matter with you, anyway?"

"Leo's after you."

It was as if a cold hand had grabbed his heart and squeezed it juiceless. "After me? What for?" he demanded harshly. Automatically his right hand flew to the gun under his jacket.

"Crise, I dunno, Tucky, honiss." She stood wringing her hands and fat tears welled up in her eyes. "He came in earlier, ask me do I know what you got up your sleeve, then he went out to have a tawk with some guy you was supposed to hadda fight with."

Tuck had forgotten his fight with Clyde and thought she was talking about Bass. He felt the chill lift and he laughed.

"Well, I hope he finds him," he said. "I've been trying to find him ever since the fight. How'd he find out about it?"

Ida deflated. Here she'd been so worried and Tuck made her feel like a fool. "Aw," she mumbled, "Leo's aw-ways findin' out things. I think he heard it from some natives. But lissin, Tucky, he's got an idea you're pullin' a fass one. You ain't, are you, Tucky? Leo gets awful mad when somebody pulls a fass one. I don't want nothin' to happen to you, Tucky. I'd die if somethin' happened to you."

Tuck stared at her in amazement. She had never broken down like this before. "What got into you all of a sudden?" he asked roughly. Then, as she lifted her tear-stained face and he saw the cow-like adoration in her eyes, he said quickly, "Nevermind, nevermind. Just tell me one thing—did Leo go out alone or did he have one of his goons with him?"

"He went alone. He took my cah or I woulda follud um. I wasn't gonna let'm do nothing to you. I wasn't gonna let'm do nothin' even if he is my own brotha," she added meaningfully.

"That's okay, kid." Tuck patted her lightly on the cheek. His mind was working furiously. Suppose Leo got to Bass before he did! That would mess things up. Leo would take the kid apart like a fried chicken and once Leo got his hands on Menagh, he wouldn't even leave crumbs. Still, there was a way around that, too. Let Leo do the work, then take Leo. The only catch there was, by then Leo would probably have a half dozen of his goon squad around him. Leo wasn't a boy to take chances when the stakes were actually on the table.

Ida suddenly became tremendously important to him. He leaned down and kissed her briefly on the cheek, then took her by the arm. "Let's go up to your suite," he whispered.

She said, "Oh, Tucky!" and leaned against him. He could feel her trembling.

Fine. That was just the way he wanted her. She clung to his arm as they rode up in the elevator and walked down the corridor and the moment they were inside her suite, she threw her arms around his neck and kissed him passionately. There were no tricks this time, no fake moanings, no deliberate writhings, no squashy lips. He pried himself loose without seeming to. He knew he had to keep her ardor fanned until he could find out what Leo was up to. He knuckled her chin the way she liked him to.

She cried, "Oh TuckyTuckyTucky ..."

"Would you do something for me, honey?" he whispered, making it sound like an endearment.

"Anything, anything, Tucky!"

"Find out what Leo was up to this afternoon." He had to phrase it carefully so she would understand every word. "Not that I'm worried, you understand. I haven't been pulling any fast ones. But this guy I had the fight with might have a grudge against me and Christ only knows what he might tell Leo. Just to get even. You understand what I mean?"

Ida's eyes were huge. She nodded. Holding a grudge was something she could understand.

"When Leo gets back," Tuck went on still carefully, "find out everything you can, then come and tell me. I'll be in my room. Will you do that for me?"

"You know I will, Tucky! You know I will! Kiss me, Tucky, kiss me, please kiss me!"

He bent toward her and enclosed her in his arms as his lips met hers. The force and depth of her answering emotion actually startled him. Before this, love to her had always been a caricature drawn by a savage pen, a grotesque—but this time she did not bite or scratch or pull his hair in a dreadful pretense of ecstasy. Her emotion flowed out to him. It was as if in thinking of someone other than herself for the first time in her life, Ida had opened door after door into new depths within her and in the sheer joy of this self-revelation, she became a woman with an infinite capacity for love.

For the first time, her response was whole and flowing. Even her mouth was different.

There was only one trouble. She disgusted him.

## INTERLUDE
## CHAPTER FOURTEEN

If there was one thing Joe Menagh dreaded, it was the coming of night in the swamp. With the falling of darkness, all the things that lived by day seemed to creep out of sight and the night prowlers came out of their lairs, stretched, and began to stalk through the thick foliage. Even the sounds of the night were different. They were closer and pressed down on him, lurked just outside the circle of light thrown by his fire.

The swamp was a fearful thing. It was alive. It was itself an animal, bigger and more savage than the biggest, most savage animals that lived within its murky depths. Even on the brightest moonlit night the swamp was dark. Only at its top, where the trees moved against the sky, was there light. Below in the dark, in the sluggish waters, was where the swamp life flourished and each night, it seemed to Joe, it crept a little closer to him, inched a little farther in toward his fire.

When the frogs began to shrill, he always knew night was coming and he hurriedly built his fire.

The fire leaped into a roaring blaze and Joe stayed as close to it as he could despite the roasting heat. He kept his gun on the ground beside him, where he could reach it fast. At night the minutes dragged by like things on broken legs. The only thing Joe had to look forward to was Bass' nightly visit. Bass came every night, sometimes bringing something Mrs. McNulty had cooked, sometimes just groceries, sometimes a stack of newspapers. When darkness fell, Joe just sat beside the fire in a tight, defensive squat and waited for the sound of Bass' boat coming up the river. He sat staring into the bright fire, trying to hear only the crackle of burning wood but with each wild night cry in the swamp, his eyes rolled and he hunched a little tighter in his squat, visibly shuddering.

Something screamed in the swamp and Joe at the same moment saw a movement at the edge of the rim of darkness around him. He stared fearfully and saw the movement again. His hand stealthily felt for the gun on the ground at his side.

It moved again and he knew what it must be. A snake. A huge one. Here in the swamp they grew as thick around as a man's neck. Perspiration burst from every pore in his body at once. It dripped coldly down his ribs from his armpits, it ran down his face, it made his hands clammy. Keeping his eyes glued to the slowly-moving snake, he raised his gun, steadied it on his knee and fired. He knew he had hit the snake but it kept moving toward him. He fired again. Still it moved toward him. He fired and kept firing until the hammer fell with a dry, empty click on a spent shell. He kept working the trigger, swearing— but before the terror could consume him, he realized it had not been a snake he was shooting at but an old cabbage palm log, animated by the shifting shadows of the fire. He knew that old palm log as well as he knew every bush and tree that fringed the clearing. He looked down at the now useless gun in his hand. He suddenly began to cry.

This was the end. Nothing could be worse than this, not even the men who were waiting outside with guns for him. He'd give them back what he had taken from Guastella's body. That was all they wanted. He'd give it to them. They'd beat him up maybe but actually all they wanted was what he had taken from Guastella. They didn't give a damn about him and he no longer gave a damn about anything other than getting out of this swamp. He'd go out tonight with Bass ...

Clyde hid the speedboat in the mangrove on the mainland east of the little island in the mouth of the bay. Here it could be reached quickly and easily and unless you knew it was there, you'd never see it. He glanced up at the sky. The full moon had already risen. It was going to be a bright night. He hoped Bass would go out in his boat tonight so he could have something to call Leo about. Clyde didn't actually think Bass went to see anybody, just went out after bullfrogs.

Clyde felt the thick wad of bills in his pocket and sighed. For the first time since he could remember, he had more money than he could possibly spend in a night. His tastes were simple. A bottle of whisky when he was in funds (a quart of mule when he wasn't)—and an audience. The whisky he could get in the gin mill opposite the fish house, the audience in the same place.

There were about twenty fishermen in the gin mill when he walked in. Four of them were playing an earnest game of shuffleboard at the side of the room, with another half dozen standing around with beers and kibitzing. The room fell quiet as Clyde walked in and, though no heads were conspicuously turned, every eye watched him. The voices rose to a hum but there was a tenseness in it.

Clyde waved his hand, said, "Evenin', chumps," and walked to the end of the bar near the window that overlooked the road. He glanced through the window to make sure he could see both the dock and the McNulty cottage from his position against the wall, then threw a ten dollar bill on the bar and called for whisky.

The barkeep brought it and said cautiously, "What'll you have for a chaser?"

"Make it a beer."

Clyde drank moodily for a few moments, then began to look around him. There was one man standing beside him but most of the crowd had drifted to the other end of the bar. The man next to him was drinking beer. Clyde tapped him on the shoulder.

"Ever see a face like this before?" he said, tapping his chin with his forefinger. "What would you do if you had a face like this?"

The man half turned and looked at him sidelong. "I've seen worse," he said warily.

Clyde scowled at him and was about to reply but suddenly thought the hell with it, leaned back against the wall and settled down to watch the McNulty house and the dock.

## THREE-HANDED DEAL
### CHAPTER FIFTEEN

Leo had been in a jovial mood ever since he returned to the hotel and Tuck found it more disturbing than if Leo had come back with a grouch like a wet wildcat. The grouch was Leo's normal temper, in varying degrees, but this jovial mood meant something had happened.

All he said, however, was, "Come on up the suite for a couple rounds a pinochle, boy. Long time since we had any pinochle, hey?" He patted Tuck's shoulder and chuckled.

Tuck said, "Sure," and watched him narrowly.

Leo cleared the cocktail table of debris and they played there, Tuck and Ida sitting side by side on the sofa, Leo facing them, seated on the edge of the armchair he had dragged over. Tuck brought a bottle of Scotch from the bathtub and put it on the floor beside him. He didn't drink just to drink now. He drank to keep up that fine edge he had acquired. Ida sipped gin. Leo drank nothing but that was not unusual. He sat stockily upright as he solemnly dealt the cards.

It did not take Tuck long to find out that nothing conclusive had happened that afternoon. Whatever had occurred had merely been the prelude to something, though what it was he could not discover. Leo, usually a hard player, handled his cards with an abstracted air and appeared to be waiting for something. His attention wandered.

Once he said casually, "We can have a nice long evening, boy. I called the desk and told them to put any calls for you through to Ida's phone up here."

Tuck shrugged.

Ida took Leo's jovial mood at face value and was happy. Everything was all right again. Leo wasn't after Tuck any more. She was filled with contentment. She couldn't keep her eyes off Tuck. She was drifting in a rose-colored reverie. She had been stirred deeply that afternoon and was still under its enchantment, remembering every little motion and sensation. It was going to be like this all the time, she knew. All the time, just her and Tuck.

Leo guffawed and roared at her, "Didn't you ever see the guy before in your life? The way you gape at him, you'd think he was Greg'ry Peck or something."

"Drop dead," said Ida happily. She touched Tuck's knee and smiled at him.

There was a tremendous secret between them and Leo was now the outsider. Tuck scowled at her intimate touch and reached for the Scotch. He wanted to get out suddenly. He wasn't getting anywhere and time was passing. Furthermore, he knew Leo was keeping him there deliberately—and not to play cards, either. He had the feeling something was going to break and that he would be left outside. It wasn't anything he could put his finger on, nothing Leo had actually said, but it was in Leo's manner.

"What's the matter?" said Leo suddenly. "Got ants in your pants or something?"

Under the spur of a sudden inspiration, Tuck answered with some thick-tongued gibberish, then pushed himself up out of the sofa and staggered into the bathroom. He listened at the door and heard Leo's chuckle.

"Whattaya know, the punk's soused."

Tuck turned on the water in the sink and let it run noisily for about five minutes. Then he wet his face and hair and stumbled out into the other room, wearing a sickly grin for Leo's benefit.

"Gawn moan room 'n lay down," he muttered.

Ida jumped up and ran to him. "I'll help you, honeybunch," she crooned.

He pretended to hang on to her for a moment and whispered, "Nix, nix, work on him, then come and let me know."

He pushed himself clumsily away from her. "Find moan way," he grumbled.

Ida got the idea. She let him go alone. He went quickly to his own room and straight to the whisky bottle from which he poured himself a stiff drink. He started to raise it to his mouth, then lowered it and went into the bathroom where he added half a glass of water to it. This was no time for serious drinking. He stretched himself out on the bed, propped himself up with pillows, and settled back to wait.

It was an hour before Ida tapped on the door and slipped into his room, smiling archly. She was wearing a pair of light green lounging pajamas which were all wrong with her blonde hair and fair complexion. She had daubed on some green eye-shadow and her lipstick looked purple. She had obviously made herself up for the visit.

Tuck swung off the bed and demanded, "Well, what did you find out?"

"It's nothin' at all, Tucky. It ain't got nothin' to do with you. He's just waitin' for a phone call."

He said sharply, "What kind of phone call?"

"I dunno. The guy he saw this aftanoon, I think. Somethin' he said."

"Dammit, what did he say?"

"I ... I don't remember. I din pay no attention. It din have nothin' to do with you."

"Jesus H. Christ, can't you ever get anything right?" He grabbed her wrist.

"But it din have nothin' to do with you!" she wailed.

"How the hell do you know? I told you to find out what he was up to this afternoon, didn't I? Now try to think for a minute, goddamnit. What did he say?"

Ida began to cry. "I din pay no attention. He ain't sore at you, Tucky. Honiss he ain't. Don't be like this, Tucky. I done my bess. Kiss me, Tucky, kiss me. I done my bess."

"Shut up, will you? Jesus, when they come any dumber than you, they'll make them out of wood. I don't give a damn if it had anything to do with me. I just want to find out what he was up to this afternoon ..."

Without warning, the door opened and Leo stepped in, kicking the door shut behind him. Tuck released the weeping Ida's wrist and stepped back warily.

"Got over your drunk kinda quick," Leo said heavily. He took his hand from his pocket and there was a gun in it. "You're getting too goddamn smart, that's what I think. Lay down on the bed."

Tuck balanced on the balls of his feet. "The hell with you," he said.

Leo raised the gun a little. "Lay down on the bed," he repeated.

Ida stood petrified, then with a wailing cry she sprang at Leo, grasping his gun with both hands and pulling it to her breast. "Get out, Tucky!" she cried. "Get out ..."

Leo swore and pushed her aside. Tuck took a long step forward and shot a straight right over Ida's shoulder that caught Leo flush on the chin. Leo sagged into Ida, then toppled sideways to the floor. Tuck jerked him upright, pushed him against the wall and pulled back his fist.

Ida screamed, "No!"

Something in her voice made him turn his head and she was standing there holding Leo's gun on him.

"I ain't gonna let you hurt'm, Tuck," she stammered.

"He was going to let me have it."

"I don't care. You ain't gonna hurt'm."

She took three steps backward, still aiming the gun at him. "Juss tie'm up or something," she said.

Tuck took a quick breath. "Okay," he said. "I was just going to give him another smack, that was all." He picked Leo up and threw him on the bed. He went to the closet and pulled out four of his ties. He tied Leo's wrists and ankles, then tied the ankles and wrists together behind Leo's back. He looked at Ida.

"Okay?" he jeered. "Or do you want me to sit here and hold his head?"

"It's okay," she said weakly.

"I'm glad you think so. Now suppose we go to your suite and wait for that phone call he was expecting ..."

## THE IMPATIENT KIND
### CHAPTER SIXTEEN

"I think it's time we should go in honey," Bass murmured.

"So soon?"

"It's after ten, honey."

"It seems we just got here."

They were lying side by side on the roof of the cabin, drowsily happy, rocked by the gentle motion of the boat. The Gulf was so smooth it looked frozen in the white moonlight. Bass raised himself on one elbow, looked clown into her smiling face for a moment, then leaned over and kissed her lightly on the lips. It was hard to believe he was actually here, kissing her—but it seemed so natural now, so complete. She put her arms around his neck.

"It was so wonderful," she murmured.

And it was true. After they had decided to wait out in the Gulf for dark to come, they had stopped talking about Menagh, Tuck and all the rest of it. They had fished for a while but except for a few tiny striped pinfish and a small perch, nothing was biting. It didn't matter. What mattered was the way the deep feeling of peace had grown up in her. Her father was wonderful and all that but he was always dashing off some place, dashing home for a few days, telling her to pack because they were going to New Orleans or Tampa, or someplace, then leaving her alone when they got there. There had been excitement and fun but there had been no peace in it—not the way there was peace out here on the Gulf with Bass.

Bass. She whispered the name to herself. Bass. She felt a fleeting sadness at the thought that she had ever let Tuck make love to her, though it was hard to remember it clearly now. It was part of the hectic life that had gone by. She never wanted to go back to it. Her arms tightened around Bass, as if he alone stood between her and that old life. She returned his kiss but it was more than a kiss. It was a plea that begged him always to stand between her and the old way. She drew him deeper into the kiss. At first it was just a desire to hold tight to this kind of peaceful serenity but then she felt his lips move on hers and she became aware of him. Not that she hadn't been aware of him before ... this was a different kind of awareness. It was as if she had suddenly discovered there was more of him to know and she wanted urgently to know it.

Her arms drew him tighter and tighter and at first he strained back. "Honey," he said huskily, "honey ..."

But she would not let him talk. She smothered his words with her lips. Instinctively, she felt there was danger in talk. Spoken words were the language of the world back there on the dark shore, spoken words were hands reaching from the shore to pull her back, spoken words were chains, spoken words were a wall between her and Bass. And she never wanted to be separated from him so she killed the words with her lips.

His hands held her stiffly but she could feel them trembling, she could feel the coming life in them and when they started to move down along her arms, a wide tide of emotion washed over her. They were not on the cabin roof any longer, they were not even on the Gulf. They were wrapped in a pulsing darkness. It was not a darkness of mad, chaotic storm—it was the darkness of the curled bud at the moment of bursting into flower and at the bursting it was as if she, like the flower, turned her face to the sun in ecstasy.

Afterwards he said in voice that sounded almost frightened, "You're just gonna have to marry me. You're just gonna have to. I ain't never letting you go now. Never!"

"You mean you're not going to drive me away with sticks and stones?"

"Drive you away!"

"I was teasing."

"Then we can get married?"

"Right now, if you want!" she cried happily.

They lay side by side, not kissing but holding hands and looking up into the sky. There was no need to talk. It had all been said.

At length Mady spoke again. "I think," she said gently, "that you mentioned something about it's being time to go back in now."

"I purely did," he said. He did not want to go in now but he realized they must. He jumped to his feet, then held out his hand to help her up. He kissed her once again, lightly and tenderly, then they went down into the cabin and he started up the motor.

They had been drifting but he set his course due east now and the boat sped over the calm water swiftly until they were within sight of the flashing beacon at the mouth of the Sanibel jetties. Here he turned southeast and made for the mouth of Dogbody Bay.

The fish house dock was deserted when they tied up. He took her hand and they ran down the street to the McNulty cottage. As they burst into the house Bass shouted, "Hey, Ma, guess what!"

Mrs. McNulty sat at a table with a tall slim gray-haired man who looked like Bass. They were playing double solitaire. She turned, looked at Bass and Mady, then turned back to her husband.

"Well, Pa," she said, "looks like I'm gonna get that new dress before I thought. Though how you McNultys hypnotize a girl into marrying you, I'll never know. I been puzzlin' over it for years. If you don't mind my saying so, honey," she said to Mady, "you must be plumb crazy." Then she laughed. "Like the rest of us McNulty women."

Mady found herself in Mrs. McNulty's arms, crying as if her heart would burst, only these were tears of happiness, for she suddenly realized that the peace she had glimpsed out on the Gulf with Bass was all around her. It was right here in this house. Old McNulty offered his congratulations shyly and Bass broke it up finally by saying briskly, "We'll have to save the rest of it till later, Ma. We gotta go now."

"Go?" she said blankly. "Go where?"

"Well, you remember that feller up the swamp I been taking groceries to?"

"What's he got to do with it?"

"Well, we don't rightly know but we gotta find out. It's got something to do with Mady's pa."

"And you're taking Mady up the swamp in the dead of night? Oh no you're not, young man!"

Mady said, "Please, Mrs. McNulty. I've got to go."

Mrs. McNulty gave her a long, searching look. "Yes," she said finally, "I guess maybe you do."

Bass went into the kitchen for food and came out a few minutes later carrying a brown paper bag.

"Now see here, Bascom McNulty," Mrs. McNulty began in a scolding voice, "you take care when you go into that place ..."

"Stop it, Ma," Shawn McNulty interrupted. "Bass can take care of hisself. He's been doin' it long enough. And he can take care of his young lady too, far as that goes. Want me to go along, son?"

Bass shook his head. "Thanks, Pa, but we'll manage okay. There's nothin' to worry about. We'll just go up and talk to him and come right out again. That's all."

They walked back to the boat at the fish house dock with Bass and Mady.

"When's it gonna be?" Mrs. McNulty whispered to Mady. "The weddin', I mean."

"Soon, I hope."

"I'm glad to hear you say that, honey. I was afraid you might be one of them that likes a long engagement and Bass wouldn't be fit to live with during, 'cause he ain't the patient kind. Now you make him take care up in the swamp. He gets reckless."

"I will," Mady smiled.

Bass called from the boat, "Ready, honey?"

Mady put down her bag and threw her arms around Mrs. McNulty in a sudden surge of warmth. "I think you're wonderful," she whispered. Then, "I'm coming, I'm coming," she called as Bass looked up again.

She jumped and Bass raced the motor for a moment, then slipped it into gear. The boat raised its slim nose and sped down the bay toward the mouth of the river.

## STAND-OFF
### CHAPTER SEVENTEEN

Tuck was in Ida's suite when Clyde's first call came through from the fishing village. Ida was huddled in a corner of the sofa in sodden misery. Her hand lay numbly against her cheek where Tuck had slapped her when she tried to kiss him. Whatever there had been between her and Tuck, it was all over now. It was her fault. She knew it was her fault and she kept going back in her mind, trying to find out what it was she had done. She knew she must have done something.

Tuck's head jerked up when the phone rang and he crossed the room in three long strides.

Clyde's voice said, "This Mr. Leo Brunn?"

Tuck grunted the way Leo would have. At the same time he tried to place the voice. He knew it wasn't Bass but there was something familiar about it. He had heard it recently.

Clyde went on quickly, "The young guy and the girl just come in a little cabin cruiser. Looks like a Chris-Craft. Rossiter wasn't with 'em. They went up to the young guy's house and they're still there. What you want me to do now?"

Tuck did not answer. He was trying to remember where he had heard the voice. And he was afraid to speak into the phone because he couldn't possibly imitate Leo's voice.

Clyde said impatiently, "The boat's still tied up to the fish house dock but I think they're aimin' to go out again. They left the keys in the ignition. I can .... say, am I talking to Mr. Leo Brunn? Is this you, Mr. Brunn?"

Tuck chuckled and hung up. Now he knew what it was all about. The mention of the fish house had done it. Mady and Bass had come into the village waters in Mady's boat. But the voice. He couldn't place the voice. He stood frowning a moment, then started to leave. Ida raised herself on the sofa and called feebly, "Tucky, Tucky ..." He turned at the door and said, "Drop dead." Then he strode out and slammed the door after him.

She stared after him openmouthed for a moment. Then a hardness came into her eyes. "Drop dead y'self," she screamed after him.

She leaped up from the sofa in a fury and looked around wildly for something to break. She snatched up the gin bottle—then slowly lowered it again. She knew something better than that. She knew how she could fix him. She pulled herself together and went through the hall in the direction of Tuck's room where Leo lay tied up.

Clyde was frantic as he rang back and got no answer. As long as there was nothing doing, it had seemed all right, even a slick idea, to take Leo's money and give him a runaround. But now, unexpectedly, something was doing. The two older McNultys had come down to the fish house dock, as if they were seeing Mady and Bass off for some place, as if they were saying good-bye or something. Given a calm sea and the right weather, with a boat like that Chris-Craft there, Bass could run clear to Havana if he had a mind to. Something was up all right and Clyde was wishing fervently that he hadn't got mixed up in it. He had known all along that Leo wasn't anybody to fool with but he hadn't worried, because he had never thought he'd have to do anything for the money Leo had given him. He pulled his hand down over his face, looked apprehensively at the glistening sweat, then rubbed his palm on his thigh.

Clyde slapped the phone with his open hand and said angrily, "It ain't my fault if you don't answer, is it?"

He was suddenly conscious that everybody in the gin mill had turned and was watching him. He faced them, glowering, and they hurriedly went back to their beers. He heard the staccato roar as Bass started the motor and raced it for a moment. He ran out into the street. For a moment he thought of dashing out on the dock and stopping Bass by force but old man McNulty was there too and he could be a tough son of a gun when he wanted to. Clyde's face was pinched and all drawn together in the middle from the unaccustomed agony of thought. Then he sprinted down the shadowy side of the street to the rickety dock in front of his shanty and jumped into his own boat. It couldn't go anywhere near as fast as the Chris-Craft but at least he'd get an idea which way they were heading.

He was chugging down the bay when the other boat passed him with a muffled roar. The heavy wake set his light boat tossing and he gripped the gunwales to keep from being thrown. He yelled angrily after them and Bass' voice floated back, "Sorry, friend ..." Clyde gave his rackety motor all it had. It looked hopeless. Then unexpectedly, the Chris-Craft slowed. He immediately cut his throttle to idling speed. He watched and saw the slim white hull turn eastward into the mouth of the river. He cut his motor entirely and listened. The Chris-Craft picked up speed again and the pulse of the motor was steady as it receded. Clyde let out a heavy breath and licked the perspiration from his upper lip.

Tuck ran the Cadillac into the shadows beside the fish house and braked amid a spray of flying shell. He leaped out and ran to the dock. There was nothing tied up there now and no sign of Mady's boat, *Pal*. There was one boat out on the bay, he noticed, but it wasn't the *Pal*. The motor sounded like a handful of cutlery shaken up in a tin pot. A fisherman's boat.

Tuck swore savagely, then, almost immediately, he quieted down. They were gone. All right. If they had taken the time to come to the fish house dock, they must have come for a reason. The reason was easy to see. Bass must have gone to his house for something. If he had gone to his house, he must have told his mother and father where he and Mady were going. Now it was clearing up! If those two old goats knew where Bass had taken the Pal, it would be a pushover to get it out of them, even if he had to rough them up a little. He slipped his gun from under his arm and checked the loads in the cylinder. He smiled grimly and started around the side of the fish house. He heard the sound of running feet and he pulled himself back into the shadow and flattened against the wall. Within a few seconds a big man passed, running with awkward haste. The moment Tuck recognized him, he knew who had called Leo. It was Clyde, the big cracker he had beaten up at Mady's cottage.

Tuck said, "Huh," with satisfaction and relaxed against the wall. He watched Clyde turn into the gin mill.

Clyde stayed inside only a few minutes before he raced out again and pounded heavily up the street.

This time, Tuck knew, Clyde must have reached Leo on the phone. He ran out into the middle of the street and stared dumbly in the direction in which Clyde had disappeared. How could he have been so thick! Clyde must know where Bass and Mady had gone. Clyde had reported to Leo and now Clyde was going to join Leo.

Tuck sprinted down the street. He sprinted past Clyde's shack and within a hundred yards he reached a dead end on the shore of the bay. The only sounds were the quiet lap-lap of the water on the sand and the dry rustle of the breeze through the stiff fronds of the cabbage palms. Then he heard another sound and he leaned toward it to try to identify it. It was a muted roar, a sound of power, steady, increasing in tempo. A motor. But this wasn't any fisherman's boat. For a moment he thought wildly that the *Pal* was returning—but then a dark, gleaming shadow leaped out from behind the spur of mangrove, throwing a high plume of white froth behind it. A speedboat. A mahogany speedboat. And in the moonlight, Tuck saw Clyde crouched over the wheel. The boat made a sharp curve and headed toward the fish house. Tuck uttered a sharp exclamation, turned and sprinted back up the street. But when he got back to the dock, the speedboat was sitting silently on the water about a hundred feet out.

Tuck stopped short before he showed himself in the bright moonlight. Jesus, was there no end to the bad breaks he was getting? He had hoped to get to Clyde before Leo arrived, either to make a deal or force the man to take him after Bass and Mady. But—maybe it wasn't too bad. Maybe it was better to throw in with Leo once again. He melted back into the shadows of the doorway and stood there turning it over in his mind until he had it shaped the way he wanted it.

It was a half hour before Leo arrived in Ida's car. Luckily, Leo left his car out on the street before he strode toward the dock. That was the first decent break Tuck had had. If Leo had gone around to the side of the fish house, he would have seen the Cadillac and Tuck's advantage of surprise would have been lost.

Leo stood at the end of the dock and signaled to Clyde to come in. The speedboat crept in, the idling motor muttering. At the dock, Clyde steadied it with his hand against the pilings. Leo crouched to drop into it when Tuck called him.

"Hold it, Leo!"

Leo whirled with his gun in his hand. Tuck stepped into the moonlight, showing his own gun.

"It's a stand-off, Leo," he said easily.

Leo said stolidly, "You double-crossing punk."

"Uh-uh, Leo. You were the one to go behind my back and make a deal with this cracker here. I didn't want to be left out in the cold. And you were going to leave me out. I got a stake in this too, remember."

"You got a stake in nothing!"

"Have it your own way but it's a stand-off all the same." Tuck tilted his gun a fraction for emphasis. "You're making a mistake, Leo. I was never double-crossing you. Hell, man, I could have let you have it while your back was turned."

"Yeah? But what about Ida, what you done to her?"

"What I did to her! Talk sense. I'm nuts about her but she didn't give a damn about me. You were just using her to keep me on the hook."

Leo could always think short and straight to the point about everything else but Ida was his one blind spot.

"You damn fool!" he yelled. "She's nuts about you and she thinks you been stringing her along."

"No, Leo! You're giving me the business again."

"Business, hell! Why do you think she's cryin' her eyes out?"

"Christ, Leo, what a mess! How'd we get in this mess?"

"It was you, you goddamn stupid punk."

Tuck knew that this was the moment, while Leo was still wavering. He jammed his gun back into the holster and stood looking dejected but his heart was pounding rapidly. If he'd guessed wrong, this was the end.

"Go ahead," he mumbled, "go ahead, beat the hell out of me. What kind of a heel she must think I am!" That was the way to put the zing into Leo—with Ida.

Leo stood wide-legged with the gun thrust out ahead of him and for a desperate moment Tuck thought he was actually going to shoot. Then the gun slowly wilted.

"Boy," said Leo heavily, "you sure got it coming. And maybe I'll do it after this is over. Come on, get in. We got work to do."

Tuck walked toward him. He didn't have to pretend that his hands were shaking. They really were.

"Christ, Leo," he said, "I hope you know I'm leveling with you by this time. Here, take my gun. I want to prove it."

Tuck's heart sank as Leo said drily, "Thanks," and took the gun.

"Get in," Leo said, the harsh edges gone from his voice.

Clyde watched them whitely, his stomach queasy. This show of guns and hard talk had petrified him.

## GREEN TREASURE
CHAPTER EIGHTEEN

The *Pal* glided slowly over the oily dark water of the upper river. The high-growing cypress arched over the narrowing stream and little moonlight filtered through. The swamp reached out from either bank abysmally dark. Mady stood beside Bass at the wheel as he peered intently ahead for landmarks. She shivered.

"You mean," she said, "that he's actually been living in this awful place all this time?"

"It's not so awful, honey. Shucks, a man could live out here forever. There's plenty of fish and game and he could grow his own truck in a clearing."

He was so accustomed to the swamp that he scarcely heard the sounds Mady listened to—the bellowing of the big bull 'gators, the barking of foxes, the melancholy hoot of the owl.

They rounded a bend and Bass pointed to a red glow ahead. "That's his fire," he said. "He keeps it burning all night but he'll put it out when he hears us coming. He's kind of a scary feller."

"I don't blame him."

Bass chuckled and switched on the searchlight. The white beam fingered the shore.

"It's a jungle," whispered Mady, peering into the tangle of bulbous-bottomed cypress, maiden cane, saw grass.

"A man could get himself awful lost in there," Bass agreed. "Fact, they have. Never found again neither. Must of sunk in the bogs or got themselves 'gator-et or something. Man's a fool to go into the swamp."

He kept the beam of the light fixed on the shoreline until it rested on the dock at the river edge of Joe Menagh's clearing. He opened the window next to him and called out in a hoarse whisper.

"Hey, Joe!" Then to Mady, "He'll probably be hiding, seeing this strange boat. He's awful scary. Can you ease her into the dock, honey? I got to be ready to jump off with a line."

Mady took the wheel and Bass went out on deck. He stood ready and when the *Pal* lightly nudged the dock, he leaped ashore and quickly passed the line through the iron ring stapled into the log. Then he ran to the bow line and secured that.

"Cut the motor, honey," he said. "Then turn the light on me so he can see me."

Mady turned the light on him and he called, "Hey, Joe," again. The fire was embering under a hastily thrown blanket of sand but there was no other sign of Menagh.

"Come out and stand beside me, honey," said Bass. "He's gotta make sure, I guess."

Mady stood beside Bass on the bank but it did no good. Menagh remained out of sight. Bass turned the light on the clearing, then he and Mady walked up to the fire. Bass scooped off as much of the sand as he could, then heaped on more wood. The fire blazed up quickly. They stood for another ten minutes before Menagh's voice quavered out of the darkness.

"That you, Mac?"

"It's me, Joe," Bass called reassuringly.

"Who else's on the boat?"

"Nobody."

"Who's the dame?"

"My girl. Come on out, Joe. It's all right."

"Okay, Mac." Menagh's voice recovered some of his usual bravado. "But you sure take some awful chances, coming up in a boat like that without letting me know. I almost blasted you. You must be tired of living, Mac."

Bass winked at Mady and whispered, "He's making like Humphrey Bogart again. He'll wave his gun around too when he gets out—but don't pay no attention to it. He'll calm down."

"What'd you just whisper to her?" Menagh demanded.

"Nothin', Joe. I just told her not to be scared if you came out with your gun in your hand."

"Yah, she'd have reason to be scared, Mac. I got hair-trigger nerves these days. Just keep standing there in plain sight, that's all."

Bass winked at Mady again but he didn't say anything this time. They waited what seemed an interminable time, then Menagh appeared out of the brush rimming the clearing. He had his gun in his hand all right and he swaggered into the circle of light around the fire—but neither Bass nor Mady had to look too closely to see the ravages panic had made in his face. His eyes were bright and beady and his mouth was loose and trembling. It must have been the merest fragment of remaining pride that kept his back straight and his shoulders swinging in a swagger. But he could not control his face. Mady was shocked and turned away so she would not have to see it so nakedly. Menagh shoved his gun into his waistband.

"I just made up my mind, Mac," he said loudly. "I'm done with all this hiding out. I'm going out with you tonight. And I want you to know you've been a big help, Mac, and I appreciate it. It could have been a little rough without you. You're a right guy in my book."

"Sure, Joe. But sit down. We kinda want to talk to you for a minute."

"We can talk on the way back, Mac. I'm a guy—when I make up my mind, that's it."

"We're going to talk now," said Bass shortly.

Menagh jerked the gun from his waistband and brandished it. "Oh yeah?" he said. "Just let me tell you one thing—don't push me, Mac, just don't push me. I'm all on edge and I just don't feel like horsing around. Whatever you got on your mind, we'll talk about it on the way back. That's all."

Mady stared miserably into the fire.

Bass said, "We're going to talk about it now, Joe—or you're not going back!"

Menagh began to bluster hysterically and Mady suddenly realized that same little remnant of pride that had made his back stiff was now making him refuse to back down because she was there.

Bass said, "Now don't go on like that, Joe. I seen you do it before and I ain't paying it no mind."

Mady was about to urge Bass not to press it when Menagh uttered a screech and flung himself at Bass, dropping his gun and clawing with his bare fingers. Bass leaped aside and Menagh plunged past him. Menagh turned and crouched, snarling like a wild animal.

"You're taking me out of here," he gibbered. "You're taking me out of here, do you hear?"

Mady stepped between them, facing Menagh with a shaky smile.

"Please don't hurt him, Mr. Menagh," she said, forcing calm into her voice. "He's the only man I've got. You wouldn't hurt him, would you?"

Sanity returned slowly to Menagh's eyes. Her appeal had touched what was probably the last remaining spark of his ego, his pride, his self-respect. He straightened up and even managed a pitiful suggestion of a swagger.

"I wasn't really going to hurt him, lady," he said. "But I warned him. I got hair-trigger nerves these days. Most guys that went through what I did'd be nervous wrecks by this time. I'm all on edge—but I wouldn't hurt the kid. I just wanted to let him know he can't push me around, that's all."

"Thank you, Mr. Menagh, but you ... you scared me."

Menagh seemed to grow in stature before her gaze. He stood straighter and gave his pants a little hitch.

"Lady," he said, "I apologize. And I apologize to the kid, too. Hell," he waved his hand, "if you want to have a little talk before we go back, let's have it. What the hell, I got all night."

Bass had unobtrusively picked up the gun Menagh had dropped and put it into his hip pocket.

Bass handed him a cigarette, then quickly held the light. Menagh's hands were shaking too much to light his own. Menagh leaned against the trunk of the fallen water oak and waved his hand again.

"Fire away, Mac," he said.

Mady warned Bass with a glance, then said to Menagh, "I was the one who wanted to talk to you, Mr. Menagh."

"Well now, lady, why didn't you say so in the first place? We could have saved a lot of trouble. I thought the kid was just trying to act big, that's all."

"I know," said Mady contritely. "I should have said so in the first place. It's about my father. Mr. Guastella worked for him in Cuba. His name is Eric Lamont."

She watched Menagh narrowly but Joe's face remained blank. "What was the name?" he asked.

"Eric Lamont."

"Never heard of him, lady."

"But ... Mr. Guastella worked for him. Mr. Guastella was in charge of my father's Havana office. He was in charge of buying crops of tobacco and odd lots of rum."

Menagh shook his head. "I don't know where you got your information from, lady—but Guastella never bought no tobacco or rum for nobody or from nobody."

Seeing the dazed look on Mady's face, Bass said quickly, "That Rossiter feller must've lied to you, honey." Then to Menagh, "Who was Guastella's boss, Joe?"

Menagh thought for a minute. "A guy named Brown. But wait a minute. Brown didn't have to be his right name. Maybe he was your old man. A short, heavy-set guy with kind of glassy blue eyes like ice cubes. I saw him once in Havana with Guastella. That him?"

"My father was tall and slim," said Mady in a bewildered voice. "People said he looked something like Robert Taylor and ..."

"Wait a minute," said Menagh in a dawning voice. "I know the guy. He called himself Smith. Good-looking guy. Had a way of lifting his chin and grinnin' when he talked ..."

"Oh, yes, yes, that was Dad!"

"Him!" said Menagh with careless brutality. "He wasn't nobody's boss. Guastella called him the errand boy. He just kind of took messages between Guastella and this Brown that they wouldn't trust in a letter or a telegram. A messenger boy, a jerk."

Mady's eyes glazed and she looked faint. Bass said sharply, "All right, all right." Then he added quickly, "What was Guastella's business?"

Menagh looked away uneasily. "I wouldn't know," he muttered. "He never told me. I just flew him from Havana to Ft. Myers, then back again about once a month."

He began to tremble visibly. That was one thing he would not tell Bass and he wasn't going to let them make him give it up. It was the only thing he had with which to bargain for his life when he got on the outside. He was under no illusions about that. Bass was saying something but he didn't hear it. Fear had welled up in his throat, choking him. Then the girl said something. Then he felt Bass grasp his arm.

"What's the matter, Joe? You feel sick?" Bass looked really worried.

The fear receded a little. "Okay, okay," he said thickly. "Swallowed some smoke." He coughed.

Mady began, "I think we'd better go ..." then stopped with a gasp as Menagh galvanized, thrust off Bass' hand, took two plunging steps forward and froze in a listening crouch. His hearing had apparently become abnormally sharp in the swamp, for it was not until then that Mady heard the faint, muffled rumble of a motor. As she listened, it seemed to be coming closer.

Menagh said hoarsely, "Another boat!" Feverishly he began to shovel sand on the fire with his cupped hands. Bass and Mady quickly bent to help him and within a few seconds the fire was again just a heap of winking red embers.

Menagh cried, "Let's get out of here, Mac. They'll be here in a couple of minutes and spot your lousy boat."

He turned and plunged into the brush before Bass could put out a hand to stop him.

The moonlight was bright in the clearing now. Bass put his arm around Mady and they stood listening as the boat crept slowly up the river toward them. Bass glanced once at the *Pal*, moored to the dock, but there wasn't a chance of casting off and turning before the other boat would appear. The sound was too close now.

Bass whispered, "I think we better follow Joe's example, honey."

"Do ... do you think it's Tuck, Bass?" Mady shivered.

"It could be anybody, honey. Some of the boys from the village come up here sometimes for frog legs. I think we better get back in the bush, honey, just till we make sure."

"I think you're right," Mady said. "We'd better get out of the moonlight."

Bass took her hand and led her through the tangle of jungle vines, palmetto and cypress. Ten feet away from the clearing it felt to them as if they were inside a deep cave. He found a spot from which they could watch both the dock and the clearing, though no one could ever spot them except by sheerest accident, so lush was the foliage. Bass took

Menagh's gun from his pocket without letting Mady see the movement
and held it ready at the side of his leg. His other arm encircled her.

Mady whispered, "I feel so sorry for that poor man."

"Joe? Me, too."

"He was so scared."

"The poor feller ... here they come!"

The speedboat nosed out of the darkness into the path of moonlight
that ran through the clearing and across the river. A voice shouted
something and Bass gripped Mady's arm.

"That's Clyde," he whispered. "I knew he'd be up to some meanness.
And that looks like Rossiter, that big feller standing up."

His guess was confirmed a moment later when Tuck exclaimed,
"That's the girl's boat all right, Leo. The *Pal*. Here's where we must have
seen that fire. Sure. You can still see the embers."

The speedboat nosed into the dock just ahead of the *Pal* and Clyde
leaped out to tie it up. Tuck and Leo climbed cautiously up to the dock
and looked around.

"You stay here," Leo ordered Clyde. "Take this." He handed Clyde the
gun Tuck had given him back at the fish house dock. "Know how to use
it?"

Clyde nodded dumbly. He didn't want any part of a shooting but he
knew better than to say so out loud in front of Leo.

"What am I supposed to use?" Tuck demanded truculently. "Christian
Science?"

"You stay with me."

"What are you going to do, go in there?"

"That's where they are, ain't it?"

"Sure—but why stick our necks out? We can stay right here until it's
light and then we can see what we're doing."

"Are you comin' or ain't you?"

"Okay," said Tuck sourly. "Let's show them how tough we are."

They walked warily up one side of the clearing, staying in the shadows.
When they had gone as far as the fallen water oak they realized how
useless it was and Leo grunted.

"What now?" asked Tuck mockingly.

"Start up the fire again. It'll keep the bugs away."

Leo turned his back and plodded down to the dock. "Any other way out
of this hole?" he asked Clyde.

Clyde shook his head and avoided Leo's eyes. Never before had Clyde
wished so fervently to be anywhere else except where he now was. A
fight was one thing but they hung you for a shooting.

Leo grunted, "Keep your eyes open," and plodded back to the fire that

Tuck had built.

"They're stuck here," he announced. "There's no way out."

"We're kind of stuck here ourselves, aren't we?" asked Tuck nastily. "We can't stay here any longer than they can stay in there."

"You young wise guys give me a pain in the ass," said Leo calmly. "We can always send that cracker back to town for food and stuff but who're they gonna send—a bird?"

"You got me on that one, Leo."

"You'll learn," said Leo tolerantly. "I've known jerkier guys than you finally get smart and ..." He stiffened.

A voice skirled out of the darkness, "Mr. Brown, Mr. Brown ..."

Leo pulled the gun from his pocket. "Who's that?" he demanded sharply.

"It's me, Mr. Brown. Joe Menagh." Joe's voice was wheedling and hysterical. "You remember me, Mr. Brown. I was Mr. Guastella's pilot."

"I remember you," said Leo grimly.

"I ... I wanna make a deal."

Leo's eyes glinted at Tuck but he kept his smile hidden behind his thin lips. "Whattaya think we came up here for, to hunt butterflies?"

"You'll deal? You mean you'll deal?" Joe's voice was pathetically eager.

"Sure we'll deal. What else can we do? What've you got in mind, Menagh?"

"Not a thing, Mr. Brown. Honest, I don't have a thing in mind. All I want to do is get out of here. You can have the stuff and all I want to do is get out of here."

"You could of done that long ago, Menagh, and you wouldn't have had a thing to worry about."

Behind his back, he motioned to Tuck with his hand to stand up and move away from him so they could have Menagh between them when he came out of the brush.

Crouching beside Mady, Bass saw the motion but did not grasp its significance until Tuck casually stood on his feet and sauntered off to a spot ten feet from Leo.

Menagh called, "You give me your word nothing will happen to me, Mr. Brown? You give me your word?"

"Oh come out, for cri-sake. You'll be all right as long as there are no monkeyshines."

"Sure, Mr. Brown, sure. There won't be any monkeyshines. All I want to do is get out of here. I'm coming right out, Mr. Brown ..."

Bass gripped Mady's arm and yelled, "Stay where you are, Joe! They won't keep their word."

"Don't pay any attention to him, Mr. Brown," Menagh cried anxiously.

"He's just a jerky kid. He don't know nothing."

"That was the young McNulty kid," Tuck told Leo in a low voice.

Leo nodded. He raised his voice, "Are you coming, Menagh, or ain't you? I'm getting tired of horsing around with you now."

"I'm coming, Mr. Brown. Don't get sore. I'm coming."

Bass yelled, "Don't, Joe, don't!" Then he groaned as Menagh burst out of the bushes, shaking and fawning, sidling fearfully up to Leo.

"See, no monkeyshines, Mr. Brown," he gibbered, holding up his empty hands. "No monkeyshines, no horsing around. All I want to do is get out of this goddamn swamp, that's all. I'm going nuts in here. All I want to do is get out, that's all I want... I promise you I don't want any monkeyshines either ..."

"All right!" yelled Leo. "Shut up. You're drivin' me nuts!"

Menagh cringed. Tuck moved in from the right. Leo held out his hand.

"Give," he said shortly.

"Sure, Mr. Brown, sure. I got it right here. I'll give it to you right now. I got it right here ..."

Menagh fumbled at his belt, untied something, pulled up a piece of cord, then sucked in his belly and pulled out a leather pouch. Leo's eyes glittered and he reached for it. He had barely closed his hand around it when Tuck stepped to his rear and brought down a smashing forearm across the side of his neck. As he sagged, Tuck snatched the bag from his hand, bent and grabbed up the gun. Menagh screeched in terror, whirled completely around and ran straight into Tuck in blind panic. Tuck tilted the gun and shot him in the chest, then turned and sprinted for the dock. But before he could reach the speedboat, Clyde had pushed off and was midstream, starting the motor.

Tuck leveled his gun and snarled, "Get back in here ..."

Clyde crouched and gave the motor the gun, yelling, "You're not getting me mixed up in no shooting!"

Tuck pulled the trigger. The hammer clicked drily on an empty shell. It was Leo's gun and Ida had taken out all the bullets but the single bullet to give Leo a chance, too. Tuck swore and hurled the empty gun after the boat as it fled down the river into the darkness. He turned. Bass was kneeling beside Menagh. He looked across the clearing at Tuck.

"You killed him," he said. "You didn't have to but you did." He started walking toward Tuck. Tuck's eyes darted around the clearing and he leaped for the brush.

Bass shouted over his shoulder, "Stay where you are, Mady!" and sprinted after Tuck with a wild leap, flaming fury in his eyes.

He stopped at the edge of the brush and listened. From the sound, he could hear Tuck running blindly nearby. Bass parted the bushes and started in slowly. Running was no good in here as the violent crashes ahead testified. There were too many things to trip you—the spidery, arching roots of the mangrove, the running fingers of the vines, the rotting trunks of fallen trees. Bass made his way carefully and slowly, feeling ahead with his feet. From time to time he would stop and listen to the crashing around him. Then he would change his direction.

From behind him, already muted by the jungle between them, Mady's voice came thinly. "Bass, Bass ..." It sounded as if she were calling to him from the bottom of a well.

"I'm all right, honey," he called back to her. He worked his way deliberately through a thicket of mangrove, stepping carefully from one root-arch to the next. Here he had to be extra careful, for if your foot slipped down the springy root, there was another root below to catch and twist it. Bass had an idea many a man must have died here in the swamp because of a broken ankle.

At the other side of the thicket, he came out to a level spot of white sand. He stopped for a moment to catch his breath and to listen. Tuck was off somewhere to his left now.

He must have run into the false arm of the river just below the bend, Bass figured, and was working his way up the shore, possibly hoping to go around it. But there was no way around. It wasn't an arm of the river at all. It was a finger of the swamp and there was no way around.

Bass turned back into the mangrove thicket, cutting in behind Tuck. Sooner or later Tuck would realize he was merely working his way into the morass and he would turn from it. But he wouldn't try to retrace his steps because he would think Bass was behind him. So Bass cut in from the side in order to be ahead of Tuck when he turned. Bass could move silently in here, because he knew the swamp, knew the things that grew here.

He heard Mady's voice again, farther away now. With a start, he realized it was now coming from his right. She should have been off to his left. He must have turned himself around, somehow—but he could not remember where. He had thought he was going straight down the bank of the river. So this was how people got lost in the swamp!

Mady's voice called again and he could hear her growing anxiety. He turned his face toward her in an agony of indecision. If he didn't answer her, she would be frantic—but if he did, he would give away his position to Tuck.

He gave his head a shake and called, "I'm all right, honey. I'm all right."

He made his way through the mangrove but there was no firm ground on this side, only the darkly gleaming swamp water. He worked his way to his right on the fringe of the mangrove. It kept curving and he didn't like that, for it was curving deeper into the swamp. He decided to go through again, to his right, and this time his guess was good. There was firm, grassy ground, an open space about fifty yards across.

He stopped to listen again. His face tightened. He could hear only the ordinary swamp sounds—the frogs, the birds, the 'gators. He couldn't hear Tuck any longer. But it did not surprise him. There were bogs to trap a man in here, mangrove root to cripple him. Warily he crossed the grassy opening, holding Menagh's gun down at his side. Suddenly he heard a chuckle behind him and he whirled as Tuck crashed into him. He went flailing back, digging with his heels to keep his balance but he tripped over a vine strand and fell into a clump of Spanish dagger. The gun had been jolted out of his hand and Tuck, still chuckling, snatched it up. Bass lurched to his knees and stopped, one hand grasping a clump of stiff Spanish dagger leaves. Tuck was standing about fifteen feet from him, grinning, pointing the gun.

"End of the line, cracker," said Tuck and pulled the trigger. A look of furious disbelief swept over his face. Not twice! It couldn't happen twice in one day! The hammer of Menagh's empty gun made a thin, futile click. This was the gun Joe had fired until he had emptied it only a few hours earlier.

Tuck swore and clubbed the gun in his hand. "We'll do it this way," he said thickly. He began to advance slowly, menacingly.

Bass ripped off a handful of the Spanish dagger leaves and backed away. His heart hammered in his throat. It was then when he saw the killing lust in Tuck's face that it burst upon him. "You ... you killed Mady's father!" he cried. "There wasn't any Juan Nuñez. I knew you were lying about something. It was the body of Mady's father that was found in the Gulf near Ft. Myers ..."

Tuck jeered, "It sure was—but they're never going to find yours, cracker."

A red rage exploded in Bass and he leaped forward, jabbing upward with the handful of Spanish dagger leaves. The leaves were stiff and tipped with points as sharp as needles and as tough as steel. Tuck shrieked and clasped his hands to his face. He ran in an agonized circle. For a moment, his eyes gleamed at Bass from a bloody face, then he turned and plunged headlong across the open grassy lea, disappearing into the thicket of mangrove on the far side. Bass stood swaying uncertainly. Then his eye fell on the leather pouch Tuck had dropped and he bent to pick it up.

He straightened up and leaned weakly against the bole of the water oak, no longer thinking of Tuck. He was thinking of Mady and his heart was sick. He could not tell her her father was dead. No! But he had to tell her something, some convincing lie. It was better if she lived in the hope that her father would someday return and let time blunt the inevitable grief. Yes, he would tell her Tuck had told him that her father had gone to ... South America, fleeing. That was it. Her father was hiding in South America.

Now he had to get back. He turned toward what he thought was the direction of the clearing and bugled his voice.

"Ma-a-a-a-ady!"

Her answer, faint but clear, came from behind him.

He made his voice as shrill as he could so it would carry. "Keep calling, honey. Keep calling. Do—you—understand?"

Faintly, a ghost of a voice now, thin but beckoning. "This—way—Bass, this—way—I'm—over—here ..."

She understood.

Wearily he turned and started through the jungly brush again, guided by her voice. He did not go quickly nor in a straight line. Occasionally he had to stop and listen, carefully correcting his course. Once he came upon a quaking body of grass into which his foot sunk to the ankle before he could draw back—a bog he had sidestepped on the way out. It was an hour before he finally stumbled back into the clearing. Mady ran to him and he kissed her tiredly but gratefully.

He looked around the clearing and saw neither Menagh nor Leo. Instead there were two heaps of carefully piled palmetto fans. He didn't ask Mady the question. There was no need to. It seemed obvious. Both were dead, killed by Tuck. Bass felt a cold spray wash over him as he remembered how close he had been to becoming the third victim. Mady watched him anxiously.

"You're ... all right, Bass?"

He nodded. "I'm fine, I guess."

He turned and looked at the lowering mass of swamp. The fire had long since burned away, all wood gone, and the swamp growth was silver in the moonlight.

Somewhere back in the swamp, Tuck Rossiter was floundering. Bass looked at Mady and the same question—and the same answer—was in their eyes.

"No," said Bass wearily, "we can't just leave him in there. I wouldn't do that even to a feller like him. We gotta call him in." He climbed up on the trunk of the fallen water oak and shrilled his voice. "This—way—Rossiter—this—way—answer—answer ..."

He cocked his head. He couldn't be sure that he heard Tuck's answering voice, it was so filtered by the cacophony of the swamp. He called again. Mady climbed up on the trunk beside him and held his hand. When he tired of calling, she called—and after that they took turns calling. They sometimes thought they heard him, first from one direction, then from another. And each time they turned and called in that direction so their voices would carry farther. They clung to each other in gray fatigue as the dark hours passed.

By dawn, their voices were so hoarse they could barely be heard across the clearing. It was only then that they realized it was useless to try any longer. Mutely, independently they had reached the same conclusion. Whatever had happened to Tuck was all over now.

Bass climbed down from the tree trunk and held up his arms to Mady. He almost fell as she lurched into him. He stumbled over the brown paper bag of food he had brought up for Menagh the night before. He picked it up.

"There's a can of coffee in it," he said dully. "I could use a cup of that."

Mady said, "I could, too. I'll make it on the boat. There's a stove. It works."

They stumbled down the clearing and she climbed aboard as Bass threw off the lines, then followed her into the cabin. He warmed up the motor, then turned slowly and headed downstream. Mady made the coffee and they drank it steaming and black but it didn't seem to help much. There was more than fatigue weighing them down.

"Oh here," Bass remarked dully after a while. "Here's that bag of stuff Menagh was carrying. Tuck dropped it when I ... when he ... this bag's what it was all about."

Mady opened it and took out a large green stone. She studied it with a puzzled look on her face.

"It's an uncut emerald," said Bass. He retrieved the bag from her and looked inside. "The bag is full of them. Must be worth a fortune."

"Stolen?" asked Mady without interest, dropping the stone back into the bag.

"Smuggled, more'n likely. There was a case I read in the paper about a year ago. Smuggled emeralds. They come from Colombia in South America, the paper said. Emeralds're a government monopoly in Colombia. Nobody but the government down there is supposed to sell them. To keep the price up or something. But a lot of emeralds get smuggled out, like these. So that's what that Rossiter feller was and that other feller with him. Emerald smugglers. I guess that bag must be worth a lot of money, all the fuss there was about it. We ought to turn it over to the police, I s'pose—'less you want them."

"I don't. Do you?"

"Nope."

Mady put the leather pouch down on the table and turned her back to it. Bass made a listless effort to dispel the gloom.

"Remember the *Zoe?*" he asked. "The boat I want to buy for shrimping?"

Mady smiled wanly. "It looks like a fat old lady."

"Yes. By winter I think I can have the five thousand down the man wants. We can take a kind of delayed honeymoon down the Bahamas."

"But we don't have to wait till winter."

"Yes we do. I kind of lost my job and ..."

"That doesn't matter, Bass. We'll sell the *Pal* and that'll give you enough money to buy the *Zoe* outright!"

Bass said heavily, "No."

Mady stared at him. "No? But I own it ..."

"I don't care who owns it. I make my own way!" His hand pounded on the wheel. "I've always made my own way. My wife isn't going to set me up in business. If I can't make my own way, I can't afford to have a wife."

"But what's wrong with ..."

"I don't want to talk about it!"

They couldn't raise their voices because they were too hoarse, but there was shrillness in them.

Mady lashed out at Bass in a croaking voice. "If a marriage can't be a partnership, I don't want a marriage, with you or anybody else!"

Angrily, he continued to pound the ledge beside him. "I'll make my own way ..."

"All right, make your own way! And you'll make it without me!"

They stood in frozen-faced silence. He was at the wheel and she was at his side. She did not move away from him and at times they touched with the sway of the boat, almost seeming to lean together. But their faces were wooden.

Deep in the swamp, Tuck heard the far-off mutter of the boat motor. He was standing waist deep in water, some of it covered inextricably with water hyacinth. There was hardly enough strength left in him to move but as he heard the boat, he raised his head and gave an anguished croak that turned into a thin, shrill scream as he saw a rippling V cutting through the water toward him. He did not have to know much about 'gators to know what it was. And he knew it was a huge one, though all he could see was the tip of the snout and the two mounds of eyes. Tuck gibbered and floundered frantically but there was no place to go to. Fright held him to the spot as the 'gator struck.

## A PRACTICAL WOMAN
## CHAPTER NINETEEN

Mrs. McNulty was a practical woman. Bass had been sitting cross-legged on the back porch for the past three days repairing the same self-starter motor. And to her way of thinking, no self-starter motor in the world could have been that bad.

She stood in the doorway and demanded, "Will it or won't it? Or are you building yourself an automatic fish-catcher or some such invention as the McNultys are always up to?"

Bass raised his head. "What was that, Ma?" he asked without interest.

"I said, your Pa just fell off the roof and broke his watch. What is that thing you're fiddlin' with anyways?"

"This?"

"Never mind," she said briskly. "I just remembered something."

She went back into the house, took off her apron and put on her hat. She stopped for a minute before the mirror in the living room and smoothed her dress. "Hm, not bad for a woman of fifty," she mused, "provided she was thinkin' of takin' up rasslin'." She was still chuckling as she walked up the beach toward Mady's cottage.

She found Mady sitting indoors, with her hands in her lap, listening to a radio program from St. Petersburg. Mady smiled faintly as Mrs. McNulty marched in but her air was that of one absorbed in other things.

"Well, my goodness," said Mrs. McNulty, "if I'd-a known you was interested, I got a whole backyardful."

"What?"

"Periwinkles. That's what you're so interested in the man on the radio is saying."

At that, Mady did a most unexpected thing. She began to cry. Mrs. McNulty walked over to the sofa and took Mady in her arms. "That damn Bass," she said, "he's so pigheaded."

In a muffled voice Mady said, "And that damn Mady, she's so pigheaded, too."

"You have a right. You're a woman. But what's all this pigheadedness about anyways?"

"His darned old boat—and my darned old boat."

Mrs. McNulty harvested the facts in less than three minutes. "And right there," sobbed Mady, pointing across the room, "is the darned old check. I sold the *Pal* yesterday to a man from Nutley, New Jersey. And

I don't want the darned old thing!"

"That's fine, honey," said Mrs. McNulty, crossing the room. "You can just ... arrrroooo!"

The check was for twelve thousand dollars. Mrs. McNulty held it very carefully and read it twice, making sure first that it really was certified by the First National Bank of Nutley, New Jersey. She was a practical woman. "Honey," she said, "do you trust anybody?"

"No," said Mady dully.

"Here's a pen. Indorse it right here."

Mady took the pen and scrawled her name across the back of the check. Mrs. McNulty folded it carefully and deposited it in her bosom.

"Everything I have," she said vaguely, "and everything old man McNulty has will go to Bass. The Lord works in mysterious ways, though once in a while He kind of loses the way and you have to help Him back. It's the man's place," she added firmly, "to admit he's wrong whether he is or not. The woman is the weaker sex just so long as she remembers she ain't. It'll be the day after tomorrow at about twelve. If you could manage to look a little frail and sickly, it would help."

She marched out of the cottage patting at the rustling hardness of the certified check.

Mady was looking very frail and sickly at twelve noon the second day after Mrs. McNulty's brief visit, when Bass stormed in. She was lying on the sofa with a wet white towel across her forehead. He was furious.

"My own mother!" he grated. "My own mother!"

"What is it, Bass?" asked Mady feebly. "Is something wrong?"

"Wrong! Do you know what she did?" He strode up and down the room, slapping his fist into his palm. "She bought the *Zoe*. Right out from under me. Cashed in the old man's insurance, my insurance and her own—and bought the *Zoe*. That's what she did!"

"Is that bad, Bass?"

"Bad! She knew I wanted to buy it. I wanted to stand on my own feet. I don't want to run it for her. I want to run it for myself."

"Your mother's a louse!" said Mady indignantly.

"She certainly ... well, I wouldn't exactly say that." He looked unhappy. "Come here, Bass."

He looked at her sideways and approached the sofa by a circuitous route. First he went into the kitchen and had a drink of water, then came back into the living room, looked with interest at the scallop shell ashtray on the radio, then finally came and sat down at the edge of the sofa.

"Bass ...

"It was a dirty trick," he said mechanically.

"Your mother isn't so young anymore ..."

He considered it at length. "She ain't," he agreed finally.

"Perhaps she's looking for security in her old age," said Mady.

Bass stared at her in amazement. Even he couldn't swallow that one. Then a look of horror flooded his face.

"You're sick!" He put out his hand and lightly touched the wet towel across her forehead.

"Oh it's nothing," said Mady truthfully. "It's nothing at all, really."

"You're sick, honey, and all I been doing is yelling around the room. I just ain't got no sense, that's the trouble with me. What is it, honey, a headache?"

"Well," said Mady, "it was a—yes, I guess you could call it a headache—a kind of headache, anyway—while it lasted. It's just about over now, I think."

He looked down at her uncertainly. Then he blurted, "You're not mad at me anymore for the way I acted, honey?"

Mady held out her arms. "Oh, Bass ..."

Whatever else she was about to say remained unspoken as Bass bent down and took her in his arms.

## THE END

## LORENZ HELLER BIBLIOGRAPHY
(1910-1965)

*As Frederick Lorenz*

**Novels:**
A Rage at Sea (Lion, 1953)
Night Never Ends (Lion, 1954)
The Savage Chase (Lion, 1954)
A Party Every Night (Lion, 1956)
Ruby (Lion, 1956)
Hot (Lion, 1956)
Dungaree Sin (Chariot, 1960)

**Stories:**
Backbite (*Justice*, Jan 1956)
Big Catch (*Justice*, July 1955)
Living Bait (*Justice*, May 1955)

*As Laura Hale*

**Novels:**
Wild is the Woman (Rainbow, 1951)
Lovers Don't Sleep (Falcon, 1951)
Kiss of Fire (Rainbow, 1952; reprinted in Australia as
    *Kiss Of Death*, Phantom, 1953)
Woman Hunter (Falcon, 1952; reprinted in Australia, Phantom, 1953)
Desperate Blonde (Beacon Australia, 1960)
Lessons in Lust (Beacon, 1961; re-write of *Woman Hunter*)
Sensual Woman (Beacon, 1961; re-write of *Lovers Don't Sleep*)
The Zipper Girls (Beacon, 1962; re-write of *Wild is the Woman*)
The Marriage Bed (Beacon, 1962; re-write of *Desperate Blonde*)

*As Larry Heller*

**Novels:**
I Get What I Want (Popular, 1956)
Body of the Crime (Pyramid, 1962)

**Story:**
Blood Is Thicker (*Guilty Detective Story Magazine*, Mar 1957)

*As Larry Holden*

**Novels:**
Hide-Out (Eton, 1953)
Dead Wrong (Pyramid, 1957)
Crime Cop (Pyramid, 1959)

**Stories (alphabetical listing):**
...And Death Makes Ten (*Detective Tales*, June 1947)
Another Man's Poison (*Shadow Mystery*, Apr/May 1948)
Any Corpse in a Storm (*Dime Mystery Magazine*, Aug 1949)
Anybody Lose a Corpse? (*Mammoth Detective*, Aug 1946)
The Big Haunt (*10-Story Detective Magazine*, Oct 1948)
Blackmail Means Homicide (*15 Story Detective*, Feb 1950)
Bloody Night! (*Dime Mystery Magazine*, Oct 1949)
Bodyguard (*Thrilling Detective*, June 1951)
Bullets for Beethoven [Dinny Keogh] (*Mammoth Mystery*, June 1946)
Coffin Key (*Detective Tales*, Oct 1951)
A Corpse at Large (*Ten Detective Aces*, July 1949)
Corpse in Waiting (*New Detective Magazine*, Nov 1950)
A Corpse to His Credit (*Dime Detective Magazine*, May 1947)
Criminal at Large (*Suspense Magazine*, Summer 1951)
The Crimson Path (*Detective Tales*, Sept 1947)
Cry Murder (*New Detective Magazine*, Oct 1952)
The Crying Corpse (*Ten Detective Aces*, Sept 1948)
Death Brings Down the House (*10-Story Detective Magazine*,
    Apr 1948)
Death Carries the Mail (*F.B.I. Detective Stories*, Aug 1950)
Death for Two! (*Detective Tales*, Dec 1952)
Death in Dirty Linen (*Shadow Mystery*, June/July 1947)
Death in Six Reels (*Doc Savage*, July/Aug 1948)
Death in Thin Ice (*Shadow Mystery*, Feb/Mar 1948)
Death Is Where You Find It (*Suspect Detective Stories*, Nov 1955)
Die, Baby, Die! (*Detective Tales*, June 1948)
Don't Crowd My Shroud (*10-Story Detective Magazine*, Dec 1948)
Don't Ever Forget (*Detective Story Magazine*, Mar 1953)
Don't Wait Up for Me (*Triple Detective*, Fall 1955)
The Eighteen Screaming Corpses (*Detective Tales*, Jan 1948)
The Expendable Ex (*Dime Detective Magazine*, June 1952)
Face in the Window (*Detective Tales*, June 1951)
Fall Guy (*Detective Tales*, Aug 1953)
Forger's Fate (*Dime Detective Magazine*, Apr 1951)
The High Cost of Chivalry (*Dime Detective Magazine*, Dec 1951)
Home for Christmas (*Thrilling Detective*, Dec 1947)
House of Hate (*10-Story Detective Magazine*, Apr 1949)
Humpty-Dumpty Homicide (*Detective Tales*, June 1949)

If the Body Fits— (*Dime Mystery Magazine*, Dec 1947)
If the Frame Fits— (*Detective Tales*, Dec 1951)
I'll Be Home for Murder! (*Detective Tales*, Apr 1948)
I'll See You Dead! (*Detective Tales*, May 1947)
In Her Mother's Best Bier! (*Detective Tales*, Dec 1948)
Keeping Honest (*Doc Savage*, Winter 1949)
Kickback for a Corpse (*All-Story Detective*, Apr 1949)
Killer's Kiss (*Detective Tales*, Aug 1949)
Lady in Red (*Detective Tales*, Oct 1948)
Lady-Killer (*Dime Detective Magazine*, Dec 1952)
Lethal Boy Blue (*Detective Tales*, May 1949)
Love Me, Love My Corpse! (*Detective Tales*, Aug 1948)
Make Mine Mayhem (*New Detective Magazine*, Jan 1949)
Man with a Rep (*Detective Tales*, Dec 1949)
Mayhem at Eight (*New Detective Magazine*, May 1950)
Mayhem's Mechanic (*Detective Tales*, Sept 1946)
Morgue Bait (*New Detective Magazine*, Dec 1951)
Murder and the Mermaid (*Dime Detective Magazine*, Oct 1952)
Murder Never Gets Too Old (*Private Detective*, Jan 1950)
Never Dead Enough (*New Detective Magazine*, Sept 1947)
Never Turn Your Back (*Mike Shayne Mystery Magazine*, July 1959)
Nightmare (*Detective Tales*, Oct 1952)
No Dead End (*Triple Detective*, Spring 1955)
On a Dead Man's Chest (*Thrilling Detective*, Apr 1953)
One Dark Night [Dinny Keogh] (*Mammoth Mystery*, Dec 1946)
One for the Hangman (*Suspect Detective Stories*, Feb 1956)
Operation—Murder (*F.B.I. Detective Stories*, Aug 1949)
Orphans Are Made (*Mobsters*, Feb 1953)
Out of the Frying Pan... (*15 Mystery Stories*, Oct 1950)
Port of the Dead (*New Detective Magazine*, July 1947)
Prelude to a Wake (*Dime Detective Magazine*, Feb 1952)
Red Nightmare (*Dime Mystery Magazine*, July 1947)
Sailor, Beware! (*Detective Story Magazine*, May 1953)
Save Me a Kill (*New Detective Magazine*, June 1953)
Self-Made Corpse (*Detective Tales*, Apr 1949)
She Cries Murder! (*New Detective Magazine*, June 1952)
Sing a Song of Murder (*Dime Detective Magazine*, Aug 1952)
Snow in August [Dinny Keogh] (*Mammoth Mystery*, Aug 1946)
The Spice of Death (*Private Detective*, Dec 1950)
Start with a Corpse [Dinny Keogh] (*Mammoth Mystery*, Jan 1946)
There's Death in the Heir [Dinny Keogh] (*Mammoth Mystery*, Aug 1947)
They Played Too Rough [Dinny Keogh] (*Mammoth Mystery*, Mar 1946)
This Shroud Reserved (*New Detective Magazine*, Oct 1951)
Those Slaughter-House Blues (*Mammoth Detective*, Feb 1947)
A Time for Dying (*Dime Detective Magazine*, Aug 1951)
Too Many Crosses [Dinny Keogh] (*Mammoth Mystery*, Feb 1947)

Tragedy in Waiting (*Invincible Detective Magazine*, Mar 1951)
The Trouble with Redheads (*Mike Shayne Mystery Magazine*, Apr 1959)
Two-Headed Killer (*15 Mystery Stories*, Feb 1950)
Undressed to Kill (*New Detective Magazine*, Sept 1949)
Vicious Circle (*Detective Tales*, Nov 1949)
The Voice That Kills (*15 Mystery Stories*, Aug 1950)
Wake of the Ermine Chick (*15 Story Detective*, Dec 1950)
When Cops Fall Out (*Detective Tales*, June 1953)
With Hostile Intent (*Fifteen Detective Stories*, Dec 1954)
With Love and Bullets! (*Detective Tales*, Feb 1953)
Written in Blood (*Ten Detective Aces*, May 1948)
You Can't Live Forever (*New Detective Magazine*, Aug 1952)
You Die Alone (*Fifteen Detective Stories*, Oct 1953)
You'll Die Laughing (*Detective Tales*, Oct 1950)
You're Killing Me (*Detective Story Magazine*, Sept 1953)

**Dinny Keogh series:**
Start with a Corpse (1946)
They Played Too Rough (1946)
Bullets for Beethoven (1946)
Snow in August (1946)
One Dark Night (1946)
Too Many Crosses (1947)
There's Death in the Heir (1947)

*As Lorenz Heller*

**Novel:**
Murder in Make-Up (Messner, 1937)

**Stories:**
Blood Money (*Suspect Detective Stories*, Nov 1955)
A Tasty Dish (*Suspect Detective Stories*, Feb 1956)
Twilight (*Short Stories*, Nov 1956)
The Hero (*Mystery Tales*, Dec 1958)
The Last Hunt (*Adventure*, June 1959)

*As Burt Sims*

**Television Scripts:**
1953: "Death Does a Rumba" (Season 2, Episode 12, *Boston Blakie*)
1953: "Island of Stone" (Season 2, Episode 1, *Chevron Theater*)
1954: "Tailor-Made Trouble" (Season 1, Episode 11, *Waterfront*)
1956 - 1959: Seven episodes of *Sky King*
1958: "Beautiful, Blue and Deadly" (Season 1, Episode 14, *Mike Hammer*)
1958: "Texas Fliers" (Season 1, Episode 18, *Flight*)

Rediscover the hard-hitting, character-driven fiction of

# Lorenz Heller

### The Savage Chase
written as Frederick Lorenz
978-1-944520-75-5  $19.95
Combined with *Tall, Dark and Dead* by
Kermit Jaediker and *Run the Wild River*
by D. L. Champion, three noir thrillers
originally published by Lion Books in
the 1950s.
"...a sexually frank, violence packed
thriller with vividly crisp dialogue."
—*GoodReads*.

### A Rage at Sea / A Party Every Night
978-1-944520-99-1  $19.95
"In both novels the dialogue is crisp,
the story edgy and populated by
eccentric, volatile characters who just
can't get a grip on life."
—Paul Burke, *CrimeTime*.
"Lorenz's characters are what keep the
pages turning."—Alan Cranis, *Bookgasm*.

### Dead Wrong
978-1-951473-03-7  $9.99
Black Gat Books #26.
"These interesting, well-developed
characters propel this rather standard
crime-noir plot into something special
and unusual. The prose is smooth and
there's no confusion in the storytelling
despite many clever twists and turns
leading to the tidy ending."
—*Paperback Warrior*.

### Hide-Out / I Get What I Want
978-1-951473-15-0  $15.95
"Tough, gutsy novel of passion and
corruption in a small town. Sure-fire!"
—*Real Magazine*.
"In Lorenz's fiction, it feels like he
moulds the plot from organic character
confrontations, his writing is electric and
alive with unpredictability."
—Paul Burke, *CrimeTime*.


**"[One of] the real pros of suspense."** — Anthony Boucher, *New York Times*

**"He can put a story together that will have you on the edge of your chair.
[Heller] writes in a hard, fast, crisp style and he has a feel for colorful
language and characters that makes the story sing."** — *Mammoth Mystery*.

## Stark House Press
1315 H Street, Eureka, CA 95501
griffinskye3@sbcglobal.net / www.StarkHousePress.com
Available from your local bookstore, or order direct via our website.